I0727331

Once Upon a Spell

DEMELZA CARLTON

Three tales in the Romance a Medieval Fairy Tale series

Spin: Rumpelstiltskin Retold

DEMELZA CARLTON

A tale in the Romance a Medieval Fairy Tale series

One

Kempenich winced as he reined in his horse. Even that slight movement set off the pain in his chest. Truth be told, he should not be riding at all, and he knew it. But some things could not wait.

The destrier's hooves caught on something, but the horse righted himself before Kempenich was thrown from the saddle. He breathed a sigh of relief. Darkness had carried him into many battles at the order of King

Karl the Great, while the monarch had lived. Now he'd outlived his king, the time had come for what might be his last battle, and he intended to ride the black beast home from this one.

He slid down to the ground. "I seek the witch!" he bellowed. It took every bit of his strength to stand tall and stride toward the cottage, as a knight should.

The witch emerged, her arms folded across her chest. There was pity in her dark eyes, but she stood firm. "I am sorry, Sir Rumpelstiltskin, but there is nothing more I can do for you. You're dying." Mistress Kun turned away.

Sir Kempenich von Rumpelstiltskin refused to admit defeat. "I may be dying, but there is still something you can do for me."

She sighed. "I assure you there is not, but why don't we go inside and discuss it? I can see you need a pain draught. That, at least, I can give you."

Kempenich followed her inside the cottage, then sank gratefully onto a bench. He would drink anything she asked, if only she would grant him one last favour.

Mistress Kun darted about the cottage, assembling what she needed to make the draught, and Kempenich summoned his resolve.

Once more into battle…not for his life, but for the future.

"Mistress, I have heard tales that you are more than a herbwife and healer. More than a usual witch. There are tales that you are what heathens call an enchantress, a woman who works magic. They say that you have power over earth and rocks, and when a child from the village fell down a well, you cracked open the very earth itself to retrieve her, then commanded the rock to return to its previous place, and it obeyed." Kempenich held his breath, praying she would confirm the story.

Kun glanced at him. "There are all sorts of tales. Why, I have heard people tell stories of unicorns and dragons and immortality to children around the fire at night."

Kempenich bowed his head. He, too, had told such tales to his children. Including one he hoped was more fact than fiction. "There is a story about an ancient king who was granted a wish. He wanted to be the richest man in the world, so he wished for everything he touched to turn to gold. It is said that gold comes from the ground, and a wielder of earth magic might be able to do such a thing."

Kun lifted a bucket of water and poured some of it into a small pot over the fire. "Then you must also know the end of the king's tale. He could not eat or drink or touch his family, and he feared his wish would kill him, so he washed his wish away in the river, and shunned gold for the rest of his days."

"I will soon be beyond such mundane things as gold or food or even days, Mistress. But my family will not. And I have spent all that I have in physic for what ails me, seeking a cure that will let me live long enough to restore my family's fortune. If I die now, I will leave them little more than the Rumpelstiltskin house on stilts my father left me, on the rock King Karl granted him for his service. Other knights are building castles along the river to secure their lands, and if my son does not have one, he will lose his lands to a richer man who does. He needs gold, and I would give anything to give it to him."

Kun sank onto a bench and squinted at him in the dim light. "You ask me to curse you. Not for yourself, but for your son, who you will never be able to touch again. You will never be able to eat or drink, and your own wife will not be able to hold your hand as you take your dying breath. You even wish to hasten that dying breath."

"Yes. I am no use to them like this. Better to be dead than to be a burden." Kempenich took the cup she offered and drained it.

Silence stretched between them. But it was Mistress Kun who broke it.

"There is some truth in the tale, but the enchanter who cast such a spell was a fool. I can restrict the spell to your hands, while you live. You may still eat and drink, as long as your hands do not touch it. But when your heart stops, the spell will spread throughout your body, turning it all to gold." Kun bowed her head. "This I will do for you, but you must swear to tell no one about the source of your wealth. Breathe a word to anyone that I cast the spell, and that breath shall be your last."

"I swear on my honour, and that of my father, that I shall tell no one," Kempenich promised.

"Then hold out your hands, palms up," Kun instructed, picking up a knife. She pricked her thumb with the point, then used the welling blood to trace lines on Kempenich's fingers, then his hands, until she swiped her thumb along the lines on Kempenich's wrists, right the way around. "By my blood, I bespell yours. Everything your hands touch from this moment until the day you die, will turn to gold."

For a moment, Kempenich's hands glowed, then lit up in a blinding flash of blue that made him turn his head away, lest the brightness hurt his eyes. When he saw his hands again, the light had vanished, and so had the blood, though the blue tinge to his fingertips had taken on a greenish hue.

Dead hands. Kempenich shivered. Did he dare touch anything with them? What if the spell hadn't worked, and he tainted whatever he touched instead?

"I would offer you a cup of wine to toast your family's fortunes, but…"

Kempenich grimaced. "No more wine for me, now. It does not agree with the draught you gave me."

Kun nodded. "I have just the thing. One of the dairymaids brought a pail of milk this morning, and it's been chilling in the cellar ever since. I mean to keep the cream for butter, but there will be more tomorrow." She rose and headed for the cellar. When she returned, she carried a brimming jug that she poured into two cups and a bowl.

When she caught Kempenich eyeing the bowl with curiosity, she shrugged. "That's for Butter. He usually comes running as soon as I go into the cellar, for he loves his milk." She raised her voice, and called, "Butter! Puss-puss-puss!"

But the cat did not come.

With increasing urgency, the witch kept calling, leaving Kempenich alone in the cottage as she moved outside.

After a while, Kun fell silent. But she didn't come back in.

Kempenich debated whether to follow her, or stay and wait. He wanted to head home before the effects of Kun's draught wore off, but even the walk to where he'd tethered Darkness wore him out these days. He knew in his bones this would be his last ride.

"You did this!" Kun shrieked, bursting into the cottage. In her arms, she cradled a piece of gold-coloured fur.

It took a moment for Kempenich to realise the fur was still attached to a feline body. "I've never seen that cat before," he said weakly. It wasn't a lie. Too late he remembered his horse stumbling as he arrived the cottage. Had Darkness lost his footing because he trod on the cat?

Kun pointed a shaking hand at Darkness. "He had a muddy hoofprint on his back that could only have come from that enormous warhorse of yours. You come here for my help, yet you kill my cat without a care? It's not my fault your ailment is beyond my powers. You, Sir Kempenich von Rumpelstiltskin, have no heart, and that is what is killing you. Take your golden curse, but know this: every male born of your blood will bear the same curse. His heart will fail him in his prime, just as yours has, and his only warning will be the curse, heralding his death. And you – " She waved her hand, and Kempenich found himself soaring through the air, to land in the saddle. "You shall have a daily reminder of the creature you killed." Another wave of her hand, and a pair of gloves appeared on Kempenich's hands.

Golden brown leather, lined with golden fur. Kempenich glanced at her, only to find the cat's corpse had vanished. He now wore it on his hands. His belly roiled, but he fought to keep the bile down.

But Kun wasn't finished. "As long as you wear these gloves, you may touch things like a normal man. Take them off, and all you touch turns to gold. A curse on you, and all who follow you!"

"Please. Curse me…kill me, do what you will with me, but don't hurt my son," he begged.

Her eyes were the cold of black ice. "Bring my cat back to life, and I will consider it."

"Please…"

She clapped her hands. "Go!" The tether holding Darkness broke and he galloped off, forcing Kempenich to cling desperately to the reins so that he would not fall off. "And don't return!" she shouted after him.

As his world dissolved into despair, Kempenich knew one thing for certain: he would never return to the witch's cottage. For if he survived the ride home, it would be a miracle indeed.

He remembered little, until something in the horse's slowing gait made him open his eyes. After several blinks, the blue-green blur before him revealed itself to be the corroded bronze lion that protected the bridge to the island where the house of Rumpelstiltskin stood.

Without thinking, he pulled off his glove and patted the lion's head, as he had done every time he returned home safely. This time, his fingers tingled at the touch, and too late he realised what he'd done. The blueish bronze was neither blue nor bronze any more, but bright, shining gold.

He shoved his hand back into the cat-fur

glove, cursing witches and their cats.

His son would die young, and so would his grandsons, because Kempenich had been a thoughtless fool who sought out a witch. He should have left things well enough alone.

But it was too late now.

What had he done? And how would he ever set it right?

As his vision faded and Kempenich slid from his horse to the ground, fighting for air that did not seem to breathe life into him any more, he had one last, fleeting thought. Even if he died before he could restore his family's fortune, at least his son would have a chance to do it. Before this curse killed him, too.

Two

And so the wheel turns. The flax would flower and fade, the ponds would fill and flow, and through it all Molina would spin and spin and spin, for how else could a woman help the prosperity of her flood-ravaged town?

She stared wistfully at the waterwheels, which never stopped as long as the water flowed down from the mountains. If Lord Bachmeier would only listen to her and let more such wheels be built, their town would be prosperous once more. His grandfather had listened to her grandmother, otherwise these wheels would not be here at all, but to hear the current Lord Bachmeier talk, it was as though nothing had changed since his many-times great grandfather had been given this land from King Karl the Great himself.

If half the stories she'd heard of King Karl, or Charlemagne as the current king called him, were true, he'd have built new wheels all over his empire before the year was out, harnessing the flood instead of complaining about it.

At least Lord Bachmeier had agreed to plant flax in the flood-ravaged fields as soon as the water went down. Which meant an ocean of blue flowers instead of other crops, but they could trade linen for food. Heavens knew precious little grain had passed through the mill this year, but that was just as well, for they needed the spare waterwheels to power the hammers to beat the flax. That had been her mother's design, but Molina had improved on it since. What Lord Bachmeier didn't know wouldn't hurt him.

Molina sighed. She could speed up some of the process, but spinning the flax still took the most time. If she could use a wheel to turn the spindle, this would be so much faster.

"Good day, Miss Molina," a male voice said.

She glanced up in time to see Hofer slap Lanik before Lanik remembered to snatch his cap off his head. "Good day, boys. How goes the spring planting?"

"Almost done, miss. But it looks like the flax on the northern slopes is almost ready to harvest, maybe as early as next week, so we might have to bring the flax up to the pools to soak, and my father sent us to make sure there is water enough up there in the millponds," Hofer said.

"The pools are full, with enough water coming down the mountain to keep the wheels turning," Molina replied.

Lanik coughed. "Beg pardon, miss, but Uncle wanted us to speak to Mister Rademaker."

Of course he did. None of the men in town would take the word of a mere woman over the miller, even if she was his daughter. Molina forced a smile. "Father is beekeeping today. He had his eye on some wild hives further up the mountain, and he thinks they will swarm soon.

He means to capture some new queens for our hives." Their hives were the only ones that had survived the flooding, so if Father didn't capture new bees, there would be no mead brewed in the town at all this year. "I'm sure he'd appreciate the help of two big, strong lads. Maybe even look the other way if a boy managed to get his hands on a honeycomb of his own."

"Yes, miss!"

"Thank you, miss!"

The boys scampered off, too eager at the thought of the possible sweet treat awaiting them to even say farewell. Boys, indeed. They were the same age as she was, old enough to marry, but she'd never see them as anything but the boys she'd grown up with. Certainly not potential husbands, though the other girls in the village didn't seem to share her opinions. Most of them were married already. At this rate, she wouldn't marry anyone, and today would be the same as every day for the rest of her life. She would sit and spin and watch the waterwheels, waiting for her father to return home for the evening meal, wishing for something different.

Today she could do something different. She'd done enough spinning for one day, and the warm breeze whispered of the summer waiting just over the horizon. Perhaps she should go check on the pools herself, and have a swim while she was up there. If the pools would be full of flax next week, this might be her only chance.

She set her spinning inside and dug out a cloth she could use to dry herself afterwards. Flinging it over her shoulder, she set off up the mountain, following the stream to the source of all its bubbling secrets.

Three

Lubos had changed his mind, he decided. Marriage was indeed the happiest state in the world, for if he were at home with his chosen wife, he would not be here in this predicament.

He almost wished he'd simply closed his eyes and agreed to the first girl his father thrust toward him as a possible bride. Instead, he had to endure the company of what felt like hundreds of girls exactly the same as the first. Oh, they might look different, with blonde hair or brown, or even a redhead or two, but whatever colour their eyes had been, he had not noticed. For every girl's eyes held the same look: wide and on the verge of tears. For each girl had been little more than the object of their father's ambition. He wanted her to marry the prince, therefore she was dangled in front of a prince, and it was her duty to ensnare said prince, or forever dishonour her whole family. He did not want to be a duty. He wanted a wife who wanted him, not merely a crown. Yet it seemed once women knew he was the crown prince, the crown part was all they saw.

Lubos had had his fill of such girls at court, which was why he'd happily agreed to his father's suggestion that he accompany the tithe collectors on their rounds this year. Father had told him he suspected a conspiracy among his lords and barons, who were cheating him of his rightful percentage. Lubos, however, smelled a different plot. The recent floods had affected them all, and all of his father's kingdom was poorer because of it. If the tithe was smaller this year, it was because the lords and barons had less to give. Well, to the king, perhaps. Every man among them with a daughter old enough to be out of swaddling clothes wanted to push the poor girl toward the prince, and it was worse than court. Lord Bachmeier was by no means the worst of them, but Lubos had to give him credit for being the most persistent. His four daughters were all old enough to be married, and it seemed the girls had a competition among themselves to see who could win the prince. Lord Bachmeier had boasted about the quality and quantity of linen his lands produced, and it seemed that every lady in the land was employed in making the stuff. His own daughters went everywhere with a spindle in one hand and a distaff in the other, linked by a length of thread. This thread they then used to ensnare him in any way they could.

Why, only last night Lubos had woken from a terrible nightmare. The four girls had turned into spiders, venom dripping from their fangs, as they spun webs to entrap him the moment he moved.

Unable to bear the feeling of fine wool or linen, for it reminded him of his nightmare, in the morning he dressed in his coarsest clothes.

But he'd almost screamed when Lorelei let her hair trail over his hand as she filled his cup.

To escape her wide eyes and even wider mouth, for Lorelei had evidently never heard a man utter such an unmanly squeak before, he'd made his excuses and bolted.

He headed to the town at first, a place where the girls did not go, for they believed it was beneath them, or at least their father did. But as he descended into the valley, Lubos noticed a stream with a well worn path beside it that led up the mountain and into the forest. There might be good hunting up here, he thought, which would give him a good excuse to flee from Lord Bachmeier and his daughters in the future, if he needed it.

As he climbed, Lubos heard a strange creaking sound. Like a sign blown in the wind, but it was not a back-and-forth sound. It was as though the wind had picked up the sign and carried it forward, protesting all the way, as it moved ever onward.

Lubos laughed aloud at the thought. Why, the sign was him – moving ever onward from vassal to vassal, protesting when presented with a possible bride at each new castle.

Lubos emerged from the shelter of the trees, and saw the truth. The creaking was driven by water, not wind. Nor did the wood move onward. The giant waterwheels, spinning on their axles in the stream's turbulent flow, could go nowhere. They were anchored in this place as marriage would make him a fixture in his father's castle, for the rest of his life.

A small bridge arced over the millstream, leading to a building as big as any manor house Lubos had visited on his travels. This belonged to the miller, or at least it did now. Perhaps Lord Bachmeier's family had once lived here, before moving to their current castle. He considered crossing the bridge so that he might take a closer look at the house, and perhaps obtain a cup of ale, for climbing this path had been thirsty work. But if this house belonged to Lord Bachmeier still, then any of his daughters might be lying in wait for him there, or one of his servants who might send a runner to find the girls. Either way, his solitary walk would be over.

Instead, Lubos dropped to his knees beside

the stream, cupped his hands, and drank. It was cold and sweet, tasting of the mountains it had descended from. Better yet, it slaked his thirst enough to make him choose a higher path – the one that led further up the mountain, following the stream. For if the water tasted so good in the lower reaches down here, how much purer would it be in heights? Determined now, he followed the stream to its source.

Four

Molina trekked up to the pools, panting a little as the slope grew steeper. The track led to the topmost pool, the biggest and deepest of the three. The cool, blue water tempted most newcomers into taking a dip, but Molina knew better. The glacier fed stream was ice cold still when it fed the top pool, and the overhanging trees did little to let the sun in to warm the water. The second pool was little better, for it was cut into the cold stone of the mountain itself, which seemed to drink the warmth the water gained from the sun glittering across its surface.

The third pool, however, was an overflow for the other two. When the snowmelt was too much for the top two pools to take, the water trickled down over the rocks into what was now a third pool, but after Midsummer, would be little more than a depression in the ground, where the softest, thickest grass grew.

Now, it was waist deep – perfect. No trees grew around this pool. The rocks left them no place to take root.

Molina clambered down to the bottom pool, before she stripped off, laying her clothes out on the rocks. She was under no illusions that the water would be warm, and she would appreciate her sun warmed clothes when she donned them again.

She stretched her towel out on the biggest, flattest rock, where it would be within easy reach.

From up here, you could see almost clear to the other side of the valley and all the town in between. If anyone approached, she would spot them at least a mile away, as they took the road leading out of town – more than enough time to dry off and dress.

So she plunged into the water, hissing at that first, cold contact, before she grew used to the temperature and began to wash. She used the soap on her body first, lathering and rinsing as she surveyed the valley below. Then, checking that she could still feel her feet, she decided to take advantage of the afternoon sun to wash and dry her hair, too.

Unbinding it took some time, and washing it even longer, for the thick, dark mane was her only vanity, not that anyone noticed. Most of the other girls in the village had hair in varying shades of flax. The darkness that made her different didn't appeal to any of the village boys. Not that she wanted it to, Molina reminded herself. When she was satisfied that her hair was hidden under the thick layer of creamy lather, she lay back, floating on the surface of the water as she rinsed the soap from her hair. She combed her fingers through it again and again, sending bubbles over the lip of the little waterfall which in turn fed the stream that turned her father's waterwheels.

She squinted at the turning wheels, which

looked like toys from this distance. If she could only attach a spindle to the axle of one, and yet keep the distaff close enough…

Molina shook her head and ducked under the water. Under the surface, the world was murky and green, much like the strange ideas that wanted to take shape in her head. Watermills for spinning and weaving. Why, even Lord Bachmeier thought her daft, having such ideas. Perhaps he was right.

No, she was not daft, she told herself firmly, surging out of the water. Her father listened to her, just as he had listened to her mother. Her ideas were new and different, much like Mother's, and the town did not like different. The floods had proved that. The floodwaters might have washed away crops and buildings, but it seemed the swirling waters had taken some people's sanity with it, too. Once things settled down again, perhaps then they would be open to new ideas. Lord Bachmeier could not live forever.

She used her towel to dry herself off as best she could and squeezed the water from her hair. She pulled on a shift to cover her nakedness, then began to comb her hair. When the tangles were gone, she stretched out on the rock where her towel had lay, letting the sun dry her hair, before she braided it back into a style more suitable for a virtuous miller's daughter. Resting her head in her hand, once again she watched the waterwheels turning, the cogs of her mind turning with them.

A spindle, a distaff, and a wheel…all placed together so that she had no need to hold them, leaving her hands free to spin, and spin faster…

She found a fire pit, long since extinguished, where the farmhands heated up their dinner on flax harvest days, and dug out some charcoal. A piece of bark, caught between two rocks on the edge of the pool, sufficed as her canvas, and Molina began to draw the design taking shape in her head.

A rabbit hopped across the path, and Lubos found himself reaching for his bow out of habit. By the time he nocked an arrow to the string, though, the creature had vanished. It was for the best, he mused, for he was not truly on the road between castles at the moment. If he were, the rabbit would be a welcome addition to the evening stewpot, but if he brought it back to Lord Bachmeier's kitchen, it would surely be wasted, for the man kept a fine table already. Just looking at his four plump daughters could have told Lubos that.

There must be something wrong with him that such examples of beautiful womanhood did nothing for his libido. But his father's vassals were determined to get a betrothal out of him, so he returned home with a bride.

Another rabbit hopped past, slower this time. Lubos pulled out his bow and managed to fire before the creature disappeared, but all he hit was grass.

He cursed. Unlucky in love, and unlucky in hunting. He could do little to improve the first, but the second was within his power. Lubos emptied his quiver, setting the arrows point-first into the ground at his feet. He surveyed his surroundings, and settled on a tree fifty yards away to be his target.

Lubos let the first arrow fly, followed by the rest, before going to retrieve them and try again. He hit the tree more times than he missed, but he could improve. He could.

He fired arrow after arrow all afternoon, until his arms ached and his sweat-drenched tunic stuck to him in the unseasonable spring heat.

His desire to find the stream's source redoubled, and he packed away his bow and arrows so that he might take the mountain track higher still.

A trickling waterfall seemed to be the source of the stream's flow, and he stopped to cup his hands beneath it. He brought the water to his lips and drank. But instead of the pure, sweet water he'd tasted in the lower reaches, this had the distinct taint of something like soap.

Lubos spat it out and wiped his mouth. Had he climbed the mountain in search of pure water, only to find a washerwoman at work? Even now, luck eluded him. He would have to climb higher to find what he sought.

The path curved away from the waterfall, and Lubos took it. He rounded a particularly large boulder and found himself in a positively enchanted clearing, where dappled sunlight filtering through the trees glittered on the surface of a deep pool. A pool with no sign of washerwomen or their work.

Lubos edged closer, until he was near enough to cup his hands and drink. The freezing water numbed his hands, but it tasted so fresh he had to drink more. A sound from below drew his attention, and he peered down the slope.

Ah, he'd thought there was only one pool, when there were actually three. The lowest pool had clothes laid out on the rocks to dry, but there was no one in sight. Perhaps the washerwoman would return?

Lubos paused for a moment. Reaching the third pool would require climbing down rocks. He'd do it, and he could see adventurous youngsters doing it, but a weary wife, burdened with a bag of laundry? He hadn't met a woman yet who wanted to make her work harder.

So he climbed down, determined to satisfy his curiosity, even if he had to wait all day for the washerwoman's return. Either the clothing belonged to a remarkable woman indeed, or there was an easier path he couldn't see from up here.

"Where did you come from?" an imperious voice demanded.

Lubos lost his grip and slid down the last few yards. Thankfully, he managed to land mostly on his feet before he whirled to face his interrogator.

For a moment, he didn't even see her, until he looked down. One of the creamy underdresses was…occupied.

The girl sat up and folded her arms across her breasts. A good thing, too, for the fine linen showed more of them than was decent. "How did you get here?" she demanded.

Lubos had to open and close his mouth several times before his voice came out. "From…from the road from the castle. Lord…Lord…" He couldn't for the life of him remember the man's name, and the more he stared at the girl's dark hair, blowing free in the breeze, the less he could think of anything but her.

"You came from Lord Bachmeier's castle? One of his new labourers, I imagine, as you can't even remember his name. Did he send you with a message for the miller? I'll take it, but next time, you should go straight to the house. No one is to touch the millponds without the miller's permission."

Lubos stared at her outstretched hand, trying to work out what she wanted him to place in her palm.

"Did Lord Bachmeier send you?" she repeated.

He fixed his gaze on her gown, stretched out on a rock. It was as fine as those worn by any of Bachmeier's daughters, though she didn't look anything like them. Her hard curves were half the size of their soft ones, and her dark hair and eyes were midnight to the daughters' cloudy morning light. Exotic. Irresistible. Like no woman he'd ever seen before. And wearing nothing but a shift, as if she wanted to tempt him.

"He must have known I would come here. Made sure you were waiting for me. I must say, if you are the woman he had in mind to warm my bed, Lord Bachmeier's hospitality has definitely improved beyond measure," Lubos said, taking a step toward her.

She was nimbler than he expected, leaping to her feet. In three strides, she was close enough to snatch up her gown and use it to cover her shift.

"The only bed I'll warm is my own, and Bachmeier knows that well," she said with a dangerous glint in her eye. "If he sent you to make trouble for me, then he must truly hate you. A man with no honour, who has not even the courtesy to turn his back when he stumbles across a woman in a state of undress…perhaps this is the first time I will share Bachmeier's opinion."

A washerwoman with a fine gown, so close to the manor house by the mill…this was the miller's wife. And he'd just treated her like a common harlot.

Feeling his face grow hot, Lubos bowed low. "Forgive me, Mistress Miller. I was struck dumb by your beauty." He kept his eyes firmly on the ground at his feet.

"Dumb means you cannot talk. You may have a problem with your tongue, but that is not it," she said gently. "You are new here, so I will forgive you this once, farm boy, as long as you do not say such things again."

Farm boy? Lubos almost laughed, then realised she had based her assessment on his clothes. If he told her who he truly was…

Then she would be less forgiving, for a prince should know better.

"Thank you, mistress," he said.

He waited, but received no response. Finally, he lifted his head, only to find the girl had gone. She'd dressed and disappeared. Leaving nothing behind.

Something blew from behind him, and he reached out instinctively to catch it. It was a piece of bark, bleached in the sun until it was as pale as parchment. But it wasn't the bark that held his attention. It was the sketch on it. A few lines, scrawled in charcoal, but he could clearly make out the shape of the waterwheels below, connected to what looked like a spindle and distaff. Her work, it must be…

Tucking the piece of bark inside his tunic, he began to make his way back to Bachmeier's castle. But he saw nothing of the road, no matter how many rabbits hopped across his path. All his vision was occupied by a pair of glittering dark eyes that belonged to the miller's wife.

Six

Her father was jubilant about getting three new queens for the hives, and Helga had made a particularly fine stew with dumplings before heading back to the village for the evening, so Molina did her best to forget the strange encounter with Lord Bachmeier's new farmhand. For a moment there, she'd thought Bachmeier had sent the boy to kidnap her and force her to become his bride.

But Bachmeier wouldn't do such a thing, surely. He'd asked, she'd refused, and he'd insisted she would regret her decision when he chose another. He'd said it dismissively, as though he cared little what she regretted, for he would have shifted his affections elsewhere, if indeed they existed at all,.

"The village boys still fear you. What in heaven's name did you do to scare them so?" Father asked.

Molina considered her response carefully before she said, "Oh, they think I'm a witch, because I know how the waterwheels work." Actually, it was more likely they blamed her for that Easter festival when she and a few of the other people her age had drunk too much wine and decided to celebrate some ancient pagan fertility festival that Rikard insisted was celebrated at the same time. They'd all paired up, taken their clothes off, and proceeded to see how fertile they were. Two of the girls fell pregnant that night, but when Rikard entered Molina, she'd cried out so loudly at the pain that she'd killed his desire, too. He claimed she'd cursed his manhood with her barrenness, and as she was the only girl not carrying a child, the others believed it.

But she had no intention of telling her

father that.

"Bachmeier won't wait forever. A lord like him will lose patience eventually, and decide to take what he wants. You should choose a husband, and marry the man soon. Then Bachmeier will turn his eyes elsewhere."

Molina shrugged. "None of the village men are a better choice than Bachmeier, for if they were, I'd be married already. My passion is for waterwheels and what we can make with them. Machines, not men."

"That's what your mother said, too. Did you know the first time I kissed her, it was behind the mill? And one day when we went swimming in the millpond together…"

"I know, I know, you've already told me," Molina interrupted, not wanting to hear about the first time her parents got naked together. It reminded her too much of the disturbing events of the afternoon. "Does Bachmeier have some new workers up at his farm?"

Father frowned. "Not that I've heard. Plenty of boys here in the village who would jump at the job, for Bachmeier offers married quarters for the men who work for him. Better than sharing a house here in the village with several generations of your family, or so they say." He brightened. "But the king's tithe collectors are on their way. They've been to the other provinces and we're bound to be next. If you have your heart set on a man not from the village, one of the king's men might be your best chance. Especially if he takes you back to the capital. Bachmeier might not listen when we tell him what our waterwheels can do, but I'm sure the king will care."

"I'm not seducing one of the king's soldiers," Molina objected.

"How about one of the king's knights? Or a nobleman from court? The tithe is the most valuable thing in the countryside, and he sends his best knights to protect it. Have you ever seen a man in armour?"

Molina considered for a moment. "No, but I can't see how armour is meant to be attractive. I mean, you cannot see his face under the helmet, and what if you cut yourself on the metal trying to undress him? Marrying a knight sounds like a good way to get hurt."

Father shook his head. "Once again with all

the thinking. Your mind never stops. Your mother would be so proud, but she'd be telling you even louder that village life will never be enough for you."

"It was for her!"

Father smiled sadly. "She stayed for me, and because she got to build the waterwheels the way she wanted them. Without a new project or someone to love, she would never have stayed. The waterwheels are as good as they will get, yet I know you have ideas almost daily. Tell me what you thought of today."

Father knew her too well. Molina relented. "Today I got sick of spinning, so I designed a machine that holds the spindle and the distaff and turns the spindle with a wheel. You could attach it with gears to a waterwheel so it spins at just the right rate…"

Father laughed. "Show me."

Molina felt in her bodice, where she usually stashed her sketches, but found none. "Damn. I must have left it up by the pools. A man came and distracted me, so I came home earlier than I intended. I'll go up there tomorrow to retrieve it so I can show you. I really think this will work. I would have to build it and try it first, but I think this can easily halve the time I spend spinning. It all depends on the speed."

"If Bachmeier agreed to let you try half the things you think up, no one in the village would have to work at all. He's a fool for not listening to you. His only redeeming feature is his good taste in wine. And women, for he did choose you over the other girls in the village." Father poured himself a cup of wine and leaned back on his bench, until his head touched the wall. "If you were younger, I'd tell you one of those fairytales, where a knight in shining armour comes to woo the lovely young miller's daughter, carrying her away on his horse. For all that I wish there were such a man for you, even I doubt it in this day and age. All the modern knights seek fame and glory in tourneys or crusades, not love. Yet I wish it for you with all my heart."

Molina forced herself to smile, for her father's words reminded her of the loneliness that made her heart ache at night. "I have you and your love, Father. I am lucky to have the love of one wonderful man. To have the love of two…seems to be asking too much of fate. Perhaps we should not tempt her so."

Father leaned forward. "Or perhaps that is exactly what we must do. Tempt fate, so that she might change something to make your life more interesting. Maybe not a knight. Maybe a man with rank equal to Bachmeier, who will treat you as you deserve, and listen to your schemes. You know, the ancient goddess of fate here was a spinner. Your new spinning wheel might be just the thing to get her attention. Tomorrow, you must find that sketch, and tell me everything, for we will build it together."

Molina's heart lifted. It had been a long time since her father helped her with a project. "Thank you, Father. That sounds perfect."

Seven

Dinner with Lord Bachmeier and his daughters didn't fill Lubos with dread as it had yesterday. He barely noticed when the girls brushed against him, though he could not deny his relief when Bachmeier sent his pouting daughters to bed.

When Lubos rose to retire, Bachmeier held up his hand. "Please, let me share some of my best vintage with you, Your Highness. Such fine wine is not fit for women, but for the likes of us, who can appreciate such things…"

Lubos wondered whether the miller's wife

liked wine, fine or otherwise. Perhaps he could send her a cask of the stuff on the morrow, to make up for his rudeness today. He suspected it would need to be a very rare vintage indeed to gain her good opinion, if she even liked wine.

"Did you enjoy your day, Your Highness?" Lord Bachmeier asked, pouring the wine into two goblets.

"Yes," Lubos said absently. "I have heard much about the watermills here, and I wanted to see them for myself."

It was a lie, but one that made the other man preen with pride.

"They were built by one of my great uncles, who saw such things on his travels," Lord Bachmeier boasted. "A younger son, so he had no hope of inheriting the castle. He travelled widely and brought home a wife from foreign parts. Eventually, he made a home for himself and his descendants in the old manor house beside what is now the millstream."

Lubos cursed himself. That made the miller's wife the highest woman in Bachmeier's lands, second only to Bachmeier's lady, if she'd still lived. Probably nobly born, judging by her clothes. Trust him to insult her.

He glanced up to find Lord Bachmeier staring at him, as if waiting for a response. "I'm sorry, it has been a long day. Could you repeat that?"

Lord Bachmeier didn't seem to be offended, though perhaps his near-empty wine cup had something to do with that. "I asked if you met the miller. Rademaker is a good man. 'Twas his idea to plant flax when all our autumn sown crops washed away. We have the finest linen anywhere, and now there will be even more of it!"

"No, I did not. I will return on the morrow to see him." And her. Lubos prayed he would not make a fool of himself again. He pulled the bark out of his tunic, and held it out. "Perhaps you can tell me something. Is this contraption the secret of your linen production?"

Lord Bachmeier squinted at the crude drawing, his lip curling in disgust. "Our women will not sit idle while a machine does their work! That girl is delusional to think otherwise. Not a week passes that she does not come up here, nagging me about how her inventions could make this province rich if I only surrendered to one of her insane plans. She'd be better served settling down and birthing children for her husband, like the other women in the village. Rademaker will not live forever, and we cannot be without a miller." He threw the bark down on the table and poured himself another cup of wine. "Drink up, man!"

Lubos took the cup in one hand, reclaiming the bark with the other. As he sipped the wine, his mind whirled. The miller was an old man, with a young wife? As the miller's wife, he had no business thinking of her, but once she was the man's widow…

A less honourable man would help matters along, but Lubos would not stoop to murder, even over a beautiful woman.

A woman who claimed she could create wealth with her wheeled contraptions…

Lubos would return to the mill on the morrow, and ask the girl herself. Perhaps Lord Bachmeier was right and she was not right in the head, but Lubos doubted it. He'd never looked into a more lucid pair of eyes than hers.

"What is the madwoman's name?" Lubos asked casually.

"Molina," Lord Bachmeier muttered. "Bane of my life, Molina. Wouldn't marry me when my wife died, either."

So she'd chosen the miller over being Lady Bachmeier. Lubos really did need to meet the miller. On the morrow, he promised himself.

"To women, though they may drive us mad," Lubos announced, lifting his cup in a toast.

Lord Bachmeier filled and lifted his own. "To good women," he said.

Both men drank, their thoughts on the same woman. But only Lubos wore a smile.

Eight

"I'm going to have a son," Maja said proudly. "I visited Dalia, the witch woman in the woods today. She is a seer, you know, and she is certain the baby will be a boy. You will be a father, Abraham."

Chase clapped Abraham on the back. "Congratulations!"

But Abraham felt no joy in the news. Being born a boy in his family was a death sentence. He knew, for his time had already started to drip away. Without a word, he rose from his seat and left the hall.

The spring air still held winter's chill, as its icy breath swirled around him in the dark. No breeze could ever be as cold or dark as the invisible hand clenched around his heart as he stood on the battlements, and wished he dared throw himself off them into the river below.

But he could not. Death would find him soon enough, and hastening it would not save his son.

"Now you've done it. My sister won't stop sobbing that her husband no longer loves her. First you won't touch her, and now this. What man isn't happy to know he'll have a son and heir?" Chase demanded, emerging out of the dark. "I gave her my word I would call you out if it's true, for it's my duty as your friend and your brother in law to beat some sense into you."

"Do you believe in magic?" Abraham asked.

Chase laughed. "You mean do I believe the witch? Maybe. I do not know. What does it matter? My sister knows she is carrying a baby, and that it is yours, which is good enough for me. You should be celebrating!" He shoved a cup at Abraham, but Abraham didn't take it.

"Suit yourself, then. I shall drink to your good fortune!" Chase drank it down in three gulps.

"I don't mean her. Have you heard the stories about where my family got the lion at the gate?" Abraham pointed at the statue on the bridge below. Even from up here, he could see it shine in the torchlight.

Chase shrugged. "It looks ancient, like it was taken as a trophy when one of your ancestors conquered some city or other. I mean, who would make something so big in bronze any more?"

"It's not bronze. It's solid gold," Abraham said. "When Kempenich the Cursed touched it, he called down a curse on every male in our bloodline. Or so my father told me. I didn't believe him – not even on his deathbed, when he made me swear to find some way to break the curse – but now…"

"Some curse. You have a bigger castle than any lord in the land, and more wealth than you know what to do with. A solid gold statue that guards your gate…why, that sounds like the kind of curse I would beg for, not break!" Chase laughed.

"Give me the cup," Abraham commanded.

"Now you want wine. Good thing I brought a whole jug," Chase said. He refilled his cup, and handed it to his brother in law.

Abraham took the cup, then tugged off one glove with his teeth and wrapped his bare hand around the clay cup. He lifted it to his lips and drank, wishing he could drown his dread. But Chase needed to know, for someone would have to take care of Maja and the baby when he was gone.

When the cup was dry, Abraham threw it down on the flagstones at his feet. Instead of the tinkle of broken ceramic, the cup merely clanged and rolled away.

"What in heaven's name…?" Chase began.

Abraham replaced his glove. "Pick it up. It'll be gold, like the statue, now. Like anything I touch without the gloves."

Chase whistled. "Everything you touch turns to gold? No wonder your family is so rich. Here, do my dagger." He unsheathed the knife and held it out.

"A gold dagger is too soft to be any use. Put it away. It's a curse. My family's curse."

"It does not sound like such a curse to me."

Abraham sighed. "If you could not touch the woman you love without gloves on, you would understand."

Realisation dawned in Chase's eyes. "So that's why…Maja…why didn't you just tell her?"

"Because there's more. The curse only comes when the men of House Rumpelstiltskin are close to death. None of the men in my family have lived for more than a year once they have the Touch."

Chase looked stricken. "How long? Will you live to see the babe born?"

Abraham shook his head. "That's just it. I don't know. I just woke up one morning, reached for the door of the garderobe, and the handle turned cold under my hand. If I'd touched Maja instead…" He shivered. "I haven't taken my gloves off since. My father gave them to me on his deathbed, and told me I would know when to use them. As it turns out, they're the only thing I can touch that doesn't turn to gold. They must be magic, too."

Silence reigned on the battlements, but for the burble of the river, far below.

Chase broke it. "You need to tell her."

Abraham laughed bitterly. "Tell her what? That she married a man whose family is cursed? That I'll never be able to touch her again, for the rest of my short life, and, even worse, our son will suffer the same fate? I didn't believe it, not even when my father told me on his death bed. I was a child, and thought he was telling me some fairytale about a man and a witch and a lion. Not until I saw what I'd done to the garderobe door did I think there was any truth in his tale!" He buried his head in his hands. "If I'd known, I would never have courted Maja. Never married her, never lain with her, for to visit this fate on a child…our child! I deserve my fate. And I do not have enough days to make it up to her. I will die unforgiven."

"My sister loves you, and even if she had known, I'm not sure even I could have stopped her from marrying you. And…I've seen the way you look at her. I know you would never seek to hurt her. You're an honourable man, Abraham. When you vow to do something, you do everything within your power to make sure it happens. You will not die in dishonour. Fulfil the vow you made to your father, and break the curse. For your father, for Maja, for your unborn son…for the future of your family."

Abraham didn't deserve the blind faith in Chase's eyes. And yet…more than anything, he wanted to believe his brother in law's words.

Slowly, Abraham nodded. "Though my time is short, I solemnly vow, with you as my witness, that I shall spend every waking moment I have left, working to break Kempenich's curse, so that my son will be free."

Chase leaned over to retrieve the golden cup Abraham had dropped. "I'll hold you to it, my friend. And I'll keep this as a souvenir. I always did want to drink out of a golden cup."

Abraham reached out to cuff his friend, but drew his hand back. Until he died or broke the curse, he would have to be careful of everyone and everything he touched. Just in case.

For now, more than ever, Abraham believed

in magic. He would visit the witch on the morrow, so that the seer might tell him his future. And he would not leave until she told him a tale with light at the end, not merely gold and death.

Nine

Find the wealth the barons are hiding in the countryside, his father had told him. Find it, and bring it home. The words became a litany in Lubos' head as he headed back to the mill. Bachmeier wasn't so much hiding Molina as keeping her to himself, and squandering her talents besides. If she truly could create things that would make the kingdom wealthy…make women's work go faster…

Just as men looked up to their king, a kingdom's women looked to their queen. They would do their best to fashion clothing like hers, name their children after her, attend royal events just to get a glimpse of her, and maybe receive her blessing. Even his mother, who'd done little more than smile wanly as the constant pregnancies and miscarriages took their toll. Yet a wave from her could make a crowd erupt in louder cheers than those for his father.

He'd heard tales of the legendary Queen Margareta of Aros, who ruled beside her husband as his equal. The stories said men willingly laid down their lives for her, for it was an honour to serve such a lady. It was even said that she was responsible for turning her kingdom into a great sea empire, though that could be because her dowry came with Beacon Isle. But even Lubos had heard of Beacon Isle, an independent island that was the greatest trading port in the northern sea, occupied by people who called no man king. But they answered to Queen Margareta.

If Lubos returned to his father with a wife as formidable as Queen Margareta, a woman who could hold her own against her liege lord and make the kingdom prosper again…

Well, his father would be pleased. He'd finally leave off trying to make Lubos marry some soft, insipid girl, and Lubos would be free to live the life he'd dreamed about. Well, last night he'd dreamed about it, or more specifically, her.

Dreamed of helping Molina out of that thin shift, so he could see her in all her naked glory, before making love to her as a queen deserved.

Please, let the miller be so old and decrepit he was ready to knock on death's door, Lubos prayed as strode up the path to the mill. What had the man's name been? Rademaker. A good man. Lubos prayed the man would soon receive his reward in heaven…

"You must be one of the king's tax collectors, come to inspect the mill. I had begun to think Lord Bachmeier had forgotten to mention it to you."

Lubos looked up to meet the eyes of a man who looked younger than Bachmeier, or even his own father. A man whose fine linen clothes marked him as more than a farmhand.

The man held out his hand. "I'm Rademaker, and I welcome you to our town.

We have a particularly fine watermill, thanks to my very talented wife."

Lubos' heart sank right down into his boots. Rademaker was a man in his prime, perhaps forty years old at most, with only a slight greying at his temples to show he was no longer a young man. Yet Lubos summoned a smile, for it was not Rademaker's fault he was the luckiest man in the world. "I would love to see the watermill. I came yesterday, but…"

"I was not at home. The wild bees were swarming, and I wanted to catch some new queens for our hive. They produce better honey up here on the slopes than in the lowlands of the valley, and Lord Bachmeier is particularly partial to it. Before the floods, he was often willing to trade a flagon of his best imported wine for my honey, but now that my hives were the only ones to survive the floods, I must increase production to meet the demand. And maybe even the price, too." Rademaker winked. "I fancy my honey is never part of the tithe Lord Bachmeier sends to the king, but I will happily make a gift of it for His Majesty. If you promise to make sure the king receives it, I shall give you some for yourself, too."

Lubos mumbled his thanks, forcing a smile at the thought of such sticky sweetness. He was not overly fond of honey, preferring sharp spices to season his food. Nor was he fond of wine, for the alcohol dulled his wits. It did put him in mind of the gift he'd brought, though. "I brought a gift for you, too, Master Rademaker. Lord Bachmeier's best imported wine, I believe." He held out the flagon.

Rademaker laughed. "Ah, I see why the king sent out a clever man like you. You have come to uncover all the lords' secrets. I will share ours freely, for it was my wife's dearest wish to see such watermills all over the country. I hope you will take a good account of us back to the king."

How was Lubos to tell the man it was his wife he wanted to take to the king, not tales of watermills? Lubos forced down his raging jealousy and said, "Show me, and we shall see."

Rademaker ambled up the hill with Lubos, pointing out the pools that fed the millstream, and detailing the output of the mill itself.

Lubos learned that the watermills did not just grind grain. They were used to process the flax that made the region's fine linen. Bachmeier had lied, or he did not know of it. Perhaps Molina had made the modifications to the mill without her lord's knowledge or permission. Lubos wouldn't put it past her.

Lubos looked over the waterwheels, turning swiftly in the current. All but one, that seemed more sluggish than the rest. "What's wrong with that one?" he asked.

Rademaker shrugged. "I don't know. It was fine yesterday, but something must have happened overnight to slow it down. Let's see, shall we?" He led the way up to the slow wheel. "What ails it?" he called.

A dark figure emerged from the other side of the wheel. Lubos' breath caught in his throat. Molina stood thigh deep in the water, her skirt kirtled up so as not to get wet. "There's something stuck in it," she said, peering between the paddles. "I can almost…there!" She dived through the paddles, into the middle of the spinning waterwheel.

"No!" Lubos shouted, leaping into the water to save her. He was soaked in an instant, but he did not care. He wrapped his arms around her waist and dragged her away from the wheel that wanted to crush her. Too late he realised that she wore nothing beneath her skirts, and her pale buttocks pressed against his groin woke up his libido in the most painful way.

Then something slapped him in the face, harder than any woman should be able to, and the girl wrenched out of his grasp.

Stunned, Lubos shook his head, trying to clear it.

"Get out of the water before you freeze to death, you fool!" she ordered. "Go, before I release the wheel and it wets you even more!"

Lubos blinked. She'd somehow stopped the waterwheel. She hadn't been in danger at all. Fool that he was, he'd grabbed her and now the iciest water in the world wouldn't return the blood that flooded his nether regions back to his head so he could think. Think about anything else but cupping that bottom in his hands as he made love to her…

"Suit yourself, then."

Lubos didn't have time to register her words before a wave of water hit him, knocking him on his arse in the stream as the wave washed over his head. He came up spluttering. Near drowning had cooled his ardour somewhat by the time he managed to struggle ashore.

Molina stood beside her father, her skirts let down to cover her lovely legs once more, as she folded her arms across her breasts.

"You'd best come up to the house, Master Lubos. Molina will find you some dry clothes while we dry yours, and it seems only fitting that you stay for dinner."

"We're having trout," Molina said, dropping to her knees on the grass. Lubos got another peek under her skirts as she leaned forward to slash her knife across the fat fish's throat before she rose, lifting the fish by the gills.

The fish had slapped him, not Molina, Lubos realised, touching his cheek.

"Quite a chivalrous creature, even if it is a fish," Molina added, as if reading his mind.

Red-faced, Lubos followed her into the house.

Ten

The witch had hair fluffier than a fresh-shorn fleece. Abraham prayed that her thoughts were not as woolly-headed as she appeared.

"Ah, 'tis the boy's father, come to call. And not to ask about the baby, or the chest pains, though I have prepared a draught for you, all the same." The woman smiled and gestured toward the table outside her cottage, and the steaming cup that sat beside a suspicious-looking, smoke-coloured cat.

Abraham had no intention of drinking some witch's potion. Her talk of chest pains made his ribs ache, though he was certain there had been no pain before.

"I did not curse you. It was another witch, long ago, who cursed your ancestor, but I promise you, the chest pains started when you turned that garderobe handle to gold. You just did not notice until now. And the draught is not poisoned. It will ease the pain so that you no longer notice it, at least for a little while."

"Do you read minds?" he asked.

She laughed softly. "No, Sir Abraham, I do not see into your mind. Instead, I see into the future of what will be, or what it might be. But you do not wish to ask me what will be, for you already know your fate."

His voice came out in a whisper: "Less than a year from now, the curse will consume me completely, and I will die, and my legacy will be to pass the curse on to the very son my wife is carrying, so that in his turn, the curse will consume him, too."

Her eyes were unusually hard in such a soft face, but they arrowed into his soul. "So tell me, Sir Abraham. If you know the future is so certain, why have you come here? What can you possibly want to ask of me?"

It was on the tip of his tongue to say that such a strong seer would surely know the words before they left his lips, but as he gazed into her knowing eyes, the urge left him. To let her speak for him was to let fate have her way with his life, and he would surrender to fate no longer.

"I have come to ask how to change my fate. To break the curse that kills my family, for a crime so far in the past none of us can remember it. A way to save my son, and fulfil the oath I made to my father."

"Save the boy, or save yourself?" she asked sharply.

Abraham did not flinch from her gaze. "Both of us, if I can. But if I can save the boy from sharing my father's fate, it will be enough."

"Would you give your life to do it?"

For a long moment, Abraham could not answer. Finally, he said, "All men die. If I do nothing, my time is already short."

She nodded slowly, as if this answer seemed to satisfy her. "Drink the draught, Sir

Abraham."

He reached for the cup, clenching his gloved hand around it, and downed the contents. Heat seared his throat, bringing tears to his eyes as he coughed and…ah, now his chest hurt. But it was a small pain, too small to mention. He slammed the cup back on the table. "Satisfied?" he growled.

"It is not my good opinion that matters, brave knight, but a girl who you have yet to meet." The witch closed her eyes. "You must go to the capital, and as you cross the bridge into the city, look up. You will see a tower, and there you will find the girl. She will be in danger, though she may not know it yet. You must keep her alive, no matter what happens, in order for her to break the curse. She must break it willingly, of her own free choice, even though she does not know how to do it. She is your only hope, and if she dies, then all hope is lost."

"Does this girl have a name?"

The witch shook her head. "I cannot control the visions, Sir Abraham, nor can I know everything. You have a time and a place to be, and the certainty that she is the right person. I cannot tell you more than I can see."

Despair welled up in his breast, threatening to swallow his heart. "But I must know more. Must I leave now, or can I say farewell to my family? Will she break the curse right away, or will I have to wait? Will she do it in time to save me, or save him? What if…?"

There was pity in her eyes now. "You will leave on the morrow, and you will have time to say farewell to your wife tonight. Once you arrive in the capital, your fate, and that of your son, will be in your hands. When and how and who…are questions I cannot answer, for they depend on what lies in your heart, and what you choose to do. One thing I can promise you. If you choose to stay, and do not travel to the capital, then both you and your son will die, exactly as you have foretold, and you will die an oathbreaker."

"I will not die an oathbreaker!"

She smiled. "Then perhaps your son will live to hold his own son in his arms. Oh, and one more thing. I cannot tell you more, but I can give you a gift that may make your task easier.

They were a gift to me, and heaven knows I have no use for them."

She headed into the cottage, then returned a moment later with a pair of extraordinary shoes. They were made of black leather so dark, they seemed to drink the light. They were not new, for dust scuffed the toes, but they seemed hardly worn at all.

"Keep them," Abraham said, waving her gift away. "I have no need for another man's cast-off shoes. My family's curse has the fortunate result of keeping us wealthy enough to afford good boots."

"Ah, but can your good boots do this?" she asked, slipping the shoes on her own small feet. She stamped her foot three times. A hole appeared at her feet, small at first, then widening, until it was large enough to swallow her. The witch grinned, then stepped forward. She dropped through the hole, which closed abruptly behind her.

Abraham's mouth dropped open and he could not seem to close it. He scuffed his foot across the ground where the hole had opened, but it felt perfectly solid to him, as if the hole had never been.

The witch's breathy laugh came from behind him, and Abraham whirled to find her standing in the doorway to the cottage with her arms folded across her chest.

"My cellar is beneath you, Sir Abraham. Or, more specifically, my bags of flour for baking. I landed on the sacks, and came up the stairs to where I am now. Such is the magic of the shoes. Merely stamp your foot thrice while wearing them, touch your toe to the point where you want the hole to form, and it shall open. It works on walls as well as floors. It will close when you have passed through it, just as you have seen." She held out the shoes. "In all the best tales, a knight on a quest receives a magical item to help him. Make the tale a good one, Sir Abraham. One that will be remembered through all the ages, so that a thousand years from now, when the nights are long and dark, someone will start to tell the tale of the man from House Rumpelstiltskin, and how he saved a princess from a terrible fate."

Abraham bowed. "I thank you for your gifts

and your sound advice, Mistress Witch, and I will do everything within my power to be the hero of such a tale." He mounted his horse, waved farewell, and headed home.

Dalia shook her head and reached out to stroke the cat on the table. "Should I have told him that when his tale is told, there are those who will think he is the villain, and not the hero, Kisa?"

"Mrow," said Kisa, angling her head to give the witch better access to her neck.

Dalia sighed. "Better that he does not know, then. The people of the future must make up their own minds, as he will, when the time comes for him to choose."

Eleven

Lubos stripped off his wet clothes, shivering in front of the fire. As if his dreams from last night weren't bad enough, now he'd have visions of what she really looked like under her dress. Even the memory of her pressed against him had him hard as rock all over again.

There was only one way to deal with this — short of bedding the girl herself, which he knew would never happen. Not now he'd made an idiot of himself twice in front of her.

He found a chamber pot under the dresser, and wrapped his hands around himself. As if in answer to his prayer, he spotted a bark sketch on the dresser, capturing in a few lines the beauty of the woman in his head. Dark hair, dark eyes, the swell of her breasts beneath her gown…

He stroked and stroked, never taking his eyes from her, until finally he groaned, "Oh my God, Molina," as he experienced that glorious release.

A breath huffed out behind him. "I'm not sure whether to be appalled or appreciative. Did you just pleasure yourself in front of my mother's picture?"

Lubos covered himself with his hands, unable to hide his flaming cheeks. Now he truly was struck dumb.

Molina stepped through the doorway, carrying a pile of clothing that she thrust at him. "You're bigger than the boys in the village. Is it because you're better fed as the king's tax collector, or is it a tribute to your desire for my mother?"

"I thought the picture was you," Lubos managed to say, then instantly regretted it.

Her lips twitched in what might have been a

fleeting smile, before her frown returned. "First watching me bathe yesterday, now pleasuring yourself in front of my picture. Most men would call you crazy, Master Lubos. Especially when you're staying at the castle with Lord Bachmeier's four beautiful daughters willing to do almost anything to catch a husband. I'm surprised he let you leave the castle confines, if you are a bachelor."

"I like brunettes," he said weakly.

"So I see," she said. "Is it supposed to rise again so fast?"

Mortified, Lubos moved his hands to cover himself again.

"Get dressed, while I take these outside to dry." She gathered up his wet clothes. "They are much finer than the ones you wore yesterday. You should have corrected me when I called you a farm labourer. Or at the very least introduced yourself."

"I…I was…" He couldn't seem to finish his sentences around her.

"Struck dumb, or so you said. Yes. Get dressed. Though not as fine as your own garments, these things should at least fit. If anyone in the village were to hear I'd been alone with a nude man on a mission from the king, all the old ladies would die of shock."

She swept out of the room.

Lubos slumped. Thrice he'd made a fool of himself. He'd never be able to look her in the eye again. Let alone her husband.

When he'd managed to cover himself up enough to satisfy even the most modest old woman from the village, Lubos crept down the stairs, wondering if he could escape without anyone seeing him. He'd trade his own clothes for these happily if it meant not seeing…

"Ah, good, they fit. I was worried you might be too big for them," Rademaker said. "One of the village boys just told me about another hive swarming, that I hope to catch. Molina can show you around the mill. No one knows the workings of this place better than she does."

He stuck a hat on his head and departed, leaving Lubos to stand with his mouth agape in the dining hall.

"So, are you truly interested in the mill, or are you and my father cooking up some sort of scheme together?" Molina asked, appearing in the doorway.

"I've never met your father," Lubos protested.

Molina laughed. "You're a strange one, Master Lubos. You were just talking to him a moment ago. Remember, the miller?"

It took a moment for the gears in Lubos' head to mesh together. "Rademaker, the miller, is your father?"

"You don't see the family resemblance? I know I look a lot like my mother. Ah, but you know that already."

Lubos felt himself reddening again. "I thought you were his wife. The one who designed the waterwheels."

"No, that was definitely my mother. Her mother designed the first one, but it was Mother who replaced it with something much more suitable. I've improved on them a little, but there's little I can do there. It's the potential of what we can do with them that I want to work with. But Lord Bachmeier won't hear a word of it."

"Lord Bachmeier said he wanted to marry

you." Lubos wasn't sure why he said it, but he did recognise the wave of jealousy rising up at the thought.

"Do you think me a fool for refusing?"

Her dark eyes seemed to see right through him. It should have made him feel uncomfortable, but Lubos raised his own eyes to meet her gaze. "No. He doesn't deserve a woman like you."

"Meaning he deserves better? Oh, you do have a way with words, Master Lubos. No wonder you're still a bachelor." She walked out.

"No, wait!" Lubos followed her, and seized her shoulder. "Please, Mistress Molina. That is not what I meant. Bachmeier is a fool, with a head as empty as his daughters'. A woman like you would be wasted on the likes of him."

Molina glanced at his hand, but did not shrug out of his grasp. "For once, we agree. Tell me something, as you seem to have untied your tongue. Did you really come here to see the mill? Do you really want the tour my father is so set that I take you on?"

Lubos swallowed. "I came here to see you,

and return the drawing you left up at the pools yesterday. I want to see…anything you're willing to show me. I know I've been a fool, but I wish to show you I am not as much of a fool as Bachmeier. If these waterwheels are truly as useful as you say, then I must tell the king about them."

"Good. Then I'll take you on a tour. My father thought I would have to seduce you and make you marry me before you'd agree to take word of these waterwheels to the capital."

Lubos froze, entranced at the thought of her seducing him. He wanted nothing more.

But she was already striding away, toward the spinning waterwheels, and he had to run to catch up. He didn't intend to lose her this time.

Twelve

A man who blushed! The sensible part of Molina's brain told her to run far and fast from this man, for she had no patience for fools. But the other part of her mind, the louder part, reminded her that everybody did foolish things on occasion. The village boys in particular, when courting a girl they fancied. Not that Lubos could fancy her after such a short time. Then again, she knew he fancied taking her to bed.

She wondered if his being a bigger man would make such a thing better or worse. Not that she intended to try him out just to sate her curiosity. Then who would be the foolish one?

Molina explained how the waterwheels worked, then pointed out the improvements she'd made. They might be small, but they were nevertheless important changes that her mother would surely have made herself, in time.

"And what of the machine you sketched yesterday?" Lubos asked, holding out the damp bark piece that had survived his dunking.

Molina took the drawing and stared at it for a long moment. "An idea that came to me yesterday. A wheel for spinning thread. By making the spinning go faster, a woman could spin more in a day, or have more time for other things. Or if every woman in town had one, and spent the same amount of time spinning, there'd be more linen than they could possibly need. Enough to sell, for there is always a market for linen, whether 'tis coarse or fine. Or if I could harness a waterwheel to power the spinning wheel, or a dozen spinning wheels, much like I've done with the hammers for beating the flax into fibres we can spin..."

Only now did she recognise the glazed over look in Lubos' eyes, and stopped. Maybe he wasn't so different to the village boys or Bachmeier after all. "I can see I'm boring you, Master Lubos."

He shook his head, and the glazed look vanished. "No, you are distracting me. I should be listening to your words, but you're filled with such passion that my thoughts drifted…elsewhere. I must apologise, Mistress Molina. No matter how intently I listen to your words, I will never be able to convey them as clearly as you can. Your ideas are…amazing. They cannot be allowed to rot in this place, like flax in the millponds. They must be conveyed to the king, while they are still fresh and new. When I leave for the capital, you must come with me."

Leave the village and visit the capital? Molina's heart leaped at the thought. No one left the village, and if they did, it was only to visit the next town over. The capital…why, it was as distant as the moon to most of them. To think she might get to meet the king, and have one of the king's own men speaking in support of her…perhaps her spinning wheels could be more than just a dream.

She seized Lubos's shoulders and kissed him. She intended it to be a chaste kiss — she knew her father was watching, after all — but the moment her lips touched his, she forgot everything. His lips were warm and willing, parting to tempt her inside, and she could not refuse. His tongue caressed hers with an ardour that spoke of more, far more, than a simple kiss. And as she kissed him back, letting her tongue dance with his, her body ached to share that ardour, pressing against him so that she could feel the heat of him through his borrowed clothes. What would it feel like to have his hands stroke her the way he'd stroked himself, crying out her name as he touched her…

Molina pushed him away before she tore his clothes off in her passion to satisfy her curiosity.

Molina took a deep breath. "I will come with you," she said, then added, "If my father agrees he can spare me." She nodded up the mountain, to the trees where she suspected her father watched, unseen, waiting for just such a kiss.

She was not surprised, when the question was put to her father, that he sat there as satisfied as a cream-filled cat as he gave his permission. "But you must swear to take good care of her, for Molina is my only daughter, and very precious to me," Father finished.

Lubos looked grave, then placed his hand over his heart. "Sir, I swear to you on my honour that I will hold her life dearer than my own for every moment she is in my care."

Neither made any mention of her returning home, Molina noticed, but chose to hold her tongue. Father imagined her marrying the man, she was sure of it, but Lubos…she wasn't sure why he would want to keep her. Perhaps to supervise the wheel building or some such thing. For a man who could resist Bachmeier's daughters was not one who allowed his passions to rule him.

She pushed away the small voice in her head that protested about how little she knew about this man, or the king and his court. This was her fate, and she would not let such an opportunity pass by without seizing it. No one could know the future, but she knew hers was twisted up with Lubos, at least for now.

And on the journey, she would have time to find out if he truly was a fool, or merely a fool in love. Was it too much to ask that her heart longed for the second?

Thirteen

It took every ounce of Abraham's will not to take Maja in her arms and kiss her like he wanted to. If he failed, he would never see her again. Never touch her…

He dropped to one knee. "My lady, I swear on my life, that I will not return until the curse is broken."

She reached for his face, but he reared back before she could touch his skin. He could not risk her falling victim to his curse.

Tears coursed down her cheeks. "You don't know he has it. You don't. Stay until the babe is born. Then, if he is cursed, as you say, you can go and seek out this witch in the capital. Please, Abraham…"

He shook his head. "You do not understand. The curse will not show until he is close to the end of his life, and then it will be too late. For him. For me. I must find this witch in the capital, for she is in danger, the seer said, and only she can break the curse. I swore an oath to my father on his deathbed. An oath I cannot break."

"What about your oath to love and protect me?"

He met her anguished eyes, and it felt like his heart had been replaced with her own, for anguish squeezed his just the same. But he could not yield. So he swallowed, and said, "This is the only way I can protect you and the child you carry. As long as I am near you, one touch could kill you. I cannot let that happen. Farewell, Maja."

He turned, hardening his heart against the heartbroken sobbing behind him, and strode out to his waiting horse.

"You're a fool," Chase said, emerging from

the shadows outside the gate.

Abraham sighed. "That I am. If I could have spared her this, I would have. Now…I will do all I can to save our son from the curse." He swallowed, wincing as his chest ached again. "Take care of her for me, brother."

"I am her brother, not yours. And a fool, too, for not protecting her from you."

"Then I am honoured to have been able to call you brother, if only for a short time," Abraham said. For in his heart, he knew he would never see Chase or Maja again. Though he would have given everything he owned to be wrong.

With a heavy heart, he spurred his horse into a gallop, leaving behind his home and everything he held dear.

<h1 style="text-align:center">Fourteen</h1>

For the first few days, Molina and Lubos rode together on the same palfrey, sometimes with her before him and sometimes behind. They made slow progress, for he stopped often to relieve himself, or so he said. More than once, she'd had to wait for him for some time while he disappeared into the woods, and she grew suspicious, for he drank no more than she did.

On the third morning, he procured a second palfrey from the inn, which he insisted was her new mount, and she was so busy managing the fine-looking but ill-tempered horse she paid little attention to what Lubos did, though it seemed to her he stopped less frequently.

The evenings did not change, though. Especially the ones they spent in the woods, between inns. At least, not until they travelled further north, where the nights were colder. One such night she woke up, shivering, despite her heavy cloak and the merrily burning fire.

"Is it always so cold, Master Lubos?" she asked through chattering teeth.

"Yes," he said gravely. "I must find you a fur cloak before winter, for you will need it in the capital. In the meantime, you may share mine." He flipped open his fur-lined cloak in invitation.

Molina hesitated for only a moment before she accepted. Rolled up in her own cloak, she was soon enveloped in his, too. Close enough to kiss him, yet separated by enough layers of linen and wool to ensure propriety.

Each night in the open, it became an oft-repeated routine. He would vanish into the woods for a little while, then return and offer to share his cloak with her. More than one morning, she'd woken in his arms, with her head resting on his shoulder or his chest. Neither of them spoke of it, but it seemed like a small enough thing, so Molina didn't mind if he didn't.

One night, when Lubos took his usual walk into the woods, Molina thought she heard him call her name. Then again, with considerable urgency. She hurried after him, determined to help him if he needed her.

But she found he did not need her help at all, for it was as though they were back in her father's house, with him holding his manhood in both hands as he said her name, over and over.

This was what he did every night, and every morning, too, Molina realised. So she wasn't the only one having carnal thoughts when they lay together at night.

"Do all men exercise their manhoods as often as you do?" Molina burst out, unable to restrain her curiosity any more. "Or is it because yours is bigger that it requires more exercise than most?"

Lubos turned and stared at her, his face reddening. Had he truly thought she didn't know what he was doing?

"I mean, every night and again every morning seems a little excessive. Most of the men in the village only do it once a night, which is once more than their wives would like, or so they say. Yet here you are, at it again."

"I can't stop thinking about you. Even in my dreams. This…helps." He turned away and resumed stroking himself.

The idea came again, the one that she couldn't stop thinking about, and this time Molina didn't dismiss it. Instead, she said, "What would you be willing to give me if I…if I helped you?"

She almost laughed at her own awkward words. How her father believed she could seduce anyone, she didn't know. But she could not forget that kiss, or the thoughts that had come after.

"Helped me how?"

She gritted her teeth. She'd have to say it now. "If I were to lift my skirts, perch on your lap, and let you put that snake of yours inside me?"

He let out a shaky breath. "I…I'd give everything I have. My heart, my love, my protection for as long as I live. I'd marry you, make you my bride, and love you all the days of my life. But I'd want you more than just once, Molina. I'd want you always."

Always, as he loved her all the days of his life. Some sort of madness descended on her, or perhaps it was sanity. She wasn't sure. But Molina marched up to Lubos and straddled him, lifting her skirts so she could feel his skin against hers. She looked deep into his eyes. "Swear it," she said.

He groaned. "Oh, Molina, I'd make you my wife before I dared do this. Yes, I swear by my life and yours and all I hold dear. I will marry you, if you are willing."

"Good," she said, then pushed against him, feeling the heat of him as he entered her. He cupped her bottom and drove deep, and she gasped. This was nothing like the one quick fumble she'd had with Rikard. Not painful at all. This was…wonderful. "I'll marry you, on one condition," she said breathlessly.

"Name it," he panted.

"You must make love to me every night. Just like this."

He laughed. "It shall be as my lady wishes. Every night."

Her pleasure built until she could no longer control it. She cried out, clenching down hard on him. The other girls in the village had never told her about this. Maybe this was the courtly love the wandering minstrels sang about, known only to men at court.

"I love you, Lubos," she said.

"And I love you, sweet Molina. I've never seen you more beautiful than you are tonight. I would give anything to hear you scream my name like that again."

The way he moved within her, his soft kisses on her breasts and her face, his arms holding her tight…it was only a matter of time before she granted his wish, screaming his name into the night as she felt his own, blissful release deep inside her. And for the first time in her life, she was content.

Fifteen

Three times he made love to her that first night, and again in the morning. If he'd thought her passion for machines was bewitching, it was nothing compared to the unrestrained joy on her face as he brought her to the peak of her pleasure. Even in his dreams, he hadn't imagined coupling with her could be this good. And now, he couldn't imagine ever loving another woman the way he loved her.

Watching her climb astride her mare shot a pang of jealousy through his heart. He wished he hadn't bought her the horse, so that she might ride before him again, pressed against his groin as she drove him to distraction. For tonight they would spend the night in a fine inn, where they would share the inn's biggest bed, and he could show her how much better he performed in a bed instead of the cold, hard ground. He'd make sure the room had a good fire, so that he could lay her naked upon the bed, and take his time learning every inch of the lovely body he'd touched in the dark last night.

They made good time, perhaps because he'd set a faster pace in his eagerness to arrive at their destination. It was barely mid-afternoon. Perhaps he could persuade her to retire early…

He glanced back at Molina, just in time to see her almost fall out of her saddle, she was so tired. Lubos raced to her side, ready to catch her as she half-slid, half fell off the horse into his arms.

"Innkeep, your best room!" Lubos shouted.

The innkeeper himself came running out, wide-eyed. He recognised Lubos on sight. "Of course. And for…the woman?"

She was more than just some woman. Molina would one day be his queen. "Your best is for Lady Molina, my bride. We have ridden hard for some weeks now, and I fear it is more than she is accustomed to. A warm fire, water to wash with, a good meal, and plenty of rest is what she needs."

The innkeeper bowed low. "Of course. One of my manservants will take her for you, and the grooms will see to your horses. Your father has sent – "

"No one touches her but me," Lubos growled, surprising himself, but not as much as the innkeeper, whose eyes were now wide as saucers.

"As you wish, Your Highness. But your father sent an urgent missive for you, and I dare not disobey the king, whose messenger said I must give it into your hands the moment I saw you."

"When my bride is safe and warm, I will come down, and see to this missive," Lubos said, already ascending the stairs with Molina in his arms.

He laid her on the bed, then knelt to

remove her boots. She had the tiniest feet — how had he not noticed before? He pulled off her stockings, remembering the feel of that fine linen against his back as she wrapped her legs around him.

"Lubos?" Her voice was sleepy and slurred.

He'd kept her up half the night, not letting her sleep at all. And here he was, wanting to interrupt her sleep again with more lovemaking. Lubos cursed himself. He'd have her for the rest of their lives — he could certainly wait an hour or two until she was rested.

"Rest, my lady. We're at an inn. I will make sure no one disturbs you," he said.

She sat up, blinking. "An inn? Is there water I can wash with?"

As if on cue, a maid knocked on the open door and entered, staggering under the weight of two full jugs of water. She was followed by two more girls, each as heavily laden, and a third carrying a wooden tub.

The thought of Molina bathing naked stopped him in his tracks. He should dismiss the maids and offer to help her himself. Then afterwards, perhaps…

"Sir, I was charged to remind you about the letter from the king," one of the maids said, dragging him out of much pleasanter thoughts.

Reluctantly, Lubos nodded. "Duty must come first." He followed the girls down the stairs, leaving Molina alone in her chamber.

His father's missive had been long and suspicious, demanding answers about the various barons Lubos had visited, between lengthy rants about the infractions of each baron, or sometimes even the present baron's ancestors, for Father was a firm believer in bloodlines breeding true to the source. No matter how many times Lubos told him his son was not merely a younger copy of himself.

Sighing, Lubos had called for parchment and ink, and sat down to write the lengthy reply his father required, for it would be some weeks before they arrived in the capital, and Father needed to know his barons were doing their best to recover from the spring floods, as opposed to cheating him of his tithes this year.

Darkness had fallen by the time he was done, and he trudged up the stairs behind a maid bearing their dinner on a tray. She placed it on the table, dropped a curtsey, and left, closing the door behind her.

Molina was asleep, cocooned in the bed like she'd lain in her cloak beside the fire those first few nights, before he'd made his thoughtless offer to share his cloak with her. She'd chosen to unwittingly torture him by accepting.

All those nights, laying beside her and not laying a finger on her, until last night…and now he would share her bed. Dinner could wait, for Lubos could wait no longer. He shucked off his clothes and crawled into bed beside her.

She'd bathed and dressed in a thin shift, so she now smelled faintly of soap and whatever herbs and flowers she kept her linens in. And she was warm, from the combination of the merry blaze and the thick eiderdown that covered her. Almost as warm as she'd been last night…

Lubos reached down, edging up the hem of her shift so that he could stroke her thigh. Her skin was as soft as the silks he'd dress her in, once he got her to the capital. He slid a finger inside her, gasping as he found her as hot and wet as when he'd surrendered to her last night.

She moaned in her sleep. "Mm, Lubos."

He wanted to hear her scream his name again.

He slid a second finger into her, stroking in and out, before pressing his thumb against that tiny little nub that was the centre of her pleasure.

She bucked, moaning louder this time, which only made him stroke harder. Her muscles clenched around his fingers, holding him inside her, as Lubos circled her with his thumb. Her eyes flew open as her back arched up. "Oh my God, Lubos!" she cried out.

He withdrew his drenched fingers, then impulsively stuck them in his mouth, to see if she tasted as sweet as she looked. Ha, she was both sweet and salty, and he wanted more. He spread her legs wide, kissing his way up her thigh before plunging his tongue deep inside her.

God, she tasted good. He slid his fingers inside her again, sucking hard at that little nub of hers until she gasped with delight. Slowly, he took up the same rhythm as before, slower, more sensuously this time, as he relished the taste of her. Then she thrust her hips toward him, much like he'd thrust deep into her last night.

"Lubos, please!" she begged, tangling her fingers in his hair, throwing her legs over his shoulders to give him better access to all of her. "Oh please!"

She came with a scream, her back arching so far off the bed only her head touched it any more.

Before she could come down of her own accord, he seized her around the waist, easing her onto his rock-hard cock. Her heels dug into his back as he drove deep, deeper inside her than he'd ever been before. He filled her completely, his balls resting against her as if clamouring for entry, too. She felt so good, he hoped he wasn't hurting her. He risked a glance at her face.

Her eyes met his. "More," she demanded, clenching down on his cock.

He pressed his thumb against her little nub, hearing her gasp as he slid almost out of her and then right back in, where he belonged. "Be careful what you wish for, my lady," he whispered, keeping his thrusts slow and steady and powerfully deep, until his circling thumb unravelled her once more. He silenced her scream with a kiss, and threw caution to the winds. Slow and steady be damned. He pounded into her, egged on by her breathless commands for more until she clenched around him one more time, crying out his name over and over, and he was undone.

When Lubos managed to open his eyes again, Molina, the most magnificent woman he'd ever met, eased her legs down from his shoulders, to wrap them even more firmly around his waist, holding him deep inside her.

"I am not ready to do that again, my lady. We men do not have the stamina of a lady like you," Lubos apologised.

Molina gave a slight smile. "Perhaps not, but when you are ready, I will be the first to know." And she clenched deliciously around him, making Lubos wish he was ready now.

Some hours later, he awoke to find her sitting astride him, rocking her hips gently as she rubbed against his once more hard cock. Like a dream made real. One who would one day be his wife.

"I want more," she whispered.

Lubos seized her hips, chuckling as she gasped in surprise, and thrust home.

Sixteen

Every night and every blissful morning, Molina had to pry her body from Lubos'. If she didn't, then she would neither sleep nor leave their shared bed, though it was becoming increasingly hard to remember why she wanted to.

But today, Lubos had assured her, they would reach the capital, and she did want to do that. She pawed through her clothes, wanting something clean, but she'd worn all of them on this long trip. The only item that had stayed in her bag was her red petticoat, for her moonblood had not come this month. That meant she carried Lubos' child already. Good. Once they were married, they would be a family all the sooner. So much for the village boys' taunts that she was so thin, she must be barren. Or a witch, as though her skills with the waterwheels were some kind of magic and not simply something that came naturally to her mind.

Lubos wanted waterwheels and whatever she wanted to show him. And her. Oh, how he wanted her. Even this morning his loving smile melted something inside her.

"Come back to bed," he said.

She shook her head. "We enter the capital today. I want to wear my best, but everything is so travel worn, I fear I shall look like your poor country cousin."

He rose and kissed her. "You will look beautiful, as always, no matter what you wear. And you shall have all new clothes in the latest court fashions, if that is your wish. Nothing is too good for my lovely wife."

"When will we be married? Will there be enough time to have a new gown made, or to launder these?" Molina asked.

"You shall name the day. I must report to the king first, but after that, my time is yours."

"As I am yours." She melted into his arms, wishing her worries would melt just as easily. Every inn they stopped at, he proudly introduced her as his new bride, and Molina wanted to believe him with all her might. But her mind would not stop spinning with all the things that could possibly go wrong.

Seventeen

"I should change my gown before I see the king," Molina said, hanging back even as Lubos seized her hand to lead her into the throne room.

Lubos shook his head. "It's best not to delay when reporting to the king. He is very insistent about being the first to know any news. And he will not notice your gown, I promise you. Why, I can't tell if it's the same gown you wore yesterday, or if it is a new one. The only thing he would notice about your gown is if you weren't wearing one, because no man is immune to your beauty."

Molina blushed. "You should not say such things. I'm sure if I had any beauty to boast of, someone in my village would have noticed and told me of it. And he will notice this gown, I am sure of it, for I left half of the skirt in a bramble hedge beside the road when that hateful horse decided to scratch her flank against it. Why, it is nothing but ribbons all down one side!"

When she held it out, Lubos realised the gown was quite ruined, but the layer of cloth beneath seemed unharmed, as were her stockings. Her modesty would be preserved.

"I didn't notice until you told me. I'm sure he won't, either. Here, I shall walk on that side of you as we enter the throne room, and it will be quite invisible." Before she could object again, Lubos linked his arm through hers and marched into the throne room.

Courtiers passed to let them through, bowing as they recognised him. Lubos wanted to point out to Molina that nobody noticed a little dust from the road, that they saw him for who he was, and it would be the same for her, but he kept his observations for later. The sooner this audience was over, the better.

He stopped at the foot of the dais and bowed low. "Father, you will not believe what I found in Lord Bachmeier's barony."

"The skinniest, ugliest whore in the kingdom?"

Lubos heard Molina's gasp as her hand slipped from his grasp.

Father didn't seem to have noticed. "Bachmeier said he had the most beautiful daughters in the country. Plump, fair and fertile — just what any man would want in a wife. If that beanpole is one of his, then what else has he lied about?"

Lubos rose. "Father, this is Lady Molina, and she is most certainly not one of Bachmeier's daughters, though the man wanted to marry her himself. She works miracles. The things she can do with waterwheels and a wheel for spinning thread…why, if we equipped every mill in the country with one of her wheels, the treasury would be full of gold within the year. Never have I seen anything like it. Machines that can do the work of three men, using the water from the river! If you let me show you…"

The king waved his hand languidly. "I have no desire to see what some slovenly stable girl can do. I'm sure she has spread her legs and her lies far enough, for you to have been ensnared by her. Has she fucked away your wits, too, so that I will need to name your brother Xylander the crown prince instead of you?"

Lubos didn't dare look at Molina. All he knew was he had to get her out of there.

"Your Majesty will choose his successor wisely, I am certain," Lubos said evenly. "Just as you have chosen your loyal barons and lords wisely, for they have striven mightily to provide you with a tithe even in these times of hardship and floods, which took most of their harvests. As you will have already seen in the reports I sent back while I was travelling. And as you were kind enough to bring up the subject of marriage, I would very much like to discuss my marriage with you, though perhaps in the privacy of your apartments…" He glanced pointedly at the packed court behind him.

"There is nothing to discuss. As long as she is female and fertile and of a rank befitting your station, and she comes with a sizeable dowry in gold, you may bed whatever bitch you please. When the sow is pregnant, then you may go back to tumbling stable girls." Father made a shooing motion with his hands. "Get this slut out of my sight."

Lubos muttered something he hoped sounded obedient and suitably contrite, before hustling Molina out. He almost had to carry her, for her feet didn't seem to want to work until the throne room door had closed behind them.

"I must apologise for my father. His mind is not as sharp as it was," Lubos began, but Molina didn't seem to hear him.

He'd been such a fool. Gently, he took her hand and guided her to his chambers, where he could apologise to her properly without half the court hearing.

Eighteen

Molina's mind whirled worse than ever. Lubos was the crown prince. His father, the king, wanted nothing to do with waterwheels and wouldn't let them marry, for he thought she was unworthy of his princely son. Far from home, carrying Lubos' child…what was she to do?

She followed Lubos through the castle, as lost in her own thoughts as in the maze of stone halls.

Lubos opened another door and gestured for her to go through. When Molina did, she found herself in a tower room, instead of another passage. A bedchamber, if she didn't miss her guess, full of the sort of rich furnishings she would expect to belong to royalty.

Not at all suitable for the…what had the king called her? Oh yes: the slovenly stable girl who had spread her legs and her lies for the prince. Lovely. Bachmeier's snide comments about her sanity seemed almost like compliments in comparison.

"I'll have some water sent up, and a maid with fresh clothes, who will see that yours are laundered. I'll have some dinner sent up, too, for my father's great hall is not the place for you yet, I think. Not until we are wed," Lubos said.

Molina laid a hand on his arm. "When we are wed? Why, did you not hear the king? He said he would never allow us to wed. Lubos, Your Highness, I cannot allow you to commit treason. You cannot lose your head for me." And she would lose hers, too, she thought but didn't say.

Lubos grimaced. "My father is old and

prone to rash decisions, like today, but, in time, I have found he will eventually see reason. So he will over our marriage. He sent me out to find gold from his vassals, and a bride. He made no mention of wealth or dowries then, and once his ire has cooled, I will explain to him the value of your waterwheels. Then, he will demand we marry, and we will. Until then, remain here in my quarters as much as possible, except when you are working with the castle carpenter. Or is it the wainwright you need? Whoever and whatever you need, you shall have it, so that when my father wishes to speak to you again, you will have not just a picture but a real, moving device to show him."

Against her better judgement, hope kindled in Molina's breast. "These are your quarters?"

"Yes, and they will be yours, too. As my bride to be, you will be showed all the respect befitting a princess. New gowns, new shoes, a new spinning wheel…all that you ask for will be yours. Even me, for I made a vow I intend to keep." He pulled her into his arms and kissed the top of her head. "Please, be patient just a little while, my love, and everything will be as it should be. I promise." He pulled away and bowed to her. "A maid, water, dinner…I shall have it all sent up to you on my way to see the carpenter. Then I will return to share the meal with you, before we retire to bed for the night. If that meets with your approval, my lady."

Now who was struck dumb? The irony wasn't lost on her. "I…yes," she said finally. "Your Highness," she added.

He waved the words away. "There are no titles between us. You are my lady, and my equal. In my mind, you are already my bride. Anything else is just mere words and ceremony. I am yours. Never doubt that." Then he whirled on his heel and was gone.

Molina sat on the enormous bed – big enough for Lubos and all four of Bachmeier's daughters, if he'd chosen all of the girls, instead of just her – and tried to calm her thoughts. With all her heart, she wanted to believe Lubos. She placed a hand on her belly. For the future of the child inside her, she had to hope what he said was true.

In the meantime, she would work with this carpenter, and do everything Lubos said. For this court was a strange place to her, as alien as the surface of the moon, and one wrong step would see her lose not just her own life, but her child's life, too. Molina swore it would not come to that.

Nineteen

Lubos found Zimmerman in his workshop
outside the castle gates. He watched the
carpenter hammering what looked like a chair
before Zimmerman noticed him.

Down went the hammer and Zimmerman
bowed. "Your Highness. An honour."

It hadn't always been an honour.
Zimmerman had often chased Lubos and the
castellan's boys out of his workshop when they
came searching for wood to make into toy
boats to sail on the moat. Lubos grinned. "Do
you have any spare bits for boats, Master

Zimmerman?"

Zimmerman's mouth dropped open. "I'd forgotten about you boys and those boats. It seems like so long ago…but Your Highness has only to ask, and I will make whatever you wish. Though if it's boats you're after, might I suggest Bootsma, the royal boatbuilder instead? As I'm sure you and your friends found out all too quickly, my fresh planks are more likely to sink than float."

"It's not for me, my friend. I need your skills for my fiancée, the amazing woman I'll soon marry. She has the most…inventive mind, contraptions that could do the work of a man or a woman, or even a whole village. Using wheels and water and all manner of things. Truly remarkable. What Lady Molina designs, I want you to build for her. I need you to bring her drawings to life, so that my father can truly appreciate them."

Zimmerman sucked in a breath. "So the rumours are true! People have been spreading stories, that you'd found a bride somewhere in the provinces, and you were bringing her home. Some even said she had the next heir on the way."

Molina, carrying his child? He couldn't imagine a happier thought. Well, they'd certainly made love enough times on the journey for such a thing to happen, though it was probably too early to know.

"She is like no other woman I've ever met. A treasure who will one day be queen. In the meantime, I'm sure she will keep you and every other carpenter in the kingdom busy improving the place. Now would be a good time to take on an apprentice or two."

Zimmerman bowed. "It will be an honour to work for the future queen. Something to tell my grandkids, if my daughters ever get around to having any."

"That it will be," Lubos promised him, before heading back into the castle.

He found his father in his private chambers, dressing for dinner, as usual at this time of day. "What do you want?" Father demanded. "Come to tell me you've gone and married the stable girl against my wishes, so I'll have to cut off her head? Don't test me, boy – I'll do it, no matter how pretty she is. Our treasury needs gold, not girls."

"I'll bring you the gold you ask for, Father, you'll see. Many of the provinces were hard hit by the spring floods, and they have little to spare. But what I discovered out there…ah, you should have seen it, Father. They were using the floodwaters to power the millwheels, and to make linen, and all manner of things. Almost miraculous. I'll ask Zimmerman to put together some models so that you can see these things in action. I'm sure you'll see how useful they will be. For while a machine mills the grain, the men can plant another crop. Triple the size of the usual flax crop, ready to spin into linen thread in half the time it normally takes." Lubos almost added that it was all thanks to Molina, but held his tongue. When his father saw the models and truly appreciated their value, then he would tell the king that she alone was responsible for them.

Father squinted at him. "I thought you said the girl made them?"

"She designs them. A skilled carpenter has to make them," Lubos said. Actually, he wouldn't put it past Molina to have done the work herself back at home. But she had no need for such things here. Providing for her was his job now.

"I will see the models when you have them. Until then – where are my tithe collectors with my gold? Aren't you supposed to be with them?"

Lubos sighed. His father forgot far too much these days. "Molina and I rode ahead to bring you the news. I will return to the cart train on the morrow to see if I can hurry them along." Not likely, but it was what his father wanted to hear.

"Good. Can't leave you a penniless kingdom when my reign is over, can I? What kind of king would that make me?"

Lubos made suitably sympathetic noises, but inside, his resolve was as hard as iron. With or without his father's help, he and Molina would work to make their kingdom great again. As husband and wife.

Twenty

Abraham reined in his horse just before the bridge. With all the traffic headed into the city, including an endless train of carts that looked to be carrying either the king's tithe or enough food to feed an army, he hadn't been moving faster than a walk anyway, but now he had to stop, for the very tower the witch had spoken about loomed above him.

The windows were unshuttered in the warm summer air, and Abraham fancied he could see a shape looking out through one. A feminine silhouette, there for a moment, before it was gone.

A maiden locked in the tower, perhaps? One who would be so grateful to him for rescuing her that she would break the curse as a matter of course?

It would not be easy getting in, for the tower was part of the castle, but that was where his magic shoes would come in. He would sneak in, carry the girl out, persuade her to break the curse, and be home with Maja before the baby was born.

He would hold his son in his arms, free of the curse that had plagued their bloodline for far too long, or he would not be able to look his son in the eye, for he would be a failure of a father.

Abraham urged his horse across the bridge, his eyes fixed on the tower. Therein lay his salvation, and he would not let it slip from his grasp.

Twenty-One

Molina rose and peered out the window. Ever since the morning Lubos left, she'd been watching for him. While she worked with Zimmerman, she'd managed to put him out of her mind for an hour or two at a time, but now she had the thread spinning wheel and spindle arrangement before her, she was terrified to try it. What if it worked? What if it didn't? This was sleeker, more polished than the simple device she'd imagined, but then she hadn't expected to have the services of a royal carpenter who made ornate carved chairs for his living.

She squinted at a horseman on the bridge, but he didn't look like Lubos. She'd ridden beside Lubos enough to recognise him on sight. Yet the carts coming through the gate were more numerous than usual, so they had to be the tithe. Where was Lubos, then?

Perhaps he was even now on his way up to the tower to surprise her.

She turned away from the window, smiling. She could surprise him, too. The baby was a visible bump between her hips now, and she had this table thing. Which she had to test before he got here, for if it worked...

She found some combed flax, as fluffy as fresh-combed wool, and twisted a length of it into thread between her fingers, threading it on the spindle. When she'd secured it, she set the fluffy flax on the distaff, and gave the wheel a push with her elbow. The spindle spun and she soon had her hands full, keeping the wheel turning while she twisted the thread. If the wheel could be spun by water or even her foot, it would be much better, but she was slowly getting accustomed to this. The spindle was full almost before she realised it, and she fitted a second. This time, she spun the wheel a little faster, for she had the timing of it, and the second spindle was full in no time. Why, she'd barely been working for a few minutes, and she'd done a whole morning's work.

This would change everything.

She wanted to shout and dance and sing, but she didn't dare do any of these things in the king's castle until Lubos returned, for he should be the first one to know. So she fitted her third and final spindle, and began to spin again.

As if in answer to her wish, the door behind her swung open and the footsteps that entered were too heavy to belong to anyone but a man. Lubos was home.

"Come and see," she said. "It's even better than I imagined it could be." She didn't dare stop, for the thread would be uneven.

A hand descended on her spindle, stopping it. "Lady, you need to stop playing with that toy. For what I have to say to you is a matter of life or death if you do not." He let go of her spindle, but it no longer moved, for he'd done something to the thread that turned it yellow.

Molina stared up in horror…at a man who certainly wasn't Lubos.

Twenty-Two

The terrified girl seemed to banish her fear in a moment as she rose. "Who are you?" she demanded.

She was a princess, the seer had said, which explained her regal bearing, as well as her fine gown. Maja had nothing half so fine. Abraham promised himself that when the curse was broken, he would find a fabric merchant to sell him some rich cloth to take home as a gift for Maja.

But first he had to persuade the girl to help him, and not betray him to the king. For the king would not look kindly upon an intruder in his castle, however loyal the House of Rumpelstiltskin might be.

"Who I am matters not," Abraham said finally. "All that matters is you help me."

She edged away from him, toward the door. "You should not be here. If you wish for someone's help, you should petition the king." Her hand closed on the door handle.

"No!" Abraham shouted, lunging for her.

She scrambled away, crossing the room so that the wheeled table she had been playing with stood between them. "If my husband returns and finds you here, he will cut you down. Leave while you still have legs to run with. For if you harm me, there is nowhere you can run to where he will not find you."

Harm her? He had to save her!

Abraham stared at her for a long moment before he could find the words he needed. "I have not come here to hurt you, Princess," he said slowly. "I need your help, and I will pay handsomely for it. So handsomely, you will never need to spin your own thread again." He reached for the spindles of spun thread he recognised, for Maja had used similar ones, and closed his fingers around them. In a moment, the common white thread turned to pure gold. He held out the transformed spindles. "You see?"

"What have you done?" she demanded.

"I will make you richer than you have ever dreamed, if only you help me," Abraham said. He thought he heard footsteps on the stairs. He would have to be quick. "Come with me. I will tell you everything you need to know, and once you have helped me, I will fill your chamber with enough gold to last you a lifetime."

"I don't want gold or riches. I want my husband, and no one else. Get out!" she said fiercely.

The footsteps were getting closer. "Please, Princess!" Abraham pulled on his gloves and offered her his hand. "All the wealth you could ever want, and all I ask is a night of your time."

"No!"

The door handle moved. Abraham was out of time.

"I shall return on the morrow, and ask you

again," he promised, before stamping his foot three times to conjure a hole large enough for him to escape through before the door opened.

Twenty-Three

Lubos wanted to skip all the way up to her chamber, as she'd named the empty room above his own that Molina had claimed for her workroom. He settled for racing up the steps, something he hadn't done since he was a boy.

He threw open the door, and there she was. For a moment, she seemed transfixed with shock, before her thunderous expression cleared and her beaming smile blinded him.

"Lubos!" She dashed across the room and threw her arms around him, kissing him with such fervour he wished he'd thought to commission a bed for this chamber.

He did not want to break the embrace, but he knew he would have to. His father expected him in the throne room, and he would have to explain his delay.

Gently, he pushed her away from him so that she stood at arm's length. "I must report to the king, and I cannot take you with me. Not yet." One day, he promised himself.

"No, not yet." She wrapped her arms around herself and shivered, though the room was not cold. The king had that effect on many people, it seemed.

Lubos cast around the room, and his gaze lit upon the wheeled table he'd seen in her drawings. "Did Zimmerman manage to make one for you? Does it work?"

She smiled. "It took several tries, but yes, he finished this for me today. I sat down to spin, and it seemed but a moment, yet I did a whole day's work in that time. I've never spun so much in my life. Spinning with a wheel is easily twice or thrice as fast as spinning by hand. Look how many spindles I filled." She waved a hand at the table, and the pile of what Lubos had to assume were spindles.

Lubos gathered them up, then kissed her quickly. "I'll take these to my father, and tell him you have a machine that can make miracles. I'm sure it will please him. I told you we will help him see reason."

Before he could surrender to his desire for her again, he forced his feet to carry him out of her chamber. "Once I have reported to the king, I am yours, my lady. I have a great number of kisses I mean to share with you, in our bedchamber below," he called over his shoulder as he headed down the stairs.

"I will be waiting," he heard her say.

Grinning, Lubos marched to the throne room, only to find his father had dismissed the court for the day. Sighing, he headed back up a different set of stairs to his father's solar.

He heard his father's muttering before he entered the room, and strained his ears to hear the words. Something about demanding his son for marriage, when he'd offered his daughter. His father didn't sound likely to accept the proposal, whoever it was for, and Lubos breathed a sigh of relief.

"Good evening, Father," he said loudly, as he entered the solar. No courtly bows were required here, for there was no audience to impress.

"Is it?" Father eyed the window suspiciously. "Have you caught my thieving barons yet, boy?"

Lubos shook his head. "No, not yet. They all seem to be a loyal lot. But I do bring good news. Lady Molina has perfected the miraculous spinning wheel she promised, and look what she has made!" He set the three spindles on the table before his father.

They didn't look particularly impressive. For a moment, Lubos wished he'd brought Molina and her spinning wheel along, too, but then he remembered his father's tastes ran to women like Bachmeier's daughters, not his lithe lady.

Father picked one up and examined it, then took it to the window, where the sunlight might better illuminate Molina's work.

"Who did this?" Father demanded.

"Lady Molina, the lady I wish to marry," Lubos began.

"How?" Father interrupted.

"With a miraculous spinning wheel of her own design. She takes some combed flax, spins the wheel, twists the flax through her fingers, and turns it into that. Faster than you can believe," Lubos said proudly.

"She shall show me on the morrow. If it is truly as you say, you must marry the girl. Marry her, before someone else does."

Lubos hardly dared believe his luck. "Marry her on the morrow? Father, thank you!"

Father glared at him. "I did not say that. Tomorrow she will prove her claims, while you finish the quest I have twice sent you on, but you have failed at. When you have found the barons cheating me of my share, and restored their tithe to me, then you may marry her. Meantime, I shall keep her close. She cannot be allowed to escape. Make sure you lock her in her chambers tonight."

There would be no need to lock her in anywhere, Lubos thought but didn't say. He could happily keep Molina confined to the bed until the morrow, and she would be his willing prisoner. Especially when he told her he had his father's permission to marry on his return.

He bade his father a good evening for the second time, and sped to the chamber where Molina waited for him.

Twenty-Four

The moment the bedchamber door closed behind him, Molina opened her mouth to share all her worries with Lubos, not least of all the strange man who'd stopped her spinning wheel, but Lubos pressed a finger to her lips.

"I must leave in the morning, to finish my quest for the king. The sooner I go, the sooner I may return and we can be married. I know you have much to tell me — I could tell you much about my travels, too — but neither is important right now. We have one night together, and I wish to spend it sharing as much love as possible, so that the memory will warm us both when we are far apart." He looked longingly into her eyes. "I will make love to you any way you wish, from now until dawn, and I swear the next night we spend together shall be our wedding night. My father has agreed, and so it shall be."

The very thought of him inside her once more kindled a fire within her brighter than she'd imagined possible. Why, it seemed her insides burned to feel him again. Lubos was right. She didn't want to waste these precious hours with words.

She hitched up her skirt, layers of silk and linen, until she was bare to the waist, but for her stockings. She hooked one leg around his hip, sliding her hand up under his tunic for his hard length. Her fingers tangled with his, intent on one purpose – uniting them. He thrust inside her, cupping her bottom as he lifted her, pushing deeper to her moaning satisfaction.

"Oh God, Molina," he said as he backed her up against the wall. "So long I've been dreaming of you like this."

She fastened her legs around his hips, holding his gaze as he filled her. "And I you. Make the first time hard and fast. If we have all night, we can take our time."

He chuckled. "Hard and fast you shall have, but I think you have forgotten something. My lady must come first." He pinned her to the wall, as full of him as she was with child. Without taking his eyes off hers, his thumb found precisely the right spot at the apex of her thighs, rubbing hard and fast until her vision dissolved into stars. Only then did he move again, maintaining the same rhythm until they cried out for joy together.

She was too busy gasping for breath to protest when he withdrew from her. But then he carried her to bed, and began to unlace her gown. He peeled away layers of fabric until he'd bared her breasts, which he covered with kisses. With her nipples already far too sensitive, thanks to her pregnancy, the moment he decided to suck on one was almost enough to send her over the edge, and she cried out.

"Did I hurt you?" he asked immediately,

pulling away.

"No, of course not. Please, don't stop," she said.

He grinned and lowered his lips to her breast again. His hands dipped lower, bunching her skirts up until he'd bared her legs. Legs she parted willingly at a touch, for she knew the magic that dwelled in his fingers. Magic that soon made her cry out his name, over and over, until she was too hoarse to speak.

Only then did he finish undressing her, dragging her skirts down and throwing them to the floor, heedless of what happened to them. When she wore nothing but her silken stockings, he paused.

"Would you like me to take them off?" she asked, feeling incredibly self-conscious as his eyes devoured her otherwise naked body.

"No. They stay," he said, sitting on the bed beside her. "Now, come sit in my lap and help me take my clothes off."

He didn't wait for a response, lifting her easily so that she sat astride him, just like on their very first time together. And he was rock hard between her thighs, ready for her. She reached down, ready to guide him inside her, but Lubos caught her hands and lifted them to the buttons at the front of his tunic. "I'll take care of that. You see to my clothes."

Her hands shaking with anticipation, she worked at the fastenings on his tunic. Never had it taken her so long to free three buttons from their loops, and she almost cried when the third one finally came free. As if that was his cue, Lubos thrust into her partway, holding tight to her hips when she tried to squirm down the length of him to drive him deeper inside her. "My clothes," he reminded her.

Reluctantly, she pulled his tunic up over his head.

He slid in an inch deeper.

She took a deep breath, tugging his under tunic off, too.

He filled her completely and she let out a sigh of pleasure.

"Don't forget my hose," he said, grinning.

Molina glanced over her shoulder. Sure enough, he wore thick woollen hose, the cloth scratchy beneath her bottom. Yes, they had to go. She managed to get them down past his knees by rising up onto her own knees, but in order to pull them off entirely she'd need to lean right back. One glance at his grin told her he had no intention of helping.

Wrapping her legs securely around his waist, she bent backward, arching her back up as she stretched her arms behind her to push his hose down his calves and off his feet.

"My God, you're beautiful, Molina." His finger stroked the nipple of one upthrust breast. A delicious sensation that made her cry out again. "Here, I'll help you up." One strong hand splayed across her back, while his other fastened around her hip, crushing her against him. But instead of lifting her up, he fell back on the mattress, pulling her with him until she sat astride him while he lay supine on the bed. "If I had a choice, I would spend every moment of the rest of my life like this with you. Hard and deep inside you, while you ride me to the peak of your own pleasure, with your breasts bouncing just like that." With his hands on her hips, he lifted and lowered her, thrusting up to meet her until she caught his rhythm, leaving his hands free to caress her breasts until she screamed.

But they didn't stop.

Not until dawn stole him from her, and she collapsed, empty and aching, in his lonely bed. For nothing was quite as heartbreaking as holding her husband to be and losing him, all in one night.

Twenty-Five

"Get her up and dressed. Now!"

The male voice giving orders wasn't one Molina recognised. But when unfamiliar hands seized her arms and dragged her from her bed, it no longer mattered.

"Unhand me!" she demanded. "Do you know what Prince Lubos will say if he discovers you have laid hands on his bethrothed?"

"Nothing good, I'm sure, but it doesn't matter, miss, for my orders come from the king."

Someone threw open the window shutters and Molina blinked in the bright light. The man who'd spoken, giving orders that came from the king, was the king's guard captain, who'd stood at the king's side in court. A man of honour, or so she'd thought.

He caught sight of her, too, and turned his back. "Avert your eyes, men, and let the lady dress!"

His men obeyed, and Molina hurried to don the clothes Lubos had stripped from her last night. Dropped from the very heights of passion to this rude awakening.

When she was decently covered, she asked, "Where are you taking me?" She did her best to hide her dread at what the captain might answer.

"To another room in the castle, where the king wants you to demonstrate your spinning skills. When your work is done, I have orders to return you to the prince's chambers."

That didn't sound so bad. Spinning for a day was no harder than what she did at home. Molina managed to summon her best smile as she pulled on her boots. "Then shall we go,

Captain?"

He nodded, looking relieved, and gestured for his men to follow behind them. He led her to an older part of the castle, with narrower passageways and uneven stairs leading ever upward, until he opened the door to another tower room, nowhere near as handsomely furnished as the prince's. No tapestries adorned these walls, and his bed would not have fitted here. The windows were little more than arrow slits, where they were visible at all, for the walls were stacked high with baskets of flax, waiting to be spun.

In the middle of all this sat her spinning wheel, fitted with a new spindle. A box containing dozens more sat on a stool that was evidently where she was expected to sit while she laboured.

It would be a challenge, but she suspected that with the aid of her wheel, she could have it all spun before the day was done. If not…well, it wasn't as though Lubos waited for her. The bed would be cold without him, so what was an evening's work if she had little else to do?

She thanked the captain and set to work, barely noticing when the door closed, so focussed was she on her work.

Hours passed and Molina spun, turning the wheel faster now she knew how to work the machine. Basket after basket emptied between her nimble fingers, but she did not stop. She was determined to show the king what her contraption could do in well-trained hands. A week's work in a day, that's what, she told herself, as she lifted the last basket. Her hands ached, but there was so little left, it would be but the work of a moment. And it was – in no time at all, she reached for the door, ready to return to the prince's chamber, only to find the door was locked.

She rapped smartly on the wood. "Captain, I have finished spinning all of the flax!" she called.

She heard the scrape of bolts being drawn, before the door swung open. "Truly?" the captain asked, looking relieved.

He hadn't believed she could do it, Molina realised. Well, she'd proved him wrong, too.

His face fell when he looked around. "But

where is the gold?"

"Gold?" Molina looked blank, then remembered what Lubos had told the king. "The gold comes from selling the extra linen made this way. You can't honestly believe I am a witch who spins flax into gold directly, surely!"

"What I believe matters not. It is the king's command that you remain here until you have spun all the flax into gold thread, as you did yesterday." The captain held up one of yesterday's spindles, still full of the yellow thread that horrid man had touched.

Realisation dawned on her. He hadn't tainted the thread – he'd turned it into gold, thinking it would persuade her to help him. Instead, it had landed her in terrible trouble.

"But I can't…I didn't…" she began, then closed her mouth. She could not tell this guard captain that she'd been visited by a man who wasn't the prince in the prince's very chambers. The man's very presence placed her and her child in danger, for if the king had even the faintest suspicion that the child was not fathered by Lubos, there would be no marriage…instead, she'd be tried for treason. And likely die, along with her unborn child.

"Did you lie to the king yesterday about spinning this thread?" the captain demanded.

"No," she whispered forlornly. "I spun it, with that wheel."

He shoved the golden thread at her. "Then spin the rest like this, and I can return you to the prince's chambers." He left, slamming the door behind him. This time, Molina heard the bolts shoot home, locking her in.

Molina fell to her knees and wept. If the king intended to keep her here until she spun gold from flax, then she would die in this chamber, and never see Lubos again.

Twenty-Six

When the following day came, Abraham had to hunt for the girl. She was not in the tower chamber, nor the bedchamber below it. All day he peeped into rooms all over the sprawling castle, but she had hidden herself well.

It wasn't until after dark that he spotted a light in the maidens' tower that hadn't been there last night. Abraham gazed up at the flickering light, and all the pieces fell into place. She'd been frightened, so she'd taken refuge in the highest, most defensible tower in the middle of the castle. It was heavily guarded, too — she was taking no chances. Guards at the door, in a chamber partway up the tower, and more outside the door to her chamber at the top. If it weren't for his magical shoes, Abraham would have no chance of reaching her.

After making more holes in her tower walls than he'd find in a mountain cheese, finally he emerged in her chamber. Just as before, she was alone with her spinning table toy, and several baskets filled with spindles of spun thread.

The girl herself sat on the floor, weeping.

Abraham hesitated. He had little experience with weeping women, and he did not think this one wanted to be kissed as Maja had.

"I have come for your answer, as I promised," he announced. "Will you help me?"

She raised her red-rimmed eyes. "When you are responsible for all this? Why would I help you?"

Perhaps he hadn't explained himself well enough yesterday. "Because both I and my son will die unless you break the curse that afflicts my family."

"What about me?" she demanded, rising. "I will die because of what you did! If I do not turn all this thread into gold like you did yesterday, the king will have me killed. If you want my help, then fix the mess you have made!"

"You wish me to transform this thread?" Abraham hardly dared to believe it could be so simple.

She glared at him. "The king demands that it be done, after seeing the thread you transformed yesterday."

This must be the danger the seer had spoken of.

"So if I simply turn your thread into gold, you will agree to help me?"

If anything, the fire in her eyes burned even more deadly than before. "If you work your magic on it, then perhaps the king will let me live long enough to consider helping you. For if you do not, he will execute me in the morning."

He would have to save her.

"Very well." Abraham peeled off his gloves, and plunged his bare hands into the nearest basket. Spindle after spindle he touched, until they were all transformed, and then he started on the next one.

Behind him, he heard the girl tip out the basket he'd finished with. Checking his work, no doubt. But she would find no impurities in his gold. Its magical nature required no refinement.

He reached for the third basket.

"You've missed two." She held out the spindles, their pale thread seeming ghostly compared to the shimmering gold of their companions.

Abraham didn't dare risk touching her, especially not without his gloves. "Set them there," he directed, pointing at the wheel table.

"It makes much more sense to do them a few at a time, then place them in the basket once they're done. As I did, when I spun them," she said. "Then you won't miss any."

"I didn't miss any. I just may not have touched them for long enough for the spell to work," Abraham said.

"Well, the second basket had seven you didn't touch. That's ten you've missed. A systematic approach would be much more efficient. Yours isn't the only life depending on this being done right, you know."

Growling, he reached for a fourth basket and dumped the contents on the stone floor. He seized two in each hand, transformed them, then tossed them in the empty basket. "Happy now?"

"I won't be happy until the king releases me, and my husband returns. But at least now I might live another day."

Just as Abraham would not be truly happy until he'd saved his son and could take Maja in his arms again.

"What is this curse someone has cast on you?"

Her question surprised him. Could she not see?

"Someone cast it on one of my ancestors, and it follows his bloodline. So it was passed down to me, and my son. I did nothing to deserve it but be born into the wrong house."

"But what does it do?" she persisted. "You said it will kill you, but..."

"When my death is close, and I have less

than a year to live, everything I touch turns to gold. Unless I wear these gloves." Abraham jerked his chin at the fur lined gloves on the table. "And then one day…or one night, in my father's case…it is over."

She nodded thoughtfully. "So you are given a year to improve your family's fortunes before you die. It does not seem like such a curse to me. All men die, and at least you have more warning than most."

Did she not understand? "We die young. In our prime. Leaving a young wife and child behind, who we cannot touch from the moment the curse takes hold. My family have called it the Touch, for that is the one thing we cannot do. Touch anyone we love. You cannot imagine what it is like!"

"I cannot touch my husband, for the king has sent him on some quest, while he keeps me locked up here. I do not know how long it will be before I can touch him again, or even see him again, for I do not know when he will return. So I know very well what it is like, though my misfortune is the work of men, you and the king, not some mysterious witch casting a curse!"

She was right, curse her, though he didn't dare say it. He set the last golden spindle in the now filled basket. "There. This one is done. On to the next."

She reached for it. "I shall check it first."

He sighed. He could not argue with that, either.

Twenty-Seven

Molina woke up on the floor, surrounded by gold-filled spindles. The strange man was gone, but he'd done his work well. True to his word, he'd turned all the thread into gold. The king would have to be satisfied now.

She rose stiffly and made her way to the door and banged her fist on it. "Captain, I am done," she shouted.

"I will fetch the captain, mistress," came a voice through the door. There was a pause, then a muffled, "It may take some time to find him."

Molina settled down to wait.

By the time she could hear someone unbarring the door, the sun had reached the arrow slits that passed for windows and it streamed down on the artfully piled up spindles, setting the whole room aglow.

The men in the doorway had to shield their eyes against the brightness, so it took them a moment to register her presence. "The king's work is done, Captain, and I would retire to my chamber now," Molina said pointedly.

A man stepped through the door, blinking. The guard captain looked like he'd been woken from a sound sleep.

"I…ah…yes, mistress. Two of my men will see you safely to your chambers. I must…must report this to the king."

Her arms felt leaden after all the spinning she'd done yesterday, so she was relieved when the guardsmen didn't take her arms like they might a prisoner. Instead, they walked behind her, letting her lead the way. As though she truly was Lubos' wife, and not some girl who hoped the king would allow her to marry him. For the madman Lubos had introduced as his father, the king, was not a man she could trust to keep his promises. Unlike his son.

Vowing to hide in Lubos' chambers until he returned, Molina sank into the prince's bed. She had only a moment to wish the prince lay beside her before sleep claimed her for its own.

Twenty-Eight

The following night, Abraham returned to the maiden's tower, where he found the girl sitting at the wheeled table, spinning flax into thread. The walls were stacked with baskets of the stuff, waiting to be spun.

Before he could ask, she said, "The king is not satisfied with what I gave him this morning. He insists I must spin even more. He expects the impossible. No one could spin this much thread in a day, even with a spinning wheel."

"If you merely break the curse, I will leave

you to your work, and never disturb you again," Abraham said.

She slammed her hands on the table and rose. "I know nothing of curses, unless you are one! Even if I can spin the fibres into thread, I cannot turn it into gold, no matter what the king thinks. Only you can do that. I wish you had never come to me at all, for you will surely get me killed!"

"If I help you again, will you break the curse?" Abraham asked.

"Why won't you listen to me? Why won't any of you stupid men listen to me? I do not know how to break curses, spin straw into gold, or work miracles! I understand waterwheels and spinning wheels and mills, but men's minds spin in such strange ways it is a wonder you can survive at all!" A tear trickled down her cheek. "Yet it is my life at stake, because none of you will listen."

Abraham swallowed. The seer had been certain. Only she could break the curse, no one else. For she had been alone in that tower room until he arrived. "Please," he said simply. "I am sorry for whatever trouble I have caused you. If I make amends, if I help you, would you be willing to at least try to help me break the curse?"

She stared at him for a long time before she said, "Once my work is done, maybe I will be of a mind to help you. Though this will take us all night and into the next day, I am certain."

He wanted to shake her, to demand her word, but he could not bring himself to harm the girl. He had less than a year to live, but if she did not do this task the king had set her, he would outlive her. And any hope for his son.

Her wheel whirred into life – she had no time to spare, waiting for his answer when there was work to be done.

Sighing, Abraham set to work.

Twenty-Nine

A night and a day and half the next night it took before Molina finished spinning, as the strange man turned her work from linen to gold. She must have fallen asleep on the spinning wheel, for her back ached from sitting on the stool before it for so long.

The door swung open – the sound of it unbolting must have woken her. The guard captain had returned.

"Get her up. The king wants her moved. Bring the table, too."

"And the stool, sir?"

"All of it."

Molina wished it were a dream, but as two guardsmen took her aching arms, she knew this was worse than any nightmare.

They marched her out of the castle and down the cobbled streets to where she could hear the rushing water of the river. Did they mean to throw her in?

Two men unbarred a massive set of doors, large enough to drive a cart through, which is what someone must have done, for the space she entered stretched for what seemed like miles in the light of the guttering torches. The vaulted ceilings told her she was in some vast storehouse or cellar, filled with baskets of flax.

Distantly, she heard the sound of something being set down on the stone floor. Her spinning wheel and her stool.

"By the king's order, you will stay here and spin, until his warehouse contains nothing but gold," the captain said.

She folded her arms across her chest. "And what if I cannot?"

"Then by the king's command, you shall be put to death." There was pity in the guard captain's eyes. "We all serve the king, mistress, and you must do your duty as I do mine. Set to work, and I will see that a good meal is sent up from the castle kitchens. The crown prince would not want you to starve." He hustled the other guards out, and the heavy bar on the door clanged as it dropped into place.

Molina wanted to cry, but she had no tears left. So she did the only thing she could — sit down and spin, for such was her fate.

Thirty

Day blended into night, for there was no light down here, except that which came from the torches, which guardsmen replaced every day when they brought Molina's meals. The food was not so fine as the fare she'd enjoyed in Lubos' chambers, but it was no worse than some of the things she'd cooked on the nights Helga spent with her family.

Until one morning, when the smell from the stewpot curdled the contents of her belly and she had to bring her dinner back up again.

Too weak to work, she'd lay down on her

straw pallet, pushing the food as far away from her as possible.

If she did not work, she would die down here in the dark, she told herself, but the words were not enough to rouse her. Some illness had laid her low, and she did not know if she would survive it.

Thirty-One

The next night, the girl was not in the crown tower nor the maiden's one, and Abraham despaired of finding her. He searched the castle in vain for three days, until he stumbled across the guard captain carrying a meal out of the castle gates. Curious, he followed the man to the tithe barns by the river, and that was where he found the princess.

Abraham hid in the shadows, waiting for the guard to leave before he stepped inside the barn.

He didn't see her at first, for the place was

stacked with baskets, much like her chamber in the maiden's tower. But what he'd seen in the maiden's tower was a mere millpond compared to the endless sea he saw here.

She sat slumped over her wheeled table, with a half-full spindle beside her. The basket of filled spindles at her feet told Abraham she'd been labouring for the king again, until she fell asleep.

"Princess?" he said, then repeated it, a little louder each time, until he managed to rouse her.

She sat up, blinking. "You," she managed to say before she slumped over the wheel again with a groan. This was more than simple tiredness.

She vomited into a bucket at her feet, then rose unsteadily. "Must…lie down…"

Abraham caught her before she fell. "Are you ill?" he asked, dreading her response. For he might be able to save her from some foe, but illnesses were not something a man could fight with a sword. He laid her gingerly on the pallet she'd been headed toward and backed away.

"Not ill. 'Tis just the baby. The sickness mothers get..." She coughed, and Abraham handed her the bucket just in time.

Maja had been the same, he remembered now. Ill and swearing she was not, until she'd seen the seer and admitted she was carrying his son.

Childbirth could kill a woman in more ways than a sword could. And that was without a king who'd threatened to execute her if she didn't spin straw into gold.

So much for her breaking the curse quickly.

And now he couldn't.

Abraham stared around the barn, and the piled-up baskets of flax. Even if she could break the curse now, it would cost her her life, for without his curse turning the stuff to gold, the king would kill her.

No wonder she didn't consider it a curse.

If he wanted his son to live, he would have to do the work for her. Saving her, and his son.

Abraham sat down on the stool she'd recently vacated, twisting the thread between his gloved fingers as he spun the wheel experimentally. Long ago, Maja had tried to teach him how to spin, but she had not done it with a wheel like this princess did. The thread broke, stuck between his fingers, and Abraham swore.

Too late he remembered the princess was present, but she had fallen asleep and not noticed his foul language. Fortunately.

He tried again, but every time, the thread caught on his gloves and broke. He would have to take them off.

Perhaps it was a good thing the king wanted his thread spun into gold, for between Abraham's bare fingers, the thread glittered as it wound its way around the spinning spindle.

The hours galloped past, but Abraham focussed only on his work. He rested occasionally, making up a second pallet in the shadows at the far end of the barn, where the guards would not see him when they brought the princess her meals.

One day, he woke to find her at the spinning wheel, her nimble fingers working faster than his could, though her slumped shoulders said she did not wish to.

"Let me do that, Princess," he implored.

"You are in no state for such things. Return to your bed and rest."

Her eyes seemed sunken, or perhaps it was a trick of the light. "I will rest when I am dead, which will be soon, if the king has his way. You said once you wished to save your son. Well, I wish I could save my daughter. It seems we will both fail at our respective quests." She stroked her belly wistfully.

That's when it hit him. All the times she'd refused him, told him she could not break the curse. What if it was not the princess, but her daughter? Her daughter would be a princess, too.

"Were you carrying the child when we first met?" he asked eagerly.

"What does it matter to you, bringer of bad fortune? Because of you, she will die when I do."

"Please. I mean you no harm, Princess. Truly. Whatever sins I have committed against you, I pray you will forgive me."

She looked at him long and hard. "I pray I will, too. But not yet. And if it matters, though I have no idea why it might, yes, I was already carrying my husband's child the night you invaded my chamber and made the king think I can work miracles."

Abraham shook his head. "Your husband did that, not I. I was listening when he presented your work to the king. Miracles is his word, not mine. Come with me now, and I will save you from the king and your thoughtless husband, and when your child is born, I will see she is treated like the princess she is."

"I will not leave the man I love. Not for the king, or you, or anyone." She coughed, and reached for the bucket. "Prince Lubos will return. He will help me, and will marry me, just like he promised." She rose shakily to her feet, staggered to her bed, and fell face-first into the straw. After a long moment, she moved so she lay more comfortably. "I must rest. When I wake, I will…work more."

"Swear to me you will give me the child when she is born, and I will spin all the straw in this room into gold," Abraham said. "You will live and stay with your husband, and your sacrifice will save my life and my son's.

The princess coughed again, but she did not reach for the bucket. It took Abraham a moment to realise she was laughing. "Give up my child to you? A strange man I neither know nor trust? You are a fool. No. You shall not have her."

Abraham folded his arms across his chest. "Then I will not help you."

The standoff did not last long. The princess fell asleep, and Abraham went back to work. For he could not let the girl and her daughter die, not if one of them could save his son. And as long as he stayed, he would keep trying to convince her. She would agree eventually. She had to.

Thirty-Two

While the princess slept, he spun. When she awoke, sometimes he would sleep, and at others, he would ask her again. Her answer never changed – she would not give him her child.

Until finally, after several days of being unable to leave her bed as the sickness laid her lower than usual, she said the words he was waiting for: "Yes. If you can spin every bit of flax in this place into gold before the king executes me, then the child is yours."

He wanted to cheer and dance, but

Abraham knew he could not stop working. For while there was work to be done, he could not stop. Because the pain in his chest was increasing, and his days were numbered. If he did not finish his task before the curse claimed him, then this would all be for naught.

Abraham spun until his fingers ached, and then he spun some more. Twisting flax into gold, watching the spool fill, then swapping it for another.

Until he reached for a fresh basket…and found they were all empty. A warehouse full of flax, spun into enough gold to last a kingdom for a century.

He set the last spindle on the pile and searched through the baskets again, but found nothing left to spin.

His work was done.

Abraham rose from his stool, his legs stiff from sitting so long, and staggered over to the wall. He opened a hole in the wall, and made his way back to the cottage where he'd taken up lodgings when he first arrived.

The bed was narrow and hard, little better than the pallet in the warehouse, but he fell facedown on the cool linen, pulled a blanket over himself, and slept the sleep of the dead.

Thirty-Three

Lubos had never ridden so much in his life. He lingered in each barony only long enough to hear the tales of this summer's low harvest and see the truth of it for himself, before heading to the next one. Molina was in his mind, every day and every night. A dozen times a day, he'd turn to see her riding by his side, only to find he rode alone. At night, he'd wake to a bed that was cold and lonely without her. Life was cold and lonely without her.

The faster he fulfilled his quest, the sooner he would stand with her at his side in the new cathedral as his bride.

But the longer he rode, the more he realised his father had sent him on a fool's errand. There were no grounds for his father's suspicions, as he would know if he stepped outside the castle long enough to see the farmlands for himself. Signs of the spring floods were everywhere for anyone with eyes to see. Could his father be so blind in his old age that all he saw were the slights of the past, when what the kingdom needed was a man firmly grounded in the present who could look to the future?

If only his father's body was as unsound as his mind, but Lubos could not recall his father ever knowing a day of ill health. The man might go completely mad, and yet still remain king.

So Lubos filled his saddlebags with written reports about every nobleman he visited, careful to take note of everything he saw, so his father would have no excuse to send him out again. He needed Molina, and he liked to fancy that perhaps she might like to have him home as well.

Or perhaps she was so busy ensuring every woman in the capital owned a spinning wheel and knew how to use it, that she had no thoughts to spare for him at all. Lubos smiled at the thought of a woman who loved machines more than men. At least, most men. He knew she loved him, and that was all that mattered.

When he finally rode across the bridge into the capital, he raised his eyes to the crown tower, where they'd set up her workroom above his bedchamber. Above the bedchamber they shared, he corrected himself, as his body ached to feel hers twined around him once more. Soon, he promised himself, and her, for if she happened to glance out the window, she would surely see him returning.

If only he could go to her first, but his father would want to know the news, and he might withdraw his consent to the marriage if Lubos favoured his bride over king and country. So Lubos trudged wearily to the throne room and made his report, then answered questions until even his father was satisfied.

Afternoon faded into evening before Lubos ascended the steps to the crown tower, and Molina. He'd ordered food to be sent up, for once he entered his chambers, he had no intention of leaving her until the morrow, at least.

He threw open the door, but the chamber was cold, without even a fire to chase out the chill in the autumn air. Strange. Unless Molina had taken to sleeping in her workroom above. Lubos hurried up the stairs, only to find the workroom empty, too. No fire, no spinning wheel, no Molina…where was she?

His father would know, for only his father could order the men of the castle to ignore the crown prince's orders to care for his bride.

Had he sent her home? Forced her to marry that fool, Bachmeier? Or perhaps his half-brother, Xylander? Or worse, had some terrible fate befallen his stepmother, so that the king took Molina for himself? By all that was holy, Lubos prayed this had not happened. For if it had, he would be honour bound to kill his own father, for Molina could not have gone to him willingly.

Lubos broke into a run, headed for the throne room. His father had gone too far now.

The doors to the throne room were closed, and Schuttmann, the captain of the guard, stood in his way.

"Let me pass," Lubos demanded.

Schuttmann shook his head. "You are the heir to the throne. His rages have already driven your brother and sister away. If I let you pass, he will turn his rage on you, and if he orders me to kill you as a traitor, I shall have no choice. The kingdom will need you to take the reins when he is gone. Besides, he has almost forgotten about the girl. If you did not return this week, I would have risked freeing her myself."

"You know where she is?" Freeing her meant she was imprisoned somewhere, not married to someone else. Lubos dared to breathe again. "Take me to her!"

"Yes, Your Highness. She was taken to the maiden's tower, and then to one of the tithing barns."

"Why in heaven's name would she be in a barn? They should be full of..." Too late

Lubos realised there would likely be several empty barns, after this year's poor harvest. But still it did not make sense.

Schuttmann ducked his head. "This one was full of flax, Your Highness. Flax the king commanded her to spin. She has not been harmed, I swear it."

Lubos regarded the guard captain for a long moment. He was a man of honour, who would rather die than be forsworn. A man Lubos would rely on in the future, when Lubos was king. Better to start relying on him now, for the future was coming faster than Lubos liked.

"Take me to her," Lubos repeated, more calmly this time. He followed Schuttmann down to the river, pulling his cloak tighter around him as the evening chill seemed to rise from the very stones beneath his feet.

By the time they'd unbarred and unlocked the doors, it was full dark, and Lubos lit a torch to take inside the pitch-dark barn. A wall of baskets greeted him – empty baskets, which had once contained unspun flax, judging from the fluff clinging to the sides of some of them.

"Molina?" he called, but heard no answer.

He hurried to the end of the makeshift wall, lifting his torch high above his head to illuminate the cavernous space. His breath misted before his face, for he could feel the wintry chill stealing its way through his cloak. The cold was fine for storing food, but this was not the place for Molina.

He stepped deeper into the darkness, until the pool of light from his torch touched something other than stone and baskets. Something that shone back. Golden…balls? Lubos reached down to pick one up, and realised it was not a ball but a spindle, wound around with golden thread. Thousands of them, piled up in a great mountain that stretched nearly to the ceiling.

It would have taken an army of women months to spin so much. Molina could not have done this in the time he'd been gone. Unless she had an army of women, armed with her miraculous spinning wheels…

He rounded the pile, expecting to see the machines, lined up ready for production. But there was only one, sitting in a puddle of light, all alone.

Molina had done this with only one wheel. Working day and night, never ceasing…for how else could she accomplish such a thing? His father had enslaved a free woman. His betrothed.

"Molina?" he called again, louder this time.

The sound he heard was so quiet, he might have imagined it, but Lubos was certain he had not. The smell of damp was stronger here, and there was moss underfoot. He called her name again, and something rustled to his right.

If it was a rat getting his hopes up, he'd skewer it on his sword, Lubos swore, striding forward until he met a pile of mouldy-smelling straw. And amid the straw, a familiar boot. Dropping the torch, he rushed forward to extract the half-buried woman from the straw. Molina's eyes opened slowly, shadowed as though she had not slept for weeks. Then she lifted a thin hand to her lips and coughed hard for what seemed like an eternity.

He waited until the coughing fit subsided before he lifted her in his arms, having to hide his horror at how much lighter she felt. "Were they starving you, my lady?" he choked out.

"I know the castle kitchens regularly sent food, or they did. She hasn't touched this, and it looks two to three days old." Schuttmann nudged a plate with his foot, which sat beside a full jug of water. "The king must have forgotten about her after all."

"Then she can stay forgotten, but I'm taking her home." Lubos wrapped his cloak around her, but he couldn't stop her from shivering. "Summon a physician to my chamber."

"Yes, Your Highness." Schuttmann hurried off into the dark, his torch bobbing as he ran.

Lubos didn't dare run, carrying such a precious burden, but he strode with such purpose not even the gate guards dared to get in his way.

When he reached his chamber, he was pleased to see that someone had lit the fire, and a pot of something warmed on the hearth. He lay Molina on his bed and dared to look at her properly for the first time.

She had not been plump before, but her bones showed through her skin now, and he hadn't imagined the shadows beneath her eyes. He'd seen corpses with more colour, but her laboured breathing told him she still lived.

He peeled off her clothes, worn thin from overuse, and dressed her in one of her new linen shifts before tucking her properly into his bed. Only then did he ladle a bowl of stew from the pot by the fire and bring it to her bedside. He tasted a spoon of the stuff to make sure it wasn't too hot before offering some to her.

"You must be hungry, my lady. You haven't eaten for days. This will help you keep up your strength," he coaxed.

Her eyes fluttered open. "Lubos?" she managed to say before another coughing fit engulfed her.

"The very same," he said lightly, setting the bowl down so that he could support her. "What did they do to you while I was gone? I swear if I had known, I would have come right home." An empty promise, and they both knew it. He could not change the past, no matter how much he wished he could.

"Is he gone?" she asked, peering around.

"Who?" Whoever had frightened her, Lubos intended to see him dead by dawn.

"I do not know his name," she said.

Lubos did not need to know the man's name before he executed him.

"What did he do to you?" he demanded.

She sank back against the pillows. "Nothing. Not yet. But I don't want him to take my child…" Her hands slid down to her belly. Only now did Lubos realise it looked rounder than usual, though she'd lost weight everywhere else.

His fury burned white hot. "This man with no name got you with child?"

Molina smiled wanly. "No, the child is yours. Ours. No man but you has ever touched me like that."

"No other man ever shall," Lubos vowed. "My father said we could marry when I returned. Now I'm home, you shall name the day. As soon as you are well enough to leave my bed, if only for a few hours."

"Your Highness should not have brought some sick girl into your own bed. Heaven knows what diseases she may carry! Send her to the church, where the nuns take care of such charity cases." The physician sniffed.

"And burn all the bedding."

In three strides, Lubos stood before the fool, hauling him up by his collar until his feet dangled above the floor. "Have a care how you speak about the woman I am to marry, for one day she will be queen, and it is your job to make sure she survives. For if she dies, so shall you."

The physician's eyes went wide with terror. Good. "Y-yes, Your Highness," he said.

Lubos dropped him, then pointed to the patient. "Make my wife well again." He stood by the fire, with his arms folded across his chest, and watched.

The physician scurried to Molina's bedside, where her eyes had drifted closed once more. Perhaps it was for the best, as all that poking and prodding could not have been comfortable. Lubos prayed she didn't wake up until the man's examination of her was done, for to see a strange man so close to her would surely terrify what little life she had left out of her.

But Lubos' prayers went unanswered. The moment the physician touched her belly, her hands came up to shield herself. "Don't you take my child!"

The physician muttered something. Lubos only caught two words, but they were enough. He covered the distance between them in a moment, and felt a sense of satisfaction as his fist collided with the insolent man's jaw.

"Call my wife a whore again, or our child a bastard, and they will be the last words you ever utter," Lubos promised him.

The physician rose to his feet, rubbing his jaw. "Are you sure the babe is yours, Your Highness?"

Lubos did not hesitate. "Absolutely. Just as certain as I am when I tell you that if you are responsible for the death of a future queen and the king after me, I will make sure you die a traitor's death."

The physician paled and edged away from Lubos to examine Molina again. He took longer this time, though perhaps that was because he could feel both Molina and Lubos' eyes on him. Finally, he said, "I shall stop by the apothecary's on my way home and ask him to prepare some healing draughts for the girl. I will also give you a list of things a woman in her condition should eat and drink for the best health of the child, so that your castle cook can provide such things. If you should lose her or the child, it is God's will, not mine, for I have done everything I can." He scribbled something down on a roll of parchment and dropped it on the bed. "Your Highness." He bowed and departed.

Molina reached for the paper and unrolled it. "Most of these are just hearty foods. Plenty of meat, and things from the dairy. He left off lamb's lettuce. In the village where I grew up, expectant mothers all had to eat lamb's lettuce every day. To help stave off illness." The paper fell from her fingers and she lay back on the pillow again, paler than before. "I am…so tired, my love. Would you mind if I rest?" She closed her eyes, not waiting for permission.

Lubos smiled. She had been through enough, and she would need plenty of rest in order to recover from whatever she'd endured in his absence. He swore he would make things right, whatever it took.

Thirty-Four

Days passed. Lubos helped Molina to eat a little or take some of the numerous draughts the apothecary sent, though she managed to keep very few of the noxious potions down for very long. Her coughing grew worse, until she barely managed to swallow a thing without coughing it back up again. Lubos despaired as she seemed to grow even thinner before his eyes.

Hourly, he sent orders to the castle kitchens for the nourishing foods on the physician's list, but nothing could nourish her if it didn't make it down her throat.

The only thing the cook did not send up was lamb's lettuce, for the cook claimed to know nothing of a food by that name.

Lubos wanted to weep, or break something, or tear his own hair out by the roots. He was being forced to watch the woman he loved die, and there was nothing he could do about it.

Captain Schuttmann made the mistake of visiting and Lubos almost pitched him out the door again. Almost, but some spark of reason far in the back of his mind reminded him that without Schuttmann, he would never have found her, so Lubos sank back on his chair and simply stared balefully at the guard captain instead.

"How is she?" Schuttmann asked.

Lubos waved his hand at the bed. "See for yourself."

Schuttmann's expression said it all. "I am sorry we were too late to help her. I came to tell you that the king has given you permission to marry the girl, now she has spun to his satisfaction."

Lubos wasn't sure whether he wanted to

laugh or cry. "She can't keep her eyes open long enough to speak the vows, and as long as she cannot eat anything without bringing it back up again, she cannot gain any strength. And to make matters worse, she's carrying our child!"

Schuttmann's eyebrows rose. "She is with child? My wife had terrible morning sickness with our first child. Couldn't eat a thing for weeks, and she didn't have the strength to leave her bed, either. I ate in your father's hall most nights, for she could not cook. When she carried our second child, she caught a chill, much like your girl here, and I thought I'd lose them both, but there's a witch who lives over on the south side of the mountain, and she has medicinal plants that grow nowhere else but her garden. I paid a fortune for some leaves from a plant called a rapunzel, which she said would help my wife to fight the illness. Watching my wife eat leaves like a rabbit, I thought it a foolish notion, until she began to improve. They say physicians and priests and prayer are all we should need for health, but sometimes we need to go back to the old ways, and the old gods, for witches know things that priests and physicians would never dream about."

Lubos stared at his sleeping lady. The lady who might never wake again. "Can you get this miraculous plant for me? I dare not leave her. Any moment might be her last."

Schuttmann shook his head. "Nay, that I cannot. Witches have their ways, and I dare not cross one. Whether a king or a commoner, if you want something from a witch, you must ask her yourself. It's half a day's ride – if you leave now, and ride through the night, you might be back in time to feed your lady leaves to break her fast on the morrow."

And if he did not, and she died during the night, he would never forgive himself. Lubos planted a kiss on her fevered brow, praying it would not be the last, and headed out of the room, towards the stables. He would find the witch, persuade her to part with the plant, and return on the morrow to save Molina. And when she recovered, he would marry her, like he'd promised.

Thirty-Five

Darkness had fallen by the time he arrived at the walls around the witch's garden. This had to be the place, for the rest of the mountain was covered in vineyards and these stone walls looked positively ancient. There was just one problem: the gates were closed, and no matter how loudly Lubos knocked or shouted, no one came to open them.

All his frustration and fury at losing Molina bubbled up. He'd ridden so far, willing to do anything to save her, and the witch wasn't about to let the crown prince of the realm she lived in through the gates?

To hell with that.

Lubos found a spot where the wall looked easier to climb, and started up. It had been some time since he'd climbed anything, but it was a skill, once learned, that a man never forgot. A handhold here, a toehold there, stretching for a new one, one limb at a time, until he could haul himself over the top of the wall.

From the surprisingly wide top, he had his pick of trees to climb down to reach the ground below. The garden stretched out as far as a vineyard in the moonlight, carved up into beds by myriad paths that went everywhere. It was a labyrinth with a thousand ways through to your destination – much like the capital, but with patches of plants where the buildings should be.

Each plot had a little post with a sign on top, that was surprisingly easy to read in the moonlight. It must be some sort of magic, Lubos realised, glancing around. What other spells lurked within these walls?

He was so intent on finding the sign with

rapunzel on it that he nearly missed the right plot, for the sign said lamb's lettuce. He snorted to himself. Molina was correct, as usual. He peered at the sign again, and was surprised to see that it had changed so that it clearly said rapunzel. Magic for sure. Lubos shivered.

Well, whether it was rapunzel or lamb's lettuce, this was what he needed. He stooped to pick a handful, and the whole plant came up, like a turnip. He shook the soil free, then opened a sack and slipped the plant inside. He stared at the remaining plants for a long moment, debating whether he dared take more. For if one was not enough…he would not have time to ride back here for more.

In the end, he took three, reasoning that if one had been enough for Schuttmann's sick wife, then he would need at least two for Molina. Three…just in case.

He'd brought a bag of gold coins to trade for the plants, and he emptied the pouch into one of the holes he'd left, as payment. Though he'd climbed the wall at night and taken the plants without asking the owner, he was a prince and a man of honour, not a thief. That much gold would feed a family for a year. More than enough payment for three plants.

Tying the sack shut, he flung it over his shoulder. Now he had another decision to make: back over the wall, the way he'd come, or through the gate, which surely opened from the inside?

Leaving the gate open would surely alert the witch that she'd had a visitor, but Lubos had never intended his visit to be a secret. She'd know once she reached the rapunzel beds, regardless.

He strode confidently toward the gate, holding tight to his precious sack of plants.

Only to find a figure stood in his way.

The witch lifted her lantern. "Who dares steal from Mistress Kun?"

Lubos swallowed. "I am Crown Prince Lubos, heir to the king, and I have left fair payment for the plants I took. Let me pass, for a woman's life depends on them."

The witch did not budge. "I decide what is a fair price, not you." Her eyes seemed to glow blue in the darkness. "What is it you have taken? Ah, the rapunzel. You lie, Prince. More than one life depends on the plants you hold."

Lubos hung his head. "'Tis true. The woman I love is carrying our child. We were betrothed to be married, but she has fallen ill, and I fear for her life." He paused, then added, "And for the child."

"What is this woman's life worth to you?" the witch demanded.

"She is worth more to me than everything I own, including my own life," Lubos said without hesitation.

"What would you give me, if I let you leave with your pilfered plants, and my solemn promise to you that both the woman and her child will live long and healthy lives?"

For Molina? "Anything," he said.

The witch smiled and named a terrible price.

Thirty-Six

"That's the last of the lamb's lettuce. I hope it is enough, for we have no more," Lubos said. He sounded…cheerful.

Molina struggled to open her eyes. They felt as heavy as the rest of her, as though they had not moved in far too long. Her hand flew to her belly, checking that it still swelled with the child growing inside her. She lived, and Lubos was home. She blinked against the bright morning light, and came face to face with a plate of leaves.

Lamb's lettuce, her mind supplied. She'd

never liked it in the past, but now she had the most irresistible craving to devour every last leaf. She reached for it.

"It worked!" Large, warm hands seized hers, and a man's bearded face loomed alarmingly close for a moment until she recognised Lubos beneath the scrubby beard. Then he kissed her.

She batted him away weakly. "It scratches," she complained.

"I'll shave immediately," he promised, then stopped. "Though I should feed you first."

Molina waved her hand. "I can manage these leaves. You…get rid of that horrible hedge."

He laughed and bowed low. "As my lady commands."

She'd almost finished her salad by the time a servant came with warm water and soap, so Molina sat back and watched Lubos shave in the bronze mirror by the window. Her heart soared to see him again. All the darkness…all that drudgery…but that was done now. It must be, for she was back in his chambers, just as the guard captain had promised.

"Molina, can you tell me what happened?

Why you were in that barn full of baskets and balls?" Lubos' eyes gazed at her from his reflection.

She swallowed. She could lie and say she did not remember, but she was no coward. She could not shrink from the truth, especially when Lubos asked for it.

So she told him about the tower room, and the barn, and the spindle he'd given his father that inspired the king's commands. To her surprise, even as she told him about her exhaustion, the pain in her hands from working all hours, and every hardship she had endured, the weight on her shoulders seemed to lessen. Almost as if her ordeal no longer had the power to hurt her.

When Lubos sat beside her on the bed and pulled her into his arms, she did not resist. She'd craved his embrace for longer than she'd wanted those leaves, and she loved him. Loved him with all her heart and soul. And when her body had healed, she'd love him again with that, too.

If he forgave her for what she'd done.

Reluctantly, she pulled away from him.

"There is more. The spindle you gave your father wasn't ordinary thread. It was gold thread, pure gold."

"That's not possible," Lubos said. "No one can spin flax into gold. You told me that. Gold comes from selling the linen…"

Oh, how his thoughts mirrored what her own had been. But no more. "Without magic, yes. But there was a man. That first day I managed to get the spinning wheel working, he came into my workroom. Just walked in, and I first thought he was you. He…he begged to me to break some curse, saying I was the only one who could, and some seer had told him so. He begged me to come with him to do it, and I refused. He offered me all the wealth I would ever need, so I would never need to spin again, and placed his hands on my spindle. The one you took to your father. And then he heard you coming, and he walked through the floor, just as you came in. I barely believed my own eyes, for how could a man walk through solid stone without magic?"

Lubos nodded. "You seemed…agitated, but you told me you were excited at having the wheel working."

"It was true. I was excited. And then he came in, said nonsensical things, and left. I thought perhaps I had gone mad, and did not wish you to know you had promised to marry a madwoman, so I did not tell you. Not that you gave me much time. You were so excited, you grabbed the spindles off my wheel and took them to your father. All filled with gold thread."

Molina took a deep breath. "I did not notice it was gold. Neither did you, I assume. But your father did, and after you left…he had the guard captain take me to a room filled with flax, and he told me to spin. I did, spinning until my fingers cramped and I could scarcely see straight, until every spindle was full of fine linen thread. I'd worked a miracle — doing a week's work in a day, but it was not enough for the king. He had a spindle of gold thread, and my work wasn't done until I'd spun it all into gold."

Lubos gritted his teeth. "My father will rot in hell for this, I swear it!"

Molina hushed him. What happened to the

king after his death was no business of hers, and the same fate might await her, too, for what she'd done. And she still hadn't told Lubos yet. "The strange man appeared, walking through the locked door as though it wasn't even there. He asked me if I'd thought about his offer, and I…I lied, told him I was still considering it, but I would be able to think better once he'd turned the thread to gold, just like he had the other one the day before. All he had to do was touch the thread, and it turned to gold. It was…magic, truly. I was allowed to return to your chamber to sleep, but the next day, I was marched to the tower room again, and forced to spin again. Once more, the man appeared, and begged me to break his curse, which was to turn all he touched into gold, but I told him I could not until he had turned all the flax, too."

A sob caught in her throat, and Molina took a moment to wipe away her tears before she could continue.

"The next morning, the guard captain took me across town, down to the big warehouses by the river. It was full of flax – more than I could spin in a year, without the spinning wheel. I protested that no one could complete this task, and the captain told me the king's command was that I had two choices. I could spin this flax into gold, and when I was finished, I would be allowed to marry his son. Or I could refuse, and I would be executed for daring to disobey the king." She swallowed. "I had no choice, so I sat down and spun. It was not so bad at first, for some of the flax was poorly combed, and not suitable for spinning. Enough to make a bed for me on the first night, and one of the guards brought me food and drink. But one day the food did not smell quite right, and some strange sickness seemed to stop me from rising from my bed. I could not…could not keep food down, nor water. This went on for some days, until I was too weak to move. I think I slept, but I do not know. I awoke to find the strange man kneeling beside me, coaxing me to eat. For I had to break his curse, he said, and I could not break it unless I lived."

Lubos held out his arms. "I am so sorry, my lady. I should have been here, to defend you from strange men and from my father."

Molina shook her head, refusing the comfort he offered. He did not know everything yet. "He fed me, and he did my work for me, spinning that flax into golden thread. He wore gloves when he fed me, but when he spun, he took them off. It was the touch of his bare hands that turned things to gold. I saw it happen with my own eyes so many times, I could not doubt it. And then in the middle of it all, he demanded I repay him for his hard work, and break the curse. I was forced to admit that I was not a witch, and I did not know how to break a curse, but I told him it was his cursed hands that had landed me in this mess, and if he did not spin all the flax into gold like that first spindle, then his hands would be triply cursed with my blood, and that of my unborn child."

Now she wept freely, for she knew she would lose Lubos when he learned what she had done.

"When I told him about our child, his anger faded, like clouds after a storm. He muttered something about how it must be the child, not me. And he refused to finish the work he'd started, unless I promised to give him the child. Our baby. He swore he would care for her as though she was his own daughter, in a castle just as grand as this, but if I did not, then I was cursing him and his son to death, and my death, and that of my daughter, would be on my head, and not his."

Lubos closed his eyes. "You accepted his offer, and promised him the child."

Molina nodded, tears coursing down her cheeks, as words deserted her.

"Curse my father to hell for forcing you to make such a terrible choice. I wish I could thank your stranger for helping you when I could not, but perhaps there is time for that yet, for he will come to take the child when the baby is born, will he not?" Lubos asked. He seemed far too calm. He should be cursing her, not accepting this. She had given away their child to save her own worthless life.

Lubos pulled her into his arms, and kissed the top of her head. "Do not worry about it. Rest, recover, and think only of our wedding, which will be as soon as you are strong enough to leave this bed. When the man returns, I will defend you, and the baby. He shall not take the child from you, I swear."

Molina sniffled and stared up into his eyes. Lubos was a man of honour, who did not break his oaths. For him to swear such a thing… "You are too good for me," she whispered.

Lubos did not reply, but he leaned down to kiss her, wrapping her arms more tightly around her, and for that moment, she forgot everything but the love they shared.

Thirty-Seven

A baby's cry roused Abraham from a sound sleep. "Has your time come already?" he mumbled, forcing his eyes open.

But the eyes he met were not those of the princess. They were accusing, and they belonged to Chase.

"Why aren't you protecting Maja?" Abraham grumbled, rising.

"Because her time came early. She stumbled on the steps and fell. She bled so much, it was a miracle they managed to save the baby. Isaak, she called him. The son you do not deserve."

Chase pointed.

Abraham's gaze followed the direction of his brother in law's finger, to where a strange woman held a baby to her breast. "Maja?" It couldn't be.

"Maja is dead. Giving birth sapped what little life she had left, but she was adamant that the child must live. That you might love him as you never loved her." Chase's fist slammed into the table. "Tell me you have succeeded in your quest. That my sister did not die to give you a son you will kill through carelessness."

Abraham hung his head. "I have not broken the curse yet. I do not know for certain which princess —" He stopped as realisation dawned. The girl he'd found spinning was not a princess, for she had yet to marry the prince. But the child she carried... "The princess has not been born yet," he breathed, so softly he wasn't sure Chase heard.

Chase made an exasperated sound. "You have pinned your hopes on a princess and a witch? You are an even bigger fool than I thought."

"The girl's mother has promised to give the

child to me the moment she is born. She will —
"

"You have a child! Your son! You need to care for him, not some royal bastard you have stolen!" Chase roared.

"You must…engage a wet nurse. She can care for the boy. While we watch and wait for the princess to give birth. I mean…the lady. The prince's bride. And the baby will…."

"Wail and cry and be of little use, as all babies are until they grow up! You truly have lost your wits."

Abraham stared at his brother in law. "The princess will save my son. She is the only one who can. Have faith, my friend, and all will be revealed in time." He wanted to believe his own words, but for the first time, he feared he would not live to see his prediction come true. For the princess might be the only one who could break the curse…but it might be many years before she could. Years he did not have.

"We will watch and wait," Abraham said with finality. What more could he do?

Thirty-Eight

Molina woke slowly, revelling in the feeling of Lubos' warm body pressed against her back as he reached around her to cup her breasts. "More, my lady wife?" he whispered in her ear.

"Of course," she murmured back, sighing with pleasure as he eased into her from behind. Her belly was too big now for the frenzied lovemaking of their first nights together, or even on their wedding night, but still he'd found a way to fulfil his promise of making love to her every night, and every morning, too. His hands knew her body so well he soon had her gasping, then crying out his name, as the first wave of pleasure crashed over her. As ever, he waited for the third time before his shout for joy drowned out hers. An amazing lover and a loving husband – Molina could not ask for more.

He withdrew from her and helped her wash, before cleaning himself up, too. Lubos set a fresh log on the fire, warming the wintry room so that she would not take another chill. Then he crept back into bed and stroked her belly, eliciting an angry kick from the child inside.

"Do you think he will come today?" he asked.

"I hope she will," Molina replied, as she always did.

Lubos laughed then, and rose to dress for the day. He might be the crown prince and not the king, but the king's mind was definitely slipping, and more and more duties fell to Lubos now, for no one wanted to risk his head by going to the king with anything the king might consider bad news. And there was no rhyme or reason for the things he decided constituted bad news. Why, the courier who had brought word of Lubos' younger sister, Guinevere's marriage to a neighbouring king was accused of lying and hanged for his supposed crime, despite bearing a scroll that bore both Guinevere and her husband's seal, for the king had no memory of agreeing to such a marriage.

"Bar the door, until I knock," Lubos warned her as he left. Molina rose to do as he commanded, for that was the only way to protect her from the king, and the guards who were still loyal to him. The only times she opened the door were to allow a maid inside to bring her meals, or to let Lubos back in once his day was done.

Thirty-Nine

Small pains had bothered her for days now, but when her contractions truly started, Molina knew without a doubt that her baby was coming. She seized the bell rope and yanked on it, hearing the jangle of alarm bells summoning the servant who stood watch outside her room, ready to bring the midwife. She heard the patter of running feet as another contraction gripped her, leaving her gasping.

When the pain had eased, Molina turned her attention to the door. She needed to unbar it to let the midwife in. It took her two tries before she managed to heft the bar from its brackets, and a third to tip it onto the floor so that the door could open. Then another contraction seized her, and she fell to her knees.

For a long moment, she knew nothing but pain, and then, she was free. She staggered to her feet, headed for the bed.

"Molina? My lady, are you all right?" Lubos' voice had never sounded so heavenly as it did right now.

She fell heavily into bed, landing on her side so she didn't hurt the baby. "No. Your baby is determined to escape today."

The door flew open, and his eyes shone as bright and eager as the morning sun. "It is time?"

Molina attempted to nod, but all she could manage was a grimace as the pain came again.

Huge hands gripped hers, strong and reassuring. "The midwife is coming, and I have told the physician to stay away on pain of death. What do you wish me to do?"

Molina managed a smile. "Have the baby for me?"

"If I could take the pain from you, I would, but only a woman can bear a child. Men were not made for such things, I fear. But seeing as you will do all the hard work, you must name him. I hope you have some suitable names for a future king picked out."

"Daughter," she bit out before crying out in pain.

When she opened her eyes again, the midwife was there, accompanied by several maids carrying armloads of linen and buckets of water.

"Time to go, for this is no place for men," the midwife said, attempting to shoo Lubos from the room.

As Lubos' hand slipped from hers, Molina only gripped it tighter. The strange man's words came to Molina again, reminding her that she might not live to see or name her child.

She waited for the next pain to pass, before gasping out, "What if I do not survive the birth? Many women die. What if this is the last time I ever see you?"

Lubos leaned down to kiss her forehead,

lowering his voice so only Molina could hear him. "I swear to you, both you and the child will survive. When you were ill and I feared you would not live another night, I went to a witch for your lamb's lettuce. She bespelled the leaves, promising you and the child a long and healthy life. So worry not. Today is not your time."

A witch? For such a powerful spell, she would have exacted a terrible price. All the gold in the tithing barn, perhaps, though witches were not known for their fondness for gold. No, her price would be far higher.

"What did it cost..." she began, before another cry of pain was all she could utter.

Lubos bowed, blew a kiss to her, and departed.

And Molina descended into what could only be described as hell, a realm of pain and pushing and panting that went on for an eternity, until she heard a lusty wail that had not come from her own throat.

"She's perfect, the little princess," someone said.

Molina felt a surge of triumph. She was

right, and the baby was a girl.

Forty

"Sir? The midwife has been called up to the castle."

Abraham blinked. He couldn't have slept away half the day, could he? He just felt so tired all the time, and the pain in his chest was constant now. He didn't have long left. So to lose a day to sleep…

"You promised a copper coin, sir, if I brought you news," the small boy reminded him.

Abraham fished in his pocket and pulled out a silver coin. "Thank you. Now, go back to the midwife's house and tell me when she returns, and I will turn that coin into a gold one."

The boy's eyes grew round. "Truly?"

Abraham nodded gravely. "Truly."

The boy raced back toward the city.

Childbirth took a long time, or so Abraham believed, so he would have time to take the pain draught he'd bought from the apothecary before he had to head into the castle to claim the child. The stuff was terribly bitter, so it was best drunk mixed with wine, and he would need a clear head when he confronted the princess, for the girl had married her prince now.

He poured the powder into a cup, then waited for the wine to warm over the fire. He'd thought his castle was cold, but it had nothing on this cottage. Even with the fire blazing, the tips of his fingers were blue.

When steam curled up from the pot, he poured the wine into his cup, stirring it with his finger until the bitter medicine dissolved. Then he drank it down and lay back against the wall. He could hear the thump of Chase's arrows hitting the target in rapid succession.

His brother in law had always been an expert marksman. Why, he could shoot the very flies from the air. He hoped Chase would teach Isaak to shoot, when the boy was old enough to draw a bow.

Despite his best efforts to stay awake, Abraham drifted off into sleep again.

Forty-One

"The princess has given birth to a beautiful baby girl," the midwife said, rousing Lubos from his doze. He wasn't sure what day it was, or when he'd chosen to lay down to sleep on the cathedral floor, before the very altar, but he had enough sense to know he should get up before one of the priests discovered him and kicked him out of the house of God.

"Is she well?" he asked, scrambling to his feet. Despite his words to Molina, he still didn't trust the witch. Not when he had yet to pay her price. If she chose not to honour their bargain…

"Princess Molina is very tired, for she has been in labour a day and a night, but once she has rested, she should be well. It was an easy birth."

The cries she'd uttered said otherwise, but Lubos did not correct the midwife. Molina would tell him the truth of it, and whether she wanted the same midwife again next time. For there would be a next time. There had to be, for he would need an heir.

"Can I see her?" he asked timidly. It had been a long time since he'd asked anyone for anything, but the realm of women and babies was new to him. He didn't want to do something wrong.

"She is sleeping, and should not be disturbed," the midwife said.

His heart sank, but only for a moment, as he realised she hadn't actually refused him. Could a midwife give orders to the crown prince?

He rose to his full height, hoping he could manage to look regal despite not having shaved after sleeping on the floor. "I must see her, and the child."

The midwife sighed. "Yes, Your Highness. But for only a moment."

Lubos had not run through the castle so fast since he was a boy. He startled several servants, but today he did not care. He was a father, and Molina lived.

He found her tucked up in his bed, amid layers of fresh linen. The faint smell of blood lingered, but a maid brought in a fresh basket of rushes and proceeded to lay them on the floor, and then he could smell only the aroma of summer hay, as out of place in the heart of winter as he was in the women's domain this room had been, only hours earlier.

The cradle moved, just the tiniest bit, though no hand or breeze had touched it. Lubos held his breath and approached.

The baby's eyes were closed, her head crowned with an abundance of dark curls. She lifted a tiny fist from the blankets and waved it in the air, as if cursing something in her dream, before lowering it again.

"So tiny. So perfect," he breathed.

"Isn't she?"

Lubos started. Molina's eyes were open, and

she wore a tired smile. Yet her expression glowed with happiness.

"I wished for a girl," she said softly. "But you must protect her. Swear to me that you will not let the strange man have her. You must take her away, hide her from him, and stand guard over her, until I tell you it is safe. Please, Lubos."

The words came easily. "I swear no strange man shall steal her from you."

"Take her. Take her now, for surely the whole kingdom knows about the birth, and he will come for her soon." Molina reached into the cradle and scooped out the little bundle, no larger than a loaf of bread. A tiny person. "Take her!"

Still Lubos hesitated as the baby was thrust into his arms. "I'm afraid I will drop her," he admitted. "She's so tiny."

Molina's eyes burned with determination, despite the dark circles framing them. "You are her father, and you will neither drop her nor allow her to come to harm. You swore an oath, Lubos, and you will not break it."

He held the child tightly, his heart sinking.

Yes, he had sworn many oaths, and he would break none of them. Even if it broke his own heart to do so.

"She will be safe," he promised himself as much as Molina. He had to believe it.

Forty-Two

Every hoofbeat felt like a nail hammered into his own coffin, but still Lubos rode on. He had sworn he would give anything in exchange for Molina's life, and he could not lose her now.

The massive stone walls rose up sooner than before, or so it seemed. The gates swung open for him today, though he saw no one who might have pushed them. Magic, he told himself, and shivered. This made the child squirm against his chest, as though she felt his fear. Lubos wrapped a protective arm around her, though the swaddling wraps bound her securely to him. He would fulfil his oaths to Molina and to the witch, for he was a man of his word. Even if Molina hated him for it when she found out.

"Enter, Your Highness," the witch called, emerging from a tiny cottage Lubos had not seen nestled under four huge trees. A sacred grove from ancient times, his brain supplied, and he shivered again.

He stepped forward, refusing to give in to his fear. He was a prince, and not a coward. "I come to fulfil the bargain we made. You promised that my wife and child will live long and healthy lives."

She seemed younger than the first time he'd seen her, barely more than a girl, but her eyes glittered with the same ancient secrets he'd glimpsed on his first visit. "And they will. Your queen will outlive you, and hold her son's heir in her arms when your son takes the throne."

Lubos let out a breath he hadn't known he'd been holding. "And the child? Our daughter?"

The witch grinned. "The little weaver. I have waited a long time for this moment." She held out her arms. "Give her to me."

Lubos crossed his arms over his chest. "Not until you swear to me she will be treated like the princess she is, and cared for as well as her mother might."

The witch laughed. "Princesses are raised to be pawns in a much larger game, married off at the convenience of their fathers to cement this or that alliance. Much like your sister Guinevere, married to a man she does not love. Your daughter will be much more than a bedwarmer and broodmare for one of your allies. She will shape the future of many kingdoms, like one of the ancient queens of legend. I will take her to a place so safe, no one will ever find her to steal or harm her. She will outlive her mother, though she will not bring any kings into the world."

"I will have your word." Lubos would not give her the child without it.

"Yes, you are a man of words, when there is so much more to the world. Yet you shall have mine. I swear upon my own life that I will do everything in my power to prolong her life and health. No other girl child will be as precious to her mother as your child will be to me."

Lubos wanted to trust her, if only because she promised so much of what he wanted. Yet even as he untied the baby from her bindings, taking her weight in his arms for what might be the last time, he did not want to surrender her.

"Give her to me!" the witch demanded, her eyes glowing blue.

Unwillingly, Lubos held out the child.

It took only a moment, and his arms were empty. The next moment, he blinked and both the witch and the baby were gone, leaving him alone in the garden.

Tears streamed down his cheeks, and Lubos longed to throw himself to the ground and weep, but he dared not. He had done what he had to, and there was more to come.

He had to tell Molina that in order to keep the girl safe, she could never see her daughter again. So he forced himself back on his horse, and it felt like every hoofbeat landed on his chest, breaking through his ribs and crushing his heart beneath them.

Molina would never forgive him for such a betrayal.

Forty-Three

Abraham took the stairs slowly, but he was still out of breath when he reached the top, so he took his time to recover before he entered the princess's chamber. When he no longer felt dizzy, he tried the door, which opened at a touch.

He stepped inside, then stopped to survey the sleeping girl in the bed. Only her face was visible, but it was no longer skeleton pale, like he remembered it. The dark circles were there beneath her eyes, but she'd been in labour for a day or more, so the sleeplessness was to be expected.

How he could have believed she was a witch, capable of breaking the curse…he had taken the seer's words too seriously, and it was not his fault he'd mistaken her for the princess she would become. A capable woman whose courage knew no bounds. Yet she was not a witch, but an ordinary woman. Her husband was a lucky man.

But a man who would have to beget another daughter, for his firstborn was promised to Abraham. Abraham took a deep breath, and crept deeper into the room. To the cradle that stood beside the princess's bed, within easy reach. All he had to do was reach in, take the child, and leave, but he could not bring himself to steal her.

The princess had gone through so much…she deserved to know the truth, all of it, about why he needed her daughter. And…where the child would be, and that the girl would be safe. For she was no friend of the king's, and if the princess ever needed a place to shelter from the king's wrath, then his home was open to her.

And perhaps she wanted to say farewell to her daughter. Abraham owed the young mother that much.

He slid his gloved hands into the cradle, intending to pull out the child with all her blankets to insulate her from the cold, but the blankets were empty. The child was not here.

Abraham closed his eyes. He had failed. Failed himself, and failed his son. All those days and nights spinning straw into gold to placate a mad king…wasted. He might as well have stayed home with Maja.

"She is gone where you cannot reach her," the princess said.

Abraham's eyes snapped open, to meet her gaze. "You promised her to me. She is the only one who can save my son. I spun you a king's ransom in gold, ten times over, so that you would help me. Faithless woman!"

Her eyes widened and he realised he'd raised a hand to strike her. He lowered it quickly. He had never struck a woman, and he had no intention of doing so now. She could live with the shame of breaking her oath.

"I am Sir Abraham von Rumpelstiltskin, and

my son Isaak will be the last of my line, because of you. Many years ago, my ancestor was cursed with the Touch, and he passed it down, father to son, until it came to me. I know not what my ancestor's crime was, but I have done nothing to deserve this fate. My son is but a baby – a few weeks older than your own daughter – and he is innocent. He does not deserve to die young, and see everything he touches turn to cold metal. I beg you, Princess, have pity on a father who only wishes to save his son." Abraham fell to his knees in supplication.

Tears trickled down the princess's cheeks as she shook her head. "I am sorry, Sir Abraham, but I cannot. My husband has taken her I know not where, and he will defend her with his life. I could never save you or your son, no matter how much I wish I could. I am merely Molina, a miller's daughter from a barony far to the south of here, with no special powers and no title until the prince married me. My only skill is with a spinning wheel. If I could spin a wheel and change your fate, I would, but fate is a weaver and I have no skill in that. I thank you for everything you have done for me. If not for you, both my daughter and I would be dead at the king's hand. I only wish I could return the favour."

"Then we are lost." He rose to his feet, waiting until the light-headedness faded, before heading for the door. He had pinned all his hopes on the princess, and she had dashed them in one blow.

"What are you doing in my son's bed, slut? And who is this vagabond? Is his chamber your whorehouse now?"

Abraham lifted his eyes from the flagstone floor to meet the gaze of an angry old man. An old man wearing a robe woven from gold thread.

The mad king. If it had not been for him, Molina would have told Abraham the truth long ago, and neither of them would have spent the summer locked in a barn, spinning their fingers raw.

If not for this man, Abraham might have had the time to find a way to save his son.

"Get out. Both of you!" the king snapped. "Guards!"

Abraham pulled off his gloves. "Are you the one who wanted straw turned into gold?"

The king looked smug. "I have all the gold I need. We are now the richest kingdom on the continent. But if I need more, my son's wife will provide. Which is why this slut will get out of his bed, for that is where his wife should lie, while he begets an heir on her!"

The mad king did not even recognise his son's bride. The girl who had almost died for his greed. As Isaak would die for it.

Abraham let his fury rise up, his blood heating to boiling until it felt like molten gold in his veins. Perhaps it was.

"The princess will spin no more for you. Take your gold, and I hope it makes you happy in hell!" Abraham laid his hands on either side of the king's face, and the king began to scream. The sound still rang in Abraham's ears, long after it had stopped, and he opened his eyes to view his handiwork. The king was surely the ugliest statue Abraham had ever seen, and that was with his clothes on. Abraham touched the king's robe and boots, until they, too, were solid gold.

He turned to find the princess standing on the bed, backed up against the wall, her eyes wide with terror. "You…you killed the king!" she breathed.

"He deserved to die," Abraham said simply. "My son will be avenged."

He heard the clatter of running feet on the stairs. The guards the king had summoned, he guessed. Abraham knew he had little time left, and he had no intention of spending it in a prison cell in this castle for killing the king.

Abraham stamped on the floor three times, then touched the spot with the toe of his shoe. The flagstones opened up, and swallowed him.

Forty-Four

Lubos had hoped to find Molina asleep, but she sat up the moment he entered their chamber. "Where is Tessarina?" she demanded.

"Who?" he asked. Grief and a long day's ride had surely addled his wits.

"Our daughter," she said. "You said I might name her, and I thought…"

"It's a lovely name," Lubos soothed her.

"But where is she?"

Lubos swallowed. This was the part he'd dreaded most. "She is with the witch who saved your life when you were so sick. She swore she would protect her, keep her safe, and treat her better than any princess. A witch who can defeat death itself will protect her far better than you or I could, especially against a man who can walk through walls and turn things to gold at a touch. When your strange man comes – "

She cut him off. "He has come and gone, stamping a hole in the floor through which he vanished. I have never seen anything like it. I know not where he has gone, but I hope he never returns. When I told him he could not have her, he flew into such a temper, I was certain he would kill me." She smiled wanly. "But instead, he saved me from your father."

Lubos did not believe what he was hearing. "My father? The king?"

"The late king. Abraham von Rumpelstiltskin killed him." Molina pointed at the door. No, at a statue by the door.

Lubos swallowed. The man had turned his father into a statue? He didn't want to get closer, but he had to be sure.

The statue appeared to be a perfect replica

of his father in one of his most violent rages. Bulging eyes, mouth wide open as he spat vitriol based on the delusions of his own mad mind, with his finger pointed at the long-gone target of his rage. Not the way he would want to be remembered, and definitely not the way Lubos wanted to remember him, yet here he was. It looked like Molina's strange man had encased his skin in bronze. No, gold, like the thread he'd helped her spin.

"Is he truly made of gold? We should try to get him out of it, to see if he still lives," Lubos said. But how did one extract a man from his own gold skin?

Molina shook her head. "He is solid gold right the way through, and much too heavy to move. Just as the thread von Rumpelstiltskin spun was pure gold."

Rumpelstiltskin? He had heard of such a place. A barony he'd visited, surely. Lubos racked his brain, searching for the memory. A castle on an island, in the river close to the western borders, protecting the richest trade routes to the west. Its owner was a wealthy man, one of the few who had turned in his regular tithe this year, the last man likely to be making a nuisance of himself here in the capital. Even his father had no quarrel with the man or his ancestors, loyal since the days of Charlemagne.

Well, he'd had no quarrel before. If he'd still lived, Father might not be so peaceable toward the family now. Now it would fall to Lubos to exact justice for regicide. To think Molina had been alone with the man…he should have been here, protecting her, instead of riding around the countryside meeting with witches.

He cupped Molina's face in his hands and pressed his forehead to hers. "My queen, can you ever forgive me?"

She blinked several times in surprise, before she responded, "My king, there is nothing to forgive. If you swear our daughter is safe, then I must trust you. I will miss her, but she will never be safe here while von Rumpelstiltskin lives. You must do as you think best. Such is the burden of a crown."

A crown. Thank the heavens his father had not been wearing it when he entered Molina's chamber. "A burden we shall share. With my queen at my side, we will rebuild this kingdom from the ruins my father left it in. Together. With spinning wheels, waterwheels, and my best men scouring the country for the villain who killed my father, for I will see justice done for such a heinous crime."

"Call the guard captain. You will need his help in this. And…together, maybe you can take the body out of here." She eyed the statue of the late king and shivered. "The king would have killed me, if he had laid hands on me. When you find your father's killer, be merciful. He deserves a quick death, with as little pain as possible. For all his faults, he saved me from your father's wrath four times."

Lubos seized her hands and kissed them. "It shall be as my queen commands. My father might have lived for many years longer, letting his madness ruin the kingdom completely. Von Rumpelstiltskin has done us a great service, taking matters into his own hands. Fate has the strangest ways of making things turn out well. Now, rest, for I have much to do, including planning our coronation in the cathedral. I will be the happiest man in the world when I place my mother's crown on your head."

He helped her lie back on the pillows, then rushed from the room, shouting for Schuttmann.

Forty-Five

Chase heard the horse approaching, and he headed outside to meet Abraham. He had to see for himself if the man had really stolen the crown prince's child.

Abraham slid down from his horse, then fell to his knees in the snow. His arms were empty.

"So you are not as much of a fool as I thought," Chase said. He took the horse's bridle, intending to take the animal to the stable.

Abraham seized his cloak. "I am a fool. Such a fool. The princess is his only hope.

Isaak's only hope. When I am gone, you must take the boy to her and tell her. The king is dead. And the princess…the princess…the seer was right about the boy. She cannot be wrong about the princess. She is Isaak's only hope."

Chase shook himself free. "Go inside, and warm yourself before the fire. I will see to the horse, and you should see to your son."

He took the animal inside the tiny barn that passed for a stable, and removed the saddle and bridle before brushing the mare down. No matter how hard Abraham tried to hide his ill-health, Chase knew him too well for that. Abraham was dying, and the sickness had taken his mind already. His body would be next. Thank the heavens Maja had not lived to see the man she loved go mad.

When the horse was properly cared for, Chase returned to the cottage. Abraham sat on the chair by the fire, holding out his bare hands to the flames to warm them. His fingers were perpetually blue these days.

"Oh, Maja," Chase heard Abraham say.

Chase turned away, giving Abraham the

privacy to mourn.

Isaak's wet nurse, Ida, slept in the loft above, but Isaak's cradle was here where it was warm. The boy was the very image of his brother Heber's children, even sucking his thumb like Aran, the eldest, had. "Come and see, Abraham. Doesn't he look like Aran?" Chase asked, beckoning.

But Abraham did not answer.

Chase turned to see what had distracted his brother in law, only to find his chair was empty. A pair of dark shoes lay on the floor, full of gold coins that spilled out in a puddle on the flagstones. A pile of coins sat on the chair, too, topped by a pair of familiar golden brown, fur lined gloves. Of Abraham, there was no sign.

Forty-Six

"Your Majesties, we've found him," Captain Schuttmann announced. He lowered his voice so only the king and queen could hear. "And he had a child with him."

Molina half rose from her throne, before Lubos' hand on her shoulder gently pushed her back into her seat. She shot a glance at the packed court – would she ever get used to having an audience for everything she did? – and made a show of adjusting the cushions beneath her before planting her bottom firmly on them.

Most of the court knew nothing of Tessarina, or her pregnancy, and if anyone did, they'd probably heard the same story that circulated among the castle servants: she'd lost the baby. So if the queen wept, the servants knew the reason for her grief, or at least they thought they did.

Two guards marched a man between them, dropping him to his knees before the dais. Another guard came forward with a peasant woman, carrying a squirming bundle in her arms. The child's wet nurse, Molina guessed. Could it be Tessarina? She hardly dared hope, and yet…

"You won't find him." The kneeling man's voice was harsh as he gazed unflinchingly at Lubos, though he knew better than to rise with two guards standing over him.

Molina's breath hissed out of her. She did not know this man. They hadn't caught him after all, and the child could not be her daughter. The witch still had her.

"Find who?" Lubos asked.

"Sir Abraham von Rumpelstiltskin, the man who put down your father like the mad dog he was." The man glared. "Your Majesty," he spat, as though the title was an insult. Perhaps it was to him.

"Where is he?" Molina asked.

The man's pale eyes turned to her in surprise.

When he did not answer, Lubos said, "Your queen asked you a question, and you will answer it. Where is von Rumpelstiltskin?"

"I do not know. Out of your reach, far beyond your borders."

Lubos nodded. "Then who are you? His squire? His servant?"

The man spat on the floor. "I am Sir Chase of…of nowhere now. I left my lord's service to escort my sister to her new home, where I thought she would be safe. Alas, Maja is dead, and my former brother in law decided to commit regicide, and catch some of the old king's madness, it would seem."

"And what of the child?" Lubos asked.

"The boy is Maja's child by Abraham, her husband. Before the madness took him, he swore to give his life for the boy, for he would let no harm come to him. The last thing he asked me to do was to ensure the boy was cared for, to take him to the princess." He jerked his head toward Molina. "That would be you, I guess. If he ever regains his senses, I am certain he will come for the boy, if only to check that I kept my word."

Lubos met the man's eyes, and it seemed to Molina that he gave the tiniest of nods. He raised his voice. "The child will be placed in the royal nursery, and raised as a ward of the crown. If he shows promise he will be allowed to become a page, then a squire, and perhaps even a knight, like his father. I will keep his lands in trust for when he comes of age to be one of my loyal barons." For as a hostage in this household, he would have no choice. "Does the child have a name?"

"Maja called him Isaak," Sir Chase said. "I believe she would thank you for your kindness, Your Majesty, if she could."

"If you swear fealty, I may allow you to take him as your squire when he is of an age to do so," Lubos said.

His tone was careful, calculating, with no emotion in it at all. The tone of a monarch,

Molina realised with a shiver.

Sir Chase smiled faintly. "I thank you for the offer, Your Majesty, but we both know that is not a good idea. If Abraham were to return for the boy…ah, tell him I am far away, serving some foreign lord or court. It shall be the truth." He pulled a pair of gloves out of his pocket and threw them down on the steps. "He wanted the boy to have these. The queen will know when the time is right, I think."

Molina recoiled. She knew those gloves well, for von Rumpelstiltskin had worn them, only taking them off when he wanted to touch something to turn it to gold. Yet she nodded curtly, and gestured for a servant to pick them up and bring them to her. She didn't want to touch them. "Bring the child to the nursery. I shall…inspect him there." She beckoned to the guard with the wet nurse, as she rose from the dais and made her way out of the throne room.

Lubos found her in the nursery later that evening, watching the boy sleep. They were alone, for she'd sent the wet nurse down to the kitchen for dinner.

"Did I make the right decision?" Lubos

asked. "Or did I mess up?"

Molina smiled. In court, he was every bit the king his father had trained him to be, but in private he was the same man she'd met by the millponds. "I don't know. I don't want to ever see him again, and if we have his son, I imagine we will. Yet the boy has no one, and if he grows up, he will inherit what I understand are prosperous lands. It makes sense to raise him under your roof, so that he will see you as more of a father than the man who deserted him. And there is the matter of the princess Sir Chase spoke of. Von Rumpelstiltskin could not have meant me, for he knew I could not break his curse. Perhaps he believed Tessarina could. If his father never returns and the boy becomes a knight, you can send him out to find her."

Lubos hung his head. "I sent guards back to the witch's cottage, but they found nothing and no one. Not even the garden I saw. As if somehow…magically…it all vanished. The walls were broken ruins, yet I remember climbing them. If I had known the witch would take our daughter and disappear, I would have..."

"You would have done exactly what you have done. You have not lied to me yet, and you will not do so today. You pledged her to save my life and hers, just as I did. We are both equally culpable in this, and will suffer for it, as we deserve. Perhaps, one day, there will be other children."

Lubos blinked. "Other children? You mean...but the midwife said..."

"To wait until I am ready," Molina finished for him. "It has been some weeks since she was born. I believe tonight I might be ready to take you into my bed, so that you can fondle these before they return to their normal size." She cupped her breasts through her dress.

"Will the boy be all right alone here?" Lubos asked, casting a longing look at Molina.

She shrugged. "I have never cared for a child before, so I have no idea. The wet nurse will return soon, and he's asleep now. If his lungs are as strong as Tessarina's, he will soon wail loud enough to let someone know if he wants something."

"Then let us go to bed, and see if I can give

you an heir by morning," Lubos said eagerly, taking her arm.

"Or tomorrow night, or the night after," Molina said.

"Or any night after, for I swear I will make you happy again, Molina, happy ever after."

And she smiled, because she knew he spoke the truth.

Forty-Seven

Chase sold Abraham's horse for a good price, and tucked the coins into the pouch at his waist. He had enough money to get him to almost any kingdom in the civilised world, and for the first time in his life, he was free to choose who he served.

King Erik's court in Aros was famed for its tourneys, and he could win any archery contest with his eyes closed. Perhaps it was time to aim high and attach himself to a royal court, to see how his fortunes fared there. Better than his brother's fortune, he'd wager, for Heber's land was not so fruitful of late, or so his last letter had said.

Yes, he would go to Aros.

There was nothing left for him here. His beloved sister was dead, and his brother in arms was gone. Time he was gone, too.

Sir Chase mounted his mare, and set off on his quest for fame and fortune.

Kiss:
Frog Prince Retold

DEMELZA CARLTON

A tale in the Romance a Medieval Fairy Tale series

One

If Philemon never felt the scorching desert sands beneath his feet again, he would be a happy man. "How much further?" he demanded.

The camel driver turned and bowed apologetically. "At least half the night, Your Highness. If you had not decreed a slower pace, we would be there already."

"Perhaps, but I would have left my blackened balls somewhere in the desert, for they would have bounced off at the pace this beast was going before."

Philemon heard sniggering from behind him, but it was hard to discern one man from another, silhouetted against the setting sun and all. Ah, let them laugh. He'd served with the guardsmen until his father had died, forcing him to assume the throne.

Philemon continued, "There's little point taking one of the Sultan's daughters as my bride if I cannot consummate the marriage on our wedding night. If I cannot give the city an heir, you'll find yourself a new Prince of Tasnim, I am certain of it!"

The laughter was louder now, for they all knew as well as he did that he was the last of his father's line, and they'd need to look outside the city walls to find someone of sufficiently royal blood to take his place. Whether they liked Philemon or not, he was still their prince, a man of Tasnim.

Which was why he gave the orders, not the camel driver. "We must set up camp, rest for the night, and we will reach Tasnim on the morrow," Philemon finished.

"But there is no water, Your Highness," the camel driver protested.

Philemon fought to keep his temper. Did the camel driver think he was blind? "I can see that," he said with forced calm. "Take us to the nearest oasis, and we will camp there."

The camel driver spluttered. "But…Your Highness…the nearest oasis was the one we left this morning. The only water for miles is in the wells of Tasnim itself, unless some magical wadi appears before us."

Philemon laughed, but not for long. The man's idea of magic had merit. Philemon rubbed his ring, the one symbol of his sovereignty he carried with him everywhere.

The djinn appeared, bowing low. "What do you wish, Master?"

"Make me an oasis here," Philemon commanded.

The djinn snorted with laughter. "My master jests. The best I can make for you is a puddle, if I drink a good skin of wine and piss on that rock." He tugged at the loincloth he wore, as if he intended to do just that.

"I need water for my men and the camels to

drink. Now," Philemon insisted.

The djinn spread his arms wide. "I have told you what I can do. Maybe you should have found yourself a different djinn, someone more powerful who can command water instead of stone. Fat lot of good he'd be, when it comes to opening the gates of Tasnim, but he might be able to fetch you a drink."

A different djinn. And Philemon had such a thing. "Fetch the genie of the lamp. The one you found in the oasis outside the city gates," he said. "I have a task for him."

A servant appeared, bowed, then offered Philemon the dented, tarnished bronze lamp. Philemon rubbed his thumb across what appeared to be a scorch mark on the scored surface. Back and forth, back and forth…until blue smoke began to stream from the lamp's spout.

The enormous djinn abased himself on the sand. "How may I serve you, Master?"

"Make me an oasis right here, big enough to quench the thirst of every man and beast here twice over, and still have enough water for me to bathe," Philemon ordered. He waited for this djinn to say the same words as the servant of the ring.

"Your wish is my command, Master. It shall be done."

And for that moment, Philemon knew he was the most powerful man in the desert.

Two

Anahita knew the very moment she lost her sense of fear. One moment, she was screaming, her broken arm splintering into a million needles of pain to the unholy delight of her new husband, and the next, the whole world went silent.

He would beat her to death tonight, whether by accident or design, her dreamy mind told her. She should have been afraid, but death would be an improvement over the endless round of beatings that inevitably ended in rape. Her father had given her to this man in an attempt to bring peace, but Sheikh Fakhri did not understand the meaning of the word. He attacked her father's people to capture women to replace his dwindling number of wives, and he beat her every time her father's men fought back.

The only way to end this was to stop him.

The sheikh cupped his hardening manhood and grinned.

No. She would not submit to him tonight, or any other night. If she was going to die, she would do so without that final indignity.

Anahita dragged herself to her feet. "You're a coward, a man whose only courage comes from beating women. I hope when my father's men cut you down, they feed your body to pigs. Female pigs," she said.

He shouted for his guards, and two enormous men rushed into the tent.

Anahita knew them both – men the sheikh had assigned to watch her so that she did not run away.

"Hold her down, so that I can cut out her lying tongue," he ordered, and the men moved toward her.

Anahita had one chance. "Don't touch my arm. It's broken," she implored, cradling it to her chest. Her husband might be a monster, but these two were merely men.

The guards looked uncertain. A moment's hesitation was all she needed. She crumpled forward, righting herself just before she fell, feeling the leather hilt of her salvation in her good hand.

She might die tonight, but she would not die alone. She lunged.

The guard's blade pierced Fakhri's throat, and Anahita thrust it in deeper, before ripping it out. Fakhri fell to his knees, clutching his gaping throat, but the lifeblood sheeting down his chest told the tale's end for him as he gasped his last.

When the light went out of his eyes, he pitched over sideways, his limp dick flopping onto the tent floor.

He would violate no houris in the afterlife, either, Anahita vowed, putting her borrowed blade to work again. She threw the pieces of hacked-off gristle onto a brazier, while blood leaked sluggishly from his groin.

Only then did she turn to face the guards. Without fear, for if she died tonight, she died victorious. She held out the bloodied blade, but it slipped from her hand, to land point-down in the sand.

Powerless. That's what she was now. That's all she had ever been.

"Do your worst," she said, falling to her knees. But she kept on falling, into darkness that rose up to claim her.

Three

The final stage of the journey home seemed to take hardly any time at all, or perhaps that was because Philemon spent most of it wondering what he would call his new oasis. After all, it was his – created at his command – so he should have the pleasure of naming it.

His first thought was the most obvious name for the place, but calling it Lake Philemon wasn't enduring enough. Philemon was hardly a rare name, even for a prince, and he wanted no confusion in anyone's mind that the oasis belonged to the Prince of Tasnim.

But to call it Tasnim Oasis implied that it belonged to the whole city, instead of its ruler. It was true that the wealth of water it contained would belong to the people of the city who travelled outside the city walls, for it was within his territory, but…the Lake of the People took away from the magic of making water appear in the desert.

Well, the djinn had performed the magic, but no one wanted the place named after a slave. Even if Philemon had known the slave's name, which of course he did not. There were far more important people for him to remember.

Including Fadi, his vizier, who was waiting for him in his apartments when Philemon arrived back in Tasnim.

Philemon sighed. He would have preferred his concubines to be waiting for him, but they would have to wait. The city came first, before Philemon's desires.

"I trust the city continued to prosper under your care?" Philemon asked, beckoning for a servant to bring refreshments for himself and the vizier.

Fadi bowed. "I do my best, as always, Your Highness. The city has endured under your family's rule and enjoyed good fortune for many years as a result. But a strange thing happened this morning…" He accepted a cup of wine and sipped from it.

Philemon paused to savour the first taste of a particularly fine vintage, before he replied, "Ah, this is Tasnim. Did a cat chase a dog? Did my jewelled garden grow? Or did a bird fly out of a well?"

Fadi managed a smile, but it did not reach his eyes. "I fear it is nothing so small as a bird, Your Highness."

Philemon felt the first twinge of unease in his belly. "Then spit it out. Tell me what has befallen my city, so that I may set things to rights."

"It's the wells, my prince. Yesterday, they were fine, but this morning, none of the buckets would reach the water."

"Then they need more rope! I am certain there is plenty in the storerooms. Have someone fetch it and the wells will soon be set to rights. Perhaps the ladies of Tasnim have bathed more often of late, or this summer has been a thirstier season than most." Philemon forced himself to smile, even as a chill crept around his heart. Water was life, and the lifeblood of Tasnim. If something happened to their water supply...

"I already have, Your Highness. It took a dozen yards of rope, but we struck water again." Fadi swallowed, as if he hesitated to say more.

Philemon knew his vizier, for the man had loyally served his father for longer than Philemon could remember. He waited in silence.

Finally, Fadi continued, "I set my clerks to search the records, looking for reports of this ever happening before. So far...they have found nothing. The waters of Tasnim have never dropped by so much. Ever. I fear...magic, or some sort of curse. Forgive me, my prince, but have you somehow angered someone powerful in your trip to the capital? Through some small act, insignificant to you...aroused the enmity of some sorcerer?"

Philemon burst out laughing. "Fadi, I visited

the Sultan for one purpose alone: to secure a wife from among his daughters. His matchmaker assured me that the Sultan finds favour with my proposal, and will send an appropriate girl as soon as I send word we are ready for her. Unless some sorcerer has set his heart on the same girl the Sultan intends to give me – chosen by the Sultan, not me, for surely he knows his daughters best – I cannot imagine what offence I have given anyone. And if I have…why, let them come! They may bring an army to Tasnim's gates, and we shall stand, as we always have, undefeated."

Fadi returned his smile. "Perhaps you are right, my prince. Maybe the earthquake we felt last night is the reason for it. It shook dust from the ceilings, and spilled soup from my bowl, but little else. Perhaps the water beneath the city spilled out of its vessel, too."

"That's the spirit. Tasnim will not fall while men like us rule her!"

Fadi left soon after, and Philemon headed to the garden, where his favourite concubines waited among the jewelled trees. The sound of soft music and feminine laughter lifted his spirits like nothing else.

Yet later, when both he and his concubines were sated, he dismissed them back to the harem, and lay alone in the darkness with his thoughts.

Tasnim would not fall, he swore to himself. He was the prince of this city, and he would defend it to his dying breath.

He padded out to where his bags had been brought in, and dug out the dented lamp. When the djinn appeared, Philemon didn't give him time to ask for orders. "I command you to fill the wells of Tasnim to where they were before I left the city," he said.

The djinn eyed him. "You want me to bring the water back?"

Philemon swore. "You stole the water from our wells? Then yes, I do want you to bring it back! Immediately!"

"I hear and obey," the djinn said, and vanished.

Satisfied, Philemon headed back to bed, and a peaceful night's sleep.

It would be the last peace he would know for a long, long time.

Four

"Just leave her, and let's go!" a male voice hissed.

Pain stabbed through Anahita's arm again — that's what had woken her — and she whimpered, her throat too hoarse to scream. She forced her eyes open, but the hulking shadow bending over her blocked the light. The only thing she could be certain of was that he was the one hurting her.

"Stop," she croaked, batting at him with her good arm.

"When I have bandaged this properly, or

you will be crippled for the rest of your life," the man said.

Anahita blinked and turned her head to get a better look at what he was doing. True to his word, he was bandaging her arm, which was already splinted so that it would heal straight.

"Take me home, where it will not matter. Servants will take care of me," she said.

The men exchanged a glance. "Your home is probably destroyed like ours was, and every other village Fakhri attacked. Your home is gone."

"Haidar, we have to go. Leave her. She will only slow us down." The second man glanced around nervously. "They'll blame us for this. We cannot be here when the body is found!"

"And where will we go? Our home is no more, cousin. If we leave her, she will surely die, for Fakhri's men are no better than he is. I will not leave her to pay the price for justice for Nasrin. She deserves better."

"Take me home to the capital. Tell the Sultan about Fakhri. He must know," Anahita insisted. She grabbed the first man – Haidar's – arm and heaved herself to her feet. Up she went…and down again, too, for her legs would not hold her. But she would not give up. She eyed the tent wall, and the inch-wide gap between it and the sand. Fakhri's tent stood at the edge of camp, where fewer people would be disturbed by the screams of his women. For once, this would work in her favour.

She grabbed the jewelled cup Fakhri had swilled wine from and used it to shovel sand away from the tent wall. Soon enough, she'd dug a dent big enough for her to squirm through. "If we go this way, and keep to the shadows, we can reach the camels without anyone seeing us. Do you know where they keep supplies? We'll need food and water – it's a long journey."

"Well, you heard the lady," the second man said. He threw himself into the shallow ditch Anahita had created, and after some widening of the pit, managed to leave the tent. "Come, cousin. Freedom awaits."

Haidar eyed Anahita. "What do they do to escaped slaves in your city, lady? Is it worse than what the desert people do to murderers?"

Anahita wet her lips. "I do not know,

but…but…if you are the Sultan's subjects, then surely he will free you for bringing word of what Fakhri did to your village. I swear I will do everything I can to see you freed, for you should never have been slaves in the first place."

"I will take a small chance of life over none at all. You first, lady, and I will follow after," Haidar said.

Anahita nodded, and followed Haidar's cousin. She hissed in pain as her broken ribs protested at bearing her weight, but she did not stop. She could not make it back home alone, and these men could help her.

When she reached the cool night air, Anahita forced herself to her feet, ignoring the pain and the swirling in her head. If she showed weakness now, they would leave her behind. So she gritted her teeth, and headed for the camels.

A heavy hand landed on her shoulder, yanking her back. "What are you doing?" he hissed.

Anahita glared at him. "If we want to get out of here, we'll need a distraction to hold their attention. Releasing the camels to stampede through the camp should do it."

"Or a fire," Haidar said cheerfully, rubbing his hands together as he rose to his feet.

A wisp of smoke curled up from the tunnel they'd crawled through.

"Fool!" Haidar's cousin growled. "I'll get us some supplies. You get her to the camels. If she's not there when I get back, we go without her!" He darted off.

"Shall we?" Haidar asked.

Anahita nodded, and led the way to the camels on the outskirts of the camp. She selected four who had been part of her entourage when she arrived, and led them away from the rest. "Stay here with him," she told them, pointing at Haidar. To him, she said, "These were my father's. They will carry us home." Then she untied the rest. "There is food hidden in the tents, with the men," she said. "Trample the tents and you will find it, but hurry!"

Heads lifted, and they stared at her uncertainly for a moment.

"Food. The men in the camp, the ones who

beat you, they are hiding it!" she said. "Go and get it!"

A cloud of sand surrounded her, as the grunting beasts rose to their full height, then lumbered off toward the camp to wreak havoc. Screams erupted. The screams of men, not women, for once.

"Yes," she whispered, elated.

"What did you do?" Haidar demanded.

A shriek sliced through the sandstorm. A sound Anahita recognised. "Vega!" She ran toward her.

"Come back here, girl!"

Haidar's hand reached for her, but Anahita dodged and ran on. She could not leave Vega here. But in the dark, the eagle's tethers were impossible to untie.

"Give me your knife," she said, holding out her hand.

"We need to go back to get Asad," Haidar said.

"I'm not leaving Vega. She is my hunting falcon, and she's coming home with me." Anahita glared at him. "Give me your knife, and help me cut the others free. They will help with the distraction."

She felt the cold hilt in her hand, and closed her fingers around it. The sharp blade sliced through Vega's jesses, and the bird rose into the air with a triumphant shriek.

"You may hunt in the morning. For now, stay with me," Anahita told the eagle, who settled obediently on her shoulder. She made quick work of the other birds' restraints, too.

The other birds eyed Vega warily, not budging from their perches for fear of what the eagle might do to them.

"Attack the men. They keep you prisoner. Once you are free, you may hunt, and all your prey will belong to you, and no one else. I will keep you safe from this eagle," Anahita told the birds. "Fly!"

The falcons rose, a mismatched flock with one deadly purpose. Vega clicked her beak in frustration, and Anahita reached up to stroke the eagle's feathers. "You will fly free at dawn, I promise. But we must get far from here."

She hurried back to the camels, where both men stood, waiting.

"What did you do?" Haidar asked. "I've

never seen animals obey like that."

Anahita smiled. "Magic."

"You're a witch?" Haidar's eyes showed white with fear.

"What's that bird for?" Asad asked, pointing at the eagle.

"Vega is what you would call my familiar. My friend." Her only friend out here.

"She'd better not scare the camels," Asad said, climbing onto the lead animal.

Anahita chose the smallest camel and struggled to climb onto her back. Between her broken arm and Vega, she was exhausted as she sank into the saddle.

"A drink for you, lady, for we will not have time to stop until we reach the next oasis," Haidar said, passing her a water skin.

Anahita nodded her thanks, uncorked it, and drank.

Wine coated her tongue, a welcome wetness as it trickled down her raw throat. Then she tasted the bitterness behind it, and it was too late. She tried to curse, but the words wouldn't come.

The opium stole her wits and darkness

engulfed her again.

Five

Day after day, the water level dwindled, despite Philemon ordering the djinn to refill the wells every night. One well ran dry, then another, and what had once been whispers became loud enough for even the prince to hear his citizens' concerns.

Philemon summoned the djinn door guardian. "What do you know about the other djinn?" he asked him.

The djinn shrugged. "He is the slave of a lamp, like I am the servant of your ring of office. He's powerful enough, but I don't trust him. My treason has long since passed into legend, but what is his crime? What did he do to deserve eternal enslavement? What if he is here to serve some other master, who wishes to bring Tasnim low?"

"You're right. I don't trust him either. Every night, I have ordered him to rectify our water woes, and every morning, they are worse. What does one do when a djinn is not following his master's orders?" Philemon asked.

The djinn shook his head. "I have never heard of such a thing. It should not be possible. He must be in service to someone else who means you and the city ill. Someone whose orders are more powerful than your own. The only permitted reason for refusing an order is because a djinn lacks the power to do what he's asked. Otherwise, I would fill the city's wells myself, but you know I cannot."

"So what do you suggest?" Philemon couldn't believe he was asking the djinn for help, but this djinn was once a vizier as loyal to the city as Fadi. And who knew djinn better than one of them?

"You can only fight magic with magic, and you need the help of someone more powerful than the lamp slave. I can let it be known among magical circles that you are looking for the help of a powerful enchantress, and you are willing to pay a high price for it."

It was on the tip of Philemon's tongue to ask how high a price, but it didn't matter. The only price too high to pay was the loss of the city, and its water supply. If it cost him all the gold in the treasury, so be it. The city's wealth was in its water. Without it…the city would die.

"Do it. Find an enchantress powerful enough to save Tasnim from this djinn."

While Philemon waited for the door guardian's return, he sent camel trains to the as yet unnamed oasis, to bring back water for the city. His concubines grumbled at having to surrender their bath to become the household water supply, but Philemon left them no choice. Once a place where water was plentiful, for the first time, Tasnim became like other desert cities, where every drop was precious.

Finally, the door guardian returned. "I have brought your enchantress, Master," the djinn announced. "Allow me to present Lady Zuleika."

She was his height, and she wore her hair uncovered, though it was twisted into a complicated knot on the back of her head, held in place by pins or magic, he wasn't sure. From her proud bearing, she could have been a princess, not just a mere lady.

The door djinn didn't seem to care about introducing him. Philemon sighed. If he wasn't enslaved to Philemon's ring of office, he would have sent the djinn away long ago.

"I am Prince Philemon, a humble prince in need of your help to control a troublesome djinn," Philemon said, bowing deeply.

"What sort of man sends a djinn to find an enchantress to solve his djinn problem?" Lady Zuleika asked. "It seems like a particularly sadistic task to set your poor slave."

Philemon jerked up from his bow and met her amethyst gaze. He'd mistaken her for one of his own people, but her pale eyes and unnatural height marked her as the child of some northern barbarian from the lands where it snowed in winter. He'd heard tales that the northern women fought as warriors alongside their men, much like the women warriors who had once been garrisoned here, and her manners made him believe it. A pity, for the enchantress was young and pretty. She'd make a lovely wife, were her tongue not so waspish.

Those purple eyes blazed. "Look at me like that again and I will leave," she snapped.

Too late Philemon realised his lust had leaked out of his usually controlled expression. Or perhaps this witch had read his mind – he had heard tales of powerful enchantresses who could do such things.

Philemon cleared his throat, trying to clear his mind of thoughts of this girl's body. "This djinn is not the problem. It's the other one. The slave of the lamp. He drained the wells of Tasnim dry and refuses to repair the damage he's done."

Lady Zuleika nodded. "Ah, no wonder the price you offer is so high. Gold is nothing compared to water in the desert. A djinn who makes it disappear must be stopped." She waved a hand. "Show me the djinn who caused the trouble."

Now? It would take his servants some time to make their way to the treasury in the lower levels of the city to retrieve the lamp and bring it back. Time he did not want to spend in the enchantress's company, risking offending her again.

"Summoning the djinn will take time, and you must be tired from your long journey here," Philemon said smoothly. "Allow me to accommodate you in one of the finest guest chambers in the palace. Servants will bring you refreshments, water to wash with, and anything else you need. My other djinn will be your guide in the city, showing you anything you wish to see."

She inclined her head. "Thank you. I have heard great things about the generosity of desert hospitality, but this is the first time I have had the opportunity to experience it for myself."

"You'll have to wait until the water's back before you can use the bathhouse," the door djinn said.

Philemon was struck with the irresistible image of the young enchantress in the harem bathhouse. Desire stirred, and more besides.

"I'll be in my chambers," he called after her and the door djinn. It wasn't a lie. He would be — after a detour to the harem to find a willing concubine or two to sate his desire. Because more than anything, Philemon knew he needed her magic more than he needed another girl in his bed.

Six

Late the next morning, Philemon emerged from his bedchamber, aching in all the right places. Now he could face the enchantress without being distracted.

"Your Highness, Lady Zuleika wishes you to meet her in the lower treasury," a servant said.

Philemon stared. "Before I have broken my fast? The woman is mad. Tell her I shall be with her when I am ready."

The servant bowed and hurried away.

Philemon took his time over breakfast,

knowing he needed to calm his irritation before he faced the enchantress. At least until she had restored their water supply. When he felt he was pleasantly full and he'd regained most of his good mood, he set off for the deepest level of the city.

"Ah, perfect timing," he heard the enchantress say. She beckoned without looking at him. "Philemon, come here and order your djinn to remain in his lamp until his master summons him."

Philemon wasn't sure which was the greater insult – her familiarity, or the fact that she deigned to give him orders.

She made an impatient sound in her throat. "It's the last step of the spell. Once you've said the words, the djinn will not be able to trouble you again. Even if he was ordered by your enemy to destroy the city, as his new master, your orders will take precedence. Hold the lamp in your hands and issue your orders."

Grudgingly, Philemon stepped forward and lifted the lamp in both hands. He cleared his throat. "Slave of the lamp, you are ordered to remain within the confines of your lamp until I summon you." He set the lamp down on a chest by the back wall.

She wrinkled her nose. "Not as precise as I'd like, but it will do. Now, Kaveh told me this is your personal fortune, and not the city's wealth?"

Philemon nodded. "Indeed. The city treasury is on a different level. These rooms hold the gifts personally given to the many generations of princes who have ruled this place."

"So, when you offered half of your personal fortune for an enchantress who can fix your problem here, you meant half of that?"

It hurt to agree – losing so much gold was a blow to any man – but Philemon forced himself to nod. "Half of my fortune for saving the city, yes."

"Good, because I've enchanted all of it. Your half and mine. Anyone who enters this chamber will be filled with such irresistible desire for the gold they see that does not belong to them, that they will not notice the lamp, nor wish to take it from you. Therefore the djinn will remain under your command and inside the lamp, unable to do any further harm to your city." She glanced around. "Perhaps I should ward the door, too, so that no one can open it. Or just you."

Philemon shook his head. "The gold here belongs to the crown – to me, now, but to my successors, should I succeed in siring a son. And princes do not open their own doors. We have servants to do it for us. Here." He rubbed his ring and the door guardian appeared. "If you must enchant the door, make it so that only this djinn can open it. He is the slave to my ring of office, which passes to my son in his turn."

She shrugged, bit her lip, and waved her hand. A faint hint of lavender dust flew through the air and sparkled on the door for a moment before it faded. "There. The djinn will trouble you no more!" She turned her amethyst eyes on him. "Now, I would like to take a small part of my fee with me, but leave the rest here, for this is as safe a place as any." A bag appeared in her hand, sturdy enough to hold a great deal of gold.

So fast? Philemon smiled. "Now you have

returned our water to the city, you have more than earned your fee, Lady Zuleika."

Her eyes grew wide. "Water? Do I look like a water witch? You hired me to deal with a powerful djinn, not fill your water tanks. Which I have now done, so as soon as you pay me for my services, our business will be concluded."

"Unless you restore the water supply to our wells, I will give you nothing!" Philemon shouted. He grabbed the enchantress's arm and dragged her into the corridor. Then he pointed at the door guardian. "Seal the door to the treasury, and do not open it unless your master commands you to do so!"

The round stone door rolled into place behind them.

"Now fix our water, witch!" Philemon said.

Lady Zuleika snatched her arm from his grip and returned his glare. "One you have paid me for the services already rendered, then perhaps I will consider taking a second commission. Until then...I will not help you, and nor will any witch, once they've heard what I have to say."

"I will not pay you a single copper coin until you fix our water supply!"

"And I will do nothing for you until you pay me for what I have already done!"

The door guardian broke the tense silence. "Master, it is unwise – "

"Silence!" Philemon roared. "Remove this woman from the city, and see that she does not return. Then find me a witch who will do as I ask!"

"Then you sentence your city to a slow death by thirst, because of your treachery. No witch will help you now!" Lady Zuleika said.

"What are you waiting for? Seize her, slave!" Philemon snapped.

The door guardian's expression was one of wide-eyed panic, but he could not say a word. He wrapped one arm around the enchantress, pressing his hand to her mouth so that she could not draw the blood she needed to cast a spell. Without magic, her strength was no match for the djinn's as he carried the struggling girl up to the gate.

"Good riddance!" Philemon called after them.

Seven

The sun reminded Anahita of her sister, Maram, the way it wanted to worm its way into her good graces, and Anahita was having none of it. Every bit of her hurt, and the sun would only blind her if she opened her eyes, anyway. Not to mention the gentle warmth she felt now would turn into a raging blaze that seemed to set the very sand on fire. Yet it was as relentless as Maram when she wanted Anahita awake, for she was one who always got her way. No one could resist her for long.

But Anahita would hold out as long as

possible, for they had played this game for as long as she could remember.

An impatient clacking sound got the better of her – Vega did not click her beak lightly.

Finally, Anahita opened her eyes.

Vega flapped her wings, as if to gesture toward her haul. Two fat ducks lay on the sand, and some sort of scurrying creature Anahita could not identify – all dead.

"You've been a busy girl. Which would you like?" Anahita asked, reaching out to stroke the eagle's feathers.

Vega cocked her head to one side, so that one fiery eye could better regard Anahita.

Ah, animals did not understand the nuances of likes and dislikes. Spending so much time among humans without an animal to talk to, she'd forgotten.

"Which is the tastiest?" Anahita asked instead.

Vega did not reply. She closed her beak around the dead scurrier's neck and tugged it closer to herself, opening her wings in a protective mantle over her meal.

"Good choice. Thank you for the ducks,

then. They will break my fast nicely." Anahita reached for them, only to realise there was something else she'd forgotten. Her splinted arm was a pointed reminder about the previous night's events.

"I wondered when you would wake," a male voice said.

Reflex made Anahita reach for a veil to cover her face, but Haidar shook his head.

"No need for that. Asad and I are no longer men. That bastard Fakhri saw to that." He spat on the ground at the mention of the man's name. "May he rot in hell like all the damned for what he did to our village."

"What did he do?" Anahita ventured, though she suspected she knew.

"A few of his men attacked our camp at dusk, luring our warriors out of the village. As the two best warriors, my father left us behind to guard the women and children until they returned. But no one returned, and he had an army hidden in the dunes that descended on us when it was dark. Asad and I are good, but not against so many. He and his men captured everyone who was left, and dragged them back to his camp — even the girl children. He used the little ones first, making us carry out the corpses once he'd finished taking his pleasure of them. I thought he was a demon then, before he started on the women. And my wife…"

"Which one is your wife?" Anahita asked.

Haidar just shook his head and buried his head in his hands.

Asad approached. "Haidar's wife was with child. That bastard tried to cut the child out of her before he took his pleasure of her. She bled to death beneath him in his bed, before he made us carry the corpse out. I'd never been so happy not to marry, but my sisters…ah, we buried them all, until we were the only ones from our village left alive. He was preparing to attack another camp when you arrived and…distracted him." Asad shuddered.

Anahita was silent for a long moment. Finally, she said, "Why did you stay with him? I understand wanting to protect what was left of your people, but if you are all that is left…"

"Because we're slaves. Escaped slaves, now.

Anyone may kill us on sight, or return us to his camp."

She wet her lips. "But…his last order was to guard me, was it not? Take me home to my father, and I will see to it that you are freed. Then you may serve whoever you please, for you will be free men again."

Haidar let out a hollow laugh. "We are no longer men, and we will never be free. My wife and unborn child will haunt me until the day I die."

Asad nudged him. "Anything is better than serving the man who killed them. Where does your father live?"

Anahita smiled faintly. "My father has a grand palace in the capital."

Asad swore, then apologised. "What manner of man sends his daughter to marry a dog like Fakhri?"

"My father has many daughters. I am…the least of them, for my mother was a concubine and not one of his wives. I think he hoped my marriage would bring peace to the desert, to further his trade interests. And perhaps I will, though not the way he thought." Anahita smiled more broadly at that. Playing at politics was the sort of thing Maram did, not a nobody like her.

Haidar fell to his knees on the sand and bowed until his forehead touched the ground. He gestured for Asad to do the same. "Then we will serve you, for we owe you a debt. We swore vengeance on Fakhri, both of us, yet it was you who exacted it. Free or enslaved, we serve you."

Anahita shook her head. "When we reach my father's palace, I will return to the harem, where no men are allowed to enter. You are fighters, warriors, protectors – enlist in my father's guards. He always needs more good men."

Haidar lifted his head. "We are no longer men. Fakhri took from us what you took from him."

It took Anahita a moment to understand what he meant, though he'd said the words before. "You mean he cut off your…?" She couldn't utter the words.

"He made eunuchs of us, yes," Asad supplied. "Guards of his harem. Guarding them against everything except that which would kill them – him."

Anahita didn't know what to say. What did you say to a man who'd had his manhood forcibly removed? Or lost everything he loved, and been forced to serve the man who'd destroyed it?

"Man or not, I vow on my wife's grave that no man will ever hurt you again while I live," Haidar said. He grinned. "My wife would have taken great pleasure in seeing what you did to his corpse."

"And I," Asad added.

"Now all we need to do is get home," Anahita said.

"We will get you there, or die trying," Haidar promised. "What is your name, lady?"

"Anahita," she said slowly, "But in the harem, I was just Ana." She stared down at the rough robes she'd donned to cover herself against the fierce desert sun. She might be a sultan's daughter, but now she was no different to these two men, all fugitives in the desert. "Just Ana," she repeated softly.

Eight

As Philemon returned to his apartments, he found his people staring at him. They'd all heard his argument with the enchantress, then.

"I will address the people of the city at sunset, in the great hall cavern," he said, repeating the words over and over as he ascended the tunnels to his own dwelling.

It wasn't until he reached the privacy of his own chambers that he allowed his stiffened shoulders to slump as despair overwhelmed him. What was he to do now?

Philemon heard the crash of the main gate

slamming open. No one but the djinn door guardian should have been able to do that.

A lesser man would have sent a servant to investigate, but Philemon was the Prince of Tasnim, and he would confront this threat head on.

He rubbed the ring, summoning the djinn guardian. Just because he wasn't a coward, didn't mean he was stupid.

The entry hall was full of dust, turning the people running through it into ghosts and shadows. But ghosts and shadows bent under the weight of whatever it was they carried. Philemon's blood ran cold.

"They can't leave! Don't let them take my treasures!" he shouted.

"As you command, Master," the djinn said, bowing, before disappearing into the gloom.

"Wait. You have to close the door!" Philemon called, but the djinn evidently hadn't heard him, for he didn't return.

"I would only open it again. You can't keep these people here to die," a female voice said. The enchantress.

She strode out of the dust, haloed against

the open doorway like some sort of avenging angel. Philemon shrank away from the fury written across her face.

"You don't deserve this city, or my help, or any magical assistance at all. You demanded my assistance, then lied to me, blaming the dried-up wells on everything but your own stupidity. The djinn of the lamp told me everything. You commanded the djinn of the lamp to destroy your own water supply, not some imaginary enemy. Even after I sent him back into exile, you dared to refuse payment for my services. To evict me from your city. It is your city no longer. Your people flee, for the source of its wealth – the water – is gone, and they cannot live here any more. You deserve this."

Philemon couldn't help himself. "The djinn tricked me! He didn't tell me making that oasis would drain the city wells dry. My princess will never marry me if I am the prince of a city of no people. Make him fix it. Or use your powers to fix it!"

Lady Zuleika shook her head. "I do not take orders from you, Prince of Tasnim. Or should that be prince of a dead, dry cave?"

"Fix it!" he shouted. "You said you would help me!"

"I did help you. And I will do you one further favour. The only way for you to understand what has happened to your city's water supply is to inspect it personally, and you shall!" Purple light erupted from her hands, knocking him back against the wall of the well. But the magic kept pushing at him, leaning him back, until…

Philemon screamed as he fell backward into the well, arms flailing for something to stop him from falling to his death, but the well somehow gaped impossibly wide, and he could not grasp anything.

The fall should have killed him, but it just knocked the wind out of him, so all he could do was lie there on his back in a shallow puddle, listening to the sounds of his people deserting him.

A head appeared above. Hers, of course. "Fix your own plumbing problem. But even then, no woman in her right mind will want a toad like you, prince or not. If you ever find some princess who will take pity on you, take you to her bed and willingly lie in your slimy arms until dawn, maybe I'll find it in my heart to make you human again. For her sake."

And then she was gone.

Philemon reached for his ring of office, to summon the door guardian to lift him out of the well. But his fingers were bare — the ring had somehow fallen off.

He screamed in frustration, a sound that should have echoed around the underground chamber, striking fear in every heart. But the only sound he heard was a forlorn croak.

Nine

Anahita was naked, covered in blood, and Fakhri came for her again, his body glowing red in the light, his jutting cock as long as he was tall. She screamed, and once she started, she couldn't seem to stop.

A hand came from nowhere, pressing down on her mouth so hard she swore there would be a fresh bruise to add to those Fakhri had already given her. She flailed about, trying to fight her way free.

"Hush, Lady Anahita, you are safe. We swore an oath, but we cannot keep it if you scream so loud everyone in the desert hears you."

She knew that voice. Anahita blinked her eyes open to make sure. Yes, it was Haidar. She blew out a breath she hadn't known she'd been holding. "Thank you," she said shakily. "I dreamed…"

Haidar cut her off. "As we all do." He grimaced. "There are some hours to go before nightfall, when we will travel under the cover of darkness again. Try to sleep, for you will need your strength."

She shook her head. "I cannot. Not after such a dream. If his men come after us…"

"They will not. And even if they do, they will not get past Asad and I," Haidar said.

It was on the tip of her tongue to say that Haidar hadn't been able to protect his own wife, the woman he loved, when Fakhri's men had come for her, but she had no desire to remind the man of his loss. Instead, she said, "I got past you. To kill…to kill…" She couldn't even say the sheikh's name, though she had only to closer her eyes to see his evil grin, gleaming above that monstrous cock.

"You were not a threat," Haidar said.

She glared at him. "Enough of a threat to kill him."

"Because he did not see you as a threat, either," Haidar replied. "If you came at me with a knife, you would not kill me so easily." He gazed at her, as though sizing her up for something. "If you truly do not think you can sleep any more, perhaps you should try." He produced a knife from nowhere and offered it to her, hilt first.

Anahita took it. The blade was barely bigger than her eating knife – much smaller than the one she'd killed her husband with.

Haidar backed out of the tent and beckoned for her to join him. "There is more space for a blade dance out here."

It took Anahita longer to join him, between her broken arm and what she suspected were also broken ribs, but no matter how much she hurt, something within her would not let her back down from this fight. She refused to let any man dictate what she could or could not do, ever again.

She stood for a moment, taking in Haidar's

relaxed stance as the afternoon sun set his face aglow. Then she rushed at him, raising the knife above her head.

His arm shot out and slammed against her wrist, sending the blade spinning across the sand.

Her wrist throbbed, already covered in dark bruises from Fakhri, and she cradled it to her chest, fighting back tears. She met Haidar's gaze squarely, refusing to bow her head.

He was the one to look away first, striding across the sand to retrieve his knife. Anahita expected him to tuck it back into its sheath, but he held it out to her instead. When she wrapped her fingers around the hilt, he shook his head. "No, you're holding it wrong. It's easy for someone to knock it out of your hand if you do it like that."

Haidar wrapped a warm hand around hers, showing her how it should be done.

"And don't hold the knife up high like you did just then. He'll see you coming, and have plenty of time to defend himself. Strike from below, like you did the first time. If he doesn't see it coming, he won't block, and your blade will have a better chance of finding its mark. A man rarely looks at what is under his nose, and if you extend the line of his nose down to the ground, you will see where he is blind." He drew a line down his nose and pointed at a spot on the ground. "That is where you lift your blade to do the most damage." He wrapped his hand around Anahita's and brought the blade up to his throat. "Or keep it low, to hit his heart, or his belly." He touched the blade tip to those places on his body, then released her. "Now try it again."

She did, and he corrected her, a sequence they repeated over and over until he was satisfied.

Anahita tried to hand his knife back, but Haidar refused to accept it. Instead, he produced the sheath, and insisted she wear it now she knew how to use it.

"Thank you," she said in wonderment.

"Are you finished with your foolishness now, so that we can be on our way?" Asad asked.

"Teaching her how better to defend herself is not foolishness," Haidar objected.

"She has a broken arm and plenty of other bruises from the bastard's blows. She wouldn't last five minutes in a proper fight." Asad pointed at the fire. "You'd be better off teaching her how to cook. Now that's a more womanly skill."

"She killed a man, with that broken arm, and the other injuries. You couldn't have done it," Haidar said.

Asad shrugged. "I don't have the advantage of being a tiny girl he's beaten into submission more nights than that bastard could count. She surprised him, that's all."

"And us," Haidar said. "You never saw it coming, either, or you wouldn't have let her take your blade. Next time, she may need more than the element of surprise. She's as much a warrior as any of our people were."

"She's not Nasrin," Asad said softly. "Your wife is dead, cousin. Nothing you do now can change that."

Haidar brought up his stubborn chin. "You think I don't know that? That tiny girl avenged Nasrin, and all our people. Her. Not you or me. And she did it after a beating, with a broken arm. That takes courage. You swore to protect her, just as I did. Giving her a blade and training her to use it is part of that oath."

"You're still a fool." Asad turned away to put some more kindling on the fire.

"I'd rather learn to fight than to cook," Anahita said. "I will sleep more soundly for it, even after I am home. Besides, it is Vega and I who do the hunting. It is only fitting that someone else cooks our catch."

Haidar burst out laughing. "The lady is right! A true huntress, and she has trained that bird well."

Anahita considered telling them that she hadn't trained Vega at all, but she wasn't sure how they would react to her ability to speak to animals. Best to keep that a secret a little longer.

"So, shall we practice some more while Asad makes our breakfast?" Anahita ventured with a hopeful smile.

"As my lady commands," Haidar said with a bow. Neither of them paid any attention to Asad's grumbled complaints as he threaded meat onto a knife to cook over the fire.

Ten

When Anahita lifted her gaze to survey the open city gates, she nearly wept for joy. Never had she seen anything so beautiful as that dusty portal. And yet…a princess did not weep before her people, so her tears died the dry death that befell all who did not know the ways of the desert.

"Stop," she commanded, and Asad and Haidar did. More than that, they stared at her in surprise. She summoned the same courage that had driven her to seize the knife that set her free, and said, "This is my father's city. The people must make way for his daughter. One of you must go before me, and the other behind, as befits a princess." She moistened her lips. "All the way to the Sultan's palace. My home."

Haidar coughed, but Asad laughed outright. "Do you truly expect us to believe that? The Sultan would not sacrifice his daughter to an animal like Sheikh Fakhri! Tell us the truth, now, Ana. Which house really belongs to your father?"

If they didn't believe her, who would? "My father is the Sultan, and you will address me as Your Highness Princess Anahita. At least until you are free, and our bargain is fulfilled."

Haidar wouldn't meet her eyes. "And if the guards do not let us into the palace?"

She had not come this far to be denied her home. "Then you will tell them to fetch Princess Maram. My sister will recognise me, and take me to my father."

Haidar grasped her arm. "What will you tell the Sultan?" Panic widened his eyes.

Anahita shook off his hand. "I will tell him the truth. That Sheikh Fakhri is dead at my hand. My father sent me to forge peace with the sheikh, and so I have. He will never attack our people again. Now, please pretend you are my official guards, and make the people make way for their princess."

Haidar grinned. "Never thought I'd get to meet the Sultan. Go on, Asad. You heard the princess. You lead the way, shouting orders to her people. I'll keep watch from the back."

"And if the Sultan has us killed?" Asad hissed, not convinced.

Haidar's grin never wavered. "It is a better death than what we faced in the desert. We should have died with our people. The only reason we're alive now is because Ana stole your knife. She's not afraid of the Sultan. How are you going to live out the rest of your life, knowing you have less courage than that girl?"

Asad glared at his cousin. "If this is a ploy so that you can see Nasrin sooner, I will torment you in the afterlife. I swear it. You will never know a moment's peace." Then he took his place before Anahita and drew in a deep breath. "Make way for the princess!" he bellowed. "Make way for Her Highness

Princess Anahita!"

Anahita straightened her shoulders, wishing she was taller and more impressive, and followed Asad into the city.

The palace gates presented no problem, and they walked straight in. It wasn't until Anahita reached the audience chamber that she realised today must be a public audience day, for the hall was packed.

"Now what?" Asad whispered.

Anahita unfasted the straps that held Vega to her. "Fly home, and see that the falconer gives you a good dinner," she said, lifting her arm high so that the bird might fly. Vega did not hesitate, soaring over the palace to where her meal awaited. If everything went well, Anahita would hunt with her again on the morrow. If not…

"We seek an audience with my father. Make the crowd part," she said, praying they would. The rest of the city had responded as though she was Maram, and not some forgotten concubine's daughter.

A path opened, and Anahita plunged ahead, her men trailing behind her. When she reached the foot of her father's dais, she threw herself down on the floor, blessing the cool marble beneath her forehead. She raised her voice, "Father, I bring news. Sheikh Fakhri is dead."

Silence fell over the hall, stretching for an eternity. Anahita didn't dare look up.

Then she heard the rustle of her father's robes. "Today's audience is at an end. Return tomorrow."

The sounds of a herd of grumbling, shuffling people echoed off the arched ceilings, so only Anahita and those closest to the Sultan heard his words: "Have refreshments bought to my private chambers. I will speak to her there."

Servants helped Anahita to bathe and dress in finer clothes than she'd ever worn before. Long silken sleeves hid her bandaged arm, now wrapped in fresh linen, as gentle hands combed and oiled her hair. It was like being a bride all over again, but there was no fear in her belly this time. Only determination.

When she reached her father's chamber, Anahita prostrated herself again.

"When I announced I was sending one of

my daughters to Fakhri to be his bride, I was advised that I was sending the girl to her death. I was begged to reconsider, for the only language the Sheikh understood was violence. But I kept my word, and you were sent. Now, you return, bringing word of the Sheikh's death. Such a thing is impossible. Therefore, I ask you to explain how it is possible."

"A miracle," Anahita said weakly.

The Sultan sighed. "Get up, girl. I can't hear you when you talk to my rug. Now, tell me everything. Did you marry the man?"

Anahita rose and met her father's eyes. The eyes of the man who had sent her to be beaten to death by Fakhri.

Haidar was right — she'd faced death in Fakhri's eyes, and she had no fear left for her father, the man who'd sentenced her to that fate.

She settled herself on a cushion and poured herself a cup of whatever her father was drinking. She drank half of it down, barely tasting the cold juice, for there was not enough sweetness in the world to dull the bitterness on her tongue.

Anahita took a deep breath, and told her tale.

She left nothing out. Not one blow, or the trials she and her men had endured in the desert. Until, finally, she was done.

Her father opened his mouth to respond.

Perhaps she was not done, after all.

"Sheikh Fakhri deserved his fate, and if you marry me to a pig like that again, I swear I will gut him like the animal he is, too," she said fiercely, then added, almost as an afterthought, "Father."

"Ana!" a female voice shrieked, and a flash of silk and gold flew across the room to embrace Anahita. "You're alive!"

Anahita wanted to warn her sister about her broken arm, but despite Maram's apparent excitement, she had taken great care not to touch Anahita's right arm. Realisation dawned – Maram knew all that had been said and done since Anahita entered the palace, and she'd chosen her time of arrival perfectly.

Maram's tone was one of girlish delight. "Father, you must give her the apartment beside mine. The harem is for virtuous wives, not the likes of us. What reward did you offer the two heroes who carried her home to us?"

If Anahita had not known before, now she was certain Maram's spies had told her everything. For she had not seen Haidar or Asad since the throne room.

She opened her mouth to ask, but both her father and Maram seemed to have forgotten her. No, not Maram, who broke from her chatter to say, "Oh, you must be exhausted! Go and rest – the chambers beside mine, mind, not in the harem. I must discuss my new jewels with Father, but when we are done, I will come to you directly."

Dismissed – by her own sister! – Anahita was too tired to protest. She followed a servant to her new chamber, only to find it larger than the one she and Maram had shared in the harem. But the size didn't matter – all she cared about was the bed, that heavenly soft surface that embraced her as it promised rest.

It seemed but a moment since she'd closed her eyes, but the stiffness of Anahita's limbs told a different story. It was Maram's voice that had woken her – her sister sounding annoyed, which didn't happen often.

"Don't be ridiculous. She is my sister. You wouldn't deny me the chance to be reunited with my dearest sister, who I thought I would never see again?" Maram wheedled.

Haidar sounded chagrined. "No, mistress, I mean, Highness, but our job is to protect Princess Anahita, and unless she says she wants to see you…" A long pause, and Anahita imagined he shrugged. "My deepest apologies."

Anahita staggered to her feet. "Let her in," she said hoarsely, then swallowed and repeated the words.

Haidar stuck his head through the doorway. "Are you sure? I think she's trying to cast some sort of spell. She's bitten her lip bloody. I wouldn't want you to come to harm. First day officially on the job and all, but I'm not that stupid."

Spells. Maram. Seduction spells, surely. Would they work on a eunuch? Anahita was one of the few who knew of Maram's magical talents, for she'd seen her use them often enough.

"Maram, stop. Boys, please let her in. She's

telling the truth. Maram means me no harm," she said.

All three of them entered the room, to Maram's obvious annoyance.

"I will not tolerate the presence of that man's sworn men," Maram said loftily, dismissing them with a wave of her hand. "Begone."

"We are sworn to the Sultan now, more than ever before. The only oath I swore to that whoreson was that he'd die screaming, drowning in his own blood. So when Princess Anahita here delivered the blow that fulfilled my oath, we became her men. Until death." Haidar bowed in Anahita's direction, and Asad did the same.

Only then did Anahita realise they wore guard uniforms, instead of the clothes they'd arrived in. "But you're free…aren't you?" she asked.

Asad laughed. "Free as we ever were. But oaths are tricky things, best not broken. Our village is gone, and we have nowhere else to go. Palace guard seemed like a good idea. Especially if we're to protect the princess outside the harem."

Maram gasped. "They're common desert herders? And your lovers? Are they any good?" Her gazed raked over Asad, then Haidar.

It was Anahita's turn to gasp. "Surely you haven't taken a lover. Not after your mother…"

Maram smiled. "Ah, you haven't heard. Of course I have. While you were off adventuring in the desert, I have been training to become a courtesan. The best the world has ever known. For it will soon be my turn to travel, as Father's ambassador to far-off lands. I would have gone sooner, but Father hesitated, doubting my advice. Now you have returned, he will not doubt me again. I told him Fakhri could only be stopped with weapons. He should have believed me. Sent an army instead of you…" Her hands fluttered in genuine distress. "Is it true that he broke your arm? Where else are you hurt?"

Anahita waved her away. "I'm healing fine. Besides, you don't want to hear about my blisters from walking across the desert. Instead, tell me about your travels. Will you go north to where ice falls from the sky?"

"I hope so." Maram's eyes lit up. "Oh, you would not believe half the things Mistress Kun has taught me. A thousand ways to seduce a man, and a thousand more to enslave him without his knowledge."

Asad hurried out of the room, followed by Haidar.

Maram smothered a laugh. "There. It is good to have you home, Ana. I thought I'd lost you forever. Now will you tell me about your lovers?"

Anahita shook her head. "Asad and Haidar aren't my lovers. They're eunuchs, men Fakhri enslaved from the camps he slaughtered. I've told my tale to Father, and I'm sure you heard all I have to tell. But you have done so much since I left. What of your lovers?"

Maram blushed. "Well…"

Anahita listened, entranced, as Maram spun a tale that seemed like an airy fantasy, of men who could make her body sing, as she learned the arts to bring a man pleasure in equal measure. Yet even as Maram spoke, Anahita fervently wished that such men did exist. Somewhere.

Eleven

Philemon feverishly searched every inch of the cavern twice over, and still he did not find the ring. He shouted until he was hoarse, but only ominous silence greeted him from above. He feared the city was empty but for him. And the water beneath it was draining away. Even now, the pool that had broken his fall had dried to a couple of shallow puddles.

No matter how high he leaped, he could not catch the lip of any of the wells, which taunted him from above.

But he would not die down here. He was a

prince, by all that was holy.

If he could not return to the city, then he would find another way. The water here had travelled some sort of path between the city and the oasis, and where water went, so could he.

He'd follow the water to the oasis and make his way back to the city across the desert.

He set off along the tunnels, following the sound of flowing water in the darkness. If he faltered, he only had to remind himself that he was not destined for an ignominious end, all alone in the tunnels beneath his city. As long as he lived, so did Tasnim. Step after tentative step, he would reach the oasis.

Hours passed, or perhaps it was days. The darkness was as timeless as the desert above, but it would not defeat him.

When he finally did stop, it was because water barred his way. Not the puddles and shallow stream he'd splashed through, but a pool so deep he could not see the bottom. Yet the water glowed as if lit by some magical underground sun.

No, not an underground one, he realised.

One that burned down from the sky above. He'd found the oasis, but he would have to swim to reach it.

So be it.

The water was cool against his skin, a sweet caress urging him on. He swam for longer than he expected, but not so long that he felt the burn in his lungs from holding his breath too long. When he surfaced into brilliant sunlight, he let out a shout of triumph. No witch would be the end of him!

Was it his imagination, or did the oasis appear bigger than before? Philemon wasn't sure, but the swim seemed to take as long as his walk through the tunnels. But determination drove him, now more than ever before, and he reached the shore.

Desert sand compressed underfoot, gritty and crumbling between his toes. Huh. He must have lost his shoes somewhere in the dark and not noticed until now. Philemon glanced down, but he couldn't see his toes through the dislodged dust swirling through the water. He stepped out.

Pain burned the soles of his feet, like the

fires of hell itself. He bit back a scream and hurled himself back into the water. Slowly, the fire in his feet extinguished in the lapping waters of the oasis.

He would bind his feet with scraps of cloth torn from his robes, the way beggars did, Philemon told himself. Beggars in other cities, for there were none in Tasnim.

He reached for the hem of his robe, but he clutched only air. Now he looked down again, really looked, and this time he couldn't tear his eyes away. No amount of water could hide the green tint to his skin, or the peculiar shape of his feet.

Philemon held his hands up to his face, praying that they would be normal, but his prayers were not answered. His green hands had only four fingers each.

A toad, the witch had called him, not a prince.

She'd turned him into one.

He let out a scream of fury, but all that came out was a croak.

Swearing he'd hunt down the witch and force her to fix the mess she'd made, he sank beneath the surface. Watching. Waiting. For frogs could not survive in the desert alone – he would need to find a travelling party to join to take him back to Tasnim. Or, better yet, to where he could find the witch.

A caravan would come, he told himself with confidence. And when it did, he would be ready.

Twelve

"I have not left the palace for weeks, and now Vega's found herself a mate, she's not leaving the nest any time soon. I want to go hunting, and to hunt I need a new bird. A hawk this time, smaller than Vega, and not so heavy." Anahita looked from Haidar to Asad. "I saw a new caravan come into the city last night. A new caravan means new birds, or at least I hope so, and who knows what else. Who's coming?"

Asad and Haidar exchanged a glance. "As long as we don't end up spending hours at the goldsmith again," Asad began.

"We weren't there for hours. And it would have been a much shorter visit if you hadn't been fondling that new blade of yours and scaring the man," Anahita said.

"I was testing the edge!" Haidar protested.

"Mm. Testing the edge while wagering how many blows it would take to cut a man's hands off." Anahita set her hands on her hips. "I still don't believe you could do that in one stroke. All that bone…it would take at least two."

"It only took one to deal with that thief who tried to take your purse last time," Asad said.

Anahita waved his words away. "That was you, with your sword. Not Haidar with a knife. And you took off half his arm, not just his hand. Please don't do that again."

Asad looked aghast. "You'd prefer to let thieves steal from you? Your father would assign you a squad of guards, convinced we are not capable of protecting you."

"I'd prefer not to have a screaming man lying at my feet, bleeding all over the place, while the marketplace erupts into chaos and closes before I have finished my shopping,"

Anahita said drily.

"You shall have it. Now no one dares get close enough to us to risk losing their arm, too," Asad said.

Anahita nodded. She had to admit, he had a point. Better that they had a reputation for being fearsome than having to deal with a squad of her father's guards, like Maram did, or being forced to defend herself. If a princess hacked off someone's hand in the marketplace, Father would never marry another daughter off again. Though that might not be a bad thing…

Anahita mentally shook herself. Just because she only knew the undesirable kind of husbands, did not mean her sisters could not be happily married to good men. Fakhri had been the worst, but her other three husbands had not been much of an improvement. Well, unless you counted the fact that all three had not had the opportunity to enjoy married life for very long, and she'd been widowed without any broken bones or significant bruises. True to his word, Haidar had taught her well. So well that she was never without a blade or three within reach.

"Have you changed your mind?" Haidar asked.

He read her expression well. As he should, after so many years together.

"No. Just…a widow's memories are not always pleasant," she said.

Asad laughed. Inside her palace apartments, he knew better than to speak freely, for every wall had ears. He would have to wait until they went hunting to say what was on his mind. And he would, she was certain. For though they kept up the façade of mistress and her sworn men, they were her friends more than anything. The only two truly good men she'd ever met, eunuchs or not.

Maram laughed at her cynicism, as well she might, for Maram charmed men as easily as breathing. But Maram was off travelling again, on some diplomatic mission for her father. Furthering trade somewhere in the far north, where ice lay on the ground for half the year. Anahita shivered at the very thought of it. She was a desert princess, only comfortable when the heat rising up from the sands was warmer than her blood. And boats? Ugh. Give her a camel any day, a creature she could communicate with that would do whatever she said.

But today was for birds, not camels.

"So, are you coming?" she asked.

Despite their initial grumbling, once they were in the bazaar, both men spent more time looking at the wares for sale than she did. Strange foreign blades, cloth so heavy it was a wonder anyone could walk while wearing it…these must have come by ship from the northern lands.

She prayed they'd brought some new creatures. If not a bird, then perhaps something else. One of the wives in the harem had a particularly fat cat that slept on her bed at night, for she abhorred mice and would go nowhere without the beast. Anahita had often wondered whether her father tolerated the animal on the nights he favoured that wife, but she'd never been brave enough to ask.

Maram would know. She knew every secret in the harem. Perhaps the ships had brought her home, too…

But there was no word of Maram's return in the marketplace, as there certainly would be, for she was well known. Instead, the people talked of a sheikh raiding their borders, enslaving those he did not kill. His men had run afoul of a party of crusaders, but the northerners were weak from hunger and war, and the sheikh's men had taken everything from them before leaving them in the desert to die. No one liked the crusaders much, but it was the height of dishonour to let them die in the desert instead of killing them outright. And the stories about this new sheikh made him sound like a second Fakhri.

An affronted shriek drew Anahita's attention from the marketplace gossip. An avian shriek, she was certain, though it didn't sound like a bird she knew. Anahita quickened her pace.

She reached the menagerie, only to discover she'd somehow left Asad and Haidar behind. She debated whether to retrace her steps or simply wait for them to appear.

"What are you looking for today, mistress?" the stall owner asked, offering her a deep bow.

Veiled and shrouded in widow's garb, Anahita didn't bother to correct him. "A hunting bird," she said.

The man's eyes widened. "A song bird might amuse you more, mistress. I have here a bird from the far north with a song so sweet, it will bring tears to your eyes."

"Her Highness has shed too many tears of grief. She delights in hunting, and wishes for your best hawk," Haidar said, appearing at Anahita's elbow.

The man threw himself down on the ground, wailing his apologies and other boring things. Anahita's attention was caught by a prickly ball that suddenly moved. It unrolled, revealing a downy belly and pointed face.

"What is that?" she asked, pointing.

The man clambered to his feet and puffed out his chest. "It is a most rare creature, found only in – "

"It's a desert hedgehog," Asad said flatly. "You'll find a dozen of them at any oasis. I'll catch you one next time you go hunting, Your Highness."

The man deflated. "I assure you – "

He was drowned out by a shriek just like the one that had drawn Anahita's attention in the first place.

This time, she could see the source. And what a source.

The hawk was small, her chest patterned in an intricate mosaic of brown, gold and white. She opened her silvery beak to shriek again, flicking her talon at something pink on the floor of her cage. A baby mouse or rat, Anahita decided.

"Are dead mice not good enough for you, beautiful?" she asked the bird.

"He has given me nothing suitable to eat for many days. I am hungry and this is not food!" the little falcon said. "I must be free to fly and hunt!"

"That is a crusader falcon, from the north," the salesman said smoothly.

Asad shrugged. "I've never seen a bird like it. Have you?"

Haidar shook his head.

"She belonged to a foreign king, who gave the bird as a gift to his mistress, who could not bear to look upon the creature after he died valiantly in battle," the salesman continued. "She was taken prisoner by a vicious sheikh, the same man who killed her paramour, and the bird is pining for his mistress. He needs a new mistress, as royal as the first…"

"My master sold me to pay his passage on a ship home," the bird said. "He knew good food. Fresh food, from the hunt!"

For once, Anahita was glad of her veil, for it hid her smile. "The bird looks thin and hungry. But it's not eating. Is it sick?"

The man began to sweat. "If Her Highness wishes for a more robust bird, may I suggest – "

"How much for the sick bird?"

"For Her Highness, I recommend – "

Haidar named a price that was far too low for the sweet little falcon.

Five minutes later, they left the stall, with Asad carrying the falcon's cage.

Not jewels or silks or the costliest carpet could catch Anahita's eye after that. She made one more stop, at a stall selling snacks and drinks, before demanding that Haidar and Asad accompany her out of the city.

She'd made sure to buy a selection of their favourite cakes, so neither man complained as they took her to one of her favourite hunting spots.

Thirteen

Darkness had descended by the time Anahita headed back inside the city gates. The guards called a challenge, but the moment they spotted Haidar and Asad, they moved aside, bowing to let them pass.

Anahita cradled her new bird to her chest, stroking her feathers as the falcon slept off her fresh-caught feast. Anahita had never seen a bird fish before, but this one seemed born to it, plucking fish and frogs out of the oasis faster than she'd seen her little brothers gobble treats. The bird had laid the first corpses at her feet, and Anahita had thanked her, before telling her she could eat her fill today without needing to share.

As they passed through the bazaar, now lit by torches and busier than ever, there was a buzz that had nothing to do with some sheikh or rumours of distant battles. No, this was the buzz of energy that only came when Maram arrived home. Some claimed they had seen her, while others swore they would line the streets on the morrow, hoping to catch a glimpse of her on her way to the public bathhouse that would be closed for her private use.

Anahita had no idea why her sister chose to patronise the ancient public bathhouse instead of the perfectly private one in the palace, but the people loved that she did.

Anahita had her own reasons to be happy Maram was home. She would have stories to tell about her travels, gifts she'd been given by the people of the various courts she'd visited, and as the Sultan's favourite daughter, her apartments were as opulent as a queen's. So when Anahita joined her for dinner this evening – as she always did when Maram was home – it would be a far pleasanter affair than eating alone, for Haidar and Asad weren't supposed to share her meals. And of course, Maram had charmed the palace cooks like she did everyone else, so the delicacies at her table outshone even the Sultan's feasts. Not to mention the exotic things she brought home from her travels.

The next morning found her fuzzy-headed from the strong berry wine Maram had generously plied her with, but the fuzziness faded fast when Haidar opened the door to her chamber.

"A message from the Sultan, Your Highness," he said gravely.

The message was important enough to be delivered by one of the Sultan's wives. Anahita's heart sank. She was usually beneath the notice of the wives, except when a marriage was in the wind. Then, the highest ranking wife delivered the order. Unwillingly, Anahita sank to her knees. "Your Majesty," she murmured. It was a safer bet than remembering the woman's name.

The wife flashed her teeth in a mirthless

smile. "Princess, you are commanded to travel to the camp of Sheikh Basit, where you will become his bride. You will depart in a week."

Anahita grimaced. While she didn't know this woman's name, Basit was the name that had been on everyone's lips in the marketplace yesterday.

Her father intended to send her to her death again. Would he ever learn? Or perhaps he liked things this way.

Anahita mumbled something about how grateful she was to the wife and the Sultan for making this match for her. Whatever she said, it met with the wife's satisfaction, and she left.

The door clicked shut, and only then did Anahita let rip with the most colourful swear words she could come up with at this latest development.

"Another marriage?"

She looked up. Asad had managed to enter the room on hunter's feet, silent as ever.

"To Sheikh Basit."

He nodded. "Another bastard, no doubt. The marketplace was abuzz about him. When do we leave?"

Anahita didn't hesitate. "Five days. Before Father's official party is prepared, so it's just the three of us. Can you tell Haidar?"

Asad bowed, grinning. "Of course. He'll be as happy to get out of the palace as I am. Are you bringing your new bird?"

Anahita felt a pang of regret, not taking Vega with her for the first time. But Merlin, the frog-hunting falcon, would be a suitable companion for the journey. "Of course I'm taking my bird. Someone has to take her hunting. Think of all the oases on the way."

"I hope Princess Maram brought home some barbarian recipes for cooking frogs, then," Asad called back as he left.

Ugh. Merlin could keep her frogs. Anahita wasn't letting one near her lips, cooked or otherwise.

Fourteen

"This is new. See, the colour of the water? It has not lain here long. And there are no trees yet, though those will grow." Asad nodded at a clump of tiny date palms. "We will camp here for the night," he said, and neither Haidar or Anahita argued.

Anahita eyed the sparkling water, clearer than the other, muddy oases they'd seen along the way. She longed to bathe, after so many days collecting dust as they traversed the desert, and this oasis looked too tempting to resist.

Haidar seemed to have read her mind. "You bathe while we set up camp. Then that bird of yours can hunt while we start a fire to cook whatever it catches."

"Don't let her cook it, or she'll poison us all," Asad said.

They all laughed. None of them would ever forget Asad's failed attempts to teach her to cook. Anahita could manage two cooking styles – charred or raw, neither of which was particularly edible.

"I wager that bird of yours won't catch much. The oasis is too new for anything to live in it yet. Perhaps in a few seasons you will have better luck. Good thing I have plenty of dried meat to season the stew," Asad continued.

"I'll take that wager," Haidar said smoothly. "Desert creatures find water faster than you give them credit for. And that bird has sharper eyes than your dull ones."

Anahita left the boys to bicker while she went to bathe. She stripped off her clothes, folding them beside the water's edge, and stepped into the water's embrace. It was colder than she'd expected, especially after being warmed all day by the sun. For all that it was a new oasis, the waters must run deep to stay so cool.

She immersed herself fully, gasping as it felt like cold fingers reaching for her, stroking away the dust and sweat of the journey as she plunged in deeper.

"Your bird's getting jealous!" Asad shouted.

Reluctantly, Anahita set her feet on the lakebed and turned to see what the fuss was about.

"Frog! Frog!" Merlin screeched, flapping her wings.

"Set her free," Anahita commanded, striding out of the water. She looked at her discarded clothes for a moment, before deciding she wanted fresh things. She rummaged through her bags, seeking something practical among the finery. By the time she'd dug out a suitable tunic, the warm desert wind had dried her skin, so it was a simple matter to slip the garment over her head.

When she turned around, she found Haidar's eyes fixed on her, though he had a faraway look on his face.

"What is it?" she asked softly, keeping her voice low so that Asad would not hear.

Haidar shook his head, and seemed to see her again. "Forgive me, but you reminded me of…happier times."

Times spent with his wife, Nasrin, she knew. "If I could return her to your arms, and make you whole again, I would. You know that."

Haidar sighed deeply. "I know. As would I. But sometimes I wonder if I am a fool for not —"

An unearthly shriek split the air as Merlin erupted from the oasis, beating her wings frantically. She flew erratically, lurching from one side to another, as though she'd drunk too much wine.

"Merlin, come here!" she called. The bird moved toward her, still flying clumsily, and Anahita kept talking, reassuring the bird until Merlin flopped in a heap at Anahita's feet.

Forgetting everything but the bird before her, Anahita knelt down. There was something strange stuck to the bird's face. She reached out to free Merlin.

Fifteen

Something warm gently tugged at his hand, unfastening it from his death grip around the bird's neck feathers. He struggled to keep his legs wrapped around that deadly beak, but that slid out of his grasp, too, as he was surrounded by something warm and soft. It almost reminded him of that night two of his concubines had agreed to share him, and his bed had become a paradise of perfumed, female flesh…

The annoyed chittering of a bird – the same one who'd tried to eat him? – dragged

Philemon out of his delightful daydream. His harem was no more. He sighed.

"You're a strange one, aren't you?" a female voice purred. "I've never heard a frog sigh before. And Merlin tells me they don't usually scream until her master cuts their legs off."

"Then Merlin is a barbarian," Philemon declared.

She sounded amused. "Merlin is a bird. The bird whose face you sat on while you were screaming. Apparently her prey is usually more resigned to their fate. And less inclined to call her names. What sort of frog are you?"

Philemon blew out an exasperated breath and dared to open his eyes, only to find another pair, inches from his own. They were the colour of a desert oasis, wavering between blue and green like water reflecting the sky and the fringing palm trees. But perfectly calm and still, as though it didn't bother her in the slightest that she held a frog in her cupped hands – both hands, for they were not large – as she conversed with him.

The bird's barbarian mistress, Philemon decided, for she wore no veil over her dark hair, and her face was bare for all to see.

"I am not a frog at all, but a prince, under a terrible curse," he announced.

The girl chuckled, a deeper sound than he'd expected from such a small woman. "And did the curse also turn your vast kingdom into that tiny oasis? Are your people swimming about as fish in that water?"

Philemon cast her a scornful glance. "Of course not. That's a story for children, which my mother told me when I was a boy. I am Prince Philemon of Tasnim, a ruler in my own right, and one of the richest men in the region, if not the world." When she seemed unable to reply (too humbled by his high stature, he supposed), Philemon graciously added, "You may address me as Your Highness."

Those blue-green eyes danced. "I don't think I will, Philemon the frog. But my sisters call me Anahita, or simply Ana, and you may, too."

Definitely a barbarian, who had no respect for rank. Philemon sniffed. "You must take me to find the cruel enchantress who cast this terrible curse. When she sees the error of her ways and lifts the curse, you will see me in my true glory, and apologise for your disrespect, for which I will forgive you."

She nodded gravely. "A kind offer, I'm sure, but one I won't accept. I have a wedding to attend, Philemon, and unless your enchantress intends to be one of the wedding guests, you won't find her with me. I will just have to live without your forgiveness." She set him down on the sand and started to walk away.

"Wait!" The word was out of his mouth before Philemon could stop it. She was the first person he'd seen since leaving Tasnim — no one came to this oasis, and if she didn't help him, he might be stuck here for the rest of his life. How long did frogs live for, anyway? Not long, with birds like that monster Merlin around. "You must help me."

She stopped. "Why, Philemon the frog? Why must I help you?"

He hopped across the burning sand, hissing, before he reached the hem of her robe. He hesitated for only a moment before hopping onto the toe of her shoe. The relief was immediate — no more burning sand under his backside. "Because I'll die out here if you don't. I cannot leave the oasis, for I would not last long on the desert sands." He swallowed, forcing the words out. "Please take me with you."

She cupped him in her hands, lifting him so that they saw eye to eye once more.

"So you have some courtesy, after all. If you wish me to carry you across the desert, you must pay for your passage, Philemon the frog. What can you offer that might be of value to me?"

"A chest of gold from the treasury in Tasnim," he answered instantly. "Enough gold to last you a lifetime."

The girl shook her head. "There is no gold here, Philemon the frog. This is not Tasnim, and I will not take you there. For an empty promise, I will take you nowhere."

He opened his mouth to protest that it was not an empty promise at all, before he remembered that he might never make it to Tasnim without her help. He swallowed. "Very well. I will be an amusing travel companion, to make your journey easier and more comfortable, and when I reach Tasnim, I will see that you get your gold." Her hands around him felt like pure bliss compared to the baking desert. "If you carry me with you to wherever you are going, I will give you whatever is in my power to grant you."

She gave a low whistle. "Gold, a helpful travel companion, and a boon. You offer a great deal for someone so small. It seems almost too good to be true." She turned. "What do you think, Merlin?"

Philemon glimpsed the bird, a fiery-eyed hawk, on the ground behind him and flattened himself against Anahita's hands so that the bird wouldn't see him.

The bird let out a shrill chirp.

Anahita laughed. "Merlin thinks frogs are only good for eating. Her previous master was fond of the legs, grilled over a fire, and he gave her the rest."

Philemon shivered. What sort of barbarian ate frogs?

"But I prefer duck," Anahita continued, "and while I already have all the travel companions I need, one who has new tales to tell would be a welcome distraction. Do you know any amusing tales, Philemon the frog?"

He had to think about that one. "My concubines often complimented me on my wit, the quality of my conversation, and the cleverness of my tales," he said finally. They'd also complimented him on his prowess in the bedchamber, but he didn't think this girl was looking for a lover.

Her oasis eyes turned cold. "Concubines. My, you must have been a mighty prince indeed, ruling over such a harem. I cannot imagine why an enchantress would choose to curse you."

"Nor I," he said softly, daring to hope.

She sighed. "Fine, I shall help you. But if you prove to be a nuisance, I will feed you to Merlin."

He swallowed, knowing he would regret this. "Then we have an accord."

Sixteen

"Philemon, I have a proposition for you," the girl called. What had her name been? Oh, that's right – Anahita. No title, no family name, just…Anahita. He should remember that, in case he ever caught himself thinking about her bathing naked in his oasis again. It had been a long time since he'd seen a woman, let alone a naked one, and her form was pleasing enough to catch the eye of a man starved for female company.

Not her face, though. Now he'd seen it up close, he thought her plainer than ever. Her nose was crooked, as though it had been broken. Perhaps barbarian girls fought like boys did. And those strange eyes…like one of the crusaders from the north. She was probably the spawn of some crusader and a girl he stole from her family. That she lived meant her mother had lived long enough afterwards to bear the child – probably as a common whore.

How low he had fallen. A prince, deigning to listen to a proposition from some whore's bastard daughter.

Philemon lifted his head from the water, just enough so that she could see his eyes. "Do you now?"

She smiled. It improved her looks, at least a little.

"You did say you would make my journey more comfortable, did you not?"

Philemon let out a noise that sounded alarmingly like a croak.

She appeared to take this as assent. "You may start by making yourself useful tonight. This lovely oasis of yours is home to a great number of mosquitoes, which have taken up residence in my tent. Given your natural talents with flying things, you shall sit at the end of my bed and keep them from bothering me as I sleep."

It was an order, not a request, and as such, it rankled. But they did have a deal, and, besides, he had to admit he was hungry. He'd give a whole bag of gold for a well-spiced roast lamb, but his accursed body demanded a different form of sustenance.

He raised his head higher, lifting his chin in what he hoped looked like lofty condescension. "Carry me to your bedchamber, and I shall protect you in a true princely fashion."

She burst out laughing.

Philemon glared. "What is so funny?"

She took her time getting control of herself before she finally said, "You really shouldn't do that. It only draws attention to that bulging thing under your chin. On a man, it would be a prominent Adam's apple, but on a frog, it's…a vocal sac of some sort. Terribly distracting, especially when you're talking. I'm too worried it will pop like a soap bubble to listen to a word you say."

Philemon tucked his chin down firmly. "I said carry me to your bed, and I shall protect you in a true princely fashion."

She still smiled, but at least she didn't laugh. "Well, you should know you'll be the first prince to ever protect me in any fashion." She scooped him up and carried him toward her tent.

Philemon had to force himself to hold his tongue. Of course she'd never been protected by a prince before. She'd probably never even met one. But barbarian or not, he had a deal with this girl, and he would honour it, for a prince's honour was a weighty thing indeed.

"I will need a bucket of water, if you wish me to stay in your tent all night. I cannot be allowed to dry out, so I must immerse myself periodically," he said as the tent flaps closed behind her.

She set him on the floor, which was a surprisingly fine carpet. Her bed was equally surprising — as big as his own, when he'd travelled, with several cushions that looked to be made of silk. Stolen, he was certain.

"I'll go fetch some," she said, heading back out the way she'd come.

The moment she was out of sight, he leaped across the carpet for the pallet, aiming for the nearest silk cushion. Oh, how he'd missed the feel of silk against his skin. The only fabric that felt like a woman's caress, which he'd missed for even longer.

But the moment his feet touched the cushion, he experienced nothing so sensuous. No, what he felt next could only be described as every bit of his body sneezing at exactly the same time.

Seventeen

A normal princess would have brought a maid, and a whole troop of servants to see to her needs, Anahita reflected as she dug through their things for a bucket. A normal princess wouldn't have to find her own bucket, and use it to fetch water for an unusually arrogant frog.

But Anahita had never been, and would never be, a normal princess. None of her father's other children had her gift of being able to converse with creatures. In fact, aside from herself and Maram, none of the others seemed to have any magical abilities at all.

Which was why Maram was destined to be alone, and if it weren't for Haidar and Asad, Anahita would be, too. But the three of them made perfect travel companions, because they knew each other so well, and she would trade a whole palace full of servants to take these two men with her.

Servants would only complicate matters. So, with a sigh, she carried her bucket to the oasis and lugged the slopping load to her tent. For the haughty frog.

She shouldn't have agreed to let him come with them. She didn't need another pet – and this one might prove to be a dangerous distraction. Even bringing Merlin with her risked losing the bird, after the way Fakhri had claimed Vega for his own, all those years ago. What if this new sheikh was just as bad, trying to take everything from her so she would be an obedient wife?

Two words that should never be used to describe her: obedient, or wife.

As Fakhri had found out, in his final moments.

His lifeblood flowed over her hands again,

warm and sticky as the night it happened. For she would never forget. Even her arm ached at the memory.

But it was a memory – no more. No man would ever share her bed again.

Anahita took a deep breath, and another, attempting to calm herself. So that she would not appear agitated in front of a frog. She choked back a laugh. Frogs could not discern facial expressions.

She ducked through the tent flaps, stepped inside, then straightened. And stopped dead.

The bucket slipped from her suddenly nerveless fingers, splashing water up to the very roof of the tent, and soaking her to the skin, but Anahita did not feel it.

A rich, mellow voice called out, "Why, you are quite the loveliest woman I have ever seen, under those shapeless things!"

Anahita closed her eyes, but she couldn't seem to shut out his voice, which made things curl up in her belly. So she opened her eyes again, and took in the scene, as Asad had taught her to do.

A lean, muscled man, his skin gleaming in

the lamplight, reclined on her cushions, his dark eyes gazing on her with obvious approval. Other parts of his anatomy rose to salute her, too. Bits she'd hacked off and burned in a brazier…

Anahita turned on her heel and marched out of the tent.

Asad and Haidar rose from their seats by the fire.

"What's wrong?' Haidar asked. "I've never seen you look so pale."

Asad squinted at her. "Me neither. Not since that first night, when — " Haidar waved him into silence, but it was too late.

The night Fakhri died was uppermost in her mind, as it was in theirs.

Anahita fought to keep her breathing even. "There is a man in my bed. An amorous one." She couldn't suppress a shudder.

"There can't be," Asad scoffed. "We've been sitting here all night. No one could have gotten past us and into your tent without us seeing him. You must have imagined him."

It wouldn't be the first time she'd imagined such a thing, and they all knew it. Her memories sometimes rose up so strong, it would take all three of them to banish them back to the past, where they belonged. But she hadn't known this man — all he'd had in common with her long-dead husband was his mighty erection, and his unwelcome presence in her bed.

Anahita lifted a shaky finger and pointed at the tent. "Then you go in there. And tell me what you see, for I will not sleep in that tent unless I know my bed is empty."

Haidar led the way. "Real or imaginary, I will remove him. Asad will help, as he's so certain no one could have gotten past him."

Anahita folded her arms across her chest and stood by the fire, watching the men enter the tent.

The brazier silhouetted them against the tent wall as they leaned down, then came up with a third man between them.

A sob escaped from her lips, before she got hold of herself.

Then she blinked, and three men became two. The mystery man had vanished.

"How dare you!" a thin, reedy voice

screeched. "The girl herself invited me into her bed! For laying hands on me, I shall have you executed!"

Faster than any frog should, the creature leaped across the sand and back into the oasis with an audible plop, still grumbling about faithless women, jealous men and methods of execution.

Haidar emerged from the tent, looking disgruntled. "He was here, and we lifted him off your bed, but then it felt like he slipped through my fingers, and now he is gone. Almost as though we all imagined him." Haidar held out his hand. "But my hand is wet – look!" Moisture shone in the firelight.

"The cushions have wet spots, too, look." Asad stuck his head out of the tent flaps and held out a cushion.

"I spilled a bucket of water. It probably splashed on them," she said, but not even she believed her own words.

Instead, she turned over Philemon's words in her mind. A cursed prince. He might not be a prince, but there was something magical about him. Magic that had made him into a man, if only for a moment.

And on the morrow, she would insist he tell her the whole story of how it happened. That would make the unwanted journey go faster.

"Well, if he's gone, I'm going to bed," she said, and the two men moved aside to allow her entry. Sleep came surprisingly swiftly to her that night.

Eighteen

Philemon sat in the water for a long time, seething. How dare those barbarian boys lay hands on him – a prince? If it had been the girl, he might have forgiven her – she was pretty enough to suit his tastes, and for that one glorious moment, he'd been human again. Desire had flared in her eyes for that moment, too. He hadn't imagined it.

But those men had ruined everything when they seized him and he'd turned back into a frog. He'd watched them from the water, and he was certain neither was her husband. She moved too freely for a wed woman. The easy familiarity between all three of them was the sort he'd known among the city guards before his father had died and he'd claimed the crown. Like brothers. They could be her brothers, though she was tiny compared to them. The child of a second wife, perhaps.

When all three of them retired to the same tent, he was certain of it. Two older brothers, protecting their younger sister. An untamed girl who was more than old enough to wed, but had not yet been taught the proper decorum for a married woman. Her husband would see to that, he was sure of it. The men of the desert demanded much of their wives.

He'd had concubines like her. Girls their fathers could not find suitable marriages for, so they'd been given to him as part of the price for the hospitality of Tasnim. Girls who had taken to Tasnim like ducks did to water, for Tasnim was different to other desert cities.

A city he had to save at any cost, or he had no right to call himself its prince.

He could wait in the oasis for a proper caravan, but who knew how long that would take? These three were the first travellers he'd seen since he took up residence here, and he had delayed long enough already.

He'd struck a bargain with the girl, wild though she was, and something told him she would honour it. But just in case she changed her mind, he would find a place among their things to stow away. The half-filled water bucket outside her tent seemed the most sensible place, he decided, when the night air had cooled the sands enough for him to hop across the camp to investigate.

He settled in the bucket to doze until dawn.

Nineteen

Avian shrieks and swearing woke Anahita from a sound sleep. She did some swearing of her own as she stuck her head out of the tent into the pre-dawn light, where Merlin appeared to be fighting with the water bucket.

"Surrender, foul foe, or I shall drown you!" came the reedy voice of Philemon.

Merlin's head appeared to be stuck in the bucket. She flapped her wings, lifting herself and the bucket a short distance off the ground, before dropping again.

"I do not jest, minion of hell!"

Anahita strode over to rescue them both. She stuck her hand in the bucket and pulled out the frog, who had his tiny arms around Merlin's head. Again. Sighing, she pried them loose. Merlin flapped away with an indignant squawk, shaking off water.

Anahita lifted the frog up so she could look him in the eye. "You're a troublemaker, aren't you?"

The frog puffed up in indignation. "I am a troublemaker? What about that dishonourable demon of a bird, attacking a man in his sleep, no less! I was merely defending myself! Why, if I but had my sword…"

"You have a frog-sized sword? I'd like to see that," Anahita interrupted.

Could a frog glare? She suspected that's what he was doing.

"A sword fit for a prince, from before I was cursed," he said stiffly. "Of course."

"Of course," she repeated. "Are you sure you want to ride with us, seeing as I travel with Merlin?"

He drew himself up. "I am on a quest to save my city from the witch who cursed me. If you had a hundred such birds, I would still fight every one of them in order to succeed at my quest. I am a prince!"

"So you keep saying," Anahita said.

"You saw my princely magnificence with your own eyes last night. How can you doubt me?"

She burst out laughing. "Princely magnificence? Is that what you call a naked man where you're from? I'm not sure what I saw last night. You're no normal frog, but whether you are truly a frog or a man, I do not know." She thought for a moment, then added, "But no matter what you are, I am certain you will prove an amusing travel companion. You may ride with me today, and tell me all about your quest and the city you wish to save."

The frog executed a bow, or at least he tried to. "It would be my pleasure."

Twenty

Anahita refused to allow Philemon to ride in a bucket on the back of her camel, where he would be a terrible temptation for her bird, or so she said, so she and Philemon reached a compromise. He rode in the neck of a half-filled water bag that was strapped in front of her saddle.

"I feel like a wax stopper," he complained.

Veiled against the sand, still she brought her hand to cover her mouth as she giggled. "Most stoppers don't have eyes. Nor are they small enough to slip inside the water bag if Merlin decides she wants to attack you again."

He glanced around, but he could not see the murderous bird. "Where is the creature?"

"She's riding with Asad on the lead camel. Leaving me free to listen to your tales while we travel. So, tell me about your quest, Philemon the frog."

There was little to tell yet, for it had just started. "Have you ever been to Tasnim?" he asked.

She shook her head, sending ripples through the white fabric of her veil. It was too big for her — more suited to one of the men she travelled with than a delicate young woman. No wonder she took it off in camp. "This would have been my first time, but the gates were closed to us."

Her first journey away from her people, Philemon guessed. Then he registered the rest of her words — the gates of the city were closed. He breathed a sigh of relief. No one would loot the place in his absence. Good.

"Until the oasis where you found me formed, Tasnim was the only water source for miles in any direction. An underground citadel in the desert, impregnable and impossible to besiege." He smiled. He was right to be proud of his city. "No one knows who built the first tunnels, but it was used in times of war and the ancients kept a permanent garrison there. Some of the city's present day residents are descended from those soldiers." Even him, for the city's princes had sometimes taken brides from the city people instead of looking further afield, as Philemon had.

"We saw no sign of soldiers. No sign of anyone, actually, no matter how loudly Haidar knocked at the door."

A barbarian girl and her brothers could not afford Tasnim's hospitality, though it was likely there had been no one left in the city to offer it this time.

"They must have fled the curse," Philemon said. "But had they not, they still might not have opened the gates. The price for Tasnim's hospitality is high. Why, I have known men who have sold their daughters to pay the price."

Her eyes – the only part of her face he could see – narrowed. "Perhaps that is why the witch cursed you and your city. Hospitality is one of the sacred laws of the desert."

She was painfully close to the truth, and yet so far from it, too. "We offered her our hospitality, including apartments in my own palace, for a price that should have been a trifle for someone with magic. Yet she refused to cast the spell. She tried to hold us to ransom."

"Did she turn everyone into frogs? Or just you?"

Anahita was observant. Too observant. "Just me. My people…she let them leave, unharmed."

"So you offended the witch somehow. You must have been particularly rude for her to transform you. I've only heard of a few enchantresses who are capable of such complicated magic, and they would need a really good reason to do it. What did you do, Philemon the frog?"

"Why must I be guilty? Perhaps the enchantress envied me the wealth of Tasnim, and wished to take the city for herself!" Philemon said.

Those narrowed eyes did not believe a word of it. "Perhaps. What sort of wealth did Tasnim have? It just looked like a pile of rocks in the desert to me."

"Have you seen the Sultan's palace in the capital?" Philemon didn't wait for her answer. "Tasnim outshines it tenfold. Maybe more. Even the common people's houses have costly mosaics on the walls. In my own palace, no wall or ceiling is unadorned. Every ruler throughout history has commissioned artwork to commemorate their reign, some of which are in the palace, but many are in the city itself. Why, my great grandmother, the Regent Princess Khurshid, had the ceilings of all the public meeting chambers painted to resemble the sky at different times of day. Dusk and dawn, midnight, noon…ah, the work is exquisite. Even now, gazing up at them, one might think they were standing in the open air, instead of beneath a thick layer of stone."

"So you live in a state of perpetual night underground?" she asked.

"On the upper levels of the city, close to the surface, there are air and light wells that let in sunlight during the day. But everywhere there are lamps, so the city is ablaze whenever light is needed. It is not as bright as the desert sun at noon, but only a madman would wish to be out in such heat!"

This did not seem to impress her at all. "So men sell their daughters into slavery so that you might have light?"

"There are no slaves in Tasnim. No…the girls are given as gifts, and I take them into my harem as concubines," Philemon said.

If anything, this only seemed to anger her further, as her eyebrows descended even lower. "Oh, and being forced to warm your bed is better than slavery."

Forced? He'd never forced a woman in his life! His concubines had come willingly to his bed. Had she forgotten what he looked like? He had no need to force women!

"My concubines were always appreciative of my attentions," he snapped.

"I'm sure they had little choice in the matter. A concubine who doesn't have her master's favour has little power in a harem, and he may discard her at will. So of course she will lie through her teeth if she has to, just to keep the place she has."

For a girl so young, she seemed to have excessively strong opinions about life in a harem.

"You know nothing about my concubines!"

Her eyes blazed. "No, YOU know nothing about them. My mother was a concubine, and I grew up in the harem. Saw how they were treated. So don't tell me your concubines were happy, with wives lording it over everyone, knowing you could be cast aside at the merest whim, and there was nothing you could do about it!"

Perhaps in whatever desert sheikh's harem she had grown up in, but not in a civilised city like Tasnim. "I had no wives, and as my concubines, the girls who were given to me were under my protection. Unless they chose to marry men of the city. Then their husband became their protector. But some girls preferred the harem, for it was all they had ever known. Nida had learned to play every musical instrument she could lay her hands on, and her voice soared above them all, like an angel come to Earth. If she had to choose between a husband and her harp, she would pick the harp."

Anahita's eyes widened. "You didn't touch your concubines?"

It would have been easier to say he hadn't, but he refused to lie to her, even to protect her obvious innocence about the real ways of the world.

"I lay with those who wished it. Two in particular, Zareen and Simin, were skilled in the arts of love, and took great pleasure in practicing those arts. Why, they knew things I'd never heard of…" His mind wandered as he remembered nights spent with Zareen or Simin, or, on rare occasions, both girls together. He sobered when he realised he would probably never see them again. They would be welcomed as courtesans in any court, and never return to him or Tasnim. Finally, he said, "But you don't want me to talk about concubines." He didn't want to think of them, now, either. Or all that he had lost.

"You're less amusing than I had hoped, Philemon the frog," she said frostily.

He couldn't disagree, so he racked his brain for something the girls had always liked. "Have you heard about the Gardens of Tasnim?"

Twenty-One

Anahita couldn't stop laughing. "Why would anyone want a jewelled garden? Why not plants? Trees for shade and flowers for scent…precious metals and jewels have no scent!"

"Plant do not grow underground, you see. Most plants, anyway. There are mushrooms growing in one of the lower caverns, I believe. They fetch quite a high price in the markets, or so I'm told."

Anahita knew little about mushrooms, unless they found their way into her food.

"Are you sure you're not a mushroom merchant pretending to be a prince?" she asked.

The frog drew himself up, and bumped his head on the lip of the water bag. "I assure you I am the Prince of Tasnim, and as such, it is my business to know as much as I can about my city and how to help it prosper. The mushrooms have a terrible smell, and must be kept away from where people sleep, or they complain. So the mushroom caverns are surrounded by store rooms."

Anahita couldn't imagine her father knew as much about his own city as Philemon knew about Tasnim.

"What sort of prince tells his people where they can live, or grow mushrooms? I thought there were advisers and officials who took care of such things," Anahita said.

"My father was more lenient about such things – letting people choose for themselves, and move if they needed to, but the city is more populous now, or it was, so after numerous cases where I had to judge in favour of one or the other of the city's residents, I assigned an official to take care of things." He hesitated, before continuing in a rush, "One of my concubines, if you must know."

"A woman holding office in a city? How is this possible? Surely no man would accept the judgement of a woman – and a concubine, at that!"

He made a sound of disgust. "Tasnim is not like other desert cities. Our women are not nothing. Tasnim was a garrison city, and some of the garrison were women – some say the fabled Amazons from the east. They fought and died like men, and were accorded the same citizenship when the city became a sovereign principality, no longer beholden to the fallen ancient empire who had brought together soldiers from such distant parts. My own great grandmother ruled as Princess Regent until her son came of age to claim the throne as his own.

"Rahat was one of the women given to me, who did not wish to remain in the harem. I believe she ran her father's household before she came to me, and after listening to several days' petitions, she informed me that I needed to do something about regulating my city. And she volunteered for the role. Any citizen of Tasnim who had a problem – man or woman – with her judgements could still appeal to me, but I cannot recall a single time that I judged against Rahat. She was terrifying. I found out much later that the decision to hand her over to the city to pay for the hospitality of her father's caravan was hers – and that her father was most upset when he discovered it."

Now he'd piqued her curiosity. "Did she not have a husband?"

"Actually, she did. She was quite partial to a particular kind of pastry that one of my palace cooks specialised in, and she married him. I gave her a set of golden bracelets as a wedding gift. She wore them always, and the clinking sound of them terrified many, I am told."

"You allowed your concubine to marry your cook?"

The frog waved his hands emphatically. "She was never truly a concubine, not in the way you mean the word. And she was a city official, a citizen, mistress of her own destiny. I could have challenged the marriage, but only if

I'd wished to press my own suit and marry her instead. Rahat would have turned me down flat, in any case."

"What of her father?"

The frog shrugged. "He surrendered her to me, along with any right he had to decide her future. Unwillingly, as it later turned out, but by that time it was too late. Rahat made sure of that." He smiled. "To the enduring benefit of Tasnim, I must admit."

"Who lived there? Aside from you and your concubines-who-weren't-really-concubines. And your cook."

"Merchants, mostly. Men who used their share of Tasnim's wealth to go into trade, financing caravans who were entitled to the hospitality of the city at no charge, because they were owned by the city's merchants. Women who chose to marry men in the city, rather than leave the city and risk falling into the hands of a husband who would not be as civilised as the men of Tasnim. Others chose to go into business on their own. I believe the mushroom merchants were two sisters, come to think of it."

"I would like to visit Tasnim. It sounds…nice." An impossible dream is what it sounded like. And yet…from Philemon's words, it sounded very real. She needed to see it with her own eyes to believe such a place could exist. Where women could choose…

"When you visit, you will stay there as my honoured guest," the frog promised.

Oh, she wanted to believe it so much. "And what if I do not wish to leave?"

The frog spread his arms wide. "Then you will need to find a way to earn your keep until you attain citizenship. Take up a trade, perhaps, or marry one of the city's citizens. The men of Tasnim value a good cook over a pretty face, for beauty fades." He held up his hands in supplication. "Not that you have anything to worry about. A plain woman such as yourself could never be considered just a pretty face."

Plain. If even a frog called her plain, there was no hope for Anahita. Of course, she knew her beauty did not compare to Maram or some of Father's more favoured wives, but that didn't make it hurt any less.

She had nothing to offer Tasnim. A plain face and no skill at cooking. As for a trade…all she knew how to do was hunt.

"Is there a place in Tasnim for hunters who are good at hawking?" Anahita asked.

"The mews in Tasnim has been empty for as long as I can remember. No falconer could keep the birds happy in an underground city, I understand. The job is yours, if you wish it."

For a moment, hope blossomed in her chest. A life with only her birds to care for — no husband, no harem, nothing but hunting. But her father would never allow it.

But if he did not know…believed her happily married to some sheikh…

Then and there, Anahita made a vow to herself. She would help the frog break the curse — even if she had to enlist Maram's help to find and persuade the enchantress to do so — and make Tasnim her home.

She would finally be free.

Twenty-Two

"You know what he's after, don't you?" Asad asked in a low voice as he helped Anahita unsaddle the camels.

"Who? Haidar? Of course. He wants the impossible – to turn back time," Anahita said. "To have his wife back."

"Not Haidar. The frog. The one who rides with you, and fills your ears with tales of old," Asad said.

"Philemon wants to break the curse, and go home to Tasnim." After listening to him for so many days in the desert, she knew that for a certainty, for all his tales were of Tasnim, the magical city where a woman could be more than property.

"He wants you to do it."

Anahita stared. "You're wrong. He's never asked for any such thing. He only wants me to take him to where he can find the enchantress who cursed him so she removes the curse."

"Just because he hasn't asked you yet, doesn't mean he doesn't want it. It's well known that a kiss from a princess can break most curses."

Anahita burst out laughing. "In stories, maybe. But I have never heard of such a thing happening in real life."

Asad shrugged. "Ask him, then, for heavens know you're the only one who understands the croaking sounds he makes. If anyone knows how to break his curse, it's the frog."

"He says he's a prince."

Asad snorted. "If you had to ask a pretty girl for a kiss, wouldn't you say you were a prince instead of some lowly camel herder?"

"Yes, but..." What if he was a camel herder? Would that make a difference? He talked about Tasnim with the familiarity of someone who had lived there all his life. To hear Philemon say it, though, even the lowliest citizen of Tasnim could still invite her to stay inside the city as a guest…and once inside, she could lay claim to her place as the prince's falconer. "I'm sure I'm not important enough for a kiss from me to work. Besides, I don't think he even knows I am a princess, high or low. And I don't want you telling him, either!"

It was Asad's turn to laugh. "No man needs to be told. The uppity way you carry yourself and order everyone about tells the world what you are."

Anahita dropped the saddle, sending up a cloud of dust that made her cough. It took a long moment for the coughing fit to subside, before she said, "Oh yes, and I'm sure princesses regularly take care of the camels whenever they travel. If I were Maram, I'd stand by impatiently, tapping my foot, until my pavilion was ready for me, and retire in there, where my servants tended to my every need!"

"Haidar would do it, if you asked him. He'd set up your tent and help you wash, quite happily."

He would, too. But Anahita would not torture her friend so with what could never be. "I'd sooner order you to start making a meal for us. And he didn't call me pretty. In fact, he regularly tells me how plain I am."

"Then your frog's a fool. But I'd be an even bigger fool if I let you cook. I'll tell you what. I'll wager the new knife I bought in the market before we left – the one with the emerald set into the handle – that he asks you for a kiss before we reach the sheikh's camp."

Anahita eyed the water bag where Philemon travelled by day, but he'd hopped over to the shallow pool of fresh water where Haidar was filling up the water jars.

"If you're wrong, I get the knife. If you're right…I'll have a second such knife crafted to match the first, as my gift to you when we get home." And they would go home, Anahita added silently to herself.

Asad rubbed his hands. "An easy bet, I'm sure. You know what else is a foregone conclusion? What you'll do when he asks you."

Was she so transparent? Asad's assertion

had taken her by such surprise that even Anahita wasn't sure what she'd do. "What, then?" she asked finally.

"You'll feed the frog to your falcon, of course. Your father may not know it, but we do – you'll never let another man touch you again. And he might be a frog now, but whatever else he is, that one's a man." Asad jerked his chin up. "Your bird's back. Looks like she has dinner, too, so I'd better get the fire going." He headed off.

Anahita watched Merlin glide gracefully to land at her feet, before the bird laid her catch out proudly. A scurrier of some sort, and a small one, at that. Not enough to feed one, let alone three of them. Asad could cook something from their provisions tonight. "You eat it. Maybe next oasis will have more ducks."

"Or frogs!" the falcon said, neatly eviscerating her prey.

At least the bird had forgotten about Philemon, for the moment. Anahita wished she could do the same. Because despite Asad's assertion, she wasn't as sure she'd refuse him if Philemon asked her to help him break the curse. Usually the journey through the desert dragged, but with him to talk to and tell stories of the wonders of the city he loved so much, the week had flown by. She'd thought his overweening pride would have put her off, but somehow…she'd grown used to it. Maybe even liked him.

So if he asked for her help…could she, in conscience, refuse? A kiss was such a small thing, really.

Twenty-Three

From his perch atop a camel's back, safely wedged into the neck of a water bag, Philemon watched the three of them set up camp, like he had every night since he'd joined their small caravan. Haidar refilled their water supply and Asad built a fire and began to cook. Anahita sent her bird off hunting while she pitched the tent and carried their bedrolls into it, so that they might sleep comfortably. If they hadn't stopped at an oasis, Haidar would help her with the tent.

Anahita's eyes often followed the falcon's

flight, while she wore a wistful expression, as if she wished she could fly with the diabolical bird.

For the first time, he wondered what her story was. He wished he'd spent less time talking and taken the time to ask her about herself. He knew she was an experienced desert traveller, and the way she and her brothers divided up the tasks in camp so easily, she must travel with them often. She might not know it, but she was freer than any desert woman he'd ever met – including those who lived in Tasnim, for the women of his city had mostly stayed within the underground city. For all their freedom, Tasnim citizens did not spend much time staring at the sky, or even standing beneath it.

Every morning she lifted him from his bucket and into the water bag, never once flinching at his slimy skin. It wasn't that she didn't notice, either – her brothers had made comments on how they would not carry frogs as she did. She'd smiled, shrugged, and thrown a teasing comment right back at the brother in question, but she hadn't let him go.

He'd found himself racking his brain to tell her tales he hadn't shared yet — half-remembered events from his childhood, or tales of the history of Tasnim, which she'd never heard. He'd even found himself telling her about his journey through the dark to the oasis, and discovering he'd been turned into a frog. So what if he'd made it sound like a glorious adventure, instead of the nightmarish reality? Her eyes had still grown wide before she'd laughed in all the right places.

More than anything, he wanted to take her home to Tasnim, and show her all the wonders his words simply couldn't describe.

But first he would have to find a way to break the curse, and return the waters to his city. Otherwise there would be nothing but empty caverns to show her, before her bird tried to eat him again.

If only her brothers had brought her sooner, and tried to trade her for Tasnim's hospitality. Then he might have persuaded her to become one of his concubines…

Though he suspected she would refuse the honour. If her brothers had been willing to part with her, which seemed equally unlikely.

It was a foolish thought, he told himself. Better to focus on breaking this curse, and claiming his princess bride from the Sultan. Whatever beauty the Sultan bestowed on him would surely be enough to turn his thoughts away from a barbarian girl, chance met in the desert. A girl as unattainable as the rising moon.

"Will you join us for dinner, Philemon?"

Philemon roused himself from his gloomy thoughts to find Anahita standing before him, her cupped hands ready to carry him.

He could not smell the stew already steaming over the fire behind her, but he didn't need to smell it to know it would taste far better than any meal he'd eaten since that enchantress pushed him down the well. But the fire had probably drawn an inordinate number of bugs by its light, and Anahita wished him to take care of them.

"I'm not sure you'll like that," he said, stepping into her hands. "Watching a frog crunch through a bug while it's still alive is enough to put the strongest man off his food."

"I guess my stomach is stronger than that of most men. But then, I've watched my birds rip their prey apart for as long as I can remember."

Philemon shuddered. "Where is the creature?"

"Merlin is hunting. She says there are a large number of fat frogs in this oasis, and she intends to catch them all." Anahita ducked her head. "I thought you might prefer to stay with us, where she does not mistake you for food."

Ah, so she didn't want her dinner interrupted by having to rescue him from the bird again. If Philemon could but carry a blade at his hip, he would soon see the bird off, but neither Anahita or her brothers had a knife small enough to serve him as a sword.

"You are fortunate that I am a prince and not truly a frog, or I would take offence at the bird's slaughter of my family," Philemon said. "For honour's sake, I would be forced to kill the bird, and all who harbour it."

Anahita shook her head. "And that's why I know you're not truly a frog. Animals do not say such things, or care about honour. I still imagine it would be distressing to see the slaughter of your fellow creatures, especially with your human sensibilities."

She set him on a rug beside the fire. He had barely a moment to notice that it was the rug she usually draped atop her bedroll before his body seemed to sneeze again.

"He's too skinny to be a prince. Pampered princes are plumper than that," a male voice said.

It took Philemon a moment to collect his scattered wits before he realised the man meant to insult him. He leaped to his feet. "Plump or skinny, a prince defends his honour. Give me a blade and I will make you regret every word."

Someone threw a bundle of cloth at him. "Put some clothes on, so you don't put Ana off her dinner."

Philemon caught it, and he was stunned to find his own hands holding the bundle, instead of his four-fingered frog ones. "By what miracle…" he began.

"Ana's idea. Last time you turned into a man, it was in her bed. She figured it was worth a try. I bet it would work. Asad said it wouldn't. I'll share the wineskin I won off him with you if you can tell me why. Ana insists there's nothing magical about her bed, but she doesn't usually share it with animals."

Philemon shook his head. "I know not. I have never been cursed before. And if I can break this one…I hope never to be cursed again." Realisation dawned. "You can hear me. Understand me."

Haidar nodded. "Well enough to see Ana isn't telling tales about you being a man under some spell." He lowered his voice. "Put the robe on, and she'll come closer. Naked men frighten her."

Philemon's gaze followed Haidar's pointing finger to where Anahita stood, at the very edge of the firelight. The reflected flames glittered in her eyes and off her teeth as she bit her lip. Contrary to her brother's words, there was no fear in her expression.

She stalked forward, as graceful as any desert hunting cat. By the time she stepped between Philemon and the fire, he had eyes for nothing but her.

The firelight turned her thin tunic transparent, highlighting the curves it otherwise might have hidden. Beautiful. Like an angel come to earth. He wanted to say the words aloud, but his mouth was too dry for any sound to come out.

He lifted his gaze to meet her eyes, but found them downcast. Not to the ground, but to his groin. Because a prince's cock refused to bow down to a beautiful woman. Instead, it rose to greet her. Ready.

For something her wary eyes said she would never agree to.

Philemon sighed and slipped the robe over his head, hiding his arousal as he tried to think of anything but the beautiful girl before him. Beautiful. Untouchable. Unless he was a frog, when she took him in her hands and…

"Will the spell object if I sit beside you? Or will you turn back into a frog?"

Philemon's eyes sprang open to find Anahita sinking to her knees before him. No, beside him on the bedroll, close enough to touch if he took his place beside her. A place she patted, a playful expression on her face.

"I rarely bite, Philemon. Except when it's my dinner." She accepted a bowl from Asad.

"Sit down, and hide that tent in your tunic,"

Asad muttered, shoving a second bowl at Philemon.

Philemon did as he was told, telling himself that if he'd had a sister as irresistible as Anahita, he would be just as protective.

But she sat close enough for him to feel the heat of her through his thin robe, while her brothers sat on the other side of the fire, their eyes fixed on Philemon. Torture. Temptation. Both terrible and yet…

"You should have left the stew to cook for longer. The meat is tougher than I like," Anahita said.

Asad shrugged. "Use your dagger to cut it into smaller pieces. Or don't eat it. It is all the same to me."

Anahita's arm bumped his side. "What do you think, Philemon? Do you agree that Asad did not cook the lamb enough?"

Philemon turned his attention to his food. He spooned up some of the stew and brought it to his lips. The sauce was well spiced and salted, but so was the meat. Spiced lamb as good as anything he'd tasted in Tasnim. He owned it was a little chewy, but no more so than any slice of roast lamb he'd eaten in the past. Right now, it might as well have been manna from heaven, it tasted so good. Before he'd realised it, he'd finished the bowl. "Is there more?" he asked.

Too late did he realise that Anahita and her brothers might not have enough food to satisfy him, especially after so long eating like a frog.

Asad scraped a spoon through the pot, eyeing Philemon across the fire. "Maybe," Asad said slowly. "What price would you pay me for it?"

Anahita hushed him. "Philemon is our guest. It breaks the laws of hospitality to expect a guest to pay for a meal we invited him to."

"To hear you tell it, he claims to be the Prince of Tasnim. Do you know how much it costs for the privilege of a bowl of lamb stew in Tasnim?" Asad asked.

A man who drove a hard bargain. Philemon could respect that. "I will trade one for the other. A meal at my table in Tasnim, for a meal here at yours." He glanced around. "A meal for all of you, with as much of my best wine as you wish."

Asad wiped his hands. "Take note, Ana. No man of Tasnim would pay such a price for a simple meal, let alone a prince. I don't know who your frog man is, but he is not who he claims to be. A meal in Tasnim costs a prince's ransom. If he'd tossed me a gold coin for stew that would cost him two coppers in the capital, I'd have believed him." He bowed mockingly in Philemon's direction. "Perhaps you will have more luck fooling the next caravan who offer to help you. I am going to go water the dunes, and I will be a while." He marched off into the darkness, muttering under his breath.

Haidar rose from his seat and peered into the pot. "There is plenty left, if you want it. No matter what he says, Asad is as hospitable as the rest of us. It's yours." He held out the spoon.

Philemon rose and stepped forward to accept it.

On his second step, the world constricted to crush him.

Twenty-Four

Anahita watched in stunned horror as Philemon's robe fluttered to the sand, seemingly empty but for a tiny bulge she knew had to be his frog body, especially when it moved. She rushed forward and scooped him up, robe and all, then dropped him back on her bedroll. She wasn't sure what magic let him become a man there, but she intended to find out. She might not be an enchantress, but she still was a witch, even if all she could do was understand animals.

Though understanding Philemon was

proving quite a challenge. She'd never met a frog like him – or a man like him, either.

The robe ballooned out as the magic in him turned him into a man again, or at least she hoped so. Philemon groaned.

"I'm going to check on the camels," Haidar said pointedly. "Like Asad, I will be a while."

Anahita didn't pay him more than a fleeting glance and a distracted nod as she patted down the robe to find the man she hoped was inside. He felt…normal.

A sigh of relief whooshed out of her as his head emerged from the neck of the robe. "Thank heavens," she breathed.

Philemon sat up suddenly, and his face was dangerously close to hers. It was now or never.

Anahita took a deep breath, then pressed her lips to his.

Please let this kiss break the curse, she prayed to anyone who was listening.

For a second, they stayed there like that, before Philemon leaned back and broke the contact between them. "What was that?" he asked.

Her heart sank. "A kiss, of course. Asad

thinks that a kiss from me might break your curse, and as we arrive at our destination tomorrow, you might appreciate being able to walk around and talk to people as a man again, as I will not be as…available."

"Yes, I have heard that women can be quite busy at weddings. Especially if they are close to the bride," Philemon said drily.

Anahita wet her lips. Dare she tell him the truth? No, she could not risk it. "Yes, I am close to her. So if I can help you break the curse, it must be tonight."

"You must kiss me tonight?"

Curse him, it almost sounded like he was holding back laughter.

"I already did," she snapped.

He did laugh then, a rich sound that echoed off the dunes. Nothing like the reedy voice of a frog. It did things to her belly. "That wasn't a kiss. Definitely not something a spell would recognise."

Anahita pouted. "What sort of kiss does a spell recognise? Tell me and I shall do it."

"I don't know for certain, never having broken a spell with one before, but I imagine a kiss with the power to break spells would need some passion behind it. You'd need both your heart and soul in it. And your tongue."

"My tongue?" What was she supposed to do with her tongue? Lick him? Desperately, Anahita wished she'd brought Maram along. She knew about kissing, and such things. For all her husbands, Anahita had never kissed a man in her life. This idea was rapidly turning into a terrible one. But if she could break the curse, she had to do it tonight. For tomorrow would be too late. "Very well."

His face loomed close – almost too close – and he lifted a hand to her cheek. Not to capture her, like other men might have. No, his fingers brushed against her hair as his palm cupped her jaw, sensing she needed the support or reassurance. Leaving her free to flee if she needed to.

But she did not need to, Anahita scolded herself and her racing heart. Why, even her breath was coming fast now.

His thumb traced her lips. The top one, then the bottom, as she forced herself to exhale slowly.

"Don't be afraid," he said softly.

She wasn't afraid. She wasn't. By all that was holy…

Then his lips touched hers, and she forgot all else.

He inhaled, stealing her breath, before sealing his mouth to hers. Her mouth opened almost of its own accord, her lips following his. And then his tongue stroked hers, a teasing invitation to come out to play.

She wasn't afraid.

She cupped his face in her hands, and kissed him back with all of her being. Tongue, lips, breath, heart…maybe even her very soul. Clumsily at first, but when he didn't seem to care, she grew bolder, opening her eyes and raising them to meet his.

And she was lost. Utterly and completely lost, yet found, never wanting to stop…

"Ana. Ana!"

Who was calling her name at such a moment?

"Breathe, Ana."

Her face was pressed against a broad chest as a tender hand stroked her hair.

She sucked in a breath, then another, relishing the taste of him on her lips, her tongue. The heat of him, so close.

"Philemon, why did you stop?" she asked.

Laughter rumbled beneath her cheek. "What do you think your brothers would do if they knew you'd kissed a frog with such passion you'd forgotten to breathe?"

Her brothers? Anahita flicked her fingers. "Nothing, I'm sure. They hardly know I exist, so I'm sure they would not care what happens to me."

"Not so. Haven't they been watching us all evening? I'm sure Asad and Haidar care very much about you. So much that if they knew what we had just done, they would happily bury me alive in a desert grave before dawn."

It was her turn to laugh. "Asad and Haidar aren't my brothers! They're my father's sworn men!"

Haidar's voice came out of the dark. "Your sworn eunuchs!"

Philemon stiffened.

"Sworn to protect me," Anahita amended. "Ready to come at my call, should I need their help."

Philemon eased away from her. "Men who would happily remove a frog from your bed. I should find my own bed, or bucket." He rose.

Anahita grabbed his arm. "No! If any kiss can break a curse, that one should have done so. Surely. You should sleep here. I will take some of the spare cushions and things in the tent. Or take Asad's bedroll. He often complains it is too soft for him." She bit her lip, unable to tear her eyes away from his. Philemon looked so…so sad. "Tell me that kiss was enough!"

He sighed. "One kiss from you will never be enough, and yet, it must be. But yes, if any kiss had curse-breaking powers, it was yours." He pried her hand from his arm. "I thank you for your hospitality tonight, and pray that your dreams are sweet."

Her dreams were never sweet. Especially not the night before she married. Anahita turned away before Philemon could see her grimace.

"Sweet dreams to you, too, Philemon," she called over her shoulder with forced lightness as she trudged to the tent where she hoped she might get some sleep tonight.

Twenty-Five

"Oh no!" The feminine wail woke Philemon from what had been a sound sleep.

He scrambled out of the covers and blinked in the blazing sun. He'd missed the dawn, this time. Possibly because the blankets on Anahita's bed had blocked it out. "What is it?" he mumbled, wishing his mouth didn't taste like the inside of someone else's sweaty sandal. He'd drunk too much wine last night.

"The curse didn't break!" Already on her knees, she stretched her hands out to Philemon, and he stepped onto them without thinking.

"No," he agreed. He hadn't the heart to break it to her that the only kisses capable of breaking curses came from princesses, and this desert girl wasn't capable of fooling a curse into believing she was royalty when she wasn't. Besides, the witch had said something about a princess's bed being the key. Perhaps Anahita's bedroll had once belonged to some minor princess before someone stole it for her.

He was damn sure that he'd given Anahita her first kiss. He'd meant to make it quick and light, but the moment her natural passion had asserted itself, pushing aside her initial awkwardness, he hadn't been able to let her go. It had been like drowning, with her lips breathing life into him for the first time. And yet, they'd been so intent on each other, they'd forgotten to breathe.

"You don't have time for that today. You need to get dressed, so we can head out," Haidar said, holding out the water bag Philemon usually rode in.

Philemon hopped into the cool water. Darkness engulfed him as someone stoppered the bag, but he wasn't worried. He'd push the stopper out once he felt the sway of the camel beneath him, when they were under way.

In the meantime, he dreamed of Anahita's kisses, and how he might manage to keep her forever.

The bag lurched to one side, then back, water sloshing around Philemon as the camel rose cumbrously to its feet. The ride began bumpily at first, until the camel settled into a steady pace. Finally.

Philemon set his shoulder against the stopper, pushing until he felt it pop free.

"So what does a frog have to promise a lady to be invited to her table again tonight?" he asked, peering up.

Haidar shook his head. "I don't speak frog, so save your croaking. Her Highness has no time for pets today. Even her precious bird rides with Asad."

Philemon leaned out further so that he might see the truth of Haidar's words. Before them rode Asad, with the bird on a perch strapped to his saddle. And behind them…

Philemon swallowed. The white veiled

desert maiden was no more. Instead, she wore the colours of the desert, a bright reddish orange stiff with gold embroidery that made her glitter in the sun. The rich robe draped over the saddle so extravagantly that the silk hid both her and the saddle completely. As the sun rose higher, the cloth canopy above her would shelter her from its heat, but now the only shadow it cast landed on her face, so he could not even see her eyes.

She looked like some desert queen out of legend, ready to lead an army into immortality. No, to accept a defeated army's surrender. Dressed so, she was clearly no warrior. Her Highness…so she was a princess after all? Or was it all a pretence?

A stolen bedroll, stolen clothes…was she a pretend princess, or a very real one? He wanted to ask, but Haidar would not understand him.

Philemon stared at the regal statue that had to be Anahita for a moment longer before he retreated back into his water bag, pulling the stopper into place behind him.

Twenty-Six

Muffled shouting as the camels drew to a halt caught Philemon's attention first. The rough descent as his camel sank to its knees confirmed it. They'd arrived somewhere. Their destination, perhaps? A long moment passed, but no one unloaded his water bag, so he pushed at the stopper to peep at his surroundings.

A desert nomad camp stretched out across the sand, brightly coloured tents huddled together against the surrounding dunes. The men who had assembled to greet the small caravan wore clothing as patched as the tents. Despite its size, this was not a prosperous camp.

A clinking sound drew everyone's attention away from the new arrivals.

Could it be Rahat?

The crowd parted to let a man through. A man who looked like he'd raided his mother's jewel chest and had no idea how ridiculous he looked, wearing his mother's treasures. Gold bangles covered his forearms, and countless gold chains weighed down his thick neck, some of them dangling as low as his protruding belly. The silk robe he wore looked like he'd stolen it from some courtesan, for surely no one else would wear such a garish shade of purple. Except perhaps a fool in the Sultan's court.

But no man knelt before a jester, like these were now. Whoever this fool was, no one dared mock him.

Even Haidar and Asad, who stepped forward to press their foreheads to the dust at the man's feet.

"Most Honoured Sheikh Basit, we bring a

gift from the Sultan. Your bride, Her Highness, Princess Anahita."

Anahita's camel was the only one still standing, so she towered above all of them, including – Philemon swallowed back bile – her incensed future husband.

"A good, obedient bride does not sit higher than her husband. She must abase herself," the sheikh announced.

Philemon smirked. Anahita wasn't the abasing kind. This would be interesting.

Asad and Haidar rose and headed for Anahita. A command from Asad made the camel kneel, so that Anahita could dismount, but the girl didn't move. Instead, Asad and Haidar each took one of her arms and lifted her off the beast, carried her several feet, then deposited her on the sand. Her robe puddled around her feet, spreading into a train that swept along the sand behind her as she crossed the distance between her and her hideous husband-to-be.

To Philemon's astonishment, she dropped to her knees, then threw herself facedown on the sand.

The sheikh smiled. Then he lifted his slippered foot and brought it down on her neck.

Philemon gasped, but no one heard. He wanted to storm across the sand and shove the sheikh away from her, but as a frog, he couldn't do anything.

So much for Haidar and Asad claiming to be her sworn men. They weren't anything of the kind – a man sworn to protect her would have killed the sheikh by now, yet he still stood there, ready to break her neck with one stomp of his foolish foot. They really were eunuchs.

Was this why Anahita had tried so hard to break the curse last night? So that he could help her, when no one else would? No wonder she'd despaired when she discovered her kisses hadn't worked. She knew the fate that awaited her.

Poor girl. Philemon couldn't begin to imagine what thoughts were going through Anahita's mind at that moment. Of one thing he was certain: she must be terrified.

Twenty-Seven

If she slipped a blade out of her wrist sheath, she could reach up and sever his Achilles tendon. Both of them, if she was quick. Throw a handful of sand in his eyes as she jumped to her feet, and run. Anahita's instincts urged her to do just that, but she knew she could not. Not yet. For if half the marketplace gossip about this man was true…she could not risk leaving him alive.

Running could wait until after the deed was done. Until then, cold calculation would occupy her mind, as it always did. Haidar and

Asad had taught her well.

In the meantime, she allowed herself the small fantasy of choking him with the very shoe he'd balanced on the back of her neck. Watching his face grow red, then purple, then blue as he gasped for air that would never again reach his lungs…

"Take her to the women's tent, where they can prepare her for our wedding. If she pleases me tonight, you can carry word back to your master on the morrow. If she does not…" The foot pressed against her neck, making it hard to breathe. "Perhaps I will make her head MY gift to the Sultan, and the next gift the Sultan sends will be more acceptable."

The sheikh did not know how wrong he was, but Anahita had no desire to enlighten him just yet. His time would come, and she would enjoy it. For now, she forced her face to appear blank as Haidar and Asad took her arms and hauled her to her feet. She itched to brush the dust off her embroidered gown, but that, too, could wait. Some servant could deal with the damage when she returned home. She would not wear this again, if she could help it.

She would have enough to do, finding another way to break Philemon's curse. Once this current task was complete. First, she had to grind Basit's face in the dirt.

Asad thrust her through the flap of the largest tent in the camp, from blazing light into darkness. It took her a moment for her eyes to adjust, which was time enough for Haidar to drop a bag of her things at her feet and inform the women of their sheikh's orders for her.

Then the tent flap closed entirely, leaving her alone with what looked like a hundred women, curious about the newest of their number.

Anahita relaxed. She knew her place in a harem – even this one. She allowed the women to lift her dusty robe off, and pretended not to notice their exclamations at the quality of the work or the quantity of dust on it.

"She's so small!"

"He'll break her on her first time."

"She looks terrified."

"Such a pretty tunic. Are the jewels real?"

Anahita let their words wash over her, not uttering a word except to nod occasionally if someone asked her a question. A new bride in a new home was supposed to be nervous. Never mind that she outranked all of them – once she married their sheikh, her place would be his to dictate. So she surrendered to them for now.

"Should we tell her? Warn her, maybe?"

"Can't risk it."

"She should save herself if she can. What if she suffers the same fate as Inbal?"

Inbal, a girl who could not have been older than ten, Anahita discovered, had had her tongue cut out for saying something that displeased the sheikh.

Anahita resolved to avenge the girl.

"Make her so beautiful he cannot resist."

"Oh, isn't the silk lovely? So fine, you can see quite through it!"

"That will not last the night."

Women washed her with cool water, then applied perfumed oils to her skin, before helping her into her wedding clothes – the contents of the bags Haidar had brought. Sheer silk so thin that in the right light, you could see through it, but only her husband would see that, in the privacy of his tent tonight. She fastened the bells onto her bracelets herself, while two small girls did the same with her anklets. A thin chain of bells clipped to her belt, and her dance clothes were complete.

"Do you think they will succeed?"

"They must! This cannot go on."

"Don't forget to oil her hair. You know how grabby his hands can be. At least give her a chance."

They combed, curled and oiled her hair, a luxury Anahita had not allowed herself while they travelled. Hair oil seemed to pick up every speck of dust in the desert, but tonight its glossy sheen would catch the light once she took her veil off. She knew she was too plain to attract him with her beauty – even Philemon had said so.

"Wish we dared poison the wedding feast. He and his favourites alone will eat it – this poor mite won't eat a bite."

"Better that way. What would he do to her if she vomited her food at his feet?"

"Don't even think it. Whoever does the

deed will have my thanks."

"And mine."

"Who is it, do you know?"

"One of the men. They all want the honour of delivering the final blow."

"Of course they do. They know what it means."

Over the gossamer silk, they placed another heavily embroidered robe the blood-red colour of her marriage bed. Jewels had been sewn into this one – dark rubies that glittered in the light, drawing attention to the curve of her breasts beneath it.

"When will it happen?"

"After the feast, when he takes her to his bed."

"Actually IN…?"

"Shh, she looks scared enough. Don't frighten her further. It must be tonight."

The matching jewelled veil completed her bridal clothes, covering Anahita's hair and all but her eyes.

"Doesn't she look a vision?"

"He will not be able to resist."

"Good."

A gentle hand landed on Anahita's shoulder, and she met the pitying eyes of an older woman. "It's all right to be afraid, chick. All brides fear their wedding night. Just stay silent, lie back, and submit to whatever he wishes. It will be over quickly."

Anahita's heart sank as the woman didn't say the final line of bridal advice she'd heard so many times in her father's harem: "You might even enjoy it." No one here enjoyed Sheikh Basit's attentions.

No wonder they were plotting a coup tonight.

A coup that could not succeed if the sheikh was already dead at her hands.

Did she have the right to take vengeance away from these women? Stolen from their fathers, husbands, families, to serve his pleasure?

Ah, but none of the women would deliver the blow. And she had her answer.

She didn't need a man to save her. Anahita would save herself. And all of them. The moment that arsehole put his foot on her neck, he'd sealed his fate.

Twenty-Eight

Philemon sat, forgotten, with the camels and other animals. Would this be his fate forever? Even the passionate kiss of the princess he loved had not been able to break the curse. If Anahita couldn't do it, then could anyone? Or would he be alone forever?

The sounds of feasting and merriment came from a well-lit tent near the middle of the encampment, beside the women's tent where they'd taken Anahita. Women walked between the two, carrying platters of food or what remained of it after the men had devoured everything.

He hadn't heard a single female voice since he arrived, he realised. No laughter, no chatter – none of the normal sounds he'd expect from normal women. They might be more outspoken in Tasnim than other places, but nowhere had he ever met women who were forced into silence. It was against their very natures. There was something very wrong in this camp, and he wished he were far from it. But he could not leave Anahita here among the worst of it. With that sheikh who didn't deserve to kiss the ground she walked upon.

Whose wedding feast they were no doubt celebrating now. A feast to give the bridegroom stamina, for the true test of a wedding was whether he could keep the bride in his tent until morning, when the wedding breakfast they shared concluded the marriage ceremony.

Yesterday, he would have bet money on Anahita not staying until morning but after what he'd seen today…

Had her men drugged her? Given her something that would make her more docile?

Or cast some spell on her that had the same effect? Was that why he'd been kept away from her, and made to ride with Haidar?

He prayed they had not, but he could not be certain. Even if he was, what could he do? He was a frog.

"Are we still doing it tonight?" an unfamiliar voice whispered.

"Of course! Every day under his rule is an abomination to the honour of all good men," a second voice hissed back.

"And their wives," the first one muttered.

"Why didn't someone just poison his food?"

"Didn't you see the boys he has lined up at his feet? Their mothers cook the meals, and must feed each dish to their own sons before he tastes a single bite. That's how he foiled the first poisoning attempt. The women do not dare any more. It must be us, and we cannot fail!"

"When? There was so much arguing, I couldn't stay to find out what they decided. An ambush after the feast, when he is too drunk on wine to see it?"

"Of course not. He'll be expecting that.

Besides, did you see him drink more than a cup of wine at the feast? No, he has all his wits about him now, and he will expect an attack as he walks back to his tent with his princess. She's barely more than a child, my wife said. Would you willingly give your daughter to that monster?"

"I'd sooner kill my daughter than give her to him. It is fortunate I don't have one."

"Not yet. If you get your wife back on the morrow, I'll wager you'll be busy planting one in her belly before sundown!"

"If she still lives. She hasn't left the women's tent in weeks."

"She's the only healer left. They're probably keeping her busy, healing the girls the morning after he's had them. If he'd killed someone, we'd know about it, for who'd he send to bury her, hmm?"

"Maybe. So when will we finally be rid of him again?"

"We wait until he's distracted, deflowering his child bride, and then we strike."

"What about the girl?"

"If she gets in the way, kill her, too. No one

here will mourn her."

Philemon opened his mouth to shout that he would, but he knew it was no use. They wouldn't hear him. Only Anahita would understand him. Someone needed to warn her.

"He'll probably crush her the first time he tries to mount her. They say that's what happened to Ahmed's daughter. He broke her hip bones with his weight, and she wouldn't stop screaming, so he killed her."

"If she's screaming, he won't hear us until it's too late."

Cheers and catcalls rose from the feasting tent.

"Look out. He's heading to bed."

The plotting men disappeared into the shadows as a couple appeared on the track that ran between the tents. He held a torch aloft in one hand as his other arm encircled the waist of a girl dressed head to toe in blood red.

Anahita. It had to be.

She walked willingly, he noted – the sheikh did not need to drag her. She should be trying to tear loose from his grasp, to run away.

Philemon shouted a warning at the top of

his lungs, but she didn't seem to hear, for she kept going. To her death, he was sure of it.

Cursing his already cursed body, Philemon leaped down from the camel's back and headed after them. He had to warn her, about the monstrous sheikh and his imminent death. A warning just for her ears, for the sheikh would not understand him.

He hopped faster. He had to save her.

Twenty-Nine

It took every drop of Anahita's self control not to sink a blade into Basit's arm as he marched her away from the feasting tent. Not that she'd wanted to stay, but his meaty fingers biting into her arm would leave bruises.

Her stomach protested that she hadn't eaten, but Anahita ignored it. No one had offered her food or wine at the feast – even her previous husbands had made an effort to feed her. Then again, with Basit's greedy eyes on her, she hadn't felt like eating.

While he stuffed himself and his men drank

countless toasts to his health and virility and other such manly virtues, she'd watched the crowd. Several men had slipped out, unseen by anyone but her, and she'd witnessed whispered conversations between the serving women and some of the men seated at the lower tables.

The bloated bastard beside her was blissfully unaware of the coup his own people had planned, while she saw signs of it all around her, spreading like a sickness. Eyes watched from the darkness between the tents as they passed, but none came close enough to kill the man. No, they wanted her to distract him.

And she would, but not in the way they had planned. For she was not a pawn in anyone's game. Not her father's, not Basit's, and definitely not the strange one played by his people.

Basit shoved her through a tent flap, shouting for some guards to take their position at the entrance. Haidar and Asad, she hoped, as they'd planned.

Gaily coloured silk cushions lay in piles everywhere, not unlike Maram's bedchamber if she'd tripled the number of cushions and not cared about the colours. Or the cleanliness of them, Anahita realised, noting the stains on several of them. A patch of dried blood here, something white and crusted across two of them, something yellow that had turned part of an azure blue cushion murky green… She shuddered.

"Get your clothes off. Now," Basit growled, shoving her toward the dirty cushions.

Anahita ducked her head to hide the fury in her eyes. "In the Sultan's harem, it is traditional for a new bride to perform an intimate dance for her husband as she removes her wedding clothes. I am told it is necessary to increase a husband's pleasure."

Actually, Maram had told her it give her a way to take off her own clothes without her husband noticing how many knives she carried, but Anahita wasn't going to tell him that.

Basit threw himself on the cushions and folded his arms across his chest. "I will be the judge of that. Show me."

Anahita took a deep breath, then began to mark the beat with her feet, stamping on the ground until she had the rhythm in her head. Then she began to move, unfastening the heavy, red gown slowly as she moved her hips to swirl the skirt.

Basit grunted.

She released the last fastener and let the gown's own weight carry it to the floor, revealing the thin silk tunic she wore underneath. A twirl unfurled the skirt fully, showing off everything before the folds settled again, giving only a tantalising glimpse as she moved.

The heavy red veil was next. She turned her back as she tore the garment from her head, shaking it out so that it flew like a banner behind her as she danced. She turned to face him, revealing her face to him for the first time, and held her breath.

Plain she might be, but the women here had done their best to paint her eyes to make them look bigger, and redden her lips, too.

The obvious approval in his expression made her breathe out a sigh of relief. She danced faster, her every movement sending the bells on her belt jingling.

"Enough dancing. Take the rest off," Basit ordered.

Anahita pretended not to hear, planting her hands on her hips as she moved them again, more slow and sensuous this time.

"I said now!"

He grabbed her arm and dragged Anahita around to face him, tearing her sleeve.

Another gossamer silk tunic ruined. What was wrong with men?

Anahita met his eyes. "And I say no."

Thirty

The track between the tents seemed to stretch forever. Philemon would never get there in time to warn her. Not before that misbegotten camel herder got his hands on her…and what if he hurt her? Philemon sucked in a breath and hopped faster.

Of course the sheikh's tent was at the far end of the camp. Where no one could hear the screams of his women as he tortured them, most likely. Barbarian.

Four guards stood at the entrance. Two tribesmen, Haidar, and Asad. Philemon cursed.

He couldn't go in without her men spotting him.

He hopped around the back of the tent, looking for another way in. Maybe if he squeezed under the tent wall here, digging under it a little, he might manage…

A woman's scream sliced through the night. Then another. From inside the tent.

Anahita.

He squeezed through the gap, not caring what happened to him, and caught sight of Anahita struggling with the sheikh.

He had to stop him. Couldn't let him hurt her.

But what could a frog do?

He eyed the sea of cushions between him and the woman he loved.

Her marriage bed.

He'd make Basit rue even looking at Anahita.

Philemon leaped.

Thirty-One

Anahita started to scream, startling Basit into releasing her. She didn't hesitate, thrusting her knife up to pierce his throat. Once, twice, then a third time. Basit jerked his head up, ripping the blade from her hand, before she could deliver a final blow.

Gasping for air he could no longer breathe, Basit fell heavily against her, nearly knocking her over. Anahita fought to stay on her feet, then to push him off her. He weighed so much, but she gave an almighty heave and she was free. He tumbled back onto his soiled cushions.

Beside a naked man.

Philemon?

She opened his mouth to ask how, or perhaps why…

The guards chose that moment to charge into the tent.

Anahita thought fast.

"He killed him! He killed him!" she screamed, pointing at Philemon, as she backed into a corner of the tent and curled up into what she hoped looked like a hysterical wife pushed past what her mind could handle without going mad.

Haidar and Asad would seize him, he'd turn back into a frog, and chaos would ensue. She could retrieve her knife, and slip off into the darkness. Though if she had time, she'd still like to cut out his tongue.

"You killed the sheikh?" one of Basit's men asked shakily.

Philemon drew himself up to his full height. "I did. Honour demanded it."

Anahita suppressed a snort. There was nothing honourable about Basit's death. She'd made certain of that.

In the silence that followed, she risked another look. Basit's men had dropped to their knees, pressing their foreheads to the floor. Asad and Haidar slowly followed their example.

"Honoured Sheikh, what are your orders?" one man asked.

Philemon's mouth opened, but no words came out.

Anahita wasn't as familiar with desert politics as Maram, but she vaguely remembered something about tribes where leadership was won by being the strongest fighter, and the succession was not by birth, but by force of arms. Kill the leader, and you inherited his position. Was it like that here?

Asad seemed to think so. "Most Honoured Sheikh, would you like us to bring you a better wife to warm your bed? One who is not so…hysterical?" He nodded in Anahita's direction.

She buried her head in her hands again and whimpered a little. Her throat was already sore from screaming – she didn't want to do it any more tonight, if she didn't have to.

"This one will suit me fine. I'm sure she will calm as soon as you remove the corpse from her chamber," Philemon said. "And bring us fresh bedding."

"As you command, Most Honoured Sheikh," they chorused.

Anahita's hands clenched into fists. When she got Philemon alone, she would throttle him for this. This wasn't her plan at all.

Thirty-Two

The guards took an eternity to carry all the cushions out of the tent, or so it seemed, before they set up a bedroll big enough for a bridal couple.

Two men rolled the former sheikh in the blood-soaked carpet beneath him, then lifted the grisly bundle between them.

"Wait!" A third man made them set their burden down and open it.

By all that was holy, why? Philemon wanted to scream.

The third man pulled the knife from the

sheikh's breast, wiped the bloodied blade on his own robes, then held it out to Philemon. "Your blade, Honoured Sheikh."

It was a pledge of fealty, however informal, and Philemon had accepted enough in his time as Prince of Tasnim to know not to refuse. Gingerly, he took the knife and nodded.

It was a small blade to have taken the life of such a large man. Small and delicately curved, yet the blade was wickedly sharp. The hilt was worn from use, any sharp edges softened by the grip of how many hands? A dagger passed down through generations of desert people, until being buried in the guts of some insignificant sheikh. A dagger whose owner would surely return for such a valuable weapon.

Philemon looked up. The men were gone, leaving him alone with Anahita. He dropped the dagger where the bloodied carpet had once lay. It sliced into the sand and stood, hilt deep, as though it would murder the whole desert next.

Philemon shivered. He had to do something before the dagger's owner returned and tried to use it on Anahita, too.

"You're a fool, Philemon the frog," Anahita said, rising to her feet. "You should have stayed out of this."

Philemon seized her shoulders. "How could I? The whole camp could talk of nothing but how they would kill you and your husband on your wedding night. He could have killed you! And he'll be back, once he realises he left his knife behind. What in heaven's name made you blame his death on me? The real killer is out there, and it's only a matter of time before he claims leadership over this squalid camp for killing the last leader. What do you think he'll do to me for trying to claim his kill? Or you?"

Anahita tossed her head and met his eyes. "What else was I to do? They should have taken you into custody, and the moment you left this excuse for a boudoir – " she kicked one of the cushions that the men had missed " – the moment you left, you'd turn back into a frog, and escape. In the chaos that ensued, my men and I would be able to escape unseen. By the time they remembered us, we would be well on our way!" Her eyes narrowed. "Now, take your hands off me, or I will turn you into a eunuch like Haidar and Asad."

The shiver of steel touched his groin.

"Do your bits grow back when you turn back into a frog?" she asked.

Philemon released her, stumbling back. His eyes went to the knife, but it had vanished from the sand, as if it had never been.

She twisted the silky belt slung across her hips, and sheathed the knife. Another twist and the belt was back in place, an innocuous-seeming string of bells that hid a deadly secret.

"You killed him," Philemon whispered, not wanting to believe it. "What did he ever do to you?"

Anahita shrugged, a smile twisting her lips. "Nothing. I saw to that. That disgusting old man will never steal another woman from her husband again, or attack my father's people. On the morrow, or the next day, my men will find an excuse to slip away with me, and we will return home. I am a woman of my word – you may come home with us. But no one can ever know what I did here tonight. Or I will use one of my blades on you."

Philemon choked. "One of your blades? You have more?" He stared at her. She wore little more than the belt, and smaller versions of it at her wrists and ankles. Why, she was practically naked! Philemon averted his eyes. "How many more?" he asked, trying not the think of her smooth, curved flesh.

"Seven," she said. "Seven more."

He stared at her in horror. Her face, not the rest of her. "Seven?" His mouth was suddenly dry. For all he'd travelled with her, he barely knew this barbarian princess. He should have listened to her. Should have stayed in the waterskin, just like she'd said. Then he wouldn't know any of this, and he'd be blissfully ignorant that the woman he'd fallen in love with was some sort of demon. "Of course. Forgive me for worrying about your safety. You can take care of yourself, I see now." He turned on his heel and headed for the exit.

"Please don't go."

His foot hovered above the sand — sand that should be saturated with her bridegroom's blood — but Philemon hesitated to put it down on what was, to him, another man's grave. A man he had wished gone only hours before.

"I'm only doing what you asked me to. Returning to where I belong, to wait until we leave."

"Wait until morning. Please. It's my wedding night. I should not be alone." There was an edge of desperation in her voice – or did he imagine it?

"Then perhaps you should not have killed your husband. He could have warmed your bed. I…cannot." Because, heaven help him, he wanted her. Never mind the knives or that she'd killed a man or pinned the crime on him. If he shared her bed tonight, he wouldn't be able to keep his hands off her.

She lifted her chin. "I had no choice. Do you think I like killing? My first husband deserved his fate, a dozen times over, but I had no grudge against this one until today. But I swore an oath, and my father heard me do it. So he sends me to be his assassin, in the name of peace. He keeps his hands clean, yet mine are awash in blood. As always, on my wedding night. Such is my fate."

"It is not the fate you deserve. If you were my bride, your wedding night would be glorious, as it should be. I swear it."

She stared at him — it was her turn to be shocked.

Philemon wished he hadn't said it. To admit his weakness in front of her…why, she could stab him in the heart without needing any of her seven blades.

"Normally, my men would take me away — the hysterical bride — to calm me down, and when the nightmares invade my sleep, we are too far from the camp for anyone to hear my screams. But tonight you were here, and you made me stay. Why are you here, Philemon?"

She hadn't called him a frog. He took it as encouragement, however tiny it might be. "Because I couldn't let them kill you with him. Even let you witness what they intended to do to him. You deserve better. A wedding night to remember, for the right reasons, not the wrong ones."

She laughed softly. "I remember all my wedding nights, especially the first. I've survived five husbands, and five wedding nights I would give anything to forget."

"Let me make it up to you. Tonight." The moment the words left his lips, he regretted them. And yet…now they were out, he had nothing left to lose. "Give me one night, I beg you. From now until dawn. I will finish what we started last night with that exquisite kiss. If I cannot deliver what I promise – a wedding night like you deserve, filled with the pleasure such a lovely princess deserves – then do what you will with me. Carve me up and feed me to your falcon." He spread his arms wide and closed his eyes.

Thirty-Three

Faced with Philemon in all his naked glory, completely at her mercy…for the first time, Anahita felt shy.

She unfastened the cuffs at her wrists, letting them tinkle to the floor, followed by her belt, and finally the ankle cuffs. Naked and unarmed, her breathing short and ragged, she crossed the cushions until she stood before him.

Anahita took a deep breath, then took his face in her hands. She stretched up even as he yielded to her, and their lips met. Even before her lips parted, he stole her breath, so tender was his kiss. She could kiss him all night.

And yet…her heels dropped to the floor, so she looked up at him longingly. "I'm afraid," she whispered.

Her traitorous body reminded her what showing fear had done in the past – her body, flying through the air, from the force of her husband's blow. The explosion of pain, the fear of more, her voice silenced, her vision dulled…

Philemon's arms enfolded her. "You have nothing to fear from me. I promise. Tell me what you wish for, and I shall grant it. Your own personal djinn."

She managed a smile. "Then can we kiss a little more? And then…can I sleep in your arms?"

He lifted her in his arms, effortlessly. "As you wish, Princess."

Thirty-Four

"Do you know how to pleasure a woman?"

With Anahita naked in his arms, Philemon struggled vainly to think of anything but what he wanted to do to her. Her words made him lose the battle.

"Oh, yes. In many different ways," he began, wondering if he dared hope.

"With your fingers?" Anahita asked.

Ah, he'd forgotten she was a new bride on her as-yet unconsummated wedding night. A bride who had never known a man's touch.

He considered for a moment, before he

decided to take the risk. "Would you like me to show you?"

"Yes," she said promptly.

In the silence that followed his loss for words, she continued, "When I can't sleep and the dreams return, it's the only way to distract my mind from the memories. If I'm asking too much, Philemon, merely say so, and I will…I will attempt to take care of myself."

His imagination ran riot at the thought of her pleasuring herself in his arms, but the selfish part of him shut down that particular idea. She'd asked him for pleasure, and he intended to give it to her.

"You tell me if it is too much," he whispered, skimming his hand over her hip and between her thighs. She gave a little sigh, parting her legs wider, as his fingers found the right spot.

Philemon wrapped his other arm around her chest and pulled her firmly against him, revelling in the increasing tempo of her heartbeat as his fingers worked the only magic he knew.

Anahita began to moan softly, squirming in

his grasp to drive his fingers deeper inside her. She ground her soft little arse against his groin, turning him hard as a rock. He'd give anything to slip more than his fingers inside her. Just one thrust…

She bucked, arching her back away from him as she cried out, not once but twice, trapping his hand between her tightly clenched thighs.

When the moment ended and she lay limp and panting in his arms, Anahita whispered, "I've never…it's never felt that good before. Not even when Haidar – "

"I'm a man, not a eunuch," Philemon snapped, fighting the jealousy curling up at the mention of the eunuch's name. How could she think of any other man when she lay, sated, in his arms?

"I know." She reached down and cupped him, and he was proud to realise it took both of her hands to do it.

It took all of his self-control not to thrust into her warm hands, and demand that she reciprocate. The bliss of those soft hands stroking him, or those wicked lips wrapped around him…

"Do you know how to pleasure a woman with this?"

Philemon grinned. Oh, she was a maiden, all right. No woman who'd ever been loved by a man would have to ask such a question. "A hundred…nay…a thousand times better than with my hands," he assured her. He wanted to beg her to let him show her, but he knew that was too much to ask.

She squirmed around so that she faced him, her oasis eyes fathomless pools in the darkness. "If you can, I give you my word that you may share my bed every night until I return home."

His breath caught in his throat. Was she really asking…?

Anahita took his hesitation for reluctance. "And when we reach home, I will press my sister into finding the enchantress who cursed you, and making her break the curse. If you show me the pleasure you would show your bride on her wedding night." She moistened her lips. "Please."

He reached up to cup her face in his hands.

"On a wedding night, the pleasure must be shared," he said, then kissed her.

She stiffened at first – kissing was still too new to her – before Anahita melted into his touch, kissing him back with far more passion than he'd hoped for.

Thirty-Five

Philemon entered her slowly, as though terrified he would break her if he thrust too hard or fast.

"We only have until dawn," Anahita said, feeling it would be churlish to tell him to hurry up.

He swallowed. "I don't want to hurt you, and as this is your first time…"

She couldn't help it. She laughed. "My first time? Truly, you thought that? My first time, the bastard beat me so badly my eyes were nearly swelled shut, then cracked my head against the tent pole so I could not see him nor fight back when he raped me. I deserved the pain, for tempting him so wickedly with my body, or so he said. I learned later his man parts wouldn't work unless the woman he wanted was cowering in fear. I only wish he'd died more slowly than he did, for I know he deserved more pain than he ever put me through." She sobered. "I was widowed for the fifth time tonight, but I will never let a man hurt me again."

"And if I fail to please you, you'll make me the sixth man to die at your feet?"

"Hardly. You are not my husband. My father does not want you dead, and neither do I. You are a most agreeable travelling companion. Perhaps even more than that if you show me the pleasure you promised tonight." More pleasure than he had already.

He nodded. "Very well." And in one smooth motion, he filled her completely.

She took a deep breath, relishing the heat of him inside her, touching exactly where his fingers had stroked her to ecstasy not long before. Truly, she wanted this. Wanted him.

She didn't even need to say it. He looked into her eyes, and saw it all, from that very first thrust until he pushed her all the way to an incredible peak where they cried out for joy together.

And as he folded her into his arms afterwards, she pressed her ear to his chest, to hear his still-racing heart, beating in rhythm with hers. "Will you love me like that again tomorrow night?" she asked sleepily.

"Every night. I'll love you like that every night you desire," Philemon said.

"Mmmm. You should not say such things, you know, for after tonight, I will desire you every night, as long as I live." She smiled. "My prince."

"It will be my pleasure, Princess."

Thirty-Six

Philemon awoke to the sweet smell of the soft girl in his arms, and for a moment, he wondered whether he had died in his sleep and flown direct to heaven. But Anahita was no houri. She was a living, breathing woman he would do anything to keep.

A woman who deserved a proper husband, not one who would turn back into a frog when the sun rose. And she did not deserve to wake up beside his slimy self today, after the pleasures of last night. He should leave now, and return to his hiding place among the water skins to await their journey home.

He must have jostled her, for her hand shot out and grabbed his arm. "Don't go." Her oasis eyes reproached him.

"It is nearly dawn, and you know what happens then," he said, pulling away.

"Make love to me once more. There is still time," she said.

Philemon shook his head. "Lovemaking should not be rushed. I will turn back into a frog before we are finished, and you will throw me out of your bed in disgust."

"Never," she declared, creeping closer. He tried not to moan as her hand wrapped around his length. "You were thinking of it, too. Love me like you want to."

Despite his misgivings, he could not refuse her. And once their bodies joined, he was lost to anything but her pleasure, and his own.

Until she lay on the cushions, sated, her breasts heaving as she recovered from the exertion. Oh, how he loved her.

"Honoured Sheikh, I bring food and water, so that you may wash and break your fast. The women are waiting to tend to your wife, too, when you are finished with her." Philemon recognised the man who'd handed him the knife last night, before he bowed deeply and hid his face.

Philemon tugged a cloth up over Anahita's breasts, chagrined at the need to hide them from view. "I will never be finished with her," he said honestly.

Anahita gasped, but the man didn't seem to hear, for he ducked his head and said, "I understand, Honoured Sheikh, but the men of the camp need your leadership. With Basit gone, they look to you, and it is nearly noon. The women…they, too, need to know your orders. Basit beat them if they did not deliver the dinner he desired, and they do not wish to displease you."

Noon. How was he still human, if it was noon?

His met Anahita's wide eyes – she recognised the significance, even if she understood it no better than he did.

"My wife will instruct them," he said, his eyes begging her to agree.

A secretive smile twisted Anahita's lips

before she ducked her head to hide it. "As my prince commands."

Then the tent was full of women, helping Anahita wash and dress.

Philemon rose, clutching a sheet to cover his modesty.

One of the women bowed deeply. "For you, Honoured Sheikh." She held out what appeared to be fresh robes.

Oh, heavens be praised. He snatched them from her. He'd never dressed so quickly in his life. Yet as he reached the entrance of his tent, he hesitated. He had not stood in the sun in his own form for too long. Would the curse turn him green again once the sunlight touched him?

Only one way to find out. Philemon stepped out into the sunlight, glad of his sandals as the very air seemed to want to sear his skin off.

"Honoured Sheikh?" The knife man stood uncertainly at his side.

Enough of this sheikh business. "It's Highness, actually. I'm Prince Philemon of Tasnim." Oh, it felt good to say it. Not as good as he'd felt twined around Anahita in the throes of passion, but it was a distant second.

The man fell to his knees and touched his forehead to the burning sand. "Oh, please forgive me, Your Highness. I did not know!"

He'd burn his face off if he stayed down there, Philemon knew. He seized the man's shoulder and hauled him to his feet. "Of course you didn't, because I didn't tell you until now. What is your name?"

"Tariq, Highness," the man said, not daring to raise his eyes to Philemon's face.

"So, yesterday, who would you have expected to succeed Basit as sheikh?" Philemon asked.

"I don't understand, Your Highness," Tariq said cautiously.

"Yesterday, your people couldn't wait to get rid of him. Who did you think would take his place?" Philemon asked, watching Tariq's face carefully.

Tariq hesitated, them said, "Why, the strongest among us, the best leader, like yourself, Your Highness."

Now Philemon wished he had been the one to kill Basit. A right fearmongering bastard.

"I'm not staying, Tariq. I must return to Tasnim. I didn't leave the richest city in the world to come and lead a desert tribe. I'm not your new sheikh. Your people must choose their own leader." Philemon heard the man splutter behind him, but he no longer needed a guide – the tent where they'd held the wedding feast the previous day hummed with the sound of men's voices. Waiting for him.

He marched in, calling for quiet.

Philemon had to hide a smile when Tariq's voice rose to a roar, drowning out all other sound: "Bow before His Royal Highness, Prince Philemon of Tasnim!"

No bowing happened, but Philemon did get stunned silence. It was enough.

He explained the things he'd told Tariq, and how he would be returning home as soon as possible.

"And what about our wives?" one man shouted. "Are you taking them, too?" Half a dozen others took up the same cry.

Philemon sighed inwardly. He had no desire to lead any part of a desert tribe – or steal its women. "The only woman who will leave with me is the Sultan's daughter, Princess Anahita."

A collective sigh of relief went up from the assembled men.

"Where is she?" a familiar voice demanded.

Philemon scanned the crowd and found them at the back – Anahita's men. They did not look relieved.

"In the women's tent, I believe, seeing to our midday meal," Philemon said airily, as if it mattered little to him. Ha. His thoughts were with her every moment they were apart, though he knew she was in no danger with a pack of cowed women.

"She'd better not be cooking it herself, or she'll poison us all. I've seen the princess burn water," the man – Asad? – shouted back.

Nervous laughter erupted around him.

Philemon cast his mind back. All those nights he'd travelled with them…had Anahita ever cooked anything? He couldn't recall her preparing any food, except occasionally skinning whatever that devilish bird of hers caught. He should have noticed her skill with a blade before. Too late now.

Philemon mumbled something about

making sure, and out of the tent toward the one where the women resided.

A boy stood at the door. A guard, perhaps? His eyes widened when he saw Philemon, and his mouth dropped open, no sound coming out.

Philemon nodded and stepped into the dimly lit space.

"The new Sheikh! The new Sheikh is here!" The boy had regained the use of his voice.

Philemon held up his hands in surrender. He knew better than to invade the domain of women without explaining himself first. "I seek Princess Anahita."

"You could have waited until I'd finished bathing, and I'd had something to break my fast," she grumbled as her head emerged from a tunic as heavily embroidered as the last two she'd worn. "After last night, I'm sure you don't need me again already."

He couldn't help it. Just the sight of her brought a smile to his lips. How had he ever lived without her? "I will always need you."

She narrowed her eyes. "And what about all your concubines, hmm?"

"I have none, and never will again. The only woman I will ever need now is you." Philemon wet his lips. "I will see you crowned as the Princess of Tasnim, if you wish it."

Anahita spread her arms wide. "And what of the other women here? Basit made them all his concubines. They were wives, daughters, all stolen from their families. What will you do with them, Sheikh?" She spat the title like the worst epithet.

Philemon shook his head. "I am no sheikh. I am Prince Philemon of Tasnim, and I declare you are free to return to your families as honourable widows, with all that entails. Any man who says otherwise will answer to me."

Only now did he realise all eyes were upon him. "I told the guards this last night. Didn't they pass the message on?"

Anahita's fingers laced through his. "I said the same thing, but no one believed me. See? I told you he is not a monster." She stared up at him, and for a moment he thought she would kiss him. Then her gaze darted down. "Except when he keeps me too busy for breakfast. I'm sure there is a law against denying a new bride her breakfast!"

A woman Philemon didn't know laid a hand on Anahita's shoulder. "Take the prince to one of the common tents. Congratulations to you both. I will bring a wedding breakfast for you."

Thirty-Seven

In between bites of food and congratulations from what seemed like every man and woman in the camp at becoming their new sheikh, Anahita tried to ask him how he'd managed to break the curse. Philemon heard the question, she was certain of it, but he was too busy thanking someone to answer it right away.

And then another interruption, and another, until she wanted to scream, if her throat still wasn't raw from last night.

Finally, the tide of humanity seemed to decide to give them a moment alone.

"How did you break the curse?" she demanded.

He shrugged. "I wish I knew. Perhaps it was you. I do not remember the witch's exact words when she first cursed me, but she definitely mentioned a princess's bed, and something about dusk or maybe dawn. If we find her, perhaps we can ask her. But in the meantime, I mean to enjoy being a man again. A man who will travel home with you, as soon as possible, if your word still holds true."

"It does," she said, stung. "But why do you need to travel with us now? As the Prince of Tasnim, and the sheikh of this place, surely you can command your people to come with you, or take you wherever you wish."

He leaned close so his breath tickled her ear. "I promised to take you to Tasnim, my home, and prove that I am its prince. The witch didn't just curse me – when she came, the water supply dried up, too. I must see it restored, even if it means hunting her down."

"I will help you," she said. Because if she could go to Tasnim…she could finally be free.

Philemon took her hand in his and kissed it.

"And I will be grateful for any further assistance you wish to offer, Princess. For after seeing you break one curse, I have no doubt you will save my city as you have me."

Anahita wasn't sure about that, but another group of people came up to offer their congratulations, so she held her tongue.

Thirty-Eight

Philemon would have given everything he owned to bypass the oasis without having to look at the accursed place, but his travel companions were having none of it. Besides, with the wells of Tasnim still dry, they would need to replenish their water supplies.

He busied himself helping the other men unload the camels and set up camp. A task for servants, but Anahita had made it clear there were no servants or masters in this travelling party. A peculiar princess indeed.

She stood at the water's edge, wearing a pair

of flimsy sandals and a short tunic. They might have been the same ones she'd worn the day they met. Then, she'd taken him in her hands, lifting him out of despondency and saving him from certain death. An irresistible desire rose up within him, to take her in his arms and never let her go.

His feet carried him across the sand of their own accord, and she yielded to his embrace as she yielded to no one else. He pressed his lips to the back of her neck, tasting the salt of sweat she'd said she wanted to wash off.

"Why do you hesitate?" he asked. Even he felt the pull of the cool water, which held no dread for him when he was with her. Anahita had broken the curse once – he was in no danger of being cursed again while he had her.

"The water is not as clear as before, and the level has risen." She pointed. "Those baby date palms were well away from the edge before, but now they are submerged. Merlin insists there are frogs here, too, where there were none but you last time we were here. And now the water is warm, which it wasn't the first time." She shook her head. "I don't know what that means."

He helped her out of her tunic, and hurried to remove his own clothes. "Then we should wash, and wait for your bird to catch a frog. Perhaps you can question the creature."

Anahita smiled. "I have enough cursed princes to last me a lifetime. And I have no intention of sharing my bed with any man but you."

He kissed her. "Good."

They took their time in the water, for washing soon led to other things, which meant more washing, before they emerged. Moonrise in the twilight sky shimmered across Anahita's damp skin, before she slipped on a robe to cover herself.

"Dinner's ready!" Asad called.

Philemon hurried to don his own clothes, before heading to the fire, where the other three had already taken their seats.

"There must have been some rain in the mountains. We'll have to watch out for the rivers, and be careful crossing them," Asad said.

Philemon laughed. "How can you possibly

know that? I haven't seen a single cloud in the sky!"

"The water here. It's been muddied by floodwaters, which only come when a deluge washes things down from the mountains. And the frogs, of course. That silly bird ate so many, she's too fat to fly any more." Asad pointed at Anahita's falcon, who did look rounder than usual. He snorted. "I hope none of them were your brothers, Philemon. She ate them while you two were taking your time in the water, and I don't speak frog."

Anahita's blush was barely visible in the firelight, but there was no hiding it from Philemon, or the other men who knew her so well. "None of them spoke. Not like Philemon when Merlin caught him. They were ordinary frogs. Proper frogs, according to Merlin." She rose and headed over to the bird.

Haidar tipped the dregs of his cup out onto the sand, then poured himself another drink. "You may please her now, enough for her to accept you as her husband, but one wrong step and there are plenty of places where a body can be buried in the sand and never seen again.

Don't forget that, Frog Prince."

For a moment, Philemon wondered what it would be like to fight the man. A fair fight in the training ring, of course. Haidar was a better fighter than Anahita, and he had size and strength on his side, too, but it would be a fine fight, while it lasted. One Anahita would never allow, he was certain of it.

Philemon lifted his cup in acknowledgement. "And should I die in the desert at the point of the princess's blade, I thank you for the courtesy of a proper burial. For we both know you wouldn't deny her the pleasure of cutting out my heart, if that is her desire."

Asad exploded into laughter. "It's your manhood she'll cut off, and you'll live just long enough to watch it burn. Falling in love with her is foolishness."

Haidar threw his cup down on the sand and stalked away, muttering to himself.

"Should you go after him?" Philemon asked.

Asad snorted. "No. You're both as foolish as each other, and he knows it. But that doesn't alter the fact that he'll enjoy watching you die if you've lied to the princess about being a prince, or Tasnim. The one thing he loves almost as much as the girl herself is defending her honour. So if any part of your story isn't true, now's the time to disappear. Just take care at the river crossings, or your body will be swept away as easily as the princess has swept away your senses."

"I have lied about nothing," Philemon declared. "Which is more than I can say about you. Who ever heard of storms in a clear sky? Where is all the water you say will cause a flood?"

Asad grinned, his eyes glittering in the firelight. "Not all the water in the desert is where we can see it. Deep beneath the surface, there are underground rivers and lakes. The same sort that lies beneath Tasnim, and provides it with so much of its water. It bubbles up in wadis and springs like this one, but this is a mere puddle compared to what lies below. And with so much more water here…it'll be a wonder if your cave city isn't completely flooded."

Philemon's heart constricted in his chest.

"Tasnim has never flooded. Never. The water is gone. It cannot flood!" For if the treasure chambers on the lowest levels flooded, he would be penniless. The Sultan would not let him marry Anahita then. He swallowed. "I will show you on the morrow. My city has survived for a thousand years, and it will survive a thousand more."

Asad's smile didn't fade as he turned to stare into the fire. "We shall see, Frog Prince. For a man who didn't know about the rivers beneath the desert a moment ago, you'll forgive me if I don't believe your expert assessment of them now."

Thirty-Nine

Philemon's frantic lovemaking last night spoke of some emotional disquiet he refused to tell her. Fear had his eyes darting everywhere, above a mouth that couldn't seem to smile, as they approached his home.

It was a strange transformation. All the way to Basit's camp, he'd entertained Anahita with tales of the beauties of Tasnim, but now he seemed terrified to show them to her.

Determined to solve this mystery before she arrived, Anahita urged her camel to match Philemon's pace. Her happy travel companion was now too busy scowling at the horizon to notice her.

"Tell me about your last day in Tasnim," she said.

He glanced up for only a moment before the horizon drew his gaze once more. "Is that an order?"

"We made a deal. You amuse me while we travel, and I take you home. Well, I don't find your silence amusing. I find it…alarming. And I want to know what I'm walking into. Sometimes knives are not enough. Especially if there is an enchantress who turns innocent princes into frogs." Anahita managed a smile. "I'm hardly innocent."

"She will not touch you. If she even attempts to cast a spell in your direction, I shall – " Philemon stopped, then continued, "I shall stand in her way, and force her to curse me instead. In the meantime, your men will use her distraction to…deal with her."

"And then I will have to break the curse again, though I don't know how I did it the first time? You place great faith in me. Faith I don't share. Tell me what happened. What are we walking into that has you so scared?" Anahita pressed.

Philemon sighed deeply and buried his head in his hands. "There is nothing in Tasnim that will harm you. Not even her. I am not innocent, either. I fear…I fear I may have deserved the curse, and if there is anyone in Tasnim, they will blame me for the fall of the city, too."

Anahita persisted. "But you can't possibly be responsible for the wells running dry. It would take a powerful curse, or spell or…"

"It was a wish, granted by a particularly powerful djinn, actually. A careless wish that once granted, could not be undone." Now Philemon refused to meet her eyes at all.

But Anahita would not be diverted from her course. "What did you wish for?"

He let out a harsh laugh. "What does any man wish for in the desert? An oasis, where he might drink and refresh himself." When Anahita didn't respond, he went on: "The oasis where you found me, actually. A place where you could not resist bathing, either."

And the tale came spilling out, at first in

spurts and starts, before finally it gushed out of Philemon, a flow of words that could not be stopped.

A djinn who obeyed orders without question, creating an oasis for his master without caring about the consequences.

A city slowly starved of water until the wells ran dry.

A prince who demanded the oh-so-powerful djinn fix the problem, only to be told it required more power than the djinn possessed to refill the underwater reservoir.

A call for help, the help of a powerful enchantress who did have the power to compel the djinn to obey.

An enchantress who imprisoned the djinn, but who could not return the water to his home.

A fool of a prince who threw the enchantress out of the city, unthanked and unpaid, for she had not restored his city's water supply.

A city of people, trying to leave, and an enraged enchantress who could not be kept out.

An enchantress who cast him into a well, then led the evacuation herself, saving his people.

A fool of a prince, turned frog, hopping from puddle to puddle as he chased what remained of his city's water supply…all the way down to the new oasis, where he finally understood: no magic in the world was powerful enough to make water run uphill. Or to change the past.

"But it's not your fault," Anahita said slowly.

"It is," Philemon insisted. "I made that foolish wish, and I am the city's prince. The responsibility is mine. I know that now."

"But the djinn. He should have said something…"

Philemon shook his head. "You don't know djinn. They are slaves, bound by magic to obey their masters, without question. The only time they can refuse is if they are not powerful enough to grant their master's wish. Something I realised too late. I made the wish, so the responsibility for it is mine. Tasnim was a city of wonders, and she died of thirst in the desert because of me."

"Then what are you afraid of?" Anahita still didn't understand.

Philemon reached out and grabbed her hand. Her startled eyes met his — and an intensity she could not look away from.

"Have you ever killed a man who didn't deserve it?" he demanded.

"Of course not. All of them were bastards. Men who killed innocent men and women, not caring who they destroyed as they pursued their desires. They deserved far worse than I gave them, I promise you." Anahita tried to pull her hand back, but he held it fast.

"What do you think I did to Tasnim? I destroyed a city to grant the most insignificant desire. How am I any better than the rest of them? You should have killed me then, but you'll definitely do it when you see the ghost my beautiful city has become."

He released her and urged his camel into a gallop, putting space between them Anahita had no way to close.

It was for the best. Few people had seen Anahita cry, and if the desert drank her tears, no one would ever know how her heart wept for Philemon and all he had lost.

Because he was wrong. He was nothing like Fakhri or Basit or any of the others. None of them had ever showed a moment of remorse for their actions, or even regret.

And as the tears dried on her cheeks in the searing desert heat, she made a new vow. Men might die, but a city's life was in her people. If she could help Philemon return Tasnim to its former glory, then she would do everything in her power to make that happen. Because to turn Philemon the frog into the true prince he deserved to be, he needed his domain back. His home.

Forty

Philemon touched the stone that marked the gates of Tasnim. Twenty men could not move it, but when he laid his hand on it, it rolled aside as though it weighed nothing. Part of the enchantments the door guardian had laid on the place, in the centuries he had watched over the city.

The silence struck him first. The city should be bustling, but it was empty. Of people, of movement, of life. He had done this.

Perhaps he should not show this to Anahita now. He wanted her to see the city at its best, not the empty shell of what it once was.

But without her help…how could he ever bring it back to life?

Reluctantly, he led the way inside.

Anahita's fingers found his, lacing them together as she stood at his side. "So this is the legendary city of Tasnim. It looks like a sandstorm came through, and the people are just waiting for it to be safe before they sweep the sand away."

Sand, not water. Asad's predictions of flooding had not come to pass. He breathed a sigh of relief, but it was short lived. For the sand was deeper than he'd ever seen it.

More than one sandstorm had done this. The air vents and light wells couldn't keep the desert out for long, but it was piled up in drifts against the walls, leaving swathes of stone floor clear to walk across. How long had he been gone?

There was no way of telling down here. Unlike the sand, time had stood still.

He led the way to the well by which he'd last left the city. A quick peek into the houses along the way revealed…little. They'd been left as if their owners had simply gone on a journey, and intended to return. The beds were made up, ready for their owners' return, and some kitchens still had bags and casks of food in them, waiting to be opened for the next meal.

The well hadn't changed a bit. He must have already been a frog when he fell in, Philemon decided. He knelt down beside the low stone wall that normally kept people from falling in, and scrabbled around in the sand. He unearthed a robe. When he shook the sand out of it, he recognised it as the one he'd been wearing that fateful day. If his clothes were here, then his ring of office must be, too – and the door guardian djinn.

Desperately, he sifted through the sand, searching, but no ring emerged. He'd come back later and search, he promised himself.

"Didn't you say the water is all gone?" Anahita asked.

"Yes," Philemon admitted. "We will find a way to bring it back." If such a thing was possible.

"But I can hear it," she insisted. She knelt,

took a pebble from the floor, and threw it into the well. They both heard it plop into water that sounded too deep to be true.

With shaking hands, Philemon lowered his torch as far as he could without falling in. Again. Light gleamed on the water, not far below.

"It's real. It's returned!" he blurted out. He dropped his torch on the ground, wrapped both arms around her, and kissed her. "You did it. I don't know how, but you did!" He kissed her again, and again. He never wanted to stop.

"I didn't do anything!' she protested. "And the water might be back, but where are your people? Do they know the waters have returned?"

He reluctantly turned his mind to more mundane matters. "No, they must not. I must go to the capital and find criers willing to shout it from the rooftops that Tasnim citizens can come home."

"The capital." She did not sound so eager to go home as he thought she'd been.

"Of course. We must also buy provisions,

for I am sure the people took what they could when they left."

This didn't lift her frown at all.

"Would you like to see the fabled jewelled gardens of Tasnim? Words cannot describe their beauty – you must see them with your own eyes to fully appreciate them."

A small smile graced her lips. "I've heard so much about them."

Taking her hand, he led the way to the harem gardens, wishing with all his heart that he would find a way to make this her home.

He stepped into the hall that held the most wondrous trees known to man, lifting his torch so that she might see them better. And stopped.

"What bastard stole my garden?" Philemon roared.

Forty-One

It took time to calm Philemon down and persuade him that the capital was probably the best place to start looking for the thief, though Anahita suspected that the jewels and precious metals had most likely been melted down and made into smaller, more portable things by now.

Nevertheless, he agreed, and within two days, they'd reached the capital. A city that changed little, usually.

"That went up quickly. I didn't know Father intended to build a new palace, and we haven't been gone that long. Do you remember hearing anything about this…edifice?" Anahita asked, peering through the gleaming gates of the brand new palace.

Haidar shrugged. "Nothing at all. Palaces take years to build, not weeks. I smell magic at work."

Magic that could erect a palace in a matter of weeks was potent stuff indeed. Whoever had built this place was more powerful than anyone Anahita had ever met.

Haidar exchanged a few words with the guard, then returned to Anahita's side, his frown deeper than ever. "He said this palace belongs to the Prince of Tasnim and his wife, Princess Maram."

Anahita's mouth dropped open beneath her veil. "Maram will never marry, and the Prince of Tasnim is…" She waved at Philemon.

"Not about to tolerate imposters," Philemon said softly, marching toward the gate with murder in his eyes.

"No, wait," Anahita said. "If Maram has truly married the man, she would never refuse to see me. Or the men with me, for she knows

I am never without Haidar and Asad." She turned to Haidar. "Tell him who I am, and that I wish to seek consolation for my bereavement with my sister."

Haidar bowed low, hiding his grin. "As Your Highness wishes."

While they waited for a guard to find out if Maram was willing to see her sister, Anahita lowered her voice to share her plan. "Haidar, Asad, return to the palace, and see that my things are taken where they belong. Have the servants prepare an evening meal for me, for I will be home then. Philemon can accompany me as my guard – " she laid a hand on his arm, shooting him a meaningful glance " – until we know more. When the time is right, then reveal yourself, and lay the imposter bare."

Philemon inclined his head. "Spoken like a true assassin."

Anahita hushed him, scanning the people around to see if anyone had heard. Thankfully, no one appeared to have been listening.

The gates swung open and both guards bowed. "Princess Maram welcomes Princess Anahita to her home."

Anahita recognised the maid who met them at the door. "Yasmeen? So Maram really is here?"

Yasmeen bowed. "Yes, Princess. This palace was a gift to Her Highness from her new husband. He even built her a bathhouse so that she might not need to cross the city to use the one by the gates. She still does, of course, but not every day now." She giggled. "Her Highness does not like to leave her husband."

"So Maram is…happy to be married?" Anahita ventured.

"I have never seen Her Highness happier." Yasmeen's tone was rich with satisfaction. She definitely approved of Maram's marriage.

"And what of her husband?"

"The Master is most kind."

Master. An interesting title, for a man who styled himself as a prince. Whoever he was, he was wealthier than her own father, for this palace was grander inside than out. Quite a feat. His wealth must have been what swayed the Sultan to let Maram marry. But it would not have won over Maram.

And, unlike most other women in the

harem, Maram would not have confided her secrets to her maid.

So Anahita followed Yasmeen in silence, admiring the mosaics that rose from the floor to cover the walls and the ceiling. Whoever he was, he had an eye for detail and beauty, to command such work for Maram. Perhaps he truly loved her.

What man wouldn't?

Philemon's footsteps echoed angrily behind her, more stomps than steps. A quick glance back told her he had noticed the wealth they walked within, and it only inflamed his temper further. A man who could build such a place had no need to pretend to be a prince. He could have bought himself a small kingdom somewhere with the price he'd have paid for this palace alone.

Then why…?

Maram rose to greet them, her hair flowing like a dark river over her shoulders and her cerise silk gown. "What are you still wearing your veil for?" Maram chided, reaching for Anahita's face.

"Your husband…I thought…" Anahita

stammered.

Maram clucked her tongue. "No need to worry about him. You are among family here."

A hand seized Maram's wrist before she could touch Anahita. "No one touches Princess Anahita without the princess's permission," Philemon rumbled warningly.

Maram's eyes flared blue as the turned her gaze on Philemon. "But to touch Princess Maram is to lose your heart and mind in love for her, for you are not one of her usual men. Are you?" She lifted her captured wrist and spun in his grasp, a graceful dancer's twirl that highlighted her perfect figure as the silk swirled around her.

"Is he why you won't uncover your face, Ana? For he's no eunuch — see?" Maram pointed.

Philemon released Maram and seized Anahita instead, pulling her body against his to shield her from…Maram? Now Anahita couldn't help but notice his arousal, for it grew harder still with the close contact.

"Stand back, witch! Your foul spell will not work on me. I love only one woman, and no witch will tear her from me!" Philemon ripped his sword from its scabbard and pointed it at Maram. "Back, I said!"

After the enchantress who'd cursed him, he could see no good in any magic wielder. He would cut her down, he feared her magic that much.

No. This couldn't happen. Not Maram.

Her blades were in her hands before Anahita had time to think. One at Philemon's throat, while a second aimed for a lower target.

"Drop your sword, or you'll lose the other one," Anahita said. Tears welled up, but she stood firm. No matter how much she loved him, she would not let Philemon hurt her sister.

"Ana…" His eyes widened with betrayal.

"I swore an oath. Hurt her, and you are no better than Basit. And you shall share his fate." She begged him with her eyes. "Drop your sword."

Forty-Two

Philemon could not refuse her. He let the blade clatter to the floor.

Anahita kicked it out of reach. "Get out."

He stared at her. Surely she couldn't mean that.

"Is there anything you wish of me, my princess?" a new voice asked.

He stood in the doorway to the courtyard, too well-dressed to be a servant, yet not proud enough to be a prince. This lean man reminded him of a desert hunting falcon — tamed and kept hungry to serve one of the desert camps, waiting for his mistress's command.

The witch favoured him with a beaming smile. "My sister's man needs some air. Perhaps you could take him into the garden? He might find it cooler under the trees."

The man returned her smile, and bowed deeply. Not like a servant. More like…he was mocking her. He was the witch's lover, Philemon realised. "As you wish, Princess." He turned to the side and gestured toward Philemon. "Please, be my guest."

Philemon risked a glance back at Anahita, but her eyes still blazed with fury. She hadn't sheathed her knives.

Philemon sighed. "Very well." He followed the witch's lover.

"Men who threaten Maram tend to die gruesome deaths. You are the first she has ever invited to see her garden," the man said over his shoulder. "Perhaps it is because you are a man of the desert. The laws of hospitality are strong in the camps, or so I am told. She must be curious to discover what would make a man forget something so fundamental."

Philemon glanced down at his clothes, for

the first time realising what he must look like. He was dressed like a desert sheikh – had they mistaken him for Anahita's dead husband?

"I am not what I appear. I am, in fact, a man of Tasnim," Philemon said.

The witch's lover nodded slowly. "A city known for the high price of its hospitality." A faint smile touched his lips.

"Have you been there?" Philemon demanded.

"Once. I have no desire to return. It is a desolate place." The witch's lover dismissed it with a shrug of his shoulder.

Philemon bristled. "Now the waters have returned, so will its people. Tasnim will live again. I swear it."

"Spoken like a man who loves his home, and knows it is only home because of the people in it. I almost lost everything before I came to realise that. Without Maram, I am nothing." Another shrug, as though this man didn't care that his happiness depended on a woman – and a witch, at that.

"No man is nothing. Return with me to Tasnim, and I will show you that no man is worthless," Philemon said.

The man looked amused. "You would turn me into a man of Tasnim?"

Philemon opened his mouth to correct him, for the right to live in Tasnim was earned, not granted, except in the most unusual circumstances. Like saving the life of the prince, or some other such act of courage and service.

"Behold, the princess's garden." The man turned to the side, to let Philemon precede him. "Have you ever seen anything so wondrous?"

Philemon stepped from darkness into light – and what a wondrous light it was. Fractured rainbows, blinding, glittering, from every angle, both above and below. He shaded his eyes, squinting to find the source of so much light. The noon sun gazed down from above, but there was more to it. It was like standing in a cage of mirrors, or…

Philemon's heart turned to a burning lump of lead in his chest, firing his blood to boiling. "These are the jewelled gardens from the harem of Tasnim. Your Master stole these from me! Tell me his name, and I will grant you full citizenship of my city. He will die for this!" He reached for his sword, but the scabbard was empty. Too late, he realised he'd left the blade behind at Anahita's command, when he needed it now. "You stole these. You visited my city. How?"

A blue cloud erupted between Philemon and the witch's lover. "My Master is no thief, Philemon. I took them as my due, a price for service, as it were. And I was right to do so. Their splendour in sunlight is unmatched. You left them to be buried in dust and blown sand. My greatest creation!" The djinn door guardian spat on the floor at Philemon's feet. "You did not deserve them."

"Kaveh, that is no way to treat a guest in my house," the man chided.

"He means you harm – he threatened your life, just as he drew his sword on the princess!" the djinn insisted.

Realisation dawned on Philemon. "You're not the witch's lover. She's your wife – you're the man who was not content to just pretend to be a prince! My name, my garden…my door guardian! What else have you stolen from me?"

The man pulled a ring off his finger – a ring Philemon recognised. "I did not – "

"No!" the djinn howled, shoving the ring back on his master's finger. "You swore an oath. That ring is not to leave your finger until you pass it to your son on your deathbed!"

A djinn fighting his master? Philemon would not have believed such a thing was possible, if he hadn't seen it with his own eyes.

Philemon held out his hand. "That is my ring of office. I demand you hand it over, along with mastery of that disobedient djinn."

The djinn glared back at him. "You cast the ring aside, along with everyone else in the city, when you deserted us. Fadi sold that ring to a silversmith, so that he would have the money to feed your people. An evil wizard bought it, and gave it to Aladdin. It belongs to him and you shall not have it!"

Philemon ignored him. The fake prince was the key, he knew it. What had the djinn said his name was? "Aladdin, give me my ring, or I will tell your wife who is the real Prince of Tasnim. Let's see if Princess Maram wishes to be your wife when she knows the truth!"

"Please, enlighten me," a female voice purred.

The witch.

Philemon reached for his dagger.

"Oh, don't bother," she said. "She's gone home to her apartments in the Sultan's palace, and you've made your preferences perfectly clear. You fancy my sister, and against her better judgement and my own, she's still partial to you. She's never taken a lover before. She's more likely to take a man's life, than take him to bed. You must have been quite persuasive, Prince Philemon of Tasnim."

Philemon sagged. "Not persuasive enough, if she has left me."

Aladdin had the right of it. The world was empty without the woman he loved. He stared at the fake prince with sympathy, for the first time. The djinn had vanished.

"Perhaps not." The witch wet her lips. "Would you care for a wager, Philemon?"

"What do you have that I want?"

The witch smiled. "By the sound of things, everything. Your garden. Your title. Your symbol of office. And the woman you wish to be your wife."

She had him. "What do I have that you want?" Philemon asked, his heart sinking. He was back to promising all the wealth of Tasnim to a witch. If she turned him into a frog again…Anahita would not save him this time, he was sure of it.

"The power to make my dearest sister happy," she said. Her eyes filled with tears. "I would gamble my garden for that."

Philemon drew closer. "What do you mean?"

Maram waved her hand and a servant appeared. "Bring us refreshments. We have business to discuss." The maid scurried away.

Maram gazed into Philemon's eyes. A frank assessment of his soul, without a hint of the seduction she'd tried earlier. "You will go speak to the Sultan, and you will tell them Aladdin is your younger half-brother. And then you will tell him that seeing your brother's happiness, you must be married to another of my sisters at once."

Philemon shook his head. "Anahita will

never agree to it. You didn't see the way she looked at me."

Maram wet her lips. "That is where the wager comes in. If this works, she will be your wife, and I keep my garden. If this does not work…I will ask my husband to have another garden crafted for you to replace this one. Do we have a deal?"

Hope danced before Philemon, like Anahita on her wedding night. Tantalising, but too far away to touch. "And if she decides she wants me dead instead?"

Maram laughed. "If my sister wanted you dead, you'd be lying in a pool of your own blood in my reception room. Anahita does not hesitate…or she didn't, before you."

Could he gamble everything for love?

He stared at Aladdin, the pretend prince, who only had eyes for Maram. Her dark eyes were firmly fixed on Philemon.

"Yes," Philemon said. "Yes, we have a deal."

Forty-Three

The moment the men vanished, Maram tore the veil from Anahita's head. "Where did he hurt you?" she demanded, examining Anahita's face.

Anahita shook her head. "He didn't. Philemon has been everything I ever dreamed of until he threatened you."

"That's not Sheikh Basit?" Maram asked.

"No. Basit was old, fat, boring, and a bastard. He's also dead and buried. Philemon even tried to take the blame. Basit's people believed him." Because no one believed a woman was capable of defending herself, or killing a dangerous man. Least of all the men who'd died at her hands.

"So who is he, and where did you find him?" Maram asked.

The Prince of Tasnim, as a frog perched atop her hawk's head, soaring and screaming above an oasis. Anahita shook her head. "You won't believe me."

Maram smiled. "Would you believe I married a humble spinner's son, a man so poor he could scarcely afford to eat, who wandered into the wrong bathhouse?"

Anahita's mouth dropped open. "You mean…you married your lover from the bathhouse? I thought he was supposed to be a prince!"

Maram pressed a finger to her lips. "Father thinks so, which is why he agreed to the marriage. The palace helped, though."

"How did a man who couldn't afford food pay for this palace?" Anahita asked slowly.

"A particularly powerful djinn built it. He served Aladdin for a time, but now he is free."

Dread curled around Anahita's heart. "Djinn

are dangerous. Especially powerful ones. A djinn was responsible for the wells drying up in Tasnim. They grant wishes with no thought as to the consequences, and do not care to repair the damage they cause. If a djinn built this palace, then there is surely trouble coming. Where did he get the building materials, the artisans…you cannot trust a djinn!"

Maram's smile only widened. "I trust this one. He was a friend of my mother's. He would not make trouble for me, and now he is free…I trust him even more. Not all djinn are troublemakers. It is their masters who make the trouble, Amani told me, for djinn are slaves to their masters' will."

Philemon's words on the way to Tasnim began to make sense. "So if a djinn's former master said the ruin of Tasnim was his fault, then…"

Maram shrugged. "He's probably right. But Tasnim is not ruined — it's merely deserted. Locked up and hard to get into, Aladdin said."

"I've seen it," Anahita said. "He's right. But now the water has returned to the wells, the people can return, and Philemon…"

"He's handsome, your Philemon. What sort of lover is he?" Maram demanded.

Anahita felt her cheeks grow hot. "I…I…have little to compare him to, but…I think…he is…a fine lover…" Anahita broke off at Maram's laughter.

"You mean he truly is your lover? Ah, never have I been so mistaken. First I thought him the sheikh, then another lovesick eunuch to join the others…I am sorry I tried to seduce him." Maram looked suitably contrite, before her gaze turned thoughtful. "Though I have never been threatened at swordpoint to stop seducing a man. Usually they don't want me to stop. Instead, he grabbed you and professed his love for you. You've caught a strange one, there, Ana. Does he have other peculiarities, perhaps?"

She should never have drawn her blades. Not on Philemon. He'd been defending her, defending their love. "I told him to go away." Anahita burst into tears. "He said he loved me and I sent him away!"

"But he didn't go far. I've known a lot of men, and if he'd wanted to leave you, he would have. He'll come to find you, soon enough. Perhaps you should head home to Father's palace, and wash away the travel dust so that you can greet him properly when he does." She glanced toward the garden. "Aladdin will keep him occupied until then."

Her husband. Philemon. Tasnim. Anahita grasped Maram's arm. "But Philemon is the real Prince of Tasnim, and he thinks your husband is an imposter, pretending to be him. He wanted to kill him!"

Maram paled. "Then go. I will broker a peace between them. Diplomacy is my strength, after all. Wash, rest, and wait!" She ordered some guards to take Anahita to the palace, before hurrying out to the garden.

Anahita longed to stay, but short of fighting her way through Maram's men — a feat she doubted she'd manage without Haidar and Asad to help her — she had little choice but to go home with them, and hope her sister was right.

Maram was rarely wrong…but if this was the one time, Anahita might never see Philemon again. She prayed her sister had not lost her touch with men, or diplomacy. For Anahita's heart depended on both.

524

Forty-Four

Philemon took a deep breath as he surveyed the Sultan's audience chamber. He knew this was just a formality, for the Sultan's matchmaker had agreed to the marriage long before he turned frog, but that didn't stop his heart from leaping into his throat in fear if something went wrong.

But it would not. He was a prince – a true prince, unlike Aladdin – and a fitting husband for any princess. Or so he told himself.

A commotion at the gate told him Aladdin's servants had arrived, with his gift. The crowd parted, waves of an ancient sea at the command of a prophet. Or a prince.

"A gift to the Sultan from His Royal Highness, Prince Philemon of Tasnim!" the door guardian djinn – Kaveh – roared, his voice perfectly pitched to resonate through the hall.

Not for the first time, Philemon regretted losing the loyalty of the ancient vizier. But he didn't have time to dwell on it.

"Where is this prince?" the Sultan demanded. "Tell him to show his face, so that I may thank him for such a handsome gift."

It was identical to what he'd received from Aladdin in exchange for permission to marry Maram, even down to the livery of the servants. The Sultan was not fool enough to refuse it.

But Philemon was not Aladdin – he needed no fanfare or parade to announce his presence. A true prince commanded attention, or he did not deserve his crown.

Philemon strode into the archway that marked the boundary between the dim throne room and the dazzling desert daylight. He stood in the light, silhouetted against the morning sun. "I am here. I have come to claim my bride, a daughter of the Sultan to become the new Princess of Tasnim."

The crowd buzzed, but they did not hinder his march toward the dais where the Sultan sat.

When Philemon reached the row of prostrate servants presenting their gifts of gold and jewels, he stopped and bowed. Just low enough for his eyes to meet those of the seated Sultan.

The Sultan looked shaken.

Because of Aladdin, Philemon guessed.

"When I saw how happy my younger half-brother, Aladdin, was with his wife, I refused to wait any longer. I must marry, and it must be one of your daughters," Philemon continued.

If this didn't work, Philemon vowed he'd force Aladdin to confess the truth at the point of his sword, no matter what his witch of a wife wanted.

In the shadows behind the Sultan's throne, a woman leaned forward and whispered something into the Sultan's ear. He gave the slightest nod, then rose.

"This audience is at an end for today. I will hear more petitions on the morrow. I will meet privately with the Prince of Tasnim," the Sultan announced.

The court slowly emptied, until the golden doors closed with a clunk of finality.

Only then did the woman step out of the shadows. Her gown, which Philemon had taken for plain black, glittered in the light, for the wine-coloured linen was embroidered with jewels.

The Sultan did not miss Philemon's interest in the mysterious woman. "If you wish to discuss marriage, my matchmaker must be present. She knows which of my daughters are suitable."

Philemon nodded. The woman hadn't been so richly dressed when he last met her, but it made sense to have her there. Though he would be the judge of who was suitable, not her.

The matchmaker led the way into the palace proper, choosing a chamber that was better suited to an intimate discussion than the audience hall. One more richly furnished than the place where he'd first met with the woman, if indeed this was the same one. For the matchmaker he'd met here before hadn't swished her hips quite that seductively as she walked. Nor had she been the first to sit on the floor cushions, as this one did.

She'd surprised the Sultan, too, Philemon noticed, hiding his grin.

Philemon and the Sultan took their seats and servants brought in refreshments, before departing at a signal from the matchmaker. This door clicked shut so quietly Philemon was barely aware of it.

The woman threw off her veil and reached for a cup of wine.

Maram. Her haughty brows furrowed when she found both men staring at her. "He's family, Father. Aladdin's brother. Perhaps if we find him a wife, he'll learn to stop staring at women's faces when he is fortunate enough to see one." She sipped from her wine cup, then shot a red-lipped smile in Philemon's direction. "If my brother-in-law can tell us what he wants in a wife, perhaps I can help him."

"I want Anahita," he blurted out, closing his eyes to better resist the spell she seemed to cast simply by looking at him.

The Sultan cleared his throat. "My daughter Anahita is in mourning, for she has only recently been widowed. It will be some time before she is ready to wed again, if ever."

"And the daughter of a mere concubine – hardly fitting for such an important prince," Maram interjected. "I am sure one of Mahsa, the Moon Queen's daughters, would be far better suited. She has two daughters of marriageable age – Katayun and Mahvash. Mahvash is the image of her mother – sweet and obedient, and likely just as fertile. Katayun has been well trained by her mother in the practicalities of running a harem, and well able to keep your other wives and concubines in order. I have heard tales that the Prince of Tasnim's harem rivals my father's own, and a young, virile man like yourself without an heir…"

"I want Anahita," Philemon repeated. "I want her as my wife, and no one else. Now." He wished the woman wasn't here – her very presence set his teeth on edge, and made him most irritable. Left alone with the Sultan, he would not have announced his desire so directly, nor demanded it. There would have been conversation, negotiation…but the witch wanted him to fail. Why else would she be making this so difficult?

"But her husband has only just died," Maram snapped, eyeing him with considerable irritation.

If he failed, he'd get his harem garden back…but what use was it without Anahita? What use was anything without her?

Last night, Maram had insisted if he followed her plan, he would win Anahita back. Now, it was as though last night had never happened. Or was this woman one of Maram's sisters, identical in appearance to Maram, but not the same person?

If she wasn't Maram, then he had nothing to fear from her.

Philemon rose to his feet. "I am her husband, by the laws of the desert people. Sheikh Basit's death frightened her, and she refused to be left alone. She shared my tent that night, and the marriage was sealed by a wedding breakfast at dawn the next day. I will not leave the city until you return my wife to me!"

A wicked smile appeared on the woman's face, which dissolved into a shocked expression as quickly as it had appeared. "But one of the Sultan's virtuous daughters would not…could not…"

It was Philemon's turn to smile. "She already carries my child. And the child will be born in Tasnim, as the heir to the principality should be!" It was possible, therefore not entirely a lie.

Maram's eyes danced with mischief – for this woman could be no one else. "How do you know it is not Sheikh Basit's baby in her belly?"

Philemon drew himself up. "Because I slew the man myself before the consummation could occur."

"You killed him?" The Sultan stared.

If Philemon had ever doubted Anahita was her father's assassin, the doubts died then and there. "He encroached on Tasnim's territory, attacking towns that were under my protection, and we do not treat such things lightly." Philemon allowed the Sultan a small smile. "I'm sure if you were in my position, you would have done the same."

The Sultan looked thoughtful for a moment, before turning to Maram. "Fetch her," he commanded.

Maram obeyed.

Once the door had shut behind her, the Sultan poured himself a cup of wine and gestured for Philemon to do the same. "I had heard that Tasnim's wells ran dry."

Philemon's mouth was drier. "They did, but the waters have returned, sweeter and more plentiful than ever," he managed to say. He poured, then drank. "Tasnim is a worthy ally for anyone who wishes to travel and trade across the desert."

"So it is. But what if you were to suffer some misfortune? Who would be the ruler of Tasnim then?" the Sultan asked.

"The city will pass to the child my wife carries," Philemon said slowly.

"A child cannot hold a city, especially an

unborn one. Surely your brother would inherit instead."

Brother? Oh, Aladdin.

"Hence my need for a wife. One who has proven fertile already," Philemon managed to say, feigning nonchalance to cover the chill that had crept over his heart. Did the Sultan intend to have him assassinated so that Aladdin could steal the city?

But the Sultan's assassin was…

"Ah, Anahita. Good. I have some questions for you, child," the Sultan said.

Anahita stood awkwardly before the closed door, staring at her father. "Yes, Father?"

"Who killed Sheikh Basit?" the Sultan demanded.

Anahita wet her lips. "Why, Prince Philemon, of course. It was terrifying to see him strike the blow. Ask anyone in Basit's camp."

The Sultan seemed surprised, then relieved.

Because his daughter hadn't killed a man?

No, because Philemon didn't know that she had, Philemon decided.

"Are you carrying his child?"

Philemon closed his eyes.

Forty-Five

"Are you carrying his child?" the Sultan repeated.

Anahita shot a dark glance at Maram. Damn her spies. "Yes," Anahita admitted. "The midwife confirmed it this morning."

Philemon's child, not Basit's, but she could not tell her father that. Nor Philemon, while her father was listening.

"Take the girl, then," the Sultan said. "I wish you well of her."

Philemon rose and took her arm. "Thank you."

Anahita found herself in the corridor with Philemon. "What are you – " she began

"You are my wife, and I am taking you home," he interrupted, heading down the corridor as though he knew where he was going.

Anahita wrenched free. "What are you doing? The harem's that way, and even if my father has given me to you like some bauble, he will not let you have any of his own wives and concubines."

"Then how do we get out of this palace?" Philemon looked bewildered.

Anahita took pity on him. "This way," she said. Behind her, she heard the familiar footsteps of Haidar and Asad as they followed her, and she breathed a sigh of relief. No matter what her father said, she would never be some prince's plaything.

"If you know the way to a good inn, that would help, too," Philemon said softly, glancing around.

"Asad will know the best," she said. "But I have apartments here in the palace, and my sister Maram – "

"Has spies everywhere," Philemon finished.

A flash of understanding sparked between them. "Asad will lead the way, and Haidar will make sure we are not followed," Anahita said.

The two men moved into place, setting a steady pace that moved easily through the busy streets. Philemon was stiff and agitated at her side, but he didn't say another word until they were behind the closed door of the best room in what Asad insisted was the most prestigious inn in the city.

"Your father and your sister want you to kill me, so her husband can have Tasnim," Philemon said. He pulled his knife from its sheath and flipped it so it lay hilt-first in his hand. "Take it and use it now. I would rather die at this very moment than to be stabbed in the back when I believed I was happy."

Anahita stared at the knife, and then him, in horror. "I don't know of any such plan. Maram would never want Tasnim, for it is too isolated for her. She'd be bored without harem and court politics to play with."

"The Sultan made it clear he wants my city. He wanted to know all about the succession, should some misfortune befall me!"

Anahita touched her belly. "How did you know about the baby? Even I didn't know for sure until this morning."

"I guessed! I lied! I don't know!" Philemon exploded. "He wasn't going to let me marry you…and then, suddenly, he changed his mind and handed you to me. Like merchants trade their daughters for Tasnim's hospitality. I would have carried you to the city as its princess, a ruler who would sit at my side, but not like this." He thrust the knife at her, hilt-first. "Do it! If you are truly his assassin, cut out my heart. For it cannot hurt as much as it does now, knowing the woman I love will kill me." He tore open his shirt, baring his breast.

Anahita seized the knife and flung it, point down, into the floor. "I will not!" she said fiercely. "I am not my father's assassin! I killed men who deserved their fate — animals who would have killed me, given the chance. You are not like them, and I will not help anyone who tries to take Tasnim from you!"

He was the one talking of heartache, yet hers felt like it was ready to break. Her father has used her as a pawn to destroy his enemies, but she would no longer play politics. That was Maram's world, not hers. And if Maram could marry…so could she.

She stared into Philemon's eyes. "Marry me," she said. "And then take me home to Tasnim with you."

He dropped his gaze and her heart sank with it.

"Please," she begged, then kissed him.

The fire built between them, burning as bright as their first kiss. He wanted her – Anahita knew that. But then why…?

He set his hands on her shoulders and broke the kiss. "I cannot marry you, because we are already married." His eyes begged her to understand.

She shook her head. "We can't be. I'd remember."

Still he didn't smile. "By the laws of the desert people, when a couple share a tent for the night and share a morning meal afterward, they are married. The night Sheikh Basit died…" He shook his head. "In the panic of that night, I forgot what I should have known.

And with you in my arms…I lost my mind entirely. You are everything I ever wished for in a wife, and more. I should have left you alone that night, but I could not resist you."

Memories of that first night brought a blush to Anahita's cheeks. She had not been able to resist him, either, nor had she wanted to. As for letting her sleep in that tent alone…Anahita had begged him to stay when he'd suggested leaving. Realisation dawned. "That's how we broke the curse." The very night she'd vowed to do anything Philemon needed to break it, she already had.

"Perhaps. It was my first curse, and, I hope, my last." Philemon drew in a deep breath. "So…you aren't angry at me for wedding you without you being aware of it? Without asking for your consent to the match?" He rushed to continue before she could respond. "If you are, say the word and I will divorce you, though it would break my heart to do so. I could not force you into a match you do not desire."

"No, you wouldn't." She remembered the passion of that first night, and every night after. Until last night's loneliness, not knowing if she would ever see him again. "I came to you willingly, Philemon. Every night since, and so I intend to continue. Together, with you. No talk of divorce or cutting out hearts. I am your wife. I am your *wife*." The word tasted good on her lips.

"My one and only." Now his smile appeared, and it was blindingly bright. His arms slid around her, pulling her close. His kiss held the promise of everything she'd ever wanted.

She laid her head against his bare chest, where his heartbeat thrummed under her cheek. "Take me home to Tasnim, my Frog Prince."

"Anything for the princess who saved me."

Forty-Six

"Here she is, Your Highness," a man's voice said. Not Haidar or Asad.

Anahita settled Vega on her glove and turned to face the newcomer.

She had to look up to meet the eyes of a tall woman in purple. Even her eyes were that unusual colour.

"Who is this?" Anahita asked coolly.

The bowing servant straightened, and she was surprised to see he wore nothing but a loincloth, like some lowly slave.

"I am Lord Kaveh, once the Grand Vizier

of Tasnim, now slave to the ring that was once the prince's ring of office. My magic still runs strong through these tunnels, and the doors still open to my touch. I serve Prince Aladdin now," the man said smoothly.

The man who had made the jewelled gardens, Anahita remembered. But that did not give him the right to intrude in her private chambers. She'd set Vega on him if he woke the baby.

"I meant the woman."

He bowed again, even lower and more elaborately this time. "Your Highness, Princess Zuleika the Enchantress, Mistress of Beacon Isle, may I present Her Highness, Princess Anahita, the Princess of Tasnim?"

Anahita stared. This was the woman who had cursed Philemon and the city? She didn't look a day older than Anahita herself, and…was she pregnant? Philemon had never said anything about her being a princess, either. This wasn't the witch she'd imagined at all.

Zuleika inclined her head. "I heard that people were returning to Tasnim, now their prince had been found. There was even talk about the wells refilling. I had to see this for myself. Particularly the princess who could fall in love with a frog."

"He was never truly a frog. He didn't talk like one. And no frog has ever attacked one of my hunting falcons the way he did," Anahita said.

The enchantress closed her eyes. "Ah, you are a witch, then. Your magic is faint, but I see it now. That must be useful. Even I would have to bespell the bird for it to sit as contently as yours does. Especially underground."

"She has the freedom of the air and light wells whenever she wishes. So does Merlin, though she prefers to fish in the wells beneath the city, for she is fond of frogs. All my birds are free to come and go as they wish. I do not believe in enslaving anyone." Anahita sniffed. "I would not expect some barbarian king's daughter to understand."

Zuleika's eyes snapped open. "I am the daughter of an enchantress, not some king or prince. But I married one, and this one will be king when his uncle dies." She patted her belly. Definitely pregnant. "I have seen more of the world – and of slavery – than you ever will, daughter of the desert. I think if more women ruled this world than the foolish men who mess it up now, we might see an end to such things. But I cannot turn all of them into frogs, so it will not be in my lifetime." She smiled sadly.

Frogs or corpses – what was worse? Fakhri, Basit and their ilk would never trouble the world again, while frogs could be redeemed. Or maybe Philemon was unique in that. "It will take more than one woman to change the world. This city is enough for me," Anahita said. This girl…woman…whatever she was, was more like Maram than Anahita. One who played at politics, who had more power than Anahita could ever want.

"Keeping the Prince of Tasnim from drying up the city's wells through more foolishness is certainly enough to keep any woman busy," Zuleika said.

"At least nothing a good storm can't fix," Anahita said, thinking of what Asad had told her about the rivers that ran below the desert dunes. A wail rose from the next room. Mirza was awake. She sighed. "And teach my son to be better."

Zuleika nodded. "You should know Philemon promised me a great deal of gold for helping him. Gold which is still in your treasury, for he refused to pay me. I have no need of it now, so you may keep it. Consider it a wedding gift, or a wager, if you will, for I never thought there would be a woman willing to do what you have. Loving a frog – ha! Even my husband would not believe it. Wait until I tell him."

Anahita opened her mouth to thank her for her generosity, but the enchantress had vanished. So had the djinn.

Anahita tended to Mirza and fed him until he fell asleep, but the enchantress did not return.

And all was well in Tasnim, safe beneath the desert sands, where the wells never ran dry again.

Hunt:
Red Riding Hood Retold

DEMELZA CARLTON

A tale in the Romance a Medieval Fairy Tale series

One

"Once upon a time, a king fell in love with the goddess of love. They were very happy together, and she bore him a son.

"Though he had many older sons by his previous wives, she wanted him to name this child his heir. But the king did not.

"This king worshipped an ancient god of the forest, who had protected his kingdom for generations, and he prayed daily at the god's altar.

"One day, when he was at his prayers, his goddess wife came to find him. Instead of praying like he usually did, the king had her son lying on top of the altar, and the king beseeched his god to take the boy as his servant, to better protect the kingdom.

"The goddess was incensed – the boy was hers, he did not belong to some god of trees – so she snatched the child up in her arms. Only to discover that the boy no longer drew breath – the king had sacrificed him to his barbaric god, who relished such things.

"She raised her hand to strike the king dead, as he had struck her son, but the king's youngest son, whose mother had died birthing him, came running in, and wrapped himself about the queen's legs, for he saw her as the only mother he had known, and loved both her and his little brother dearly.

"The king feared for his son, and begged for the boy's life.

"The queen – not just a goddess, but a powerful sorceress, too – called down a terrible storm. The raging winds destroyed the palace, and lightning struck each of the king's sons, killing them instantly. All but the youngest, who she allowed to live.

"The king she turned into a white wolf, so pale the shepherds of his flocks instantly saw him coming, and chased him away until he vanished into the deep woods, high into the mountains.

"The youngest son became king, building a new capital closer to the trade routes, and he ushered in a time of great prosperity for the kingdom, because he was greatly favoured by both his father's god and the goddess of love, his stepmother.

"She favoured him so much that she allowed him to marry one of her own daughters by her new lover, and both king and queen were very happy and had many children.

"But the old king, the white wolf…he stayed in the mountains, hidden from humans, until the worst winter snows covered the towns. Only then would he venture out, his white fur blending perfectly with the snow, as he hunted for the enchantress who had killed his sons."

"But did he ever find her, Grandmother?" Rosa asked.

Grandmother flashed an enigmatic smile. "The tales never say, so I suppose he did not. Perhaps his time came, and he died, and that's where his story ends."

Rosa wrinkled her nose. "Or perhaps it is nothing more than a tale, and this king never truly lived at all."

"Perhaps," Grandmother agreed. She glanced out the window, where the late afternoon light was already turning the shutters rosy. "But it never hurts to be careful, especially on your way home through the forest. Practise your magic, too, on your way. I'm not sure what will fall first, snow or night, but you'd best be home before both. And don't forget to take the medicine for Edda. She might not last the winter, but we must help her all we can to see the spring."

Rosa thought of the ancient woman, who never left her cottage now. "Edda has seen many springs already. What good is one more?"

Another enigmatic smile. "When it might be your last, you will always fight for one more. One more season, one more day…perhaps even one more minute, for a lot can be said in that time. But I pray it is a long time before you know the truth of it in your heart. Now, go home, child, and don't forget your cloak, for you will need it in the snow."

"Yes, Grandmother." Rosa lifted the brand new cloak her grandmother had given her only hours before, and flung it around her shoulders. The fine red wool hung heavily, so that none but the strongest gust of wind could disturb it. It was the cloak of a lady or a princess, not a carpenter's daughter. All her other cloaks had been brown, to match her humble station. To wear something so rich and vibrant seemed to scream for attention from the very heavens themselves.

"The village needs to see you for what you are, for one day, when I am gone, you will be their witch, and they will need to know who to come to," Grandmother said, as if reading her thoughts.

If she was simply a healer, a woman who knew her herbs, it would be fine, but if the town knew her magic was the elemental kind, and far more powerful than her grandmother's…Rosa gulped. The other girls already thought her strange. If they knew what she could do…

"Be off with you, child! And practise!" Grandmother shooed her out of the house.

Two

For the first time in his life, Chase didn't know what to do. Now Maja was gone, and Abraham, too, he was all alone in the world. But one thing was certain: the king had made it clear he could not stay here. So, he would depart.

Chase sold Abraham's horse for a good price, and tucked the coins into the pouch at his waist. He had enough money to get him to almost any kingdom in the civilised world, and for the first time in his life, he was free to choose who he served.

King Erik's court in Aros was famed for its tourneys, and he could win any archery contest with his eyes closed. Perhaps it was time to aim high and attach himself to a royal court, to see how his fortunes fared there. Better than his brother's fortune, he'd wager, for Heber's land was not so fruitful of late, or so his last letter had said.

Yes, he would go to Aros.

There was nothing left for him here.

Sir Chase mounted his mare, and set off on his quest for fame and fortune.

Three

Rosa hurried home. She told herself it was because of the lateness of the hour, but in her heart she knew the truth. Her wild imagination had been so caught up in her grandmother's tale that more than once, she fancied she saw a shadow lurking behind the trees, following her home.

She tried to distract herself by practising, as her grandmother had said, but her magic didn't seem to want to cooperate today. Snow started falling, too, and she couldn't be sure if the flurries were her powers at work, or the natural movement of the breeze.

Snow already lay thick on the ground in the village by the time she reached it. She reached for the door of her family's cottage.

"Lule, I told you to put down your sewing and cut up the vegetables for the soup!" Mother scolded.

"Why can't Rosa do it?" Lule whined.

"Because she's still at your grandmother's, and if the snow keeps falling like this, she might not be home until morning. Your father's bringing fresh straw for our beds, and as soon as he gets home, I'll be busy dealing with that. Do you want supper or don't you?"

"Yes, Mother."

Rosa drew her hand back under her cloak. She hated cutting onions, and there were always so many for the soup. Let Lule do it for once. Rosa could take her grandmother's package to Edda in the meantime. Maybe when she came back, the soup would be ready and she wouldn't have to make it this time.

Four

Sir Chase rode through the gates, sparing a nod of approval for the stout construction of the King of Aros' castle. The thickness of the walls spoke of the kingdom's strength, while the gaily coloured clothing of those who walked within its walls whispered of wealth. Service here would suit him well.

A groom appeared to take care of his horse, and Chase dismounted. He lingered long enough to throw his saddlebags over his own shoulder before allowing the beast to be led off. He'd heard the telltale thwack of arrows in the practice range, and he fancied taking a shot of his own. One that would reach the ears of the queen.

In one gate, out another, and he found the practice field, where a trio of men at arms took their turns at a target. They certainly needed the practice – none had managed to hit more than the outer circle of the target. Chase's father would not have tolerated such sloppy shots, especially at that distance. Why, he stood three times the distance as they did from the target, and he had the perfect shot.

His bow was off his back and in his hands before he'd finished the thought. He strung it with the ease of practice, and plucked an arrow from his quiver. He drew, sighted, breathed and loosed, his thoughts following the arrow's flight between the three men, then across the field to sink squarely into the centre of the target.

Exclamations of horror came from the men as they turned to find the source of the arrow, which turned to words of wonder at the size of his bow and the strength it must take to wield it.

Chase held it out. "Here, you try," he offered. The bow was taller than the man who took it from him. But Chase thought the stocky guard might have the strength to draw it, all the same.

A pleasant afternoon of archery ensued. Chase could definitely get used to this. Maybe even call Aros home.

The sound of a throat clearing drew Chase's attention and that of his companions.

"Sir Knight, Her Majesty, Queen Margareta, requests your presence at dinner in the Great Hall," the herald said.

Chase grinned. "I'd be honoured. Is there anywhere I might bathe and make myself presentable to greet Her Majesty?"

"An apartment has been prepared. Follow me, Sir Knight."

"It's Chase. Sir Chase," Chase said.

The herald breathed a sigh of relief. "Sir Chase. Whence have you come, Sir Chase?"

Chase considered. Who knew how far word had spread about Abraham? He did not dare risk it. "I have travelled from lands so far away I doubt you have heard of them," he said grandly.

The herald's eyes widened. "Are you a Crusader, sir? Or have you come from the Holy Land? Have you fought in many battles?"

Chase chose the truth. "Many battles indeed." Fought with his brothers and Abraham in the courtyard, with sticks and then swords. Abraham had always bested him with a sword. Ah, but he would miss the man, brother in all but blood.

"His Majesty, King Erik, is fond of tales of battle. Perhaps he will ask you to regale us at dinner," the herald said.

"I fear I am no bard, or teller of tales. I speak best with sword and bow," Chase said.

The herald led the way inside. "Then you must tell what you can to one of the Queen's bards, so that he may tell the tale."

Tell Abraham's story? Who would believe it? Chase himself barely believed it, and he'd seen most of it with his own eyes. Enough to know the truth when Abraham had told him the rest.

He only had to look at his tourney armour to be reminded, for after many jugs of ale, he'd persuaded Abraham to lay his hands on the well-crafted leather. Now it was as beautiful as it was useless, for Abraham's warning that gold would be too soft for combat proved only too true. But if it would buy him a place in the royal court of Aros, he would consider his armour a small price to pay.

Five

It was nigh on midnight by the time Rosa left Edda's cottage, full of far more than soup. It had been the old woman's name day, and every member of her family had visited her with gifts and blessings. Edda had insisted Rosa eat some of the cakes Edda's toothless maw could no longer devour, and tell her what they tasted like.

Then she'd prepared the medicinal tea her grandmother had sent, and read to Edda from the great bible the Baron himself had sent her. Tales of men rising from the dead, when even the weakest witch knew such things were not possible. Magic could only accomplish so much.

When Edda's eyes drifted shut and she began to snore, Rosa dared to close the book and set it back on the table. Rosa wrapped her cloak around herself and set out for home.

Halfway there, she wished she'd brought a lantern, for the cloudy sky and blowing snow made it too dark to see, but the wind would have only blown it out. Fortunately, the cold meant everyone kept their fires burning through the night, and enough light peeped through the gaps in the shutters that she could discern the houses.

Even if she hadn't lived in the village her whole life, she'd have known her family cottage by the smell of soup – evidently Lule had made it, with some to spare. She pushed the door open, careful to make as little noise as possible, and closed it behind her.

Rosa frowned. The fire burned low in the grate – as though no one had stoked it before going to bed. Strange. And the soup still hung over the coals, bubbling sluggishly. That wasn't normal, either. Inside, the smell of soup was so strong it was almost overpowering, but there was a whiff of something else lurking beneath it, too. Something…rotten.

Like the Baron's slaughterhouse close to Midsummer feast day.

Ah, it was late. She could help her mother search for the offending piece of meat in the morning, when it was lighter. Now, she should rekindle the fire, set the soup somewhere to cool, then head up to bed.

She threw a handful of kindling on the coals, then grabbed a cloth to unhook the cauldron from the fire. She could barely lift it – why, the cauldron was almost full, as if her family had prepared dinner, then not eaten it.

Rosa felt the air behind her shift, almost imperceptibly, and whirled to face whatever had caused it, swinging the cauldron around with her.

Soup splashed out, covering the enormous, ghostly shape that was there one moment, before it retreated into the darkness again.

Rosa seized a torch and thrust it into the fire until the pitch caught, then turned to face whatever it was.

Blue eyes burned in the darkness, where someone crouched low, ready to spring. Someone, or something?

"Show yourself," Rosa hissed, hoping she sounded braver than she felt. "I said show yourself, coward!"

She hadn't imagined it. Something huge and white came soaring out of the shadows. Something with teeth bigger than any human she'd ever seen.

Rosa's grip tightened on her torch, splinters digging into her fingers, but she didn't care. The oozing blood would be the monster's undoing, not hers, as she summoned her magic and swung the torch.

The flaming end of the torch collided with the creature, and a gust of air came from nowhere, adding power to the blow so that it carried the creature past Rosa and into the fireplace itself, where the flames blazed to life.

The creature yelped, then howled, as it struggled to get up with its white fur on fire. A streak of orange and white and red, it fled for the door, hitting it with such force that the door flew open, releasing the beast into the blizzard outside.

Rosa blinked, trying to make sense of what she'd seen. In her mind's eye, it had been a giant, white wolf, like something out of a fairytale. A scary fairytale.

A red and white wolf, her memory reminded her. The red of blood…

Her hand flew to her mouth as the leaping flames lit the scene she hadn't seen until now. A pair of feet stuck out from under the kitchen table, wearing Lule's house slippers. Father lay behind the door, blind eyes staring at the rafters as his hands seemed to reach for his throat, which was no longer there.

Mother lay facedown behind the woodpile, as if the creature had brought her down as she tried to run. Her neck, too, was a bloody ruin. Beside her was a basket of straw, which had started to smoke. Sparked by the beast running past her with its fur ablaze.

Even as she hesitated, the basket flared up fully, flames licking at the curtains.

Rosa's weary mind was slow to make sense of it all. Her family was dead, some giant wolf had killed them, and now her home was on fire.

Her home was on fire. And filling with smoke.

If she didn't want to join them in death, she had to get out. Now.

Coughing, Rosa staggered for the door, pausing only to grab the poker. If the wolf waited for her outside, she'd take the bastard with her to hell for this.

But outside there was nothing but clean snow, with no sign of the beast, or anyone else, either.

"Fire!" she coughed out, hoping someone would hear her. "Fire! Help!"

Doors began to open along the street, spilling light out onto the snow.

But it was too late. By the time the sun rose the next day, all that remained of her family home was a burned out shell, where her family had breathed their last.

The other villagers headed home, to breakfast and all the normal things they did every day.

Rosa knelt in the ashes and swore an oath of

vengeance. The beast would die at her hand for what he'd stolen from her.

"Your Majesties, may I present to you, the renowned knight from far off lands, the hero of countless battles, the mighty Sir Chase!" the herald bellowed.

Glad his helmet hid his grin at such flowery exaggeration, Chase strode into the hall. His stupid armour turned his usually smooth stride into more of a stiff march, but no one seemed to notice his discomfort. Instead, all they seemed to want to stare, wide-eyed, as though they'd never seen a man in armour before.

The king – Erik, Chase reminded himself –

rose and announced, "On the morrow, we shall hold a tourney so that you may all test your skills against such a legendary hero – "

Whatever else he said was drowned out by cheers and toasts to the king's health as the hall erupted on either side of Chase.

When Chase finally reached the dais where the king sat, instinct told him to kneel, but he could not – his benighted armour wouldn't let him.

"Fool," the queen muttered, as if reading his thoughts.

Chase whipped off his helm.

A gasp drew his eye from the queen to a girl – a princess, perhaps? – further along the high table. She blushed. Definitely a princess, ripe for marriage to some rival kingdom. Before some handsome knight stole her heart and her virtue, too.

But seducing princesses would have to wait until his place here was assured. Chase bowed from the waist, praying his armour would not slice him in two.

"Your Majesty King Erik," he said. "I am honoured by your hospitality. I wish only to serve."

He knew he should reach for his sword and lay it at the king's feet as he knelt, but even if he could reach his sword, kneeling was beyond him. He thought quickly.

"I eagerly await tomorrow's tourney, for what better way to show a man's fighting prowess? Yet there is more to a knight than his sword," he continued.

The princess blushed redder than ever. Perhaps she knew more of such things than a maiden should.

Then the queen laughed.

And he could think of nothing but her. A hush fell over the hall, as it seemed every man there shared his thoughts.

Her mocking smile made him wonder once more if the queen could indeed read minds. "Pray continue, Sir Knight."

"As you wish, most beautiful queen." He wet his lips. Abraham had been the one with a way with words, especially when it came to women. He racked his brain for something that would impress the queen. "A true hero must keep his wits as sharp as his blade. His honour must shine as bright as his armour, and never be allowed to tarnish." Chase glimpsed a fly out of the corner of his eye, flicked away by the princess's impatient hand, and inspiration struck. He continued with more confidence: "So that if his liege or his lady is plagued by the most enormous monster or the tiniest gnat, he can dispatch it forthwith."

He turned to face the princess.

"Allow me, Your Majesty," he said.

He reached behind him for his bow, notched an arrow to the string and let it fly. His arrow lodged in one of the tapestries high above the princess's head, missing the fly completely. Not that anyone would know for sure without climbing the wall to examine his arrow.

Stupid armour.

He had the princess's attention for certain now. But he needed the queen to be equally impressed.

A fly circled the queen's head.

Chase drew another arrow. He'd only have one shot at this, and his aim had to be perfect. He breathed out and loosed.

His arrow arced up over the queen's head before embedding itself in the wax encrusting a lit candelabra at the back of the dais. The candles wobbled for a moment, but thankfully did not fall.

The fly, still unharmed, flew toward the princess, whose eyes met his. If the queen was a mindreader, so was her daughter. And the daughter knew he'd missed the fly twice.

He winked at her and said, "Fear not, young maiden. A knight's duty is to save every lady, not just the queen."

Chase reached for a third arrow.

The fly buzzed back toward the queen.

Chase released the arrow, just as the queen flicked her fingers to shoo the fly away.

His heart leaped into his throat. By all that was holy, please, no.

Queen Margareta leaped to her feet. "Guards!"

A thin line of blood trickled down the queen's fingers to where the arrow had lodged in the table before her. As if taunting him for his poorly timed shot, a shimmery wing was all that remained of the fly, now squashed under the weight of his arrow.

Chase didn't feel the guards seizing his arms – his armour was too thick for that – until the men started to drag him back, out of the hall.

No. This was all wrong. He was supposed to impress the queen, not shoot her.

"Your Majesty, I meant...I meant to rid you of a pest, not..." He was mortified to hear the weakness in his voice. Begging.

"Silence!" Queen Margareta thundered.

Chase had never been more relieved to obey a woman's command.

At her side, King Erik rose. "Anyone who seeks to harm my queen commits treason. Such a heinous crime is punishable by death."

No. He hadn't. He'd wanted to impress her, help her, not harm her. He'd never harm a woman. Never. Why, when his own sister lay dying, begging him to leave her to find her husband, to bring him home, Chase had not been able to release her hand. He'd learned archery so he could defend her. Like he wanted to serve this queen. Not…

"He's telling the truth!" The high, clear voice could only belong to the young princess.

She stood eye to eye with the queen over the head of the woman who sat between them. Her nurse, Chase presumed, for the woman was trying to make the princess sit down, but the girl was having none of it. "He shot a fly. Look!" The princess pointed.

A silent battle raged between mother and daughter.

Chase's own life rested on the outcome, he knew, but he couldn't think through his fascination at these two compelling women. The queen was formidable, but the princess did not fear her.

Whoever the girl married…he'd better not rule a rival kingdom, for that would mean war.

Somehow, the queen's eyes had moved back to Chase. Her voice was quiet but deadly. "Get out. This once, you may leave with your life. Set foot in this kingdom again and you will not be so lucky."

The princess had won, but he did not dare risk a glance of thanks in her direction, lest the queen change her mind.

He bowed, then fled, leaving his hopes in tatters on the flagstone floor.

Seven

"There she goes! The witch! She murdered her family one Midwinter and drank their blood with the devil and that's where she gets her powers from. Don't look her in the eye or you'll be next!"

Children shrieked and ran. All but one — a boy of perhaps nine or ten years, who dared to look her in the eye.

"Witch!" he taunted, even as he ignored his own warning.

Rosa gritted her teeth, hefting her bag higher on her shoulder, and said nothing.

It would be so easy to summon a gust of wind to lift the boy off his feet and deposit him at the top of the nearest tree, or on the roof of his equally ignorant parents' cottage, but she would not use her power for something so petty.

But surely no one would blame her for closing her eyes for just a moment and imagining the boy's panicked screams as he sat in that tree or thatch, before he begged for her help in getting him down.

The whole village might hate her, taunt her, and whisper rumours that only children dared repeat in her hearing, but when they needed help, they would still come to the cottage, hat in hand, and she would give it.

Her grandmother's cottage in the woods, since the night her parents' home had burned, but it was the best place for her now.

For in the forest's isolation, she did not have to listen to the taunts every day.

"Ah, there you are! Are the boots as pretty as the Baron promised?" Grandmother asked, climbing laboriously to her feet and brushing the dirt from her skirt. She lived in the garden most days, talking more to her plants than she did to Rosa.

Rosa's heart sank. "I'm sorry, Grandmother, I forgot the boots. I was talking to Alard, who needs another of your elixirs, and I was so lost in thought when I left the Great House…"

Grandmother's eyes were sharp, seeing into Rosa's very soul. "Is that boy of the Baron's begetting more bastards? Who is it this time?"

Rosa sighed. "Piroska, who else? It seems he cannot help himself around her."

Grandmother snorted. "Oh, I think he helps himself all too readily, and that's the problem. He should marry the girl and be done with it. Not like anyone better will have him."

Did Rosa imagine it, or did Grandmother's eyes dart toward her as she said that? "The problem is that Alard still hopes, Grandmother. No matter what I say…he is adamant that the best baroness should be a skilled healer."

"Then I shall go into town to fetch my boots myself on the morrow, and have a word with the boy while I'm at it. The best baroness is one who'll give him babies, and Piroska's as fertile as they come. His father's not getting any younger, after all." Grandmother led the way into the house, holding the door open for Rosa.

Rosa followed her in, and thumped her sack on the table. "I remembered your honey, though. Now we should have enough to start a new batch of mead. I'll make a start on it on the morrow, when you go into town."

"You're not coming with me?"

More than ever, Grandmother's eyes seemed to read Rosa's soul.

"You're not in love with that silly boy, are you?"

Rosa shook her head. "No! Alard is…perhaps the only friend I have in town, that's all. Everyone else hates me, calling me a witch and saying I murdered my parents."

"You are a witch. Their witch." When Grandmother said it, it sounded like an honourable occupation, instead of an insult.

"No, that's you, Grandmother. You cure their ills. I just deliver things, and collect the payment."

Grandmother waved away her doubts. "I do

nothing that you cannot. And while my magic is waning, yours grows stronger every day. Why, with a wave of your hand, you could clear the whole village of tonight's snowfall. They'd pay attention to you then!"

"They'd still call me a witch, only louder," Rosa grumbled, before her grandmother's words sank in. "Wait…snow? It has not snowed here since the winter my parents died! That was the coldest winter in living memory, you said, the sort that we won't see again for a hundred years. It's only been six!"

"The weather does not count the years. It merely is. And I fear this winter will be colder than any we have yet known. I think we have waited long enough. The snow is a sign from the gods, that it is time I initiated a new priestess. Will you be ready for the Midwinter rites?"

With Grandmother's eyes reading her very soul, Rosa could not lie. "No. I had thought to ask Alard, but now…I cannot imagine any man in the village I would want to share the ceremony with."

Grandmother patted her hand. "If the gods

want you for their priestess, they will provide. Who knows? Perhaps the folktales your mother loved so much will come true, and a knight will come riding into town in pursuit of some noble quest. No man could fail to notice you."

Yes, notice her and label her a witch, his voice full of venom as he spat the words. Yet, "Yes, Grandmother," was all Rosa said.

"It's settled, then. At Midwinter, you will pledge yourself fully to the goddess, as her priestess. The snow will come, and we must guard against it as best we can." Grandmother clapped her hands. "Which is why I need new boots. You don't feel the cold as I do, but when you are my age, you'll know!"

Rosa nodded numbly. Snow brought the wolves down from the mountains. Perhaps she would have her chance at vengeance this winter. If she killed the wolf who'd killed her family, then the men of the village might look on her with admiration instead. She only needed one who was willing to worship the goddess…but she had little hope of even one as things stood now. Once she'd slayed the beast, though…

There was no doubt in her mind that she could kill the wolf. It was merely a matter of how, and when.

As an untrained girl, she'd sent the wolf running all those years ago. Now, with her magic completely under her command, he'd be no match for her.

Eight

The village inn tempted Chase more than he liked to admit. He'd spent so many nights sleeping under hedges, as summer gave way to autumn and the infernal rain that never ceased, that the very thought of a night in a real bed, perhaps even a few hours seated before a fire, made his knees weak.

He counted his coins. He had enough for a hot meal or two and a bed, as long as it wasn't their best room. Abraham would have laughed at him, counting coppers like this. Then again, Abraham would have turned them to gold at a touch.

But Abraham was lost to him, and this was his life now. So Chase surrendered what remained of his wealth to the innkeeper and asked if the man knew of anyone in need of a knight.

The innkeeper scratched his head. "Don't know anyone who can afford to keep a knight, except for the king himself, and I'm sure he doesn't need any more. Not like we're at war with anyone right now. But if you're fixing to make a name for yourself so the king might hire you, you might try your hand at monster slaying."

"Monsters don't exist," Chase said.

The innkeeper's pitying look took him by surprise. "Then you're the only man who hasn't heard of the cursed wolf of the north, or the Kasmirus dragon."

Chase shook his head. "Indeed I haven't. Perhaps you could pour me an ale and tell me the story?"

"I'll do you one better. Go speak to the crier, sent out to search for a dragonslayer. He's seen the dragon himself." The innkeeper pointed at a boy not much younger than Chase, unrolling a scroll on the table.

Fighting a beast might be better than killing another man, enemy or no, Chase told himself. He'd seen enough death.

He turned his head to better read the boy's poster.

Heroes wanted, the poster read, for monster slaying of all kinds. Apply within.

Not that he was much of a hero, whatever the herald in Aros had said. Monster slaying might help him earn both his keep and a real reputation. It would at least keep his thoughts from straying to Abraham and Maja a dozen times a day.

Chase raised his voice. "Are you looking for a hero, boy?"

The boy looked up. He looked…resigned, Chase thought. As if to emphasise his point, the boy sighed.

Chase pulled the poster toward him. He tapped the crudely drawn dragon. "Where's the dragon and what's the reward?"

"Kasmirus, between the city and the river," the boy said. He didn't show a trace of fear.

Interesting. Either the beast wasn't so fearsome, or the boy hadn't actually seen it. "But I don't know the reward. Every time it kills another knight, the king increases it."

A dragon that could kill many knights was definitely fearsome.

"How big is the beast, and does it breathe fire?" Chase persisted.

Now the boy showed the first hint of fear, his Adam's apple bobbing as he swallowed nervously. "It would scarcely fit in the square outside, and its fiery breath is so hot, it has been known to melt a man's armour." He shuddered.

He'd seen this melting in person. Yet he'd survived. By running or hiding, or both, Chase decided. This boy was no dragon slayer.

A fire breathing monster who melted armour and had killed many knights. Such a beast would take a true hero to slay it — the sort of brave, foolhardy man who would undertake a quest for the sheer glory of it. Chase was too sensible a man for such things.

Chase lifted his hand and the scroll rolled up. "Which means it's impossible to kill."

He resolved to ask the innkeeper about the wolf. That wouldn't be an impossible task.

"Not impossible," the boy countered. "All creatures must die some time."

Chase stared at the boy. There was a steel to him, that his youth had hidden until now. The boy himself might not slay the dragon, but he was determined to recruit the man who could do the deed. Perhaps he'd known one of the slayed knights, a father or mentor, perhaps. He had a personal grudge against this dragon, but wasn't silly enough to fight it alone and die unmourned.

Chase grinned. "Even us. But there's nothing heroic about being roasted alive. I'm Sir Chase." He held out his hand.

"George," the boy said, clasping Chase's arm briefly before letting go.

Chase gestured to the innkeeper. "Two more ales for me and my friend here!" When the innkeeper nodded, Chase turned back to George. "Where are you headed?"

"Aros," George said.

Chase swallowed. From the maw of a fire breathing dragon to the court of Aros' icy queen? He had to warn him. "Not a good city for heroes, Aros," he managed to say. "Their queen isn't fond of adventurers." He suppressed a shudder as he took a cup of ale from the innkeeper.

George raised his eyebrows. "That's not what I heard. When they hold tourneys, the queen richly rewards the victor. She holds heroes in high regard, or so it is said." George drank deeply.

Sir Chase choked on his ale. Wiping his mouth with the back of his hand, he said, "Aye, I heard the same. Until I met the woman. Beautiful as the day is long, but cold as ice. Looking into her eyes is enough to freeze your soul, and no mistake."

He had a peculiar vision of Queen Margareta facing down a fire breathing dragon. It would be an even match, Chase thought.

Now, if it was that princess daughter of hers…the dragon would be doomed. But princesses did not fight dragons. Pity. He'd pay money to see a girl fight. Like Maja had wanted to, but their father had forbidden it. He'd like to see anyone try to refuse the princess of Aros, if she wanted to take up a sword.

"Then I'll be sure to avoid her," George said.

That wouldn't be hard. The boy wouldn't be invited to a feast where he might meet the princess.

"Wise choice." Chase raised his ale. "And I will avoid your dragon. I heard about a pack of troublesome wolves in the north. I might go see to those instead."

George clunked his cup against Chase's. "To both our good health, and long lives," he said gravely, and drank.

Without the interference of women, Chase added silently as he downed his ale. Women and wolves didn't mix, so he'd be safe in the north.

Nine

"Now, will you be all right brewing all that up by yourself?" Grandmother asked, surveying the jars of honey that covered the table.

Rosa didn't spare the table a glance. "Of course. I'd sooner brew ten times this much than go into town again after yesterday."

Grandmother shook her head. "The townspeople will never show you the respect you deserve unless you believe you deserve it. You are their witch, soon to be their priestess, far more important than the Baron and his line, for our family has been here for centuries.

You must wear your magic boldly, with pride, much like your red cloak. But today, save your magic for your brewing, for that is how the best mead is made."

Rosa bowed her head. "Yes, Grandmother." There was no point in arguing – Grandmother had earned the respect of the villagers and the Baron, but Rosa knew she could never ignore the taunts when her own head told her they were right.

She might not have murdered her own family, but their blood lay on her hands. If she'd been home, her magic might have saved them, as it had saved herself.

But she'd arrived too late.

Grandmother's eyes brimmed with sympathy. "You dwell too much on the past and what cannot be changed, Rosa. Look up, to the future, for that is where hope lies."

Not until the wolf was dead, she thought but did not say. Instead, she managed a smile. "My future is all about boiling and brewing, until all the barrels are full of mead. Which I hope will taste as good as the last batch."

Grandmother returned her smile. "Better,

I'm sure. You've learned so much since last winter, the village will have no need of me any more." She swept her cloak around herself and strode out before Rosa could respond.

For a moment, Rosa was a lost little girl again, all alone with barely a breath of magic to call upon, before she took a deep breath and reminded herself that girl had grown up. Stronger, more powerful. Powerful enough to seek vengeance when the wolf returned, she hoped.

And strong enough to brew an ocean of medicinal mead alone.

She stoked the fire, filled the cauldron from the well, and set it on the fire to boil. Then she headed outside and lit the firepits, which would be blazing hot enough to heat the other cauldrons once she'd filled them.

Her day consisted of wood, water and watching for bubbles, stirring in the honey, setting the mixture aside to cool, before sealing it up in barrels to ferment for a few weeks.

Then she could use her magic to lift the barrels up to the loft, where the warmth from the winter fire would help the brew mature.

Darkness had fallen by the time she'd stopped stoking the fires, but she couldn't leave the cauldrons out in night's chill and let ice ruin her hard work. She filled the last few barrels and sent them soaring inside with their fellows.

Only then did she allow herself to head back into the house to rest. Too exhausted to cook, she swallowed a few bites of bread and cheese.

Rosa's arms ached as she brought in wood to feed the fire for the night, but her day's work would go to waste if she let the fire go out. Not to mention Grandmother would admonish her for such laziness when she returned in the morning, for surely Grandmother had accepted the Baron's hospitality for the night instead of walking home so late in the dark.

So Rosa toppled into bed and fell asleep almost instantly, without a worry in the world.

Ten

Morning held an unfamiliar chill, forcing Rosa to reach for a shawl to wrap around her shoulders as she rekindled the fire from the coals. A cup of willow bark tea would see off the aches from yesterday's labour, before today's began.

Seeing as she'd left yesterday's milk in the cellar and forgotten about it, after today's milking, she might have enough to make cheese. She left a pot of water over the fire to boil, then headed outside to the barn where the goats slept.

Snow had turned their fertile, dark soil white. Rosa cursed, then summoned a whirlwind to whisk it away from Grandmother's garden. The spells Grandmother had cast on the clearing usually kept all but that hardiest frost away – she had an arrangement with the surrounding trees, or so she'd said – but perhaps even trees could not keep a snowstorm out completely.

No wonder Grandmother had stayed the night with the Baron. Walking through snow was…to return to trudging through despair, that winter Rosa had lost her family to the wolf. The coldest winter in living memory, or so everyone had said. She hadn't felt the cold, for she'd been too wrapped up in her grief. But now…snow sent a chill through her heart that had nothing to do with grief.

This year, her family would have justice. And snow would not touch her or hers again. Rosa bit her lip, strengthening the spell that swirled the snow away from her home so that it would not stop until the storm was over.

Better than dwelling on the evidence that Grandmother's magic was weakening.

A faint sound reached her ears, and Rosa sent a gust of wind to tell her more. The sound grew louder, until she could discern the crunch of wheels on the snow dusted road, accompanied by the low voices of the men who drove the wagon.

Milking and cheesemaking would have to wait. Rosa had time to comb her hair and straighten her cloak before the wagon trundled into view, accompanied by three guards and Alard.

Despite the freezing wind, all four of them removed their hats and held them to their chests.

Rosa's heart sank.

"Alard, what's happened?" she demanded, looking from him to the wagon and back again. Casks stood on either side of a covered lump that ran the length of the wagon. "What's all this?"

"Ah…this is my father's gift to you. And your grandmother. As thanks for all that you do for the village. All supplies from our cellar to help you through the winter. You'll need it, now that…"

"What, Alard?" Rosa couldn't keep the bite of impatience out of her tone.

One of Alard's men twitched the cloth aside. Beneath it was Grandmother's green cloak, ending in a pair of brand new boots.

"No!" Rosa doubled over. Not Grandmother. The only family she had left. "What happened?" she demanded.

"My father asked her to stay last night, but she refused. She insisted on walking home. One of the woodcutters found her this morning, lying in the snow on the road at the edge of the forest. Some cowardly creature had attacked her..."

Dread curled in Rosa's belly. There was only one creature it could have been.

Rosa reached for her grandmother's cloak, exposing the old woman's throat. Or what would have been her throat, if the wolf hadn't ripped it out.

"My father wanted to bury her in the churchyard, where our family lie, but I knew she wouldn't have wanted that. That you would want..." Alard couldn't seem to finish.

"Yes. She would want to be buried in the

woods, where she lived," Rosa lied. Alard and all the Baron's family worshipped the new religion, the one with the dying deity, instead of the multiple gods she knew lived in this part of the world. The gods her grandmother had prayed to and sacrificed to every day of her life. Grandmother would be accorded a funeral appropriate for a High Priestess who'd served the forest gods — her body would be burned on their altar, and her ashes scattered to strengthen the forest.

"My father has sent men out to hunt the creature, before it kills anyone else," Alard said. "You need not fear. I will bring you its head myself."

Rosa shook her head. "It's the wolf. The same one who killed my family. It came for her. Your hunters will not find it. It's too clever for that. When it comes, it will come for me. And I will be ready for it, this time. I will bring you its head. I'll carry it through the streets and maybe then, people will finally believe that it was a wolf, not me, who killed my family."

Alard looked alarmed. "We do believe you!

No one thinks such a terrible thing. But now that your grandmother is gone, perhaps you should consider moving to the village. I would be happy to offer you the hospitality of the Great House..." His eyes shone with eagerness.

"And who will placate the gods of the forest, with Grandmother gone? No, Alard, I will not move to town. I will stay here, where I belong." She eyed the wagon. "The supplies you brought should see me through the winter."

"But what then? I know your grandmother was a powerful witch, but you..." Oh, so earnest. Even when he insulted her.

Rosa bit down hard, tasting blood. "I am my grandmother's successor, and anyone who thinks my power is any less than hers is welcome to test it." She sent a gust of wind across the clearing, lifting Grandmother's cape from her body and making it dance as though her spirit animated the cloth, ten feet up in the air. The cloak reached the space between the firepits, and Rosa felt the faint warm air current stirring from the not-quite-dead coals.

She sent the breeze swirling through the coals, four gouts of flame that climbed higher than her house. "But not before I have sought justice for my family." She swallowed. "And Grandmother." Tears threatened, but she blinked them away. She would not cry in front of these men.

"Rosa…"

She ignored Alard. "You may store the supplies in the cellar. I'm sure if I must take up my grandmother's healing duties on top of my own, I won't have time to do it. But if your families have need of healing throughout the winter, be assured your kindness will be remembered."

Alard's men nodded and set about unloading the wagon.

Rosa let the air lift Grandmother's body, carrying it to where her cloak lay spread out on the ground, between the firepits. She gently laid the body down, like a queen lying in state. For to the forest, Grandmother had been the queen of the trees.

A power Rosa did not share, though they'd both been able to practice a small amount of healing. Rosa would have to work harder on the herb garden now, without Grandmother's magic to make it flourish.

The men carried casks, jars and sacks into the house. Rosa took stock of it all, stashing the information into a corner of her mind for later, when she could think about such things.

"There's space in the wagon for your things. Please come back to the village, so we can keep you safe. Just for the winter, until the wolf is caught," Alard wheedled.

"My place is here," Rosa said, planting her feet. She looked the Baron's son in the eye. "That wolf will die by winter's end, Alard."

He nodded once. "Yes, it will."

Eleven

The town looked no different to any of the others Chase had travelled through to get here. The only difference was the depth of the snow, which had fallen steadily until even his mare struggled through the drifts. What passed for a Great House here – the seat of the local baron, he'd been told – looked like one of the bigger outbuildings on Abraham's estate. A stone barn, not a castle.

But he didn't have the time or funds to be choosy. Winter was well and truly here, and his need for shelter at night had forced him to sell his armour, piece by piece, until nothing remained. If this town wasn't the one beset by wolves, he might have to sell his horse to make it through the winter.

No, fate would not be so cruel. She might not want him to live comfortably in the service of the royal court of Aros, but fate could not be such a bitch that she wanted him to die in a ditch halfway to nowhere. But fate was a woman, and a traitorous one at that. He wanted nothing to do with women when his business was with wolves.

He headed for the Great House, leading his exhausted mare.

"You're not from around here."

The voice came out of nowhere, until the owner appeared from behind what Chase had thought was a snowdrift. Now, he saw it was a half-buried building. A woodshed, judging by the pile of wood in the man's arms.

Chase stopped. "No, I'm not. My name is Sir Chase, and I heard your town had a wolf problem. I've come to take care of it." He hoped, he thought but didn't say.

Logs tumbled from the man's arms into the

snow. "Master Alard will be pleased to hear it." He headed for the house, and opened the door. "Boy, fetch Master Alard! A knight has come to slay the wolf!"

Chase heard the sound of running feet before the man closed the door again.

The man stuck out his hand. "I'm Wido. My family have served the Baron's for generations. But we've never had a wolf this bad. First six years ago, in that cold winter, and we thought it'd gone, but it's back, and more murderous than ever. Last time it murdered a whole family in their house as they slept!"

Chase's heart sank. That didn't sound like a wolf at all. What had he gotten himself into?

But it was too late now. He had no money left. If he did not take this job, he would starve before spring.

"Sir Knight, our saviour!" A well-dressed man of about Chase's own age appeared, his arms held wide as if he intended to embrace him. He did, kissing Chase on both cheeks. "I'm Alard. I thought we wouldn't see anyone else until the spring, though I sent riders out in every direction. Angels must have sent you!"

"An innkeeper on the road between Aros and Kasmirus, actually," Chase said.

Alard's eyes widened. "And you chose to help us instead of slaying the dragon? We are blessed indeed!"

The admiration in the man's eyes made Chase feel uncomfortable. "Hold your praise until the job is done, Baron Alard."

Alard shook his head. "My father is the Baron. I'm just Alard, for as long as my father lives. Which I hope will be a long time."

Chase could detect no lie in the man's fierce words. Perhaps Alard truly was a loving son, who had no desire to rule his father's lands. "I'm Sir Chase."

Alard's eyes shone. "Well met, Sir Chase. Tell me what you need to end this plague, and it shall be yours."

"Plague? I thought your problem was a wolf!" A wolf was one thing, but the plague was enough to send him galloping as far and fast as his mare could take him, winter snows be damned.

"The wolf that plagues us, yes. God forbid any other misfortunes befall us this winter!"

Chase breathed out a sigh of relief. "I heard there was a bag of gold on offer as reward for anyone who slays the beast."

Alard nodded. "Yes, that is so."

Chase took a deep breath. "I must ask for more than that. Board and lodging until spring, which are mine no matter how long it takes me to exterminate your wolf. Whether it takes me a week or the rest of the winter. I have travelled far, and – "

"Of course! You shall have a bed in my father's house, and a seat at his table for as long as you like. Rid us of this wolf, and my father may never want you to leave!" Alard clapped his hands. "You there – take Sir Chase's horse and see it is well cared for. Have his things brought to the house."

A man took the reins from Chase and led the mare to the stables.

"Now, join me for dinner. We'll broach a barrel of my father's best wine, and you can tell us tales of other monsters you have slain!" Alard said, gesturing for Chase to follow him.

No matter what the man had done, Abraham was no monster, and Chase had not slain him. "Better that you tell me more about this wolf. Now I am here, I am eager to start. Perhaps even on the morrow."

Alard nodded agreeably. "Of course, of course! You are a true hero, Sir Chase, to be so intent on your quest! I shall tell you everything I know."

And as the words spilled out of the Baron's son, Chase began to have an inkling of a plan. Wolves were crafty beasts, and one who sneaked into a house to kill people as they slept was craftier still. Waiting for it to appear and maybe kill again would never do. But if he could lure it into a trap, where he lay in wait with his bow, he might be able to accomplish this after all.

Twelve

Rosa could delay no longer. The ashes from her grandmother's pyre were cold on the stone altar in the forest, and she had made more cheese than she could eat in a year. The mead would not finish fermenting for some days yet, and Alard's hunters had followed the wolf's trail to a clearing in the forest, before they'd lost it.

Treating the hunters' coughs and chills from sleeping in the snow had given her all the information she needed to head out on her own hunt, along with the certainty that no one else would be out in the forest, risking his neck against the beast. The Baron's hunters didn't dare cross the witch who was now the town's only healer, who'd ordered them to rest inside for a week.

She'd sacrificed four elderly hens to use as bait, or she intended to – the old broilers were still alive, stuffed in the sack over her shoulder. Fresh blood mattered to predators, and surely this wolf was no different.

She found the clearing easily enough, though there were no wolf prints to be seen with the fresh dusting of snow the ground had received since the hunters had last been here. But it mattered not. She had no intention of tracking the beast to its lair. Instead, she intended to lure it out with the smell of fresh meat.

Rosa moved to the middle of the clearing to slaughter the chickens. Her experienced hands made quick work of the killing part, but she took her time gutting the carcasses, throwing entrails across the snow to spread the blood further.

When she was satisfied that she'd made

enough of a mess, she washed her hands and sought a suitable vantage point from which she could see clearly while she waited for dusk. The tallest tree was not the stoutest, but she was light enough to make the climb, if she kept close to the trunk. She climbed as high as she dared, before unwrapping the coil of rope she'd worn around her waist to tie herself securely to the trunk.

Only then did she string her bow, knowing speed would be her ally once the wolf appeared. The more arrows she could sink into its hide, the better chance she had of killing it before morning. Then perhaps the souls of her family would let her sleep without nightmares.

Wrapping her cloak tightly around her to keep out the cold, Rosa settled down to wait.

She must have fallen into a light doze, for she opened her eyes to darkness, or near enough. The full moon above lit the clearing, turning the reddened snow into the black of corruption. And yet…something moved across it, like a cloud, but more corporeal.

She plucked an arrow from her quiver and nocked it, ready to fire. The creature moved closer to the chickens, and Rosa loosed.

The arrow found its mark, but the creature that collapsed on the snow was too small to be the wolf. Its tail twitched once, then was still. A silvery fox, she thought, drawn by the bait. Not the wolf at all.

She slumped against the tree. Well, the fox would now be bait, too. She considered going down to retrieve her arrow and perhaps butcher the fox, to spread more fresh blood over the scene, but decided not to bother. She had plenty of arrows, and all night to wait.

Silence descended on the clearing again. Rosa longed for a hot meal, or even a flask of mead, but she hadn't thought to bring more than a chunk of ham, as she was already heartily sick of cheese.

Mead would have ruined her aim, anyhow, she told herself as she munched on the cold ham.

Something slammed into the trunk of her tree, nearly shaking her out of it, and the ham fell from her fingers to the ground below.

A second passed, and she heard the sound of chewing, accompanied by a faint whine, like a dog in pain.

Whatever it was crashed into the tree a second time. Then a third.

Rosa hung on for dear life, hoping the rope around the trunk would hold.

Then she heard the sound of scrabbling, like the creature was digging a hole in the snow.

Or a grave.

Rosa shook herself. Animals did not dig graves.

The sounds stopped, but she barely had a moment to breathe a sigh of relief before something hit the tree, harder than before. Again. And again.

On the fourth blow, the tree tipped sideways at an alarming angle, spilling Rosa off her branch into space. Only the rope around her kept her from falling.

The tree shuddered from the force of another blow, and the rope became uncomfortably tight. She flung her arms out to catch anything that might support her weight, but she dangled too far away to touch anything.

Cursing, Rosa pulled out her knife and

began sawing at the rope as another blow sent the tree toppling against the one beside it. A smaller tree that began to buckle under the weight…

Rosa sawed faster, barely noticing as she scraped her fingers raw on the rope, for her attention was directed down, in the hope that the snowdrift below would be deep enough to break her fall.

But all she could see was a pair of glowing blue eyes, staring straight at her.

The wolf, she knew without a doubt.

The beast flung itself at the tree trunk again.

Ominous cracks sounded, though whether from her tree or the other, Rosa couldn't be sure.

She could feel the rope stretching, unravelling, ready to drop her within reach of the waiting wolf, but her blood-slicked fingers hummed with power. The rope snapped, but the air caught her, as she had commanded it to. She spread her cloak, letting the wind carry her to the lower branches of the next tree.

A much sturdier tree than her first choice, though she could no longer see much of the clearing.

The wolf's eyes followed her, as if the creature could see her.

No, surely not. Wolves saw movement, and used scent to find their prey. If she stayed still against the trunk, it would lose interest in her and investigate the chickens instead.

The wolf that had let the fox go first, like some sort of scout, before attacking the very tree she sat in. Where the arrow had come from…

No. Wolves were not that clever. Men thought like that, ones skilled in battle. Not animals.

Something closed on her boot. Rosa kicked out, and was rewarded with a whine as the wolf let go. She scrambled higher up the tree, out of reach.

Why wouldn't it leave her alone? Surely now it would go and eat…

But the wolf sat down in a patch of moonlight, turning those glowing eyes up at her as if to say it could wait all night.

It could, she realised. It could wait all night and all day, its fur protecting it from the cold.

Whereas she had no food, not enough rope to secure herself, and she'd have to sleep sometime. When she did...she'd fall, and the wolf would have her.

No. If she had to climb a hundred trees and ride the air currents until dawn, the wolf would not touch her. If the creature really was a wolf, which she was beginning to doubt.

She began to climb.

Thirteen

It hadn't been a hundred trees, but she had lost count after the first dozen. She'd climbed until she could not reach any higher, then summoned a gust of wind to carry her across the treetops to another tree, which she would climb to the highest point before doing the same again.

She fell more than she flew, letting the spread cloak slow her descent, but as the night went on, her mind considered how she might improve upon her situation. Something larger and more rigid than her cloak to catch the air, big enough to lie upon full-length as it buoyed her up. But not too heavy, for the air could only lift so much.

Rosa reached for the next tree, willing herself to climb it with her aching arms, even if the wolf was no longer in sight. Until the sun rose, she knew the hunter would not sleep.

How did she know that?

Rosa turned it over in her mind, until she found the answer. Magic. Whatever had turned that creature into what it was now, it was magical. A cursed king, an enchanted wolf…what difference did it make? It was no woodland creature to fall into an ordinary trap like the fox had.

No, the creature had a man's cunning.

A man who wanted to kill her.

Who had already killed her family.

A creature that would be the next to die.

Not her.

But she would need a new plan, now she knew what she was hunting.

Dawn took her by surprise, as she reached the top of a tree that wasn't far from her cottage. She could see the stone altar below, still dusted in ash.

Grandmother, I will avenge you, she swore as she summoned a final gust to take her safely to the forest floor.

Her legs felt as soft as ricotta when she landed, but Rosa didn't dare stay here. She could not rest until the stout walls of the cottage kept the wolf out.

With a brief thanks to the gods of the wood for the gift of her magic and for delivering her home safely, she trudged toward the cottage.

Only to find that despite all her efforts, someone had beaten her home anyway.

Fourteen

Deep in his cups, Alard had grasped Chase's arm with both hands. "Promise me something, Sir Chase," he'd slurred.

Chase had nodded once, encouraging the man to continue.

"Warn the witch. She lives in a cottage in the woods. Tell her you're here at my request to slay the wolf. Tell her to stay out of the woods, where she'll be safe."

Chase had nodded again, agreeing to the man's request. What else could he say, anyway?

"Thank you," Alard had breathed, before

pitching face-first onto the table and starting to snore.

Chase had reclaimed his arm and headed off to his own bed, where he'd slept like the dead.

Now, dawn found him outside in the cold, packing enough food into his saddlebags for a week-long hunt while one of the stable boys fetched him several extra quivers of arrows from the armoury. It had been a long time since he'd last hunted with Abraham, and he missed the man more than ever. A few jokes would make his grim task so much easier, but it was not to be.

Alard and the Baron were still in their beds, as Chase would be, too, if he'd been in the Rumpelstiltskin Castle with Maja and Abraham. Or even if he'd stayed at the court in Aros.

Chase shook himself. He could no longer live in the past. He had a wolf to kill, and a new life to make. A life of his own, without Maja or Abraham or the help of some far-off court.

But first he had to find a witch, a woman who worked magic like the curse that had turned Abraham from a sane man into a mad one.

He set off into the woods, glad to find the snow lay light on the ground under the trees, unlike in town. The path was well-worn, too, as if many villagers travelled to see the witch. He wondered what the village priest would say about such things. Chase could not recall seeing a church in town, come to think of it. His father would certainly turn over in his grave if he knew.

But here, so far from civilisation, it was easy to see that the old ways would not die easily. Especially without a church to remind the people that they were supposed to believe in a new faith now.

While living in a world with numerous gods and monsters, curses and magic. Chase shivered as the town vanished from sight between the trees.

His horse felt no such chill, as she plodded onward.

He must be imagining the dread that coursed through him, he decided. He struck up a bawdy tune, and sang at the top of his lungs to pass the time.

He'd managed to sing it through three

times, or at least the verses he remembered, before the cottage came into view. Stone walls topped with thick thatch, which bore only a light dusting of snow. A small enclosure beside it held two goats, several chickens and a stable of sorts, with a carefully laid out garden in the space between. Even in the dead of winter, the garden showed signs of life, for the snow had not completely covered it yet.

Magic, the sneaky voice in the back of his mind told him, but he hushed it. It was nothing of the sort. The surrounding trees evidently kept this place clear of snow, much like they'd protected the road to reach here.

And there was the witch, crossing the clearing to reach her door, her white hair coming loose from her braid.

Chase's heart relaxed. An old, wise woman – no wonder Alard wanted her warned and protected. Her knowledge of healing herbs was surely important to his people.

Chase stepped out of the shadows, straightening his shoulders to make himself look more heroic than he felt. "Fear not, mistress. Your Baron has sent me to slay the wolf. If you but keep to your cottage, I will soon make the forest safe for a gentle woman such as yourself."

The witch whirled, sending her cloak flying out around her in a swirl of blood, for it was as red as the stuff in his veins. "Then the Baron is a fool, for who will make the forest safe for the likes of you?"

Chase's mouth dropped open, and he could not seem to close it. What he'd taken for an old woman was nothing of the sort.

Her youthful face and equally youthful figure – for her thick woollen dress only emphasised the curve of the flesh beneath it – were nothing to the blue fire in her eyes that held him transfixed.

Then she smiled, just a little, and Chase's heart turned to mush.

"Go. Find something else to slay. A dragon, or some such thing. There is magic at work here that you cannot begin to understand." She flicked her fingers in dismissal.

That flick broke the spell, somehow, and Chase's tongue unfroze. "I cannot simply leave," he said stiffly. "I have accepted a quest, and it would be dishonourable to run away before it is complete. I am a knight, and my honour is more precious than my own life. I would not expect a woman to understand matters of honour."

Her smile widened to a grin. "Then you're a bigger fool than the Baron, Sir Knight. Honour is about doing what's right, and the right thing for you to do is leave this forest. Now. While you still have your life." She opened the door of her cottage, stepped inside, then slammed it shut.

Chase opened his mouth to defend himself, but that would be pointless – she wouldn't hear a word of it. And what could he say to convince her she was wrong?

Nothing.

Deeds spoke louder than words.

So he would let his deeds speak for him. He would kill this wolf, drop its head on her doorstep, and then she'd see who was a fool. He nudged his horse to continue along the path, in the direction the witch had come from.

That wolf would die before the day was done, he swore.

Fifteen

More than anything, Rosa wanted to sleep, but sleep refused to come. Her grandmother's words haunted her — she had predicted the arrival of a knight, right in time for Midwinter. A pity she hadn't predicted the wolf, too.

If that poor fool of a knight did not take her advice and instead went hunting for the wolf…it was his body she'd find next.

She told herself she didn't care what happened to a stranger. Men could do whatever foolish things they pleased in the forest, and if it got them killed…

But it was her job to protect those who wandered into the forest. She served the gods of the forest, as her grandmother and all the witches before her had, and this was her domain.

Especially when there was magic involved.

For no one else in the village or any of the towns around was a witch.

And to serve the gods of the forest properly, to become their priestess instead of just a novice, she needed that knight. Alive.

Cursing, she rose from her bed and opened the door to see if the knight still waited outside.

To her surprise, he seemed to have taken her advice and headed back to town, for there was no sign of him or his horse.

Good.

She longed to go back inside, but her conscience would not allow it. For if the Baron had sent one fool into the woods, he would send more. And she might not be able to warn them all.

With one last, longing look at her bed, she fastened her cloak and set out for the village.

The boys who had taunted her before her grandmother's death were engaged in a snowball fight in the snowdrift beside the road, too busy to pay attention to her.

Or so Rosa thought, until a snowball came sailing her way.

Did the little brats know she'd spent all night in the forest, protecting them? Risking her life for theirs? They would never have dared to throw such a thing at her grandmother.

Magic came to her as easily as breathing now. A puff of air turned the snowball into a flurry that swirled harmlessly to the road at her feet.

She turned to face the boys. "Next time, that's what will happen to you," she said.

The boys' eyes widened in horror before they bolted.

She shook her head at the gullibility of small boys. As if she could summon a wind strong enough to do such a thing. The worst she could do to them was lift them onto their parents' roof or into a nearby tree, and they'd probably just climb down in any case.

Rosa felt eyes upon her as she approached the Great House. Before her grandmother's death, she would have tried to ignore the prickle between her shoulder blades and the person causing it, but today she was done with evasions.

She would turn and face the wolf, if that's what it was, and anyone else presented so little threat compared to the dread beast that she feared no one.

"Is there a leaf clinging to my cloak, that you stare so?" she snapped.

"You do not deserve something so fine. Not when you scarcely give him the time of day. It should have been mine," a female voice hissed.

Piroska sat outside the smithy where her father worked, her eyes burning hotter than the forge.

The silly girl thought Alard had given her this cloak? Ah, the girl's jealousy had made her foolish indeed. Especially when Rosa was certain the cloak had been a gift from the Baron to Grandmother, like many of the valuable items in the cottage. Except for the beautiful woven carpet hidden in the loft.

Grandmother had blushed like a maiden when she'd described the Crusader knight who'd given her that particular item.

Rosa had always thought there was more to that story than her grandmother had said, and now it was too late to ask. She would never know.

"Have you ever asked him for a new cloak? After all you give him, seeing as he won't even let you keep his child, surely he owes you something," Rosa said.

Two spots of red appeared on Piroska's cheeks as her hand flew to her belly. "I'm sure I have no idea what you mean."

As if Rosa had read the girl's thoughts, she knew Piroska hadn't taken the latest elixir yet, or Alard had not yet given it to her. She still carried Alard's baby.

Rosa smiled. "In a village as small as this, nothing remains a secret long from the village witch. Least of all about the girl who might one day become the next baroness."

"I'd be a better one than you!" Piroska spat.

The girl was right, but Rosa did not need to tell her that. The next baroness would need to be a brood mare, or the Baron's bloodline would die out and the king would give these lands to someone else. Someone who might not respect the gods of the forest as much as the Baron and his ancestors.

Yet another thing to confront Alard about: wolves, and now his choice of wife. If Grandmother were here…but she wasn't, so this task fell to her now, too.

Being the next baroness, to be endlessly bedded by Alard in between popping out babies, would be such an easy life compared to being the village witch. But Rosa would still be expected to waddle around the village in between births. Better that Piroska bear the babies. Or any girl, really.

Alard might one day be the Baron, but he was a bore in bed. Or was that a boor?

Not the sort of passion suitable for a priestess, anyway.

Rosa walked on, into the main hall of the Great House.

"Alard!" she shouted.

"Ngh?" A man lifted his head from the table on the dais. Had Alard been sleeping on it?

Rosa strode forward. "Alard?" She had never seen him look quite this dishevelled. Why, he looked like he needed to shave, after sleeping there all night. And here she thought he simply hadn't been old enough to grow a beard yet.

He beamed. "You came! I shall have the servants prepare a chamber for you at once. My mother's has not been used since – "

Rosa silenced him with a look. "I came to ask you why there was a knight on my doorstep this morning. A knight who believed he was on a quest to slay my wolf, Alard. Do you have any idea how dangerous that creature is?"

Alard yawned. "Of course, of course. It's a wolf that killed your family. Very dangerous indeed. Which, I'm sure, is why you are here. Accepting my invitation. I shall send someone to the next town for the priest at once, for the sooner we are married – "

"We're not getting married."

He stared at her. "Why, of course we are! Don't you remember that Midsummer when we sneaked away from the feast and lay together? We promised we would never part! I admit I should have taken you as my wife then, but Father was fine then. Now, there must be no delay."

Rosa screwed up her face. "Midsummer, six years ago? The first summer after I lost my family, and went to live with my grandmother? I was sixteen, Alard, and we'd both drunk too much mead. I'm surprised you remember anything of that night." She'd plied him with that much mead in the hope that he hadn't.

She had not been so drunk when she'd accepted the comfort his body offered. Those who had taken up the new religion believed such relations between a man and a woman to be a sin, but Rosa knew the gods of the forest thought otherwise. They expected their priestesses to encourage as much spilling of seed as possible, especially at their most sacred festivals. Particularly when a priestess in training began her novitiate, as she had that night.

Alard's kisses and caresses that night had been reverent to the point of goddess worship, which is why she had chosen him to share her mead in the moonlight before he helped her shed her virgin's blood before the altar.

One night of pleasure, consecrating her body to the fertility of the forest, before taking the bitter elixir at dawn to ensure no baby was born of the union.

"I dream of it every night, praying for you to share my bed again. There is no one else, Rosa. No one but you." He sounded so earnest, as if he truly believed his own words.

"What about Piroska?" she demanded.

"Piroska?" His face went blank. "You mean the blacksmith's daughter?"

"The same girl you asked me to mix an elixir for?" Rosa prompted.

Alard flushed. "That was nothing. I was merely doing the girl a favour. She had evidently done something untoward with some peasant boy or other and was too frightened to ask you herself, so she confided in me, begging for my help."

"Alard, half the town can hear you scream each other's names when you're rolling around in the hayloft together. Her father might be the only man who doesn't know, if only because of the noise in the smithy." She blew out a breath. "But I didn't come to talk about you and your…exploits. I came to talk about the knight, and the wolf."

Alard rose and seized her hands. "But we must. You must, Rosa. For my father…he is…he is not well, and I fear he has not long left."

"The Baron is ill?" She'd never known the man to have so much as a head cold. Grandmother had prided herself on the Baron's good health, and received many gifts from the man in thanks for it.

"After the shock of your grandmother's death, he took to his bed, and has hardly been out of it since, except last night, where he insisted on greeting the knight. I fear he already regrets it…" Alard led the way upstairs, to the private chambers.

Rosa half expected Alard to show her his mother's rooms first, but his worry for his father had driven any amorous or matrimonial matters out of his head.

"Mistress Rosa is here, Father," Alard said softly, gesturing for Rosa to precede him.

Mistress Rosa? She'd never been called that before.

Perhaps she had slept, after all, and this was a dream.

Except…in no dream, nightmare or otherwise, had she ever thought to see the Baron looking less alive than her grandmother's corpse. His skin had taken a grey cast, and no one was more surprised than Rosa when his eyes blinked open – he was not yet dead.

"Leave us, boy. See that you send the girl home with a gift befitting Mistress Saskia."

Alard frowned. "But, Father, Mistress Saskia is – "

"Always asking for more honey, to make mead. See that she has all that we have left." The Baron fixed his eyes on his son.

Alard bowed his head. "Yes, Father." He departed.

Baron Arnold turned his eyes on Rosa. "Do you have Saskia's gift for healing?"

She'd thought she had, but if her grandmother's healing magic had kept death at bay for who knew how long, Rosa didn't think she could match that kind of power. Yet she was the only witch he had, so she lifted her chin and said, "She said my magic was more powerful than hers, but I must assess your condition before I can say if I can help you."

She laid her hand on his forehead, bit her lip and closed her eyes, letting her magic sweep through his body. It reminded her of a weed-choked field, with some sort of strange growth pushing out the normal parts inside his body. In order to heal an affliction like this, she would need Grandmother's knowledge of plants and growth and her affinity with such things. Rosa could cure a cold or heal an infected wound, if she simply swept the foreign matter out of the blood the way she sent a gust of wind to do her bidding, but this…stuff…grew everywhere. Was a part of him.

Rosa released the Baron. She wanted to look anywhere but into his eyes, and yet she could look nowhere else. "What did my grandmother tell you about your condition?" she asked finally.

"That it is like a forest growing around a

castle. The walls will only remain strong for so long, but the forest will always win, in the end," he said.

Rosa nodded. "My grandmother kept the forest at bay. But now…" She didn't want to continue, for if the Baron didn't know about her grandmother's death…

"Now Saskia is gone, there is no one strong enough to fight it," the Baron finished for her. "Don't try to lie to a dying man, Mistress Rosa. As Saskia often told me, it is a witch's duty to tell the truth, however unpalatable it may be, for it will out in the end. Are you indeed a witch?"

Rosa nodded. "Of course, but my power is over air, not plants."

"Did your grandmother teach you the old ways? The ways of the forest?"

She nodded again. "She did."

"Then will you protect the village from the forest? You will take her place as priestess, when my son takes my place?"

She straightened her shoulders. "I took up my duties upon my grandmother's death, though I was helping her long before then. I do my duty not for you, or for the village, but for – "

"Hush. Saskia chose her successor well, I am sure. I never expected to outlive her, but she would not let me die, either. Even though the weeds within me grow stronger every day, she kept pushing them back. Refused to stay the night here, insisting she had to get back, to prepare you to be her replacement. If I regret anything, 'tis letting that good woman go. But I could not have held her against her will. Not Saskia."

"You are not responsible for the wolf," Rosa said. She was. And she would not shirk her responsibilities. Not in this.

"No, but I could have ordered the hunt earlier, when she urged me to, after your family was killed. Yet I did not, for we could ill spare the men. And there were no other attacks, so there was no need. Until now."

"I will not let the beast take another victim," Rosa said.

"Let the men kill it. My son boasts of a brave knight who will head them. A hero of many battles. Let the men do the work, for what else are we men for? But you…see that her spirit is appeased. When they bring that beast's body to lay it at your feet, see that it burns. For Saskia."

It might be a witch's duty to tell the truth, but Rosa could leave parts out. "When it is dead, I will see that the body burns," she said.

The Baron smiled faintly. "You are just like her. A witch, and a warrior. Make sure my son sees you safely home to your cottage with whatever he found in the cellar."

The Baron lay back against his pillows and closed his eyes. He began to snore.

Rosa took one last look at the man — for he would not live much longer, and she might not see him again — before she headed back downstairs.

Alard was waiting for her in the yard, supervising as a wagon was filled with things for her.

"I'm sorry, Alard," she said before he could ask. "At most, I can give you some medicine that will ease his pain. But there is little more I can do for him now."

He nodded. "Tell my men what you need,

and they will bring it back for you. You must stay here, to tend to him. To help him live as long as he can. I shall have rooms prepared – "

"NO!" It came out louder than Rosa expected, startling her, but everyone in the yard stopped to stare. "Alard, I will not stay here, as your wife or your kept healer. I am going home, right after I give your cook instructions so that she may prepare what is necessary to make your father comfortable in his remaining days. Nothing I can do will save your father, but if I do not hunt down that wolf, he may kill again. And I will not have that blood on my hands."

"Why do you persist in this ridiculous notion that you and only you can kill this beast? It is not a task for a girl. We have a knight, a true hero, who will do the deed. Let him be your champion. My father needs you. I need you."

She refused to be swayed by his wheedling tone.

"Either your knight will not find the beast, or he will be killed. He won't last the week, Alard."

His eyes lit up. "Then that is what I ask. A week. Stay here, safe, for a week. If the knight returns with the dead beast, as I expect, then you can go home, knowing you will be safe."

It would take her a week to work out how to outsmart the beast, but she would not spend it here. Not to mention Midwinter was less than a week away. "What will you give me in exchange for doing as you ask?"

Alard spread his arms wide, taking in the rapidly filling wagon and the men carrying more casks up from the cellars. "Anything you wish."

Rosa wet her lips. "Send for that priest. When he arrives, you will wed – "

"Thank God!"

Rosa continued, "You will wed Piroska, and do your utmost to beget an heir. For your father will rest more peacefully if he knows his bloodline will continue after you."

"Piroska? But – "

She gazed steadily back into his hurt eyes. "Forget Midsummer, and any childish passion you may have held for me. In a few days, you will become Baron, and the sooner you have an heir, the better. For that, you need a fertile wife. Fate has given you Piroska, and you would be a fool not to accept such a gift."

His voice came out hoarse. "If I agree to marry the girl, will you promise to stay safe?"

"A week, then, I agree to. A week where you may find me at home. For all the wolf attacks have been here in the village, but the beast would not dare come to the cottage." Truth, for there was ancient magic in the stones beneath it. Magic Alard did not need to know about.

Alard blew out a breath. He didn't look happy, but he said, "Very well. I shall send for the priest. But if you change your mind…"

"I won't." She wet her lips. "But warn your heroic knight that I think the beast has magic of some sort. The creature is not what it appears to be."

"Sir Chase needs no warnings. He set out early this morning with everything he needs. He swore to kill the beast, and I believe him. Have faith, Rosa."

The knight had not come back? That meant the poor fool was alone in the forest…beset by a beast he couldn't kill.

And she'd just given her word she wouldn't hunt the wolf for another week.

Cursing, she set off for home.

Sixteen

As Chase headed steadily uphill, the trees thinned, until he came upon another clearing – but this one was covered in snow. Well, mostly snow. In the middle of it was the remains of what looked like a recent kill, ringed round with feathers and bloody wolf prints.

He surveyed the trees around the edge of the clearing and nodded in satisfaction. This was the place to set up his trap. All he needed was bait.

Movement at the top of the slope caught his eye – a rabbit, tugging at a scrap of grass that grew sideways out of the vertical cliff face. Chase strung his bow, then fitted an arrow to the bowstring. Without his golden armour, he wouldn't miss this time.

He exhaled, then released, knowing the arrow would hit its mark.

The rabbit didn't make a sound as it toppled over, dead.

Chase tied his mare to a trunk just inside the treeline, before scrambling up the slope to collect his kill. The best place to set the trap was…right here, he decided, pulling out a knife. He gutted the dead rabbit, flinging its entrails across the snow, before dropping the carcass among the mess. If that didn't attract the wolf, he didn't know what would.

Now all he had to do was climb a tree, and wait for the wolf to show up.

He'd shoot it, bring it back to the witch, then drag the carcass into town to collect his reward. Easy.

Chase settled into a suitable perch, wrapped his cloak around him, set his bow across his lap in readiness, and waited.

Seventeen

By the time she'd reached home, Rosa still had no more idea of how better to slay the wolf than she had that morning, but she had thought up a plan of how to find the knight without breaking her word to Alard.

But in order for her plan to work, she needed to learn to fly before dusk, when the wolf would come out to hunt.

Rosa already knew her cloak wasn't good enough to achieve true flight. She needed something like a boat or a raft that could float on air. If her father, a carpenter, were still alive, he'd build something in moments, but she was not as practiced as he'd been with wood or tools. There had been an old door in the lumber pile, though…

She dug it out and laid it on the ground. All she had to do was fly it around the clearing. Rosa took a deep breath and bit her lip.

The door rose off the ground, but the higher she lifted it, the more magic it took, and she'd barely moved it yet. Sweat broke out on her forehead as she gave the hovering door a push. It toppled end over end before it righted itself, flying on a slight angle, before it tipped again, hanging sideways for a moment, before it plummeted.

Finally, she let it fall to earth. She could never travel atop the door if she couldn't hold it steady. Something lighter, perhaps.

A blanket flapped around the clearing with little effort, but when she tried to keep it steady, she found it impossible. The blanket rolled and folded with the slightest change of direction.

A woven screen her grandmother had sometimes placed before the fire to hide its light at night fared better, but air whistled through the gaps, so it lost height quickly, though it held steady.

The blanket pegged to the screen made its wobbly way around the clearing without falling, but the combination was almost as heavy as the door. Rosa could not fly across the forest on such a heavy raft.

Ready to give up, she carried the items back inside. It was getting late. She should start dinner soon. The knight would have to wait until the morrow, and survive on his wits for the night, such as they were.

Rosa decided to bring a smoked sausage down from the loft, and make a stew with it and some vegetables from the cellar. With the loft so full of fermenting mead barrels, she had to climb on top of them to reach the sausage. From her perch, she spotted her grandmother's prized Crusader carpet.

Thickly woven, with stiff backing, it might hold up for a flight…

She forgot the sausage and dragged the carpet outside, then spread it on the ground. If this didn't work, then she truly would give up for the day. But if it did…she would go and get the knight before dinner.

The surface undulated a little as it rose, but the carpet held steady, much like the screen. Rosa sent it around the clearing, lifting it higher as it went. The carpet did not weigh nearly as much as the screen or the door, and while it rippled a little, it did not roll up altogether, as the blanket had. She made it fly around the clearing a second time, level with the tree tops. As smooth as a bird in flight – once it had the air beneath it, it glided almost effortlessly.

Rosa laughed. What would her grandmother have said, watching her precious carpet flying about?

She would have said it was a waste of magic. What the carpet needed was a load to carry, or a passenger.

Her grandmother might have given the carpet a sack of vegetables to carry, but lack of sleep and her need to save the knight made her reckless. If she fell, she could slow her descent, she reasoned, as she swooped the carpet close enough for her to leap on.

She flung herself headlong at the carpet, clutching the edges in her desperation to stay on as she remembered to keep the air flowing beneath it, buoying her up.

She made the carpet do a slow lap around the clearing, close enough to the ground that a fall would not hurt her. Then she lifted it higher, letting it move faster. She did not understand it, but that seemed to take less magic.

Higher, then faster. The air obeyed her thought before she'd fully considered it, flying her almost to the treetops like a circling eagle.

Rosa's breath caught in her throat, her hair blowing back in the wind that seemed to claw at her eyes, but still she held on. By all that was holy, she was flying!

She let out a whoop of triumph and pushed the carpet higher, so it cleared the treetops altogether. The mountains rose up in the distance, snowy crags that gave way to naked stone, then forest, as far as the eye could see, until she turned west, where the village lay. The setting sun turned the snowy fields to fire, and Rosa could not take her eyes off the glorious scene. If she but had the skill to paint such a sight, she would be able to look upon it always.

But sunset meant more than just golden light. Sunset would give way to dusk, and she had a knight to find.

If the man still lived by the time she found him, for searching the forest at night was an impossible task for anyone, even a witch who could fly.

And if she didn't find him alive, at Midwinter…she would need to find another man.

Muttering a curse against all brave, foolish men, she headed out.

Eighteen

A scream sliced through the air, startling Chase out of his doze. Whatever it was, it hadn't sounded human.

The sound came again, accompanied by the drum of hooves that sounded exactly like a horse breaking into a gallop. Or trying to.

His horse.

Chase twisted, trying to see his mare. Moonlight lit up the clearing almost as bright as day, but it did not penetrate the canopy behind him.

Short yips and barks came out of the bushes

— the sound of excited dogs. Then a third scream, that ended in a gurgle.

The sickening crunch of bone.

The wolf had killed his horse.

The last thing he'd had left of value. Fury rose up, at fate, the wolf, and everything in between. Chase would not let them take everything from him. Not while he still had a strong right arm.

He began to climb down the tree.

He slipped a few times, including the last few yards down the trunk, but he did not care. He would kill the wolf, and buy a new horse with the reward.

Chase reached for his sword, then thought better of it. The sound of the blade sliding out of the scabbard would alert the beast to his presence. Better to use a well-placed arrow, once he could see the creature.

He took a deep breath, put an arrow to the bowstring, then peeked around the trunk he'd tied his horse to.

A pair of glowing eyes regarded him.

Then another.

And another.

Dozens of eyes glowed in the dark, all

pointed at him.

Excited dogs, his half-asleep brain had told him. Not dogs. Wolves. A whole pack of them. All staring at him over the carcass of his horse.

He bolted.

Chase clawed his way up a tree, then slid painfully down it, hearing a crunch as he landed. Then pain exploded in his leg, blinding him.

In the dark, he couldn't see the source. Had a wolf closed its jaws on his leg, bringing him down for the pack?

No. He wouldn't die here, a dog's dinner. He reached for the branches above him, hauling himself up by his arms alone, even as his muscles screamed in pain. But he could not stop – he'd seen dogs jump this high, and wolves were no different. He needed to climb higher, so they couldn't reach him. Up and up and up, until he emerged into moonlight again, at the top of the tree. He sighed and sat down heavily. Surely this would be enough.

The branch beneath him bent, then snapped, spilling him out into space. Out of the tree, and into the waiting jaws of the monsters below.

Nineteen

Rosa headed for the clearing where she'd laid her trap, figuring it was as good a place to start as any. If the knight had heard from the Baron's men that they'd tracked the wolf that far, then he might have had the same idea as she had.

A scream told her she was heading in the right direction. The wolf had caught something tonight, though that hadn't sounded human.

It was not yet full dark, but the shadows beneath the tree canopy hid much. She flew lower to get a closer look.

Her blood froze in her veins at the sight of not one wolf, but at least a dozen, tearing at their prey, which appeared to be a large buck. No, a horse, she realised with deepening horror.

The knight's horse.

The man could not be far away.

As if reading her thought, a tree shuddered violently to her right. Almost as if some large creature had slammed into its trunk, trying to uproot it like the wolf had her perch yesterday.

Something cracked. A moment of silence, before the tree shuddered again. Now she could see something scrambling madly up the tree. A tree with whip-thin branches, that even she would not have climbed, for it would not hold her weight.

The knight fell.

Rosa didn't pause to think whether she'd be able to reach him in time. She had to try.

Offering up a prayer to the gods of the forest that she would survive this stunt, she swooped beneath the branches.

Twenty

Chase was pretty sure death wasn't supposed to hurt this much. He'd remembered stories of paradise and angels, not pain. Unless he'd somehow found his way to hell. But that couldn't be right. What mortal sin had he committed to end up in eternal torment? Falling out of a tree didn't count. Perhaps accidentally shooting that queen had earned him such a punishment.

He was warm, too, which had to mean hell.

Chase sighed. Abraham would laugh himself sick. Though he was likely here somewhere, too, for killing kings was just as treasonous as shooting queens. Probably more so.

He forced his eyes open and stared up at…wooden boards, not stone. Well, the priests back home had never been able to describe hell. Maybe it was all wood, the better to burn sinners with.

But the only fire here burned merrily in a stone fireplace, which had a pot hanging on a hook above the flames.

Somehow, he'd expected more screaming in hell. Not the happy crackle of a cooking fire.

Then the door swung open and a red cloaked figure strode in.

The devil himself, surely.

Chase shrank back against the bed beneath him. "Mercy," he whispered. "I did not mean to hurt her. I swear it. Ask the princess. She knows."

Then the figure turned to hang up the cloak on a hook by the door. It wasn't the devil at all, but the white-haired witch.

"You!"

She set her hand on her hip, for the other carried a basket. "And who were you expecting, Sir Knight? Some princess, perhaps?"

He shook his head. "No, she saved me once, though I did not deserve it. She won't do it again." His mind finally caught up with his mouth. "Did you save me from the wolves?"

She set her basket down on the table. "Of course."

"Why?"

She stared at him for a moment, before saying slowly, "Because it was the honourable thing to do. Saving an innocent from the dark side of a forest he does not understand."

"I'm no innocent," Chase protested.

"No?" She scrutinised him. "So you'd prefer for me to take you back out there, into the forest? Maybe stake you out in the snow for the wolves to make mincemeat of you as they did your horse? If you don't freeze to death first, of course."

Only now did Chase realise he was naked beneath the blankets.

She'd removed his clothes? What kind of woman…

"My, what big eyes you have, Sir Knight," she teased. "Be easy. I have no intention of healing a man, only to send him to his death.

You are safe here."

"What did you do with my clothes, wench?" he demanded.

She folded her arms across her chest. "It's Mistress Rosa to you, you ungrateful lout. And 'twas not I who shredded your clothes, but you yourself, running and climbing and falling through the forest. Why, when I found you, you were wearing little more than rags. You would have died if I hadn't found you."

Saved by a woman. Again. Chase felt his cheeks grow hot. "Thank you for saving me," he mumbled.

She waved away his thanks. "No need to blush like a maid seeing her first cock." Realisation dawned in her eyes. "Is that what has you so embarrassed? No need to worry so much, Sir Knight. As a healer, I've seen many such, and I know these things shrink in the cold. Perhaps now you're warm, I can better take your measure…" She reached for the blankets, a wicked look in her eyes.

Chase clutched them like his life depended on it. "I'll thank you to keep your eyes off my cock!" he said hotly. Though now he thought about it, he wouldn't refuse if she put her hands on it…

Rosa chuckled and returned to the table. "Ah, I've already seen it. You're a fine size, nothing to blush about. But if you're the modest sort, maybe you should cover it with the blankets when I check the stitches in your leg. They should come out soon – your leg is mending nicely."

"You practised sewing on my leg?"

"Not so much practised as stitched the flesh together so it would heal." She reached for the blankets again. "Here, I can show you, if you like."

"No!"

She shrugged. "Suit yourself, then, Sir High and Mighty. I think I preferred you when you were unconscious. But now you're awake, I suppose you'll be wanting breakfast, so it's a good thing the hens laid plenty this morning."

While Rosa busied herself with making breakfast, Chase risked a peep under the blankets. Bandages covered his right leg, and encased most of his chest, as well. Broken ribs, he guessed, and his head hurt something fierce, too.

He watched the woman bustling about, and

another, more pressing question came to him. "How did you manage to save me?" he asked urgently. She was half his size. She couldn't have carried him out of there, or fought off an entire pack of wolves.

Rosa grinned. "Magic."

"Magic doesn't exist," Chase said. Even he could hear the lie in his words.

Rosa set both hands on her hips. "It doesn't, does it, Sir Knows-a-lot? Then how do you explain this? I was flying past, when I heard a commotion in the woods, and when I came in close to see what was going on, I saw a man falling out of a tree, in a fall so great it would have killed you. So I magicked you up beside me, and flew you home here, so I could tend your wounds."

"People can't fly." This he was more sure about.

She looked smug. "I can."

That could not be true. "How did you carry me here, then?" he challenged.

She jerked her head at the corner, where an old willow broom leaned against the wall. "Flew you back on my broomstick, of course. Don't you know that's how witches travel?"

Come to think of it, he had heard of such a thing. But it was such an impossible idea — brooms that flew – he'd never given it thought before. "Truly?" he asked weakly.

She shot him a look. "No, you daft thing. Sitting astride a broom is the stupidest thing I ever heard. Why, the wind would go right up my skirts and freeze the very core of me, it would. I'd need to bed a man every time I flew just to warm myself up again, and have no time for healing anyone."

He had to admit, her words conjured up such a vivid picture that he was more than a little aroused. In fact…

"Oooh, what a big – "

"Don't say it!" he begged, trying the cover the tent he'd pitched in his blankets.

To her credit, she didn't laugh this time. Instead, she shrugged. "Suit yourself, Sir Chase the Chaste. Anyone would think you'd never bedded a woman before." She considered him for a moment. "When you're healed, I could introduce you to a couple of girls at the inn who might be able to help you with that."

More images popped into his head, making him harder still.

He gritted his teeth. "Please, Mistress Rosa, can we talk about something…anything else? I was already in enough pain before this, and now…"

She blinked. "Oh, of course! You're about due another dose of medicinal. I almost forgot. I'll go down to the cellar and fill a jug. That should give you the time you need to…take care of things. Oh, and there's a bowl of water and a cloth beside the bed, so you can wash up after you're done, seeing as you're the modest sort who won't want my help with it." She winked as she knelt to lift up a trapdoor in the floor, then descended the steps until she was out of sight.

Chase shook his head. What sort of woman talked about sex as brazenly as this one? Most of the women back home had been more…modest. He didn't know what to think. One thing was for sure, though - he'd never met a woman like her.

Twenty-One

In the cellar, she sat down on a cask and laughed silently until tears streamed down her cheeks. So much for the brave and bold knights from her mother's stories — or even the show he'd put on for her that first morning. Perhaps she should not have kept him unconscious for two days, for she dearly needed a laugh.

Then again, if she'd let him wake earlier, he'd have been in a lot more pain. She'd used a fair bit of magic to heal him while he'd slept — magic the man did not believe in.

And strangest of all…he was the first man she'd ever met who wasn't eager to have a girl handle his man parts.

So much for spending Midwinter with the man. He'd probably shrink right up like a snail at the very thought.

Impulsively, she called out, "Are you finished, Sir Knight, or will you need a hand from me in finishing off?"

"I'm fine – fine! Just a moment!" he shouted back, in a fair panic.

She headed deeper into the cellar, to where her grandmother had kept the casks of medicinal mead, stronger than the usual stuff, and infused with healing herbs. Making more would take months, so she would have to be careful not to run out, but this would dull his pain better than the sleeping potions she'd given him before.

She wouldn't mind a cup of mulled mead herself, come to think of it. There were plenty of ordinary barrels she might tap. The knight would not mind a few minutes more to himself, either, she'd wager.

When she finally climbed the stairs, the

knight said, "You sure took your time. I said I was finished a while ago."

Rosa shrugged. "I didn't hear you." She set the jugs on the table.

"I shouted loud enough for them to hear me in the village. Gods, what did you do to me? This hurts! I'd give my kingdom for some wine to dull the pain."

She poured him a cup of the medicinal. "Try this. Then you'll owe me your kingdom, Your Majesty."

He didn't take the cup. "I have no kingdom. Not even a horse, now. What sort of knight does that make me?"

"One who's going to drink his medicine so I don't have to listen to you complain." Rosa thrust the cup at him, then folded her arms across her chest until he'd drained it. "There. That'll knit your bones a little more, if the magic's still as potent as I remember. Maybe your ribs will heal by the end of the day."

The knight choked. "That's not possible!"

"With magic, almost anything is possible. For a price." A blood price, usually, though she did not tell him that. This wouldn't be the first time she'd spilled blood for a stranger, nor would it be the last.

His eyes narrowed. "You sound wise for someone who looks so young. How old are you?"

Centuries, she wanted to tell him, but suddenly she didn't want to play with him any more. "I've seen twenty-two summers, but magic brings its own knowledge with it, wisdom from ages past. And witches learn young that power must be controlled, or there will be consequences."

"You're younger than me. Younger even than Maja was when…" The knight closed his mouth abruptly.

"Was Maja your princess?" Rosa asked.

The knight snorted. "Maja was my sister. She died in childbirth."

"I'm sorry," Rosa said automatically, then added, "Did the child die with her?"

"No, the boy lives. In a royal court, ward to the queen, no less. My brother in law could not have done better for his son." The knight shook his head.

To mention royalty so casually, this knight

must be highborn indeed. Ever so much higher than the Baron's family. And he hadn't said that his sister wasn't a princess — perhaps she'd married a prince, for her child to join the royal nursery. What must he think of her, and this cottage? Why, the man must be used to castles and golden plates. No wonder he hadn't wanted to take her clay cup.

She was lower than the servants who'd brought him breakfast in the morning. Speaking of which…

"I should do something with those eggs. Are you hungry, Sir Knight?"

"Chase," he said.

She mustn't have heard right.

"My name is Sir Chase. Call me Chase," he explained.

Rosa nodded. He surely understood proper protocol better than she ever could. "Breakfast, Sir Chase?"

"Yes! I feel like I haven't eaten for days. Why, I could eat a whole horse."

Did she dare mention his horse?

His face fell before she'd opened her mouth. He remembered, then.

"Just Chase. I'm hardly a knight at all without a horse. How the mighty have fallen." He shook his head. "Mistress Rosa, grateful though I am for your care and hospitality, I cannot repay you. The horse and what was in her saddlebags were all I owned in this world. Perhaps you should have left me to the wolves."

She recognised the despair in his tone. Her spirits had sunk that low at times, too.

"If you wish to offer payment, I'm sure you'll think of something suitable. I have helped far poorer patients than you, and they manage to find a way to show their gratitude. As for your horse…it seems to me the Baron owes you one, seeing as you lost yours in his service. Things are not so dark as they seem, Sir Chase. Your horse did not survive, but your saddlebags did. Your belongings are over by the window, and when you are well enough to leave your bed, you may have them back."

He half rose. "My cup? You have my cup?"

She rummaged through the bags until she found a metal cup. But when she drew it out, it glinted like it was made of gold.

Not just golden plates. Golden cups, too. This man was no ordinary knight.

"Thank you, Mistress Rosa. You don't know how much this means to me. It is all I have left of home, to remind me of them." His eyes turned pleading. "Can you stow it safely away again? I don't want it damaged."

She did as he bade her, wrapping it in the blanket that had covered it before.

She busied herself with breakfast, but bread and eggs were nowhere near enough to stop her mind from wondering what sort of man the gods had brought into her home.

Oh, he'd not harm her, she'd make sure of that, but whatever could bring a highborn knight, uncle to a prince, if he was to be believed, to hunt wolves in her woods, must be a curious tale indeed. A tale that he would tell her, she resolved, before the winter was over.

The least he could do after she saved his life.

Twenty-Two

Chase had tried sitting up while the girl was in the cellar, but his ribs had hurt so much, he'd lay back down again, heartily wishing he'd never heard of wolves or witches. Not that young Mistress Rosa was anything like he'd expected. Young and pert and far too knowing for one so young.

Unless she'd lied about her age, but he doubted that. She liked discomfiting him with the truth far too much.

Nothing he said or did seemed to discomfit her…except when she'd seen the cup. Maja's cup, that Abraham had turned to gold at a touch.

If her eyes had taken on a greedy glitter at the sight of so much gold, he would not have been surprised, but she'd looked…saddened. Disappointed, perhaps? So, out of respect for his hostess, he'd asked her to hide it again.

Her good spirits had returned as she bustled about, stoking the fire and seeing to breakfast. She hummed a little as she worked, but it was no song Chase recognised.

If he closed his eyes, he might be back in the kitchens of the castle where he and Abraham had fostered together, hoping for a treat from the cook before being sent back up to the Great Hall to serve at table, as a good page should.

But those days were gone, and Mistress Rosa's humble cottage would not yield the same fare as a castle kitchen. Likely he wouldn't see meat again until he was well enough to return to the Baron's house.

He would find a way to repay her, he promised himself. Once he'd killed the wolf and received his reward from the Baron.

"Can you sit up?" she asked, setting a plate on the table.

She didn't wait for an answer, slipping an arm behind his back to lift him with unexpected strength.

Chase gritted his teeth against the pain he expected, but it never came. He stared at her in surprise.

"That medicinal mead's powerful stuff, is it not? I told you it would heal you by dinnertime." She winked. "Ah, but there's no such thing as magic, is there?" Her mischievous eyes dared him to admit he'd lied about believing in magic. She'd seen the cup. She knew.

"All the magic I've seen up 'til now has caused nothing but grief, so you'll forgive me if I am not so ready to believe it can be a force for good," he said, turning his gaze to his plate so that he might avoid those knowing blue eyes. Yet even the plate wasn't what he'd expected — for even the Baron's table had been set with trenchers of stale bread. And what lay upon it…fried eggs, slices of some sort of spiced sausage, several slices of fresh bread, though there was no butter. He automatically looked across the table, even as he told himself he'd be lucky to get butter here.

Her sharp eyes missed nothing. She grinned as she bit into a piece of bread, thickly spread with something white. She chewed and swallowed before she said, "I wasn't sure if you'd want cheese or butter with your bread, so I set out both." She pushed two bowls toward him. "I think I put too much honey in the ricotta, so it's sweeter than it should be, but I find a little extra sweetness in the morning is not such a bad thing."

He stared at his plate. His belly growled at him to eat all that lay upon it, but he could not. "I cannot accept all this, for I cannot pay you for it. Mistress Rosa, I cannot in conscience let you empty your cellar for me. Please, take some for yourself."

She burst out laughing. "Sir Chase, if you ate ten times that much, you could not empty my cellar, not if you stayed here a year. Now. You lost plenty of blood before I got you home, and you will need your strength. Mine will be ready soon, and then I'll join you." She headed over to the fire, tipping the contents of a pan onto her own plate. Not quite as much as she'd served him, but the sausage and eggs were plain enough to tell him he'd been mistaken about her.

He waited no longer, taking up his eating knife to devour the food before him like he hadn't eaten in a week.

Then again, he wasn't sure how long he'd been asleep.

"Healing yourself does work up an appetite, for magic can only do so much. The rest is up to you. There's more bread and I can fetch more sausage, but you'll have to wait until tomorrow for more eggs. Eat your fill, Sir Chase." She handled her eating knife with all the delicacy of a court lady.

She didn't belong in a hovel on the outskirts of some tiny backwoods village.

"Who are you?" he asked. "And what are you doing here?"

She set down her knife, her eyes widening with surprise. "Why, Sir Chase, you must have injured your head worse than I thought. I am Mistress Rosa, the witch of these woods, and when you fell from a tree, I rescued you and brought you here to my home to heal you. I thought to share a pleasant meal with you before I commence my work for the day, while you rest. But perhaps I should check your head first." She reached for him.

Chase caught her wrist before she could touch him. "Not before you answer me. What have you done to me? How did I get here?"

He became aware of something sharp pressed against his throat. He glanced down, and found himself staring at the hilt of his own knife, floating in the air.

"What are you?" he whispered.

Her eyes seemed to glow. "I'm a witch who doesn't take kindly to threats. I may have saved your life once, but that doesn't mean I'll hesitate to take it back. Especially from such a poor guest, threatening your host when I have spent the last two days healing you. You're lucky I have a greater grudge against the wolves than the momentary irritation of the insult you've offered me."

It was like facing Queen Margareta in the court of Aros all over again. Except this time he had nothing left to lose. Chase sagged. "Then I must beg your forgiveness, though I do not deserve it. Magic has meant ill luck for me at every turn, so that I cannot recognise anything else. I have nothing left to offer but myself, and I am poor compensation for anything. Yet…I pledge my sword and my honour in your service, until my debt to you is paid."

Custom required him to kneel and lay his blade at her feet, but he had no idea what had become of his blade, and if he tried to get out of bed, all he would do is fall at her feet. So he bowed his head and hoped it would be enough. At least if she refused, his death would be swift, for he could still feel the blade at his throat.

"Now I know you have drunk too much of the medicinal mead. A highborn knight, pledging himself to a witch? You must have mistaken me for your princess, or someone else. I have no need of swords or service or men at all."

But he could not feel the blade any more.

"Rest and regain your strength, Sir Chase.

Maybe you'll regain your wits along the way. You may stay for the week, but then I must send you on your way, back to the Baron." Her smile held sympathy — something else he did not deserve. Then she touched his forehead and sleep engulfed him.

Almost like some sort of spell.

Twenty-Three

For a moment, Rosa almost regretted putting the knight into an enchanted sleep, but she banished the thought as quickly as it had come. She needed to take out his stitches and check how his bones were healing, instead of wasting time arguing with him.

Pledging himself in service to her, indeed! That had been the mead talking, more than the man. The only thing she could possibly use help with was killing the wolf, and what use was a man with a sword against an entire wolf pack?

But he hadn't been wearing a sword when she found him. Just the empty sheath. Oh, and he'd had a bow and quiver strapped to his back. Speaking about size, she'd never seen a bow so big. Taller than he was. She couldn't imagine how much strength it would take to draw such a thing, and he would need to heal some more before she could ask him to show her.

She changed the bandages around his ribs, noting with satisfaction that the bruising was already fading to yellow. With another dose of medicinal, they might have healed properly by the morrow.

She would have liked to leave the stitches in for another day, but she wasn't sure she'd get another chance if he woke up even grumpier than before, so she decided to take them out today, and mend the wound with a healing spell instead.

He might be a fool, blaming magic for his own ill luck, but she would not compromise her care on account of his foolishness.

When Rosa was satisfied that she'd done all she could for the snoring knight, she climbed up to the loft to check on the mead. As she'd surmised, the fermentation had finished and it was ready to be moved to the cellar to mature. That meant moving it from these casks to new ones, a task that would easily take the rest of the day, and perhaps the next, too.

By mid afternoon, she was lifting the barrels through magic alone, for her arms ached more than she cared to admit. Yet she'd dealt with more than half of the mead, so there would be less to move on the morrow.

Rosa floated the newly filled barrels to the cellar, then rolled them into place at the back of the cellar, where they would not be disturbed until they were ready.

If she had time on the morrow, she'd try her hand at turning the remaining barrels in the loft into extra strong, medicinal mead. She had to do something close to home, what with Sir Chase here in her cottage.

But such things could definitely wait until the morrow.

Sir Chase slept through the dinner hour and past dusk, so Rosa finished off the remains of the bread and sausage without cooking anything, and climbed into bed.

Her last thought before she fell asleep was that at least there was one benefit to having Sir Chase stay – it was warmer at night.

Twenty-Four

Chase could not remember the last time he'd slept in a bed so warm. Maybe when he'd been a boy, and shared a bed with his brothers on the cold winter nights. The sound of their even breathing had lulled him back to sleep then, but the sound of someone else breathing beside him set his every nerve on alert now. What was the witch doing to him?

He reached out, and his hand closed over something soft and warm.

Her breast, he realised in horror, yanking his hand back, but it was too late.

"Yes, that's a breast, Sir Chase the Chaste. Your mother had them, and if you ever find the courage to propose to a woman, your wife will, too."

He'd touched fabric, not flesh, but the thin shift had left nothing to the imagination. "Why are you in my bed in nothing but your underthings?" he demanded, feeling his desire rising even as he tried to think of something, anything, else but the near-naked woman lying in bed beside him. Close enough to touch…

"Because it's my bed, you fool. Even with you taking over most of it, there's still space for me."

Shame washed over him. Of course it was her bed. A place he had no business being, even if she'd put him here.

"I'll sleep on the floor," he mumbled, sliding a leg out from under the blankets. Cold air chilled his flesh, but honour gave him no choice.

"You will not. You'll freeze your man parts off, and other bits, besides. I haven't tended you for days to let you freeze to death on my floor."

Impossibly, her arms wrapped around him, pulling his body against hers.

Soft, warm flesh, with only a thin shift between them, her breasts pressing against his back, tempting him, taunting him…

"But…your honour…" he began, trying to pull away.

For a woman, she was uncommonly strong. More magic?

"My honour? What about yours? Isn't that the mark of a knight, his high honour? Surely you can find it in yourself to be honourable enough to share a bed with a woman without molesting her in the night. At least, I thought you would be. Was I mistaken, Sir Chase the not-so-chaste?"

The taunt stung, especially as his thoughts were anything but honourable.

"You were not mistaken," he said stiffly. "If I but had my sword, I could lay it between us, for honour's sake. Forgive me for touching you…where I did. If I had but known you were there, I would not have reached out. It will not happen again."

She laughed softly. "If I have to choose

between sharing a bed with a sword or risk being woken by the occasional caress, I'll choose you and your wandering hands, Sir Chase."

He felt the blood rising in his cheeks, and other places besides. Thank all that was holy he had his back to her.

Her breathing soon returned to the even pattern of sleep, but Chase lay awake for a long time.

When he woke groggily the next morning, he found the bed empty. A sense of loss skimmed through his mind, too fleeting to catch.

Chase shook his head. She was right. He had suffered a blow to the head, and it had turned him into a fool for sure.

Twenty-Five

For the third night, Rosa dreamed of Midwinter night, and the rite she was required to undertake if she wished to take her grandmother's place as priestess. Only a few days hence, and the gods had given her a man who would be living under her roof that very night. Almost as though they wished she would choose him.

A far better choice than Alard, for the knight would soon leave. The highborn knight probably thought peasant women shared their beds with noblemen like him as a matter of course, and he'd probably never think of her again afterward. A good thing, she told herself as she forced herself out of bed.

Rosa crept outside in the predawn light, holding her cloak tightly closed against the cold. She longed to return to bed, and see if she could wake the knight with a well-placed squeeze or caress. She'd done more than that in her dreams, and so had he. She laughed softly. No man could be as good as her dream lover had been with his hands, even if last night he'd worn the face of Sir Chase.

With Midwinter approaching, she shouldn't be so surprised the gods of the forest were sending her such dreams. Better that she spend the day working outside, for the more time she spent with the knight, the more likely she was to say something about his prowess in her dreams. Or how much she'd liked the feel of his hand on her breast last night. His touch had been surprisingly gentle, even as it set her heart alight.

She blamed her mother's tales of knights and princesses, chivalry and other such nonsense. Tales for normal girls, like Lule and

Piroska, for whom marrying some nobleman was the highest ambition they might have, but not suitable for a witch.

Her grandmother's tales had taught her far more, about the woods, and the history of this place, and magic. So much about magic.

But the tale uppermost in her mind now was about mead, and how one winter it had been so cold, the mead froze in the castle cellars. When the brewer had skimmed off the icicles and poured the remaining liquid into a new barrel, she'd found the mead more potent than anything she'd brewed before. The goddess of winter had blessed her brew, she decided, and offered up barrels of mead to her at Midwinter every year. When the longest night of the year ended, the Midwinter's Night mead was the best and strongest of all.

So Rosa had left some barrels outside last night, hoping they might freeze, and they told the truth of her grandmother's stories – frost rimed the sides of the barrels, and a thin layer of ice floated on top of the mead. She skimmed off the ice, poured the first barrel into a fresh one and dipped a cup into the liquid to taste it. Sure enough, it was stronger than the stuff she'd cellared yesterday.

By the time she was done with all the barrels, the sun was up, and the ice in the empty barrels had melted, so she left the casks in the sun to keep them from refreezing as she headed to the barn to milk the goats and fetch the day's eggs.

When she left the barn, he stood in the cottage doorway, squinting at the sun. Not naked any more – he'd found his clothes, and managed to put them on. He must be feeling better.

But that didn't mean he should be walking on that leg yet.

She opened her mouth to order him back to bed.

"Good morning, Mistress Rosa," he said, bowing, before he walked toward her.

He did not wince like a man in pain, nor did he limp. He was healed, Rosa decided, breathing a sigh of relief. Perhaps she could heal a man after all. Though that medicinal mead had definitely helped. She must make some more.

"Well met, Sir Chase. I was just fetching something for breakfast." She lifted the egg basket.

He frowned. "I should carry that for you. Leave it here. I will be but a moment..." He scanned the clearing, as if looking for something he'd lost.

Rosa smothered a smile. "The outhouse is that way." She pointed.

The knight flushed, muttering his thanks, as he loped off toward the outhouse.

Twenty-Six

Rosa's eyes sparkled with unusual brilliance this morning, like the sun glittering off blue ice. Her cheeks were pink more from cold than any blushing at his fumbling in the dark last night. Perhaps she'd forgotten it.

He wished he could. Even washing in the icy well water hadn't helped.

She finished her breakfast quickly, then headed back outside. She returned with a paddle loaded with two loaves of bread. She dropped these on the table. "Careful, they're hot," she called over her shoulder on her way out. Two more loaves soon joined the first two, whereupon Rosa enveloped one in a cloth and began to cut thick slices from it.

"Now this is what butter was made for," she said, spreading it thickly onto the heel of the loaf. She bit into it before the butter could melt. "Mmm."

Chase gripped the table with both hands. Watching a woman eat had never done this to him before. Maybe if he jumped into the well and stayed there until everything was numb, he'd manage to cool his ardour.

"Help yourself," she said. "After watching you break your fast yesterday, I hope I've made enough."

She lingered long enough to grab a second piece before she departed again.

Chase deliberately took his time finishing breakfast, thinking about all things cold and as unlike the young witch as possible.

It didn't help. The moment he was done, she entered the cottage again, this time headed for the ladder to the loft.

"Sir Chase, would you go and stand by the fire for a moment? I'd hate for you to get in the way. If I broke your ribs after all that effort healing them, I'd be a poor host indeed."

He headed for the fire, happy to warm himself while she did…whatever it was. It sounded like it involved moving something heavy. It was on the tip of his tongue to offer to help, but a gust of wind rushed through the open door. He headed to close that first.

"Oh, by all that's holy…stand aside or be it on your head!"

Chase whirled at the sound of her voice and froze, transfixed. A row of barrels floated toward him, supported by nothing but air. Headed for the door behind him.

Now her words made sense. Chase leaped out of the way, just in time, as the barrels floated outside, then landed neatly on the ground.

Rosa slid down the ladder, looking annoyed. "Did you not hear me, or did you simply not listen?"

"How did you do that?" he stammered.

She swore. "Magic, of course!" She waved her hand and another gust of wind came through the door, swept up Chase's empty plate, then dumped it into the washing up tub by the window. "Just like that!" She reached for her cloak, which flew into her hand from across the room. She fastened it as though it was a perfectly ordinary occurrence. "I should have taken you back to the Baron instead of bringing you here. Let you heal normally instead of…" She raked a hand through her hair. This close to her, Chase could see that it was pale gold, not white at all. "Pack your things. Let me know when you're ready to leave and I'll take you back to town." She turned and marched outside.

Magic. Of course. The most normal thing in the world for a witch.

For all he'd seen — Abraham's curse, then mindreading royalty in the court of Aros…he'd never truly seen magic performed in front of him. Not like this.

That first day he'd woken up in her house, she'd told him she could fly. She'd probably floated him back here like one of those barrels. So many times he'd questioned her, and she had answered. If only he'd listened.

She had more magic than Abraham and the court of Aros combined. Magic she'd used to help him.

And he owed her a debt for it. A debt he'd

sworn to pay.

He followed her outside. "You can't take me back to town. I haven't repaid you yet."

She knelt beside a firepit, watching a wisp of smoke curl up from a pile of kindling. Then she rose, turning to meet his eyes as the flames behind her leaped into the air, fanned by the wind. Rosa didn't even blink. Instead, she folded her arms across her chest, challenging him to continue.

"I pledged my service, and you said I had a week. A week to repay you." Chase took a deep breath. "I will do anything you ask of me. Just as I would for my liege lord, or lady. Anything. Just name it. But don't take me back to the Baron yet."

It shouldn't matter whether he stayed here or at the Great House, but somehow…it did.

He'd said it before, but now he meant to do it properly. Chase fell to his knees and drew his dagger, which he laid across both hands as though it were his absent sword. "My life and my blade, I pledge it in your service, Mistress Rosa," he said.

She stared at him for a long moment, before she finally said, "By all the gods, Sir

Chase…no one's ever done such a thing for me before. I'm no queen. I wouldn't rightly know what to say to that. Except…if I made a joke about the size of your sword, would you consider it a mortal insult? Because that's all I can think about right now."

"I have no idea," he confessed. "I've never made such a vow to anyone before, either." Not successfully, at least. Best if the King of Aros forgot he'd ever existed.

Rosa held out her hand to help him up. "I guess I accept, then. It feels ungrateful not to."

He wet his lips. "You should probably know that I am better with a bow than a sword. Oh, I can wield a sword well enough in the practice ring, but my accuracy is deadly with a bow."

He'd sparked her interest. "I saw your bow, and wondered…perhaps we can both use some target practice, but not today. Today, I want to try and get the god of fire to bless my mead."

That wasn't something you heard every day. "What can I do to help?"

Twenty-Seven

Loath to admit this was the first time she'd ever distilled mead on her own, or that it had been years since she'd seen her grandmother do it, she asked Sir Chase to fetch enough firewood to keep the cauldron boiling for several hours.

While he did that, he would be too busy to notice she was not as sure of herself about this as she wished. Oh, setting out the cauldron and filling it from one of the barrels of fermented mead was easy enough, once the fire was hot enough, but setting the special lid on it just right was a more delicate task. Not to mention making sure she had a cask on hand ready to take the distillate, but far enough away that the cask didn't catch fire, and the liquid didn't evaporate.

Her grandmother had always lit the firepit closest to the herb garden, and placed the cask on the far side of the garden wall, Rosa remembered, so Rosa did the same.

Then she sat on the wall to watch the knight hauling barrow after barrow of wood. He favoured one leg over the other – as she expected, for while he'd healed enough to walk, he still had not healed completely – and more than once, he'd winced as the load he carried was more than his half-healed ribs could handle. She half expected him to complain at being forced to do the work of a lowly woodcutter, especially in his condition, but the man simply smiled as he passed her and kept going.

A smile that warmed her heart, each time she saw it. Watching him work, she thanked the gods for sending her such a man in time for Midwinter. Why, she might even enjoy her initiation now.

When he'd piled up enough wood to fill all four firepits, he perched on the wall beside her and asked, "Do you think we have enough to summon your fire god now, or will he want a bigger pyre before he puts in an appearance?"

Rosa laughed. "He doesn't actually appear," she admitted. "It's more of a story my grandmother always told, about the ways to make the best mead. The recipe originally came from the goddess of bees, but the god of fire and the goddess of winter had a competition one Midwinter, to see who could make the best mead…" She stopped at the knight's sceptical look. "You're of the new faith, aren't you? The one with only one god, who cures diseases, conjures bread and fish, walks upon the surface of water without falling in and can raise people from the dead? The god of the desert people in the south?"

Chase nodded. "That sounds like the tales our priest told, yes. A faith more than a thousand years old is hardly new."

"It is new here. And the more people who believe in it, the fewer will respect the old gods, or give them their due. Then they grow angry, and it falls to we few who remain to remember the old ways, to save those raised in the new faith from a wrath they cannot begin to understand." Rosa shook her head. "Those who spread the new faith say the old gods are evil, but truly, they are not. Only when they are angered or not shown proper gratitude for their gifts do they stop caring for their people…but surely that is not evil. If you cared for someone every day, and never heard a word of thanks from them, only insults when they did not ignore you altogether…would you not turn away from them, too?"

It would be so easy to ignore the needs of the village, to live her life as she wanted, without taking up the mantle of priestess to the gods of the forest. Especially when even the village children taunted her…

"I'm a knight, not a god," Chase said slowly, "but if people hated me, I admit I would not want to help them, either. Yet…many of our priest's tales told of forgiveness, and charity, and how we should help those who needed it, not just our friends. Perhaps because if the other gods withdraw their assistance, it is up to us to perform their duties." He wiped a hand across his eyes. "Alas, I am no theology scholar. I learned to wield a sword and shoot a bow. Who am I to know a god's thoughts, or the reason they do what they do?"

His words put her to shame. Who was she to question her fate, indeed? She had received her magic as a gift from the gods, and she owed them her service for such a blessing.

"But I have heard many stories from my father's bible. What I have not heard is a tale about a mead-making competition between gods. So, Mistress Rosa, must I beg for this tale, or is it only told at Midwinter?"

A blush stole across her cheeks. "No, Midwinter is when…when they drank the mead. The tale is told whenever it's time to make it." She eyed the cauldron, which had not yet begun to steam. "I suppose we have plenty of time."

She took a deep breath. "The goddess of winter and the god of fire were drinking mead together one cold winter's night. The offering was made to the goddess, in thanks for helping a brewer, and the goddess said she would show the god of fire how to improve on the nectar of the gods, for that's what they called mead.

"She spread her magic around the jar, until ice formed on the outside. When she lifted the lid, the contents had frozen over, like a lake in winter. But just like a lake, when she smashed a hole in the top, there was still liquid inside, sweeter and more potent than before. She lifted out a jug of the stuff and shared a cup with the god of fire, who proclaimed it as his new favourite drink.

"He drained his cup, then said fire was far better than ice when it came to drink that warmed you from the inside, and he would make something even better.

"The goddess said he was welcome to try.

"So he took another jar, and built a fire beneath it. Soon, the jar began to boil. He took his sword and shield, placing the shield atop the bubbling jar, and propping it up with his sword, held upright in an empty jug." Rosa gestured at her setup. A conical copper lid with a pipe at the top, which slanted down to the empty barrel on the other side of the wall, was a far cry from the sword and shield, but if she closed her eyes, she could almost imagine it being the first such still, before time and practice had refined it to what she had now.

"My grandmother said the sword and shield were made of bronze, which glittered like gold," Rosa added.

Something tightened in Chase's expression, as if he did not like this particular detail.

Rosa hurried on. "The steam touched the shield and turned to liquid. The droplets ran down the sword until they formed a rivulet, filling the jug with what looked more like water than mead. Yet when they drank it…it burned their throats like liquid fire.

"The goddess said that ordinary mead had the power to heal, so this stuff was so medicinal, it could cure anything, so she declared that the god of fire had won the contest.

"He poured himself a cup of the sweet mead from the goddess's jar, and said the mead he'd made by fire was so strong, so pure, it should not be drunk by mortal man except on the very cusp of death. A mead most men could not drink was hardly mead at all, and he declared the goddess had won the contest.

"They then proceeded to drink more mead, as they argued about who had won the contest. By the time they had drunk all the mead, they had forgotten all about the competition, and it was time to…to do what deities do at the Midwinter solstice…so they never declared a winner." She ducked her head to hide her blush.

Chase laughed, his good humour returned. "I love it! Gods who get so drunk they forgot to pick a winner."

Rosa smiled, happy to let him believe it. If she told him why they'd been too distracted by their other duties, he would be horrified. Sir Chase the Chaste would not understand the power of fertility rituals, especially between gods.

He waved at the cauldron. "So you are making the fire mead today. Why not the ice mead?"

Rosa pointed at the barrels lined up outside the cottage. "I left those outside last night. I skimmed the ice off them while you were still sleeping, when I lit a fire in the baking oven for our bread. We call it Midwinter Night mead, for the goddess, and usually it stays in the casks for another year before it is drunk the following winter. The flavour is richer."

"And what will you do with the fire mead?"

This part was the bit she understood the least, for no matter how well her grandmother had explained it, Rosa had not been able to grasp how it was possible.

"The distillate – which my grandmother called the raw spirit, for it feels like your very soul has been ripped out of your throat when you drink it – is mixed with magic imbued leaves, so steeped in healing magic it is said they could bring a man back from the brink of death." She thought of the Baron – why had Grandmother not given him the medicinal mead? Unless she knew it would not work, for his growth disease could not be cured by it. There was so much her grandmother had not had time to tell her. "Perhaps that is what your desert god used. Maybe they knew the secrets of distilling there, too. Or your desert god stole the secret from our fire god."

"I'm not sure what intrigues me more. Gods getting drunk and stealing from one another, or magical, life-saving leaves. I wish I'd had some when my sister was dying. I might have been able to save her." Chase's shoulders slumped.

"You can't save everyone. Sometimes, it is simply their time." Rosa closed her eyes. "But sometimes, it's not. It's every bad decision you and everyone else ever made, that rips someone from you before their time. And no matter how much you wish you'd done things differently, that maybe you'd been brave enough to go instead of them, or you'd been quicker to take action in the past when it might have made a difference…it is still too late. I would give anything to have her back, and yet I still know I couldn't save her."

"Your grandmother?" Chase guessed.

Rosa nodded, not daring to raise her eyes lest he see the tears spilling down her cheeks. It did not do for a witch to show weakness.

"Was it sudden?"

Another nod. "The first snows had just fallen. We didn't even know the wolf had come down from the mountains. He killed her on the road, on her way home."

He stared at her. "You mean…the wolves the Baron sent me to kill? Your grandmother was killed by a wolf pack?"

"It was only one wolf then. The same wolf who killed my family, the last time the snows came. The same wolf I tried to kill the day before you came, but I thought it was just an ordinary wolf. I should have listened better to her stories…" Rosa shook her head, angry with herself. "It must have found a pack in the mountains and taken it over. Like…a man building an army…" Even as she said the words, they felt right. Like a man, not a wolf.

"A wolf building an army? Impossible. It was just a pack of them. Hungry, seeking food, and I foolishly left my horse where they could find it. I should never have left my eyrie. If I'd stayed up high, I could have picked them off one by one and I would have already claimed the Baron's reward." He jumped to his feet. "I shouldn't be sitting here, sharing stories by the fire. I should be out there, with my bow, fulfilling my quest."

"No!" Rosa grabbed his arm. "You're not healed yet. You've barely been out of bed for a few hours – you're in no state to go out hunting on your own. The medicinal mead may have brought you away from the brink of death, but it still takes days to heal. That beast out there is no ordinary wolf. There is magic about him, I tell you, or I would have killed him myself before you came. I tried, and failed, and barely escaped with my life. I could not kill one lone wolf, and you cannot defeat him with a pack at his back. If you were to go out there now, I might not be in time to save you again." She gestured at the still, which had started to drip. "Besides, don't you want to taste for yourself, and see which of the old gods truly makes the best mead?"

Five days. She only had to keep him here for five days. Long enough for Midwinter to have come and gone, and for her to have kept her word to Alard. But she would have to keep her word to the Baron, too, and become a priestess at Midwinter. For that, she needed the knight.

"Please, Sir Chase. You have travelled to

many places, and undoubtedly tasted many fine things. Perhaps you can settle the score between the goddess of winter and the god of fire. Perhaps they will see fit to offer you a blessing that may help you in the coming battle."

"The bishop back home would have me excommunicated for even thinking about accepting your offer."

Hope sparked in her breast. "But you are considering it, are you not?"

He stared at her, as if measuring her soul. "More because it is foolish to refuse a drink offered by a beautiful woman, than because some deities I do not believe in may offer me some kind of magical assistance."

The knight had turned the tables on her, for he was far more skilled at flattery than she would ever be. "You go too far, Sir Chase. No man has ever called me beautiful and told the truth in the same breath."

"Then it seems the men of your village are more foolish than me." He took a deep breath. "It is said far and wide that Queen Margareta of Aros is the fairest lady any man has ever seen, but I have gazed upon her face and I can honestly say you bring more joy to my eye in a moment than a lifetime spent in her presence."

Rosa didn't know what to say. She managed a shy smile. Finally, she said, "Then I thank you for the compliment, Sir Knight."

Perhaps her mother had not been wrong about knights and their courtly courtesy after all.

Twenty-Eight

He didn't deserve her thanks. He hadn't lied, but…he hadn't told her the truth about the Queen of Aros, either. Then again, no one here needed to know the truth about how he'd been banished from Aros. Least of all Rosa, whose ice-fair features were lovely enough to tempt any man. Including the Baron's son, he was sure.

A thought that shouldn't send a rush of anger through him, yet there it was. He'd experienced jealousy before, envying Abraham and Maja their happiness together, but that was nothing compared to the acid eating his insides now.

Even as he told himself he was here to complete a quest and earn a reputation, a tiny voice in the back of his mind added how wonderful it would be to win Rosa's heart along the way. To share her bed the way a man usually did with a woman, dishonour be damned.

Only he would have to leave her at the end of the winter, for he had no place here. And to break the heart of a witch who could probably kill him with a glance, or curse him for the rest of his days, did not seem like the wisest course of action.

The Baron's son was a better match for her, he reasoned. She could rule over the Great House instead of this tiny cottage, and have servants to do the work for her. And surely she had family here, for in a village so small, everyone must be related to some degree.

Unless the wolves had killed them all.

But why would a wolf do that – kill a whole family, yet leave the rest of the village untouched? Until now. It made no sense.

"What can you tell me about the wolves?" Chase asked, trying to sound casual.

"Well, there was only one until the day you decided to go after him," Rosa said.

One wolf? That's what the Baron's son had said. But for one wolf to kill so many people…

"How many men had it killed before the Baron sent for me?" he asked.

She stared at him, as though trying to decide if such a question merited a reply. Finally, she said. "He killed my parents and my sister, six years ago, and my grandmother a few weeks ago. There are tales of others he may have murdered in the past, but that was long ago. Too long for anyone to know for sure. Then there's you, and me, though he hasn't killed us yet."

"The wolf attacked you, and you got away? How?" The moment the question left his lips, he knew he'd been stupid. "Wait, I know — magic, right?"

He'd earned a smile from her as she nodded.

"Can you tell me more than that? If there is some way I can defeat it, then I must know more." He reached out and captured her hand.

"Please, Mistress Rosa. You've told me tales about gods getting drunk. Now tell me the tale about the beautiful young woman escaping from the beast."

"That is another story entirely, and not the one you want, I think. But if you wish to know the true tale of the reckless witch who went out to kill the wolf by herself, you shall have it." Rosa took a deep breath.

He listened to her tale, which sounded disturbingly like his own plan when he'd headed out to that clearing. He'd seen the feathers, but dismissed the earlier kill as something the Baron's hunting party had placed, not Rosa. The more she spoke, the more his admiration grew. If the wolf hadn't manage to knock her out of her tree, she would have been victorious, he was certain of it.

"No wonder the wolf sought reinforcements before it fought you again," Chase said in wonderment.

Rosa blinked. "But that's just it. Wolves don't do that. They are either part of a pack, or they aren't. The only lone wolves who are allowed to join a pack are either fertile females or a male so strong he defeats their leader, and any other challenger the pack sends against him. Only a man – a leader of men – would go and recruit an army to defeat a foe they cannot defeat alone. In wolves, they would see that as weakness and slink away to find a more easily conquered food source. They would not return with greater forces. Wolves don't think like men…unless magic turned a man into a wolf, as my grandmother said."

"Is that possible?" He didn't want to believe it, but after all he'd seen Rosa do with her magic, he might have to.

"My grandmother told many tales of such things, long before my gifts revealed themselves, so that I might recognise my magic when it came. Neither of us expected my powers would have an affinity for air, and it took me longer to master than others might have because it seemed like such a trivial thing at first. Then I learned I could use it to listen, and lift things and…on the night I fled from the wolf, I truly learned to fly." Rosa spread her hands wide. "So, I suppose my answer is that yes, it is possible. Transforming people into beasts is a common method of punishment, when a man commits a crime against a witch."

She said it in such a matter-of-fact way that it shouldn't have sounded like a threat, or even a warning, but Chase shivered all the same.

In a soft patch of dirt beside the fire, the cat rolled onto its back, stretching as it dozed in the warmth.

"What was his crime?" Chase asked, pointing at the cat. He could easily imagine the beast as some fat, greedy baron, taking everything from his people and leaving them to starve.

Rosa stared at the creature. "Oh, Hagen's crime is laziness. When a rat entered the cottage, he let it get away with Grandmother's dinner."

"She kept a man in her cottage to catch rats?" Now he'd heard everything.

Rosa laughed. "Of course not. Hagen is a cat, one who's supposed to be much more suitable for such things. But when he got all the female cats around pregnant so they were all busy with their litters at the same time, and Hagen would not hunt…she took his manhood." She grinned evilly. "One stroke of the knife, and no more kittens for him. I swear it made him even more fat and lazy than before, but Grandmother liked him sitting on her lap of an evening, so she tolerated him. I have yet to find a use for him. Perhaps he can warm my bed when you are gone." Now she wouldn't meet his eyes.

"Gone. Yes," Chase said vaguely. He'd barely been here a week, but already he didn't want to leave. He'd never thought such a tiny cottage could be comfortable, or even a desirable place to live, but with Rosa…he could not…nay, he did not want to imagine living anywhere else. Yet how could he already think of it as home?

He was becoming as mad as Abraham.

Better that she share her bed with a sexless cat than a less than honourable knight who half feared and half hoped he'd give in to his desires and make love to her in the night.

She'd probably turn him into a neutered cat for it, though.

Better that he turn his thoughts to besting the beast, and not her bed.

If Rosa allowed him to. She could easily have left him in her house, and gone after the beast by herself.

Chase cleared his throat. "When you hunt this wolf again, will you allow me to help you? I may not have magic, but I have yet to meet a better bowman than I. If I take care not to climb or fall out of my tree, of course."

"Modest, aren't you, Sir Knight? All right, you may show me your bow skills on the morrow. If you can match me, then I will agree to hunt with you."

From any other woman, the suggestion that he might not be good enough would have rankled. Yet the challenge he saw in Rosa's eyes made him want to rise to meet her.

Here he had no golden armour, no herald to announce him, not even a horse to ride. In his regular leather armour, with injuries that had barely healed, his fate rested on the best archery performance of his life.

Against a woman who could manipulate the very air so that she might fly.

A woman who made his heart soar just by looking at him.

Aros could keep their queens and princesses. He would give everything he had on the morrow, for a chance to hunt beside this lovely woods witch.

He inclined his head in thanks.

Twenty-Nine

Despite grimacing in pain more than once over the course of the day, Sir Chase never complained. He laboured as hard as Rosa did to keep the fire burning, the distillate flowing, and the casks moving into the cellar.

She considered telling him she usually used magic to lift the casks, but as he was already halfway down the stairs to the cellar, she didn't think he'd hear her, so she let him continue. Well, until she'd heard him swearing loudly.

"What's amiss?" she called, hurrying inside after him.

"The size of your cellar! You have enough space and supplies here to feed a whole castle through a siege, and yet there is nothing more than a tiny cottage atop it?"

Ah. "This was once the seat of an ancient king, who built a mighty fort in the forest, the home of his gods. When conquering invaders came from the south, he made an alliance with them. Their builders and architects took apart his wooden halls and walls, finding the weaknesses they could exploit in other, similar forts that held their enemies, and rebuilt his in the style of their own brick and stone palaces, so they might winter in comfort and safety in between campaigns.

"Eventually, the southerners headed home, carrying the wealth of the king's neighbours, but leaving the king his share, and the palace. The southerners never returned – my grandmother said they lost their own city to invaders, while they were out waging war here – so the king ruled alone. One of his descendants moved the capital to somewhere more convenient for trade with the northern cities, and the forest was allowed to conquer the castle."

Chase nodded. "Then why is the cellar still here?"

She hadn't thought to ask that question when she'd first heard the tale, but then Grandmother had captured her imagination with tales of battle, kings and princes. Then, she hadn't known how slowly a house fell into ruin, or how the upper parts collapsed into the cellar until…

Rosa wiped away a tear, chiding herself at thinking of her parents' house, when she should be thinking about this one.

"The kings left much of their wealth hidden here in the cellars, ordering the stones of the palace to be pulled down and carted to where the town is now, so that none might stumble across the king's treasury by accident. A cottage was built atop the entrance, home to the High Priestess dedicated to protecting the grove…and the king's people from the wrath of the forest gods."

She managed a wry smile. "Grandmother once told me the High Priestess was chosen from among the king's daughters, for the gods demanded no less than royal blood be shed at their altars for granting the king their favour. She laughed and said that meant we had royal blood, too, for she never would have been chosen as High Priestess without it. If it is true, then perhaps I am a princess, too." She stuck her nose in the air, trying to look as haughty as Piroska. "But as I have yet to hear of a princess who milks goats, I won't start wearing a crown any time soon." Or ever, she added silently to herself. Though she had played with some rather corroded ones in the back of the cellar when she was a little girl.

No need to tell the knight that the old king's treasury still hid in the secret chambers beneath his feet. Forgotten by all but herself, now.

Chase climbed the steps and stood before her. "That is a pity. A circlet of fine silver, studded with rubies, would keep your scarlet hood in place in the winter, but for summer, a fillet of gold set with sapphires the icy colour of your eyes, I think, holding back your hair so that all might see your lovely face and lose themselves in your eyes as I have. I should write a letter to the king, come spring, commanding he honour your beauty as it deserves."

She met his gaze squarely. "You're mocking me, Sir Knight. What would your princess think, if she knew you said such things to me?" She turned and headed back to the fire, for while he'd been stoking her ire, the flames were in need of feeding.

Behind her, she heard him mutter softly, "She is not my princess, and may never be." A sigh with the weight of the world upon it accompanied his words.

Her heart went out to him – for he loved a woman he could not have – but she didn't stop to offer her sympathy. If he'd meant her to hear, he would have spoken louder.

Let him think he kept secrets. Like the pain in his eyes as he hefted the next cask. The man would not be able to draw a bow on the morrow, and another day in bed might help him heal completely.

She'd give him a cup of the freshly fire-distilled mead when all was done, to help ease him into sleep tonight. She might even drink a cup herself.

Thirty

Dawn burned Chase's eyelids, while some bloody minstrel had started drumming on the inside of his head. His bladder begged to be emptied, but he had no desire to release the warm, soft maiden in his arms.

Even her hair was soft, and she smelled of honey. No surprise, given all the mead they'd brewed yesterday. And the mead they'd drunk…

By all that was holy, he hadn't dishonoured her, had he?

He should have felt a stirring in his groin at

that thought, but with her body pressed against him, as it likely had been for hours, he was already hard as a rock.

Oh, now he definitely needed to visit the outhouse.

When he returned, Rosa had already lit the fire, and she had a pan in her hand, ready to warm it to make breakfast. She pointed the pan at him. "What manner of mischief were you up to out there? Doing more damage to yourself, after yesterday?"

He flushed, torn between telling her why he'd taken so long in the outhouse, or lying and saying he felt fine.

"Bed for you, you bad boy, and if you try to get up again, I'll tie you to it," she said.

He wanted to argue, but he hurt too much to stay stubborn when he really wanted to go back to bed. If he went hunting today, the wolf would win for sure.

He climbed into the bed and pulled the blankets up to cover himself. He might have taken his time in the outhouse, but watching her walk around the cottage in a thin shift, her nipples clearly visible, would soon arouse his desire again. He forced himself to look away.

"What was in the mead we drank last night? Miners, with picks and hammers, I swear, for my head is full of them this morning," he said.

"I told you 'tis no good to dull the pain so, or to keep working in your condition, but you're a stubborn one, Sir Knight. I'll make you some willow bark tea, if you swear you'll stay in bed." She set her hands on her hips, daring him to refuse.

Why did she have to stand so, thrusting her breasts forward so he could not help but stare at those two pink pearls?

Chase squeezed his eyes shut, but still the image taunted him from behind his eyelids. "As you wish, Mistress Rosa."

A cool hand touched his forehead, forcing his eyes open. "You feel a mite hot, Sir Chase. I hope 'tis not a fever. I'll fetch you some of the medicinal mead, too." Her icy eyes fair melted with concern for him.

Chase blamed the fever in his blood. He cupped her cheeks, stretched up and kissed her.

Her lips were warm and soft, as he knew

they would be, tasting slightly of salt.

She'd broken her fast already, without him.

Disappointment welled up, and he dropped an arm around her to pull her closer. Her breasts touched his chest and he lost all reason, kissing her as though beyond her lips, she kept the very air he needed to breathe.

And she returned his kiss, yielding to his embrace as her tongue curled to tempt his, for this maiden was as skilled with her mouth as she was with her hands. Oh, to feel either of them on him, to…

She broke the kiss. "Sir Chase. I thought I'd made myself clear – I want no swords in my bed." She climbed out of his lap and resumed making breakfast with her back to him.

Swords? He glanced down at the all-to-obvious tent in his tunic, outlined by a damp patch where she'd been sitting. Either she'd shared his desire, or he'd made a mess of things. Again.

Strongly suspecting it was the latter, Chase hung his head. "I'm sorry, Mistress Rosa. You are so enchanting, I forgot myself. For a moment. It won't happen again."

She hung a pot from a hook over the fire, then glanced over her shoulder at him. "That's a pity. For you have quite an extraordinary mouth on you, Sir Chase. Not to mention a clever tongue. I imagine your princess is very fond of your kisses."

He wanted to shout that he had no princess, but the noise would have hurt his head, and she wouldn't have listened, anyway. Yesterday, she'd said she had royal blood, which meant if he wanted to kiss any princess, it was her.

Now, if Rosa had agreed to become his princess…

Chase lay back and imagined how she might grow very fond of his kisses indeed…

Thirty-One

Two days she kept the knight in her bed, and two nights she slept in his arms. More than once, she'd considered climbing into his lap, lifting his tunic and finishing what they'd started.

But she knew she could not. If she succeeded in seducing him, he would stare at her after, his eyes wide with guilt, and swear he would not let his desire overwhelm his reason again. And that simply would not do, with Midwinter approaching. If she could spend but one night as his lover, best to save that pleasure for Midwinter. For she'd be lying to herself if she thought she might want to spend the night with any other man.

So after two days of letting the magic-infused mead do its work, she didn't protest when she came in with the morning's milk to find him stringing his bow.

"I won't repay my debt to you lying in bed," Sir Chase said, his eyes on the notched yew. "I mean to help you slay that wolf, so that I may keep my word and complete my quest."

She almost told him that if he gave himself to her tonight, the longest night of the year, he would help her more than enough, but something in the stiffness of his back and shoulders made her bite her tongue. Honour and pride – a man's worst failings, though most men considered them virtues – would force him out after her if she left to slay the wolf alone. Gods only knew how that would end, especially if the pack found him first.

"I'll go clear the snow off my archery targets, then," she said lightly, heading back out the way she'd come.

He stared at her, his mouth open as if he

wanted to ask something, but the only words that came out were an abrupt, "Thank you."

Rosa scoured the ground of snow, but the archery targets were nowhere to be seen. Come to think of it, she couldn't remember the last time she'd used them. Certainly not since she'd learned she could simply fire an arrow in the vague direction she wanted, and command the wind to do the rest. Perhaps her grandmother had added the targets to the lumber pile, and they'd become buried under some woodcutter's payment for services rendered.

She finally found them atop the woodshed roof, covering holes the thatcher had not yet seen to. She set the targets up in front of the bramble hedge that would be a mass of berries when summer came, and found Sir Chase watching her from the cottage doorway.

"Most men set targets up in an empty field, or at least somewhere with plenty of clear ground to make it easier to retrieve the arrows that miss the target," he said. "I can't imagine you want to venture into the brambles, nor heal my scratches if I do."

"I never miss," she said.

He gave her a long look. "Neither do I."

Chase strode up to the furthest target, then paced the distance across the clearing. He turned, took aim, and fired.

His arrow hit high, halfway between the centre and the edge.

Before Rosa could comment on his accuracy, he fired off a second shot…one that buried itself in the very centre of the target.

By the time he'd emptied his quiver, Chase had marked his target with a cross made of arrows. Then he bowed, like she imagined a knight would to his lady-love at a tourney. "Your turn, Mistress Rosa."

She shook her head. For a moment, she'd thought…something very silly indeed. "Of course."

She took her time stringing and testing her bow, ducking her head until her blush faded. He might be a knight, but she was no lady. She was the kind of girl he might allow to warm his bed for a night, before forgetting all about her.

Rosa let her first arrow fly, biting her lip for the air she needed to carry it where she wanted. She fired off a half-dozen more, until she'd roughly marked the rune for the winter goddess on her target. The goddess was far more powerful than some deity who made fish multiply. Why, the fish themselves could do that.

"Not bad," Chase said.

Rosa folded her arms. She'd been every bit as good as him.

"Let's try again," he said. With four more arrows, he turned his cross into the rune for the fire god.

Rosa's mouth went dry. Did he know…?

"Now, your turn," Chase said, setting the butt of his bow on the ground.

Rosa lifted hers, ready to bite her lip again.

"Without magic," Chase added.

She stared at him in horror. "Why in the goddess's name would I do that? You use your strengths, and I'll use mine."

"But what if you need to use your magic for something else, and can't use it to guide your arrows? Better that you use your bow to shoot, and shoot well, and keep your magic for where it's most needed. What if you grew tired, or you ran out of magic?"

Rosa shook her head. "Magic doesn't work that way." But even as she said it, she could see he had a point. She could grow too tired to use her magic properly, or she might lose too much blood and be unable to cast another spell. And while she could summon a huge gust of wind, she struggled to control two, even if they were very small.

"Show me how you shoot, Mistress Rosa. Please."

Between the look in his eyes and his wheedling tone, she could not refuse him anything. Thank the gods he hadn't asked her for a kiss instead.

Rosa took a deep breath, released it, and focussed on her arrow. It would never reach the target from this distance without magic.

She fired anyway, seeing the arrow dip so that it would strike the dirt long before the target.

He hadn't said anything about not using magic to retrieve her arrow, though, so she dashed forward, ready to catch the arrow when it flew back into her hand.

When she'd halved the distance, she took aim once more. The second arrow reached the target, but only just. The point touched the bottom edge, then fell away, for it had not hit hard enough to stay.

Rosa cursed and summoned the arrow back.

"I'm too far from the target," she said, lifting her foot to halve the distance again.

But a hand caught her arm, pulling her back.

"I assure you, you're not," Chase said, releasing her. He held out his arms. "May I show you?"

Mutely, Rosa nodded.

She found herself pulled into his embrace, or that's what it felt like, until she realised he had his hands on the bow and arrow, not her.

A hard, muscled leg slid between hers, making her gasp, but he merely nudged her stance wider as he turned her, then withdrew.

Rosa couldn't breathe. She'd lain in his arms for several nights now, but somehow this seemed closer, more intimate. Then she felt his body hard against her back and she thought she might swoon.

He laid his cheek against hers. "Pull," he

whispered, wrapping his hand around hers as he drew the arrow so far back, his fingers touched her breast. "Aim." He blew out a warm breath that seemed to head straight down the lacings of her gown. "Loose." He let go.

Rosa's knees crumpled. Fortunately, the only thing he'd released was the arrow – if anything, his grip around her tightened, so she stayed on her feet. Barely.

"Now you try," he said. "Or do you want me to show you one more time?"

Her voice came out as a whisper. "Please."

"First, I want you to promise me something."

"Anything." She meant it, too.

"You won't go off hunting the wolf without me. When you go, you'll take me with you. I want your word, Rosa. I can't bear the thought of you going out there alone. If something were to happen to you…so I must go with you. Give me your oath on whatever you hold holy that we will hunt the wolf together."

She pressed her lips together. While her body might be going mad with desire for this man, her head still ruled her. And she knew she would be safer hunting without him. Especially after tonight.

"Give me your word, or I shall carry you inside and lock you in the cellar. Then I'll hunt the beast on my own."

"NO!" burst from her lips. "You'll be killed!"

He chuckled. "A normal woman would be fearful of being locked up, while having faith that her champion would return victorious."

She wrenched free so she could face him. Why, oh why was she breathing so hard?

"If I were a normal woman, you'd already be dead. I won't let that wolf kill anyone else!"

His stony expression gave her no hope. "Your oath, Mistress Rosa."

She closed her eyes. This was madness, yet what else could she do? "I swear on my life, and the souls of my family, that when I hunt the wolf who killed them, I shall take you with me."

With her eyes still closed, she had no warning. He seized her and kissed her, stealing her breath almost entirely. For a moment, she froze.

It's Midwinter Eve, she reminded herself. If they spent the rest of the scant daylight hours kissing, when night fell he might be the one to seduce her, and with the gods' help for the hunt, he would be safe.

She gasped, sucking in air like a woman nearly drowned, threw her arms around the knight's neck and kissed him with all the passion she could muster.

Thirty-Two

Hoofbeats, in a hurry. Chase reluctantly released Rosa, and took up a defensive position before her. He might only have a bow, but he could kill the horse and its rider before either reached Rosa. He had some honour left, after all.

The rider galloped into view, then pulled the horse to a stop, hard. "Sir Chase!" the man shouted, sliding to the ground. "We all thought you must be dead!"

Alard, the Baron's son. Chase lowered his bow. "Only thanks to Mistress Rosa here, and the good fortune that wolves prefer horseflesh to mine."

"Well, thank God for that, then, eh? Though you must be quick if you mean to kill the beast. I have sent out my men to scour the forest for it. After it attacked again…"

Rosa ducked out from behind Chase. "Who did you send? And who was attacked?"

"Mighty hunters, just like Sir Chase here, though I don't think any of them were knights. They rode off in different directions. Each man swore he would bring me the wolf's head, and win the reward." Alard looked dazed. "The beast will not survive the night!"

"You fool!" she hissed. "It's your men who won't survive the night! There's more than one wolf now – a whole pack of them, and they hunt horses!"

Alard's face turned pale, his eyes suddenly as icy as Rosa's when she was annoyed. "It's treason to show such disrespect to your liege lord, not to mention the man who will soon be your husband. Beg for my forgiveness now, and I shall not have you thrown in the stocks."

Rosa was betrothed to the Baron's son?

Why hadn't she told him?

Rosa gasped. "The Baron? He's…gone? How did the wolf manage to enter his bedchamber?"

"Of course the wolf didn't kill him. Wolves can't open doors. He died last night, on the blade of his own sword, which caused chaos in the household, for there was no priest about to administer last rites, and I feared for his soul…"

Rosa stamped her foot. "Let the priest worry about your father's soul. Who did the wolf attack, if not the Baron?"

Alard's face still looked pinched. "Piroska. We did not find her until this morning, what with all the fuss over my father. It's likely one of my riders scared the wolf off, or it might have been much worse."

"Worse than losing the woman carrying your unborn son and heir?" Rosa demanded, advancing. "Your father would be ashamed to hear you say such a thing. And you gave me your word that you would marry her before the week was out. Faithless fool, what kind of man can't even protect his own wife and child?"

Alard retreated, until his back smacked against a tree, his eyes round with fear. "She lives! She lives!"

Rosa stopped. "The wolves didn't kill her?"

"The beast dragged her into a ditch beside the road, her cloak so covered in mud no one saw her until morning, when she was half frozen. She has some bite marks on her arms, but that is all." Alard seemed to recover a speck of his former composure. "She is safe in her father's cottage, resting. He had to give her some strong drink to send her to sleep, for she was quite hysterical."

Rosa blinked, suddenly thoughtful. "Piroska does not own a cloak. She wraps herself in a shawl as she stares at me in mine."

"I gave it to her. She insisted she would not see me again until I gave her one," Alard said. "Just like yours."

Realisation dawned. That meant…

"The wolf mistook her for me," Rosa said slowly, as if reading Chase's thoughts. "If it doesn't know the difference, it will come back for her, to kill her as he did the rest of my family."

Chase found himself nodding. "Or perhaps it noticed it had made a mistake, and left her."

"It's an animal!" Alard said. "Beasts don't think!"

"Go home, Alard. Get Piroska into the Great House, then lock the doors and bar the gates. Post guards inside. We'll deal with the wolf, and maybe save the lives of your men while we're at it." Rosa flicked her hand in dismissal.

"As your husband to be, I forbid it!" Alard insisted. A stronger man might have roared the words, but Alard's voice was too reedy for it to sound like more than a whine.

Rosa lifted her chin. "You are not, and never will be, my husband. Now, get home, you fool, to the woman you promised you'd marry. Before the wolf pack comes after you and your horse."

Wind began to move through the treetops, swirling what leaves remained. Alard's horse's ears flew back, his eyes rolling in panic. The horse recognised angry magic, even if its master did not.

"I command you to come with me!" Alard said.

Chase watched in amazement as a whirlwind of leaves shot down to the ground, lifted a struggling Alard, and dropped him into his saddle. The horse bolted, its master barely clinging to its back, while the wind whipped the beast's tail to urge it on.

"His father was a good man who believed in the old gods, but paid lip service to the new god for the love of his wife. He should have taken another wife after she died, but he said he had no need, with Alard as his heir. Gods grant Alard a son who possesses all the wits he does not, though given who the mother is…who knows?" Rosa shrugged. "What he does now matters not. We need to find that wolf before it kills again."

Chase agreed. "Tonight."

She sighed. "I had hoped to wait until tomorrow, but we cannot. It seems I will definitely need your help, enacting the best plan we can concoct before sunset." She looked troubled, but didn't say why.

Probably worried about facing the wolf

again, after failing the first time. Chase certainly was.

"May your gods help us," he said solemnly. The god of his father certainly hadn't done anything for him – perhaps the old gods would be more helpful.

"They'll have to, if they ever want another priestess." Rosa beckoned. "We have a few hours until dark, and you promised me an archery lesson."

Chase wished he could lock her in the cellar, safe from harm, but Rosa probably knew another way out. She was as eager for this fight as he was.

He swallowed. No more kisses. He would bring her the wolf's head, or die trying.

Thirty-Three

"That tree," Chase said, pointing.

He'd picked the largest one, with branches so broad you could sleep on them. The wolf would not be able to knock over this mighty tree, Rosa was certain of it. She brought the carpet lower, so that Chase only had to step out onto the branch. He had his bow, a full quiver, a jar of tallow and a brazier full of coals. His armour would protect him and his cloak would keep him warm. She shouldn't worry so, she told herself, but she could not shake the memory in her mind's eye of him falling out of the tree that first time.

Remember, we both have to survive this

battle, if you want us to perform the Midwinter rites tonight, Rosa said silently to the gods of the forest, knowing they would be listening. Unless you wish to find a new priestess.

She didn't expect a response, but it would have been nice, all the same. The gods only spoke to the High Priestess, or so her grandmother had said.

She didn't have chickens as bait this time. Hagen had caught his first rat, and inadvertently showed her the nest where she'd found four more. Now their gutted corpses lay scattered around the clearing, the smell of fresh blood enough to lure any predator in for a taste.

She prayed it would be enough, and wished she'd had the foresight to demand Alard's horse to use as bait instead.

If they failed tonight, she would head straight for the stables.

She had her bow and a quiver of her own, but Chase was the true hunter tonight, not her. Her job was to be his eyes in the air, seeing what he could not, while his fire arrows would light up the clearing, bright as day.

The fire should drive off the pack, if they were naught but ordinary wolves, they'd decided, but they weren't so sure about the white wolf. Fire had saved her life the night it had killed her family, so it would surely be wary of it, but not in the way of a wild beast. No, like a man who had been burned.

Rosa flew up, high above the treetops, where she might see the clearing and half the forest. She pulled her cloak close around her, and settled down to wait.

The sun sank. The sky faded into twilight, before deepening to darkness. The moon would not rise for hours yet. All the more reason for the fire arrows.

The wind brought her sounds from every corner of the forest, whispering that wolves were on their way, and from where.

Rosa let the wind carry her own whispered words to Chase: "They come, from the west."

She thought she glimpsed something moving in the trees, around the edge of the clearing. The southern side, though, not the west. Then she blinked, and it was gone. Probably just leaves, or snow whipped up by the wind, she decided.

Chase's first arrow blazed into light, arcing up, across the clearing, to find its target in the eye of a wolf. He was a remarkable shot, and she would tell him so, when this was over.

His second and third arrows landed in the

snow.

Perhaps not so remarkable, after all.

Two more wolves went down to ordinary arrows.

Only then did Rosa realise that the shots into the snow had not missed, but the lamp oil had been slow to catch fire. A ring of flames rose up, encircling the wolf pack.

The pack panicked, milling around the clearing like frightened sheep. One picked up a dead rat, while others ran in every direction, cutting one another off as they darted around, trying to escape the flames that fenced them in.

Rosa looked in vain for the white wolf, but it was nowhere to be seen. Once again, the creature had sacrificed someone else with no care for the consequences or loss of life. A nobleman or a king for sure.

She glanced at Chase, wondering if the knight would simply slaughter the pack while they were trapped. He was a nobleman, too, after all.

But the branch where he'd sat only moments before was empty.

"Chase!" she shouted, swooping lower.

"I see it!" he called back.

She could not see him, but his voice sounded excited. She dropped further, straining her eyes to see. Was that movement on the ground beneath it? Gods, if he was on the ground…

A fire arrow dropped into the snow, narrowly missing the white wolf's tail. It started to run away.

"I have a clear shot!" Chase said, now on the tree's lowest branches. Barely two yards above the snow, level with a drift that stood between him and the beast. Almost like a defensive wall…

The wolf came barrelling back the way it had come, charging up the drift. If it leaped, it would land on the same branch as Chase, or push him off it to his death amid the crazed pack.

The wolf bunched its muscles, and Rosa dived to intercept it.

Paws scrabbled for purchase as it landed on the end of her carpet, claws digging in to the weave. With shaking hands, she nocked an arrow to her bow. At this distance, she couldn't miss.

The wolf snarled and snapped at her,

sending her scuttling back to the trailing edge of the carpet. It lunged, now half on the carpet. If it got its hind legs up, it would kill her for sure.

She fired, nocking arrow after arrow as she urged the carpet to buck the beast off.

She reached for another arrow, just in time to see her quiver roll over the side, out of reach.

Rosa gripped the sides of the carpet, closing her eyes as she turned the air into a whirlwind. She clung on for dear life as it dipped and spun, desperate to shake the wolf off before it reached her. But the beast's claws were snagged in the carpet – it just wouldn't fall.

Then something smacked into her head, and she knew nothing.

Thirty-Four

Chase watched in horror as the carpet spun crazily between the trees, Rosa and the white wolf clinging to it. If he could only get a clear shot…for he could not risk hitting Rosa.

There. If the carpet spun one more time…he fired, and had the satisfaction of seeing his arrow sink into the beast's paw, prying it loose from the carpet. The creature fell, hopefully to its death.

He turned his eyes back to Rosa. She'd slumped facedown on her carpet, which was now falling out of the sky. He raced to catch her, but she fell into a deep drift of snow before he could reach her. Chase didn't stop until he'd dragged her out of the snowdrift and into his arms.

She was as limp as a corpse, but she still drew breath. She lived.

But there was blood in her hair from where she'd hit her head. He needed to get her home, where she had that miraculous medicine that had healed him. Hopefully it would heal her, too.

He glanced around, hoping to see the wolf's body, so he'd know where to come and collect the head in the morning. But his arrows had burned out, and he couldn't see much. He found a snapped-off pine branch, sticky with pitch, and plunged that into his brazier to use as a makeshift torch.

Carrying Rosa and the torch was a struggle, but he had to make it home, and there was no other way. Her magic carpet would not fly until she woke, and he had no horse.

So he set one foot in front of the other and trudged into the forest, hoping and praying he would find his way.

Thirty-Five

Rosa woke in unfamiliar warmth, though it took her fuzzy head some time to realise why it felt wrong.

"Sir Chase?" she whispered.

A gentle hand touched her forehead. "Does it hurt?" he asked.

"No," she said. "Should it?"

"You flew into a tree and knocked yourself out on a branch, I think, so I brought you back here. I gave you some of the same mead you made me drink to help me heal."

Medicinal mead? No wonder her head felt

fuzzy. But it didn't hurt, either, which meant he must have given her a lot.

"What about the wolves?" she asked urgently.

"You shot the big one full of arrows and he collapsed in the snow, dead. The rest of the pack ran off when the lamp oil burned out." Chase paused. "I figured we could go back for the body tomorrow, or whenever, but it was more important to get you home to bed, as I didn't know how badly you were hurt."

She remembered now. She'd been so busy trying to shake the wolf free that she hadn't noticed where she was flying.

"How long was I out?"

If she'd slept through Midwinter Night, the gods of the forest would definitely be displeased.

"Maybe an hour? I came straight here, and gave you the mead, before I even put a fresh log on the fire. It's still burning, look." Chase pointed.

Relief washed over her. It wasn't too late.

"Then we should celebrate," she said, pressing her lips to his.

She half expected him to pull away, but he returned her kiss eagerly, cupping her head in his hand to prolong it.

Rosa let her hand trail down his chest to the hem of his tunic. He wasn't ready for her yet, but a few pumps of her hand and he would be.

"Hey!" Chase pried her hand off his cock. "You've had a lot of mead, Mistress Rosa. I'm not sure you're thinking clearly."

"But it's Midwinter Night," she said impatiently, reaching for him.

Chase jumped out of bed, backing toward the fire with his hands up in a shield against her. "Now, that's no reason to get drunk and give in to all our desires," he said cautiously.

Ha! So Sir Chase the Chaste had been entertaining lustful thoughts for her. Good.

"Of course it does – it's Midwinter Night!" When he still looked mystified, Rosa continued, "Remember when I told you the story about the mead competition between the god of fire and the goddess of winter?"

He nodded.

"They drank so much mead they forgot to name a winner?"

Another nod.

"That's the children's tale my grandmother told me when I was younger. You see, the goddess of winter was a maiden, and all the other gods wanted her for a wife, because she was also a fertility goddess, but she wanted none of them. She was a huntress who hunted alone. They'd all tried to woo her, but failed. The fire god, being a trickster at heart, waited until all the others had given up, and he joined her for a drink when she came back after a long hunting trip. That's when he issued his challenge."

Chase still looked puzzled.

Rosa went on. "They had their contest, each proclaiming the other the winner. And every time they did it, they toasted their win with another cup of mead. Cup after cup, until they'd drunk most of the jars dry. Then the god of fire began to woo her in earnest. Complimenting her on her beauty, her skill at the hunt, anything he could. Then he laid a wager that he could kiss better than she could.

"Of course, the drunk goddess kissed him. She liked it so much that she did it again, and again. Each time they kissed, he gave her a breath of his heat, until she was so hot inside, she took off all her clothes. But they kept kissing, so she started taking off his clothes, because his skin was as hot as hers. He let her do it, until they were both naked.

"Then she insisted upon taking him for a roll in the snow to cool him off. So she took him to the snow in the far north, and beneath him, the snow began to melt until it had formed a pool around him. Then the water began to steam and bubble, turning into a hot spring. So hot the goddess of winter feared for him, so she jumped into the pool to save him.

"She laid his body on the snow, terrified that his body had cooled too much, and tried to use her own body to warm his. Being the trickster he was, he was only pretending to be injured, so he immediately began to respond to her caresses with his own, until their shared passion overcame them both and…they melted the snow around them, which started the spring melt.

"Mortified at what she had done, the goddess went and hid her face, until winter came again the following year. She brought snow down to cover the land, hiding the scene where she'd shared such passion. But at Midwinter, the fire god returned, to share some mead with the goddess, and she wept so many tears of shame, she set off the spring melt again. But her salty tears turned the land barren, where nothing would grow.

"The following year, the fire god arrived early, and hid, where he could see her without being seen. The goddess thought he had not come, and drank the mead alone, bemoaning that the fire god was not there to share it with her, for if she was fated to melt her own snow just thinking about him, it would be better to share passion and make the soil fertile again.

"When the fire god heard this, he jumped out of his hiding place, finished off the contents of her cup, lay her down on the snow, and together they made love with such passion that all the snow melted early, washing away all the salt and making the land fertile again."

Chase was nodding once more. "I wish you could tell this to my brother. Back where I grew up, the sea flooded the land so often that whole swathes of it are lost to salt. He'd happily bow down and kiss your goddess's feet if she would make the soil sweet again."

Her shoulders slumped. He'd missed the point of the story. She would have to explain even more.

"In the villages, most people know the shorter tale, not the full story. The priestesses learn the full story as a novice, when they first spill their maiden's blood at Midsummer." She paused just long enough to see that this wouldn't be enough, then rushed on with, "But they do not graduate from novice to priestess until they have played the part of the winter goddess at Midwinter. First they must make the Midwinter Night mead, which takes a year, and when it is ready, they choose a lover.

"Grandmother said some of them chose a man from among the fire god's priests, or they were paired with a novice priest, but as the new faith took hold and there were fewer and fewer of us, more and more, the priestess picked her own lover. Unless she becomes the High Priestess, a lover is all she is allowed, for that one night of the year, so – "

"What about the High Priestess? Is she allowed to sleep with whoever she pleases?"

Rosa's cheeks glowed red. "No, of course not. On the years when there is no novice, she must take the place of the goddess. She may choose a lover, but as High Priestess, she is allowed to marry, as long as her marriage ceremony is performed in the old way, and only at Midwinter. The High Priestess and her husband reenact the goddess's first night of passion with her fire god lover, while the other priestesses…"

"Dance around naked?" Chase suggested.

Rosa frowned. "If you already knew, why did you make me tell the whole tale?"

Chase laughed. "I meant it to be a joke – I had no idea it would be true. Dancing naked in winter sounds like a good way to lose some toes, or worse. But there are stories, like witches and their broomsticks, that witches like to dance naked in the moonlight. I didn't think it would be wise to ask if it was true."

Rosa let out a breath she hadn't been holding. "All right, then."

Chase folded his arms across his chest.

"You still haven't explained what this has to do with you trying to seduce me."

Rosa pressed her lips together. "My grandmother was the High Priestess, and I am still a novice. There are no other priestesses, so I must take the role of the goddess tonight."

Silence swelled between them.

Finally, Chase said, "You want me to pretend to be some pagan fire god, and seduce you outside in the snow?"

Rosa could feel the emphatic NO about to leave his lips.

She forced a smile. "Actually, it doesn't snow much here, and as there isn't anyone else to dance or observe the rites except the gods themselves, maybe they wouldn't mind if this time, the rites take place in a bed." She swallowed. "Please, Sir Chase."

Thirty-Six

Between the beseeching look in her eyes and her nipples poking through the thin fabric of her shift, Chase didn't know where to look. He'd be a fool to say no, but what sort of honour would he have left if he said yes?

"If you don't do this, it will be a whole year before the gods have a proper priestess. In their anger, who knows what they might do to me, or the village?" She took a deep breath, and his gaze darted down to her swelling breasts again. "Worse than a wolf pack. Perhaps they will send a dragon to destroy us.

It is said the fire god alone can control the fire breathing beasts."

So he'd be honour bound to defeat a fire breathing dragon after all. Good for his reputation, if he survived. If.

Chase opened his mouth to tell her he'd do it.

"You promised to serve me. A week, you said. If you do this for me, give me just one night, I will consider your debt repaid."

By all that was holy, yes! If she brought honour into it, he had no choice.

He tried to keep his expression calm, though he was singing inside. "When you put it that way, Mistress Rosa, then it becomes a matter of honour that I do as you ask."

Her eyes lit up. "Truly? You will help me?" She whipped off her shift and lay naked on the bed. "Then take me, Sir Chase. For tonight, I am yours."

Chase swallowed. Now was not the time to admit he'd never made love to a woman before. But for the first time in his life, he wished he had, for he wanted to do this right.

If her gods helped him to make this a night

for her to remember, he would serve them faithfully until the day he died.

Thirty-Seven

Gods, Chase looked as nervous as she felt.

"So, we should maybe start with a drink, like in the story?" Chase suggested, pouring two cups brimful.

Rosa sniffed hers. "Which mead is this?"

Chase shrugged. "You're the expert, not me."

She took a cautious sip. "This is the medicinal mead. There's precious little left, and no knowing if I'll be able to make it as well as my grandmother. Best pour it back in the jug and put it somewhere safe. I'll go down to the cellar and find us something more suitable to drink." Clumsily, she wrapped a blanket around herself and headed down the stairs.

"Right. I'll…stoke the fire, so it's warmer up here, for when you come back," he called after her.

Definitely as nervous as she was. She considered backing out of the deal altogether, but she knew she couldn't. She had to complete the rites, so she could serve the gods as priestess. Nothing else mattered now.

She found last year's Midwinter Night mead sitting untouched, where she'd left it a year ago. The goddess runes on the barrels were wonky on some of them, as it had been the first year she'd made it. If she'd known a year ago that she would be using the brew in her own rite of passage…Rosa shook her head.

In her haste, she'd forgotten to bring a jug with her, so she decided to float the whole barrel up the stairs to the cottage. Probably for the best, as they might need more than one jug of mead to calm both of their nerves before the night was over.

She set the cask on the table, then knelt

down to tap the barrel. Her blanket kept slipping down, forcing her to yank it back up again, until she bunched it up in her fist to keep it in place. Try as she might, she could not tap a barrel with only one hand.

"Let me do it," Chase said, placing a second blanket around her shoulders. "You get back into bed, and warm. Unless half freezing to death is part of the ritual?"

Rosa shook her head. "I've never seen the ritual performed before. I know only the story, and how there must be mead, and sex."

Chase looked alarmed. "I'll…I'll get the mead, then, and you get into bed, ready for…the other stuff."

She felt the uncontrollable urge to laugh, but one look at Chase's face told her that might not be the best idea.

This was a mistake. Curse the gods for placing her in this position.

"If you don't want to, we don't have to," she said in a rush. "We can – "

He slammed the jug of mead on the table. "I want to."

"Oh." It was the tiniest sound, barely a

word at all, escaping without permission as she tried to assemble her scrambled thoughts.

He wanted…her?

Chase poured these cups more carefully than the first, not spilling a drop.

But when he handed a cup to her, Rosa's hands shook so badly she spilled it down her chest. She swore.

"Here, let me." Somehow, he'd found a cloth and a bowl of water, and he squeezed the water out of the cloth as if he'd been a healer all his life.

Rosa released the blanket, baring herself to the waist.

With the cloth, he traced the line of stickiness between her breasts and down her belly, then back up again, as if he couldn't decide which breast to wash first. His hand went right, but then he leaned over, peering at her left breast. The cloth rasped over one nipple as he took the other in his mouth, sucking hard.

She tangled her fingers in his hair. "Gods, Chase!"

He looked up, and his eyes were full of

mischief as they met hers. He let go, tracing a circle around her nipple with his tongue. "I'm not sure what tastes sweeter, you or the mead."

And then he kissed her mouth again, his arms around her, as he climbed into the bed beside her. She helped him undress, still kissing him, except when they had to stop to pull some item of clothing over his head.

Once he was naked, she could run her hands over his chest, stroking the firm muscles like she wanted to. Down his chest, his belly, and the hard length of him…

"Don't," Chase groaned, pulling away again.

"But…I thought…you wanted…"

He tipped her onto her back. "I want, all right, but if you get your hands on me like that, I won't last more than a moment, and I think for us to have sex, I must at least make it inside you."

She thought for a moment. "If you're so sensitive, then perhaps we should leave off on the stroking and sucking and move onto the sex."

"Are you sure? Are you ready for me?"

Before she could answer or even nod her

head, he'd slipped a finger inside her.

"Not yet." He knelt between her thighs, pushing them open wider, before he traced her lower lips with his finger, as if he was trying to memorise them. Then he touched a place that left her gasping, and she opened her eyes to see him grin. "That's the spot." He rubbed harder, and she thought she swooned, unable to focus on anything but his finger and what it was doing to her.

Her breath came in great, ragged gasps, as his finger sent ripples of desire rolling through her body. Bigger, and bigger…until she arched her back, digging her fingers into the mattress as she exploded at his touch.

She was still panting by the time her vision cleared enough to see his face. Still grinning.

"Rosa, I want you more than any other woman I've ever known. But I need to know if you're ready for me. If you want me."

He had his cock in one hand, ready to enter her, while his finger still stroked her lightly, sending small ripples through her.

Rosa swallowed. "If you're going to do that to me again, I'm not sure I'll ever be ready for it." When he frowned, she hurried to add, "But if you're asking if I want you to do that again, and to make love to me…then yes. As many times as you like."

He slid a finger inside her again. "You're wet enough, that's for sure. Tell me if I hurt you, Rosa, and I'll stop."

She nodded. The first time with Alard had hurt, but that had been mercifully quick, and from what Chase had said, this would be, too. Then he could back to doing the thing he did with his fingers.

Except…his fingers hadn't stopped, still rubbing her until her vision started to cloud again. Then she felt him enter her, in one slow, smooth stroke, stretching her but not hurting her.

But the ripples were getting bigger again, as she panted faster, clenching her muscles hard like she had before, only with Chase inside her that set off more ripples. Caught between the two, she was lost in love for him.

He started sliding in and out of her, no longer slow, and she lifted her hips to meet him, keeping pace as he sped up, until each frenzied thrust pushed her closer and closer to what felt like it would be an even bigger explosion and she couldn't stop but she wasn't sure if she could bear it when it did come and…

"Oh gods, Chase, Chase!"

Some time later, she opened her eyes to find him grinning at her again. She could still feel him inside her, but he'd stopped moving and somehow, she didn't feel quite so full any more. And she was shaking. Couldn't stop shaking. Didn't know why. And yet…

"That was amazing. I want to do it again," she said, her voice hoarse from…had she truly screamed his name?

He reached for the bowl and cloth. "First, let's get cleaned up. Then, I want to spend some time stroking and sucking, as you called it, before we find out if I'm even capable of making you scream like that again."

She winced as he eased out of her, hating how empty she felt without him. "My first time was nowhere near as good as that," she said, to distract herself from the way he stroked the cloth down his own length, before using it on her. "Are you a very experienced lover, or is that what royalty require from their husbands?"

He dropped the cloth in the bowl, then stared at her. "Well, I guess that explains why there wasn't any blood, and why I didn't hurt you, if I wasn't your first. But I wouldn't know anything about what royalty require from their husbands or their lovers. That was the first time I've ever made love to a woman, and it was better than I dreamed it would be." He filled the cups, and held out hers. "If you spill it this time, I promise you, I'll use my tongue to clean every drop that lands on your skin."

Rosa drank deeply, her hands no longer shaking. Oh, there was a little shiver of pleasure at his words, but not enough to shake the warm glow that suffused her whole body. She drank until only a few drops remained at the bottom of her cup, which she dribbled across the top of her breasts, meeting his gaze squarely with a challenge of her own.

Chase laughed. "If you hadn't done it, I was going to pour my cup over you. By all that's holy, I could spend all night just worshipping those breasts." He drained his cup and set it on the table. Then he pushed her down on the bed, touching his tongue to her nipple once more. "So sweet." A finger slid inside her, stroking, as his other hand closed on her breast. "And I want you wet for later, too, when we see if I can earn a better adjective than amazing."

"Yes. Oh, yes." Rosa wanted to say something more articulate, but with his hands, his lips and his tongue on her, she soon struggled to say anything coherent at all.

Thirty-Eight

The sound of Hagen growling woke Rosa. Hagen never growled, unless there was another cat outside. Probably sniffing at the door, wanting to come in out of the cold. She didn't blame it. Even with Chase spooned up close behind her, she could feel the chill air. Almost as though the fire had gone out, or she'd left a window open. But the shutters had been closed for weeks, and she wouldn't have left…

The door was opening. Swinging out wider, until she could see the moonlit clearing outside.

Hagen had puffed up, until he looked more like a thundercloud than a cat, complete with ominous rumbling. Yet even he backed away from the door, retreating into the shadows beside the fire.

Rosa crept out of bed, reaching for the nearest weapon – the poker. She held it before her like a sword and demanded, "Who's there?"

Something huge and pale leaped at her, knocking her down. The poker flew from her hand, clanging down somewhere out of reach.

She saw firelight glint off big eyes and…even bigger teeth…

The beast had knocked the breath out of her, and with its weight crushing her, she couldn't even draw in the air to scream.

Air…

Cold air came screaming through the open door, pelting the beast with leaves as it tried to lift the creature off her.

But the beast seemed to be pushing down just as hard, its weight more than she could bear as those teeth came closer, and closer…

And then the weight was gone, as the beast

rolled off her.

Rosa jumped to her feet, backing away as she felt around behind her for anything else she could use for a weapon. Even the poker, which was surely…

But the beast didn't move. It just lay on its back, on top of the poker. No, not on top of.

"I wouldn't have thought a poker would go straight through him like that, like a greased spit," Chase said. He nudged the beast with his foot.

A paw curled, like a fist clenching in agony.

"Pull it out," Rosa said. "It will die a faster, more merciful death that way."

Chase shrugged. "If you wish." He reached for the handle.

"Don't," the creature said hoarsely.

Except…the white fur on its belly seemed to be thinning, exposing more skin. And the paw had lengthened, almost like fingers…

"Gods, it's a man!" she said, staring.

Only the head hadn't changed, and then she realised the massive man wore a white wolfskin cloak, with the stuffed head adorning the hood so that it looked like his face. Yet he shoved it aside and she found herself facing a wrinkled, white-haired man.

"You're not Mistress Kun," the old man said. "I thought I smelled her magic, but you're not her."

"I am Mistress Rosa, and I have some healing skill," Rosa began. "If you let my friend remove the poker, I might be able to save you."

"For what? A lifetime as a wolf, seeking the bitch who turned me into a beast? Better to let me die, girl. She killed the rest of my sons, as if that might bring back the one she whelped who died in his sleep." The man coughed. "She found me offering up the body to the gods' care, ready to light the pyre. Screamed that I'd killed him, and she'd kill all my sons and tear down all I'd built. After she'd made me watch all of it, she cursed me. Said if I could find her in the doorway to death, maybe I could be a man again. Ever since, I've been searching. Neither a wolf nor a man, and all I know is the stink of magic. But whenever I followed it…the witch would rather die instead of turning me back. And only now, I realise I must have heard her wrong. It wasn't her I had to kill to turn back into a man. It was me."

He squinted at her. "You look like my daughter, Skathi. She's the High Priestess to the winter goddess – even Kun wouldn't risk the wrath of the goddess by hurting her. Find her. Tell her to make sure to give me a king's funeral. Burned before the altar."

Rosa bowed her head. "It will be done."

"And give my cloak to your man there. He looks mighty cold."

Rosa glanced at Chase. He was as naked as she was, and he did indeed look cold. Perhaps if he closed the door…

The wolf had opened the door to the cottage. She'd always wondered how he'd gotten into her family's house, for the door had been closed when she found them. She opened her mouth to ask.

The wolf king gave a little sigh and said no more. Rosa checked his pulse.

"He's dead."

She didn't know whether to be relieved or sad. For years, she'd yearned for this, and now…

So this was vengeance. She'd thought it would be sweet, but it was as bitter and bleak as the heart of winter.

"What do we do now?" Chase asked.

Rosa swallowed. "We burn the body, like I promised. I guess I'm the priestess now, so it falls to me."

"To us," Chase corrected. "We're in this together. Until the very end."

Thirty-Nine

Rosa seemed dazed, so Chase left her to pull on some clothes while he, already dressed, headed outside to find a handcart to carry the body to this altar she'd spoken of.

He should have felt as confused as Rosa, killing a wolf who'd turned into a man only to die again after telling the strangest tale he'd ever heard.

And yet…his mind was clearer than it had ever been. Seeing that beast slavering over Rosa, he'd known exactly what to do.

Even now, he could see his way forward.

knowing exactly what he wanted to do next.

He filled up the handcart with enough wood to make a pagan funeral pyre, then went inside for some other supplies. Rosa had pulled on a shift, but she seemed to be struggling with the laces.

Chase headed over to help. After making love to her tonight, he wanted to unlace her more than cover her up, but that could wait. She'd need to be dressed warmly, and if he had to dress her, he would. He found a clean overdress and helped her into it. Stockings, boots, cloak…

He left her sitting on the bed as he stripped the corpse of its cloak and carried it to the cart. The man, despite his age, had been powerfully built. No wonder he'd made such a huge wolf. As for his parting gift of the wolf head cloak…Chase could decide whether to accept it or not later, when the body was dealt with. Or leave it up to Rosa.

"Ready to go find this altar, High Priestess Rosa?" he asked.

She blinked and finally seemed to focus. "Just a priestess. Not so high," she said. She sighed. "I had everything so clearly planned out, and now…I'm lost. What do you do when you finally finish your quest?"

"Find a new one," he replied. "Or rest and recuperate for a bit, then think up something else to do."

She nodded. "Yes. I should…rest. Would you rest the winter with me?" Before Chase could answer, she continued, "Oh, but you probably have a new quest. Never mind. I would have liked…but it doesn't matter." Her shoulders slumped.

He would bring a smile back to her face. By dawn, if not before, Chase swore.

Ha. Yes, he did have a new quest.

Gods grant he would be successful in this one, too.

Forty

Together, they threw the corpse onto the pyre they'd built on the ground at the foot of the stone altar. They piled more wood on top of it until it resembled a bonfire more than a funeral pyre. Then they stepped forward together and thrust their torches into it, setting it alight.

Rosa bit her lip, bringing a breeze into the grove to fan the flames. The quicker the corpse became ashes, the better, for the night was cold and dark, and it would be many hours before the sun would warm the land again.

She moved closer to Chase, craving his warmth more than that of the fire.

"Shall we go back to bed?" he asked, wrapping an arm around her.

She longed to say yes, but she could not. "We must keep vigil until all traces of the body are gone. You go home if you wish, and back to bed. I will join you once the fire burns to ashes." But not before dawn, for it took a long time to burn a body so big.

"Isn't this what you told me about, though? In the ancient rites, where witches dance naked in the grove about a holy fire?"

He'd remembered. "In the ancient rites, the priestesses drank a lot of mead before they danced naked. And at Midwinter, they didn't dance alone. They had partners…to…warm them…" Her face warmed with an unusually hot blush.

"While the fire burns, I will warm you," Chase said, reaching into the handcart. He pulled out a pair of blankets and a jug of mead. He handed her the jug, then spread the blankets on the ground. The flames reflected in his eyes made it seem almost as though the fire burned within him. He lay her down on the blankets, then knelt before her, lifting her legs up onto his shoulders so that her skirt fell back, baring her to him. She could feel the heat of him, ready to enter her, yet he did not. "But only if you want me. Do you?" he asked, his tone so gentle it could melt the iciest heart.

As she looked up into his eyes, she knew her heart had more than melted.

In the sacred grove, before the watching eyes of the forest gods, she could only speak the truth. Truth that had dawned on her tonight, as she lay naked in his arms. "Yes. More than any man I have ever known, I love you, and I will love you until I draw my last breath." Tears sprang to her eyes. "Even when spring comes and you run off to find your princess once more, I will love you still." Such was the life of a priestess. Always a lover, never a wife.

"You wish for me to stay here, with you?"

Rosa closed her eyes, wishing she could stop the tears from falling. "Yes. With all my heart."

"But your heart and soul belong here, to the forest."

She wept. "Yes. As priestess to the gods of the forest, my body and soul belong here, to them. I can never leave. But my heart belongs to you. Only you."

"Good. Because I think you stole my heart the moment you first looked at me, and I will never love any other woman the way I love you."

At his words, her eyes flew open, staring at him, but he thrust deep inside her, and she could do little more than moan at the pleasure of it. This was nothing like the first time, or the second. Every thrust was slow and deep, like the beat of a giant heart at the centre of her world. Somehow, he'd unlaced her dress, letting her breasts spill out, and his hands were warm as he caressed her, never once changing his pace.

The world spun and stood still, air freezing her flesh even as his skin heated it to burning, while the fire within her built and built, a blaze she could not contain.

And when she screamed out, "YES!" as the pleasure of their union overwhelmed her, it seemed the whole forest shouted with her.

Forty-One

A thousand voices whispered, debating whether they should wake him up, remind him of his duties, or let him sleep a little longer.

Chase's heart sank. He'd fallen asleep in the Great Hall again, his head pillowed on something so soft it might be a maiden's breast. He didn't want to wake to find out what it really was, for he wanted to dream a little longer, about the magical maiden who summoned such a fire inside him, he could not resist her. Especially when her ice-blue eyes had glowed with some enchantment, enticing him to take what was so freely given…

He had to wake now, for his cock was far too alert for such a public place.

Chase dared to open his eyes. A pink nipple sat before him, like a berry atop sweet, creamy flesh, begging to be tasted.

"Serve your priestess, knight."

"Yesss, the High Priestess."

"You swore to serve."

Hissing whispers came from all around, but he saw no one. Trees stood sentinel on either side, their branches meeting above, like he lay in a massive cathedral.

With a lovely young woman. Rosa, the priestess of the forest.

He tried to lift his hand to stroke her hair off her face, but he could not. One arm was tucked beneath her, holding her tight to him, while his other hand was trapped between her thighs, with only his thumb free. He moved his thumb experimentally, eliciting a gasp from Rosa.

He pressed with the pad of his thumb, and it slipped inside her, her irresistible heat contracting around him just as she had last night.

His cock was now rock hard, as though he hadn't touched a woman in years, when he knew he'd made love to this one scant hours before.

"Yes," Rosa whispered, and a thousand voices agreed with her.

She shifted, rolling him onto his back so that she could sit astride him, her heat engulfing him completely. Her breasts, bouncing free of her unlaced bodice, taunted him.

He sat up, needing to kiss her, to taste those creamy breasts, to match the timing of her rocking hips with thrusts of his own.

"Yesss…"

"YES!"

"Yessss…"

"Oh, yes."

A thousand voices echoed his thoughts, until he and Rosa cried out in shared pleasure for a moment that seemed to last for ever…but not long enough.

When he could see clearly enough to look around, they were alone in the cathedral clearing, beside the ashes of last night's pyre, wrapped in her red cloak, on the forest floor.

"Hail the new High Priestess, for she has conquered the fire god himself in the sacred grove," a smug whisper hissed.

"Who said that?" Chase demanded, looking around.

Rosa blinked. "You heard that, too?"

"Of course. Now, show yourself!" Chase commanded.

"The knight cannot see."

"He sees only the High Priestess."

"So nubile is she."

Hissing laughter drowned out the rest of the words echoing around them.

Rosa ducked her head, no longer meeting his eyes as she laced up her bodice. "I should return to the house and wash." She levered herself up off Chase's lap, and cold air rushed to cool what ardour he had left. "You should…go to the Baron to collect your reward."

Chase cleaned up as best he could, and rose. "Not without you."

She shook her head. "I have no need of

coin, and I don't think Alard wants to see me. But you will surely need it, wherever you are going."

Chase folded his arms across his chest. "I'm going home, with my wife."

Rosa froze, her face losing all colour. "You never said…never mentioned…a wife." Tears filled her eyes.

No, she could not cry. Not now. Not after…

He rushed to take her in his arms. "My lady, please do not cry. If I've done things wrong, I must make amends. Tell me again how the ancient marriage rite goes. I will do it all over, until I have it right."

Her words were muffled in the folds of his shirt, but he could still make them out. "The couple would come to the altar, and pledge their love before witnesses. Then, they would spend the night in the sacred grove, to receive the gods' blessing on their union…"

"And the priestesses. How was it different for them?" Chase prompted.

"Only the High Priestess was permitted to marry, in a secret ceremony witnessed by the gods and those who served them, at Midwinter. The couple were allowed to drink nothing but Midwinter's Night mead, for they take the role of the winter goddess and the god of fire, uniting to drive away the cold and renew the land for another year. The couple were not truly married unless the gods found them worthy, by showing the couple a sign at dawn, which is why the priestess often married one of the fire god's priests..." Rosa stared at him. "But you can't have meant to marry me. You're leaving."

"I told you, I'm not going anywhere without you, and you wanted me to stay, Lady Rosa."

"I'm not a lady. Just a village witch, and maybe a priestess. Nothing more. Chase, you could have married some princess or fine lady. Why would you tie yourself to someone like me?"

"Because I love you, and I don't want some princess, or anyone else. I want you as my wife, Lady Rosa, which you are because you are a knight's lady. I pledged my life to you the first time you saved my life. And then you saved me again last night...so I am doubly indebted to you. A debt I will happily take a lifetime to repay." He took her hands in one of his, tilting her chin up with his other hand so that he might look into her eyes. "My lovely Lady Rosa, High Priestess to all the gods of the forest, will you accept a poor knight as your husband, to love and serve you until my last breath?"

Please say yes, he thought but did not say. Would it help if he dropped to his knees and begged?

"She already said yes."

"Several times."

"He was too busy between her thighs."

"Yes!"

More hissing laughter.

"Silence! I would hear her answer, not yours!" Chase snapped.

Silence fell.

A giggle escaped from Rosa. "I don't think anyone has ever told the gods of the forest to be quiet before. Only the High Priestess is meant to hear them, and even then, I thought it might be something my grandmother made up. How you can hear them, too...I do not know."

"Maybe it's the sign of the gods' favour, like you spoke of. Please, Rosa. An answer, I beg you."

The trees seemed to lean in, as though they wanted to hear, too.

She laughed. "Yes, yes, a thousand times yes! Especially if it means that last night won't be the only time we make love."

"I sure hope not!" Chase wadded up the blankets and tossed them into the hand cart, followed by the empty mead jug. "I plan on warming your bed for many nights to come, Lady Rosa, if you are willing."

Rosa tucked her arm under his. "I think I will grow accustomed to having you in my bed far faster than I will learn to like being Lady anything. But first, I'd like to cook my new husband a wedding breakfast. Something for stamina, and strength, washed down with something to sweeten his tongue…"

Laughing, they ambled through the forest for home.

Forty-Two

"And…I think she's full," Rosa said as her nipple popped out of baby Maja's mouth.

While she retied the laces of her gown, Chase carried the sleeping baby over to the cradle she shared with her twin sister, Saskia, for the girls screamed fit to wake the dead if they were parted for long.

"Do you think they'll sleep through the night?" Chase asked doubtfully, smoothing a blanket over the girls.

"My sleeping spells have worked fine so far. They will not wake until sunrise, even if they weren't full to bursting with milk." She lifted her lips for a kiss. "We have all night, the longest night of the year."

"We'll need it. We've scarcely shared a bed, even to sleep, since the girls were born," Chase grumbled as he threw a couple of blankets over his shoulder. He fastened his cloak, then picked up the two jugs of mead from the table. "Which barrel is this?"

"The Midwinter's Night mead, strong and sweet, like you, made the night you first touched my heart," Rosa said, settling her red cloak across her shoulders.

"The night I touched your breast in my sleep, you mean."

"I'd like to think the gods guided your hand," she said lightly, slipping her arm through the handle of a basket of food she'd packed to sustain them through the night. Outside, the trees whispered, as if a high wind whipped through their branches, but the night was still. "Can you still hear them?"

Chase closed the door behind him and squinted up at the trees. "Unfortunately, yes. They've been whispering all day. Your gods of the forest are randier than I am, and that's saying something."

Rosa set off with a skip in her step. "Then perhaps we should hurry to the grove, so I can help you with that."

Chase followed, but Rosa was faster, reaching the unlit bonfire first.

"Oh, it's beautiful," she whispered. Chase had edged the altar in holly and mistletoe, with a row of lit candles on both ends. "I should have thought to bring an offering, too."

Chase touched his torch to the bonfire. "Your gods of the forest were very clear about what they desire from their High Priestess."

"They told you, but not me?"

"You were busy inside with the girls. Too busy to listen to a bunch of randy trees who have taken a distinctly unholy shine to their High Priestess."

A shiver of alarm touched her. "Chase, you should not mock the gods of the forest so. If they struck you down for your insolence, I would be inconsolable. And the girls…"

"Do not fear. I may not worship your gods as devoutly as you do, but we have an understanding. As long as I keep you happy." Chase untied the laces of her gown, then pushed it down, until it puddled on the ground. The two woollen shifts she wore beneath soon followed it. Then he lifted her so she perched on the edge of the altar, well away from the holly and candles, and peeled her hose and boots off her dangling legs.

Rosa pulled the edges of her cloak closed over her nakedness. "What are you doing? We can't do this on the altar!"

"That's not what they say!" Chase raised his arms, waving at the treetops.

Now Rosa could hear their hissed words, and what she did hear made her blush.

Surely the god of fire hadn't dared bend a goddess over her own altar to take her from behind…

"Yes!"

"Please!"

"Drink the nectar of the gods, High Priestess!"

Behind Rosa, the bonfire finally caught, roaring up with a wave of heat that enticed her to loosen her hold on her cloak. She reached for Chase's golden cup, brimful of mead, and drank half of it in one draught, before handing it to Chase to finish.

Then Chase stripped off, until he stood before her in nothing but his white wolf-fur cloak. Only then did he position himself between her thighs, ready.

She lifted her glowing ice-blue eyes to meet his fiery gaze. "Oh, Sir Knight, what a big sword you have."

"All the better to…gods, it feels so good to be inside you again, my lady!"

About the Author

Demelza Carlton has always loved the ocean, but on her first snorkelling trip she found she was afraid of fish.

She has since swum with sea lions, sharks and sea cucumbers and stood on spray drenched cliffs over a seething sea as a seven-metre cyclonic swell surged in, shattering a shipwreck below.

Demelza now lives in Perth, Western Australia, the shark attack capital of the world.

The *Ocean's Gift* series was her first foray into fiction, followed by her suspense thriller *Nightmares* trilogy. She swears the *Mel Goes to Hell* series ambushed her on a crowded train and wouldn't leave her alone.

Want to know more? You can follow Demelza on Facebook, Twitter, YouTube or her website, Demelza Carlton's Place at:

www.demelzacarlton.com